Summer
Desires

Barbara McCauley

Joan Johnston

Wendy Rosnau

*First published in Great Britain 2006
by Harlequin Mills & Boon Limited, Eton House,
18-24 Paradise Road, Richmond, Surrey TW9 1SR*

SUMMER DESIRES © by Harlequin Books S.A. 2006

The publisher acknowledges the copyright holders of the
individual works as follows:

A Wolf River Summer © Barbara McCauley 2003
Hawk's Way: The Virgin Groom © Joan Johnston 1997
The Long Hot Summer © Wendy Rosnau 2000

*ISBN 13: 978 0 263 85080 2
ISBN 10: 0 263 85080 3*

081-0706

*Printed and bound in Spain
by Litografía Rosés S.A., Barcelona*

A WOLF RIVER SUMMER
Barbara McCauley

* * *

To Mary-Theresa Hussey —
an editor whose boundless energy and
unwavering dedication to her work inspires
everyone around her. This one's for you!

Dear Reader,

What a thrill it's been to tell Clay and Paige's story! Clay had been grumbling at me for some time to find him a woman – not just *any* woman, mind you. A dependable, intelligent woman who won't expect love. A woman to willingly share his bed, but not his heart. Ah, but men are such silly creatures, aren't they?

So come along for the ride. It's a wild one, with more than one sharp turn and bump along the way. And that final stop – well, you'll see…

Sincerely,

Barbara McCauley

Chapter 1

When Clay Bodine came to town, folks took notice.

It was a rare sight to see the Wolf River County rancher drive into town in his dusty, black pickup. So rare the residents called his appearances a "Bodine Sighting." Before that black pickup even turned onto Main Street, phones lines were already sizzling, ears were already burning. Curiosity had more than one store owner sweeping a sidewalk they'd swept only an hour before, and window shopping—in spite of the one hundred plus degree heat—tripled in popularity.

For the most part, the good people of Wolf River minded their own business. But small towns were small towns, after all, and the fact that Clay had made himself so scarce for the past fifteen years had created an aura of mystery around him that simply couldn't be ignored. Not that folks didn't understand *why* Bodine had kept his distance. They understood completely. But still, what happened to Clay and his family when he was fifteen was water under the bridge. Though they might not have forgotten, everyone in Wolf River had long since moved past that difficult time.

Everyone except Clay.

Today, Clay's pickup had barely passed the Papa Pete's Diner before noses were pressed to glass, everyone hoping to catch a glimpse of the elusive Texas cattleman. Inside the barbershop, bets were placed where Bodine was headed. George Simon, the barber, laid a buck down it would be Peterson's Feed and Grain. Hugh Foderman doubled the odds it would be the bank. Ronald Weeder put his money on the department store. Clay hadn't been shopping since last Christmas, Weeder said, and the man had needed new boots then.

When the dusty pickup passed the feed and grain store, then the bank, as well, Weeder grinned and stuck his hand out to be paid, only to watch as Clay drove right past the department store, too.

"I'll be damned," Weeder muttered, and all three men stared at Clay's tailgate.

"Where's he going?" Hugh craned his neck.

"Beats me," George said, scratching his ear. "'Cept the hotel, the drugstore and that little antique store, ain't much down at that end of town."

"There's the library," Weeder added.

George and Hugh both hooted at the idea of Clay Bodine going to the library, then George said, "A buck on the hotel."

"Two bucks on the drugstore," Hugh determined.

Only because he was stubborn as a mule, Weeder folded his arms and lifted one of his two chins. "I'm going with the library."

Stepping out onto the sidewalk to get a better view, the men watched Clay's pickup pass the intersection of Main and Bristle, then pull into a parking spot.

"I'll…be…damned." Weeder shook his head in amazement, then grinned at his dumbfounded buddies. "Pay up, boys."

Paige Andrews made prudent use of her lunch break from Wolf River Library by shopping at the drugstore. She'd made a list just that morning—cotton balls, hair pins, reading glasses, in-sole cushions for her work shoes, a catnip mouse for Eudora and the most recent copy of *Quilter's Monthly.* She lingered over the magazines for a moment, even picked up a copy of *Celebrity Circle* and browsed through it, but since she didn't own a television set, most of the pretty faces inside the glossy pages were unknown to her.

Paige had been thinking about buying a TV. She knew she was probably the only person in Wolf River who didn't own one. For that matter, she was probably the only person in Texas who didn't own one. But her grandmother had not approved of whiling away one's time with "that sort of horsefeathers,'' so for the past twelve years, the only television Paige had watched had been at her best friend Rebecca's house, or her ongoing Friday evening date at Bernie Pratt's apartment.

Not that anyone would exactly call take-out pizza and watching *Jeopardy* with Bernie and his mother a *date,* but at twenty-six, that was about as exciting as Paige's personal life had been since she'd finished college five years ago.

Still, Grandma Millie had not approved of her only grandchild visiting a man's house unchaperoned. Though Paige had reassured her grandmother that Bernie was well behaved, Grandma Millie had harrumphed. ''There better not be any hanky-panky going on, Paige Eloise Andrews,'' Grandma had said.

If only there were, Paige had always thought. Not that she considered Bernie her dream man. But he was always a gentleman, even when he kissed her good-night. He never groped or pushed himself on her, though she had always secretly wondered what it would be like if maybe he had been a little more...forceful.

As if I were the type to instill that kind of ardor in a man, Paige thought with a silent sigh.

No, Bernie was exactly the right type of man for her. He had a stable job at the bank. He was comfortable to be around. He was dependable. All important, admirable traits in a man. Since Grandma Millie had passed away six months ago, Bernie had commented on more than one occasion that he didn't think it was a good idea for a young woman to be living alone, which led Paige to wonder if he was working up the courage to pop the question.

But the real question, Paige thought, was what would she say if he did?

Her shopping list completed, Paige paused at the candy display and picked up a package of red licorice whips to add to her basket. She had a group of five-to-seven-year-olds coming into the library for storytelling this afternoon, and she always enjoyed giving the children a treat as much as they enjoyed receiving one.

Paige had barely reached the end of the aisle when she heard the excited murmuring of Sheila Gordon, the drugstore clerk, and Daphne Pringle, a waitress from Big Bob's BBQ, coming from the front of the store. When Paige stepped around the corner, she saw both women standing at the front glass window.

"I'm telling you," Sheila said. "I saw him go in there."

"Were you wearing your glasses?" Daphne asked. "You know you're blind as a bat without them. It could have been one of his ranch hands."

"Of course I was wearing my glasses." Sheila gave an indignant toss of her short, red curls, then straightened her thick, tortoiseshell glasses. "It was him, all right. I saw him plain as the mole on Marilyn Monroe's face."

"It's just hard to believe." Daphne shook her pretty blond head. "What in the world would Clay Bodine be doing at the *library,* of all places?"

Paige froze. Clay Bodine had gone into the library? *Her* library? Sheila must have made a mistake, Paige thought.

Clay Bodine had never come into the library before. At least, not in the five years Paige had worked there.

Wouldn't that just figure, Paige thought, stepping closer to Sheila and Daphne. The most interesting man in town comes to the library where she worked, and it's one of the few times she wasn't there.

The story of my life.

"There he is! It's him! It's really him!" Daphne grabbed Sheila's arm as Clay stepped out of the library and stood on the sidewalk. The black Stetson he wore shadowed his face, but there was no mistaking the six-foot-four-inch rancher.

"Ohmigod." Sheila uttered a low groan. "I think I might faint just looking at him. That man is *fine.*"

Paige felt her own pulse quicken as she looked at the man herself. Clay had the solid, muscular build that came from the hard labor and long hours of working a ranch seven days a week. His legs were long, his shoulders strong and wide. Today he wore a denim jacket and jeans, a weathered, soft blue that matched his eyes, Paige knew, and remembered the day five months ago when she'd opened her front door and he'd turned those incredible eyes on her....

"Ms. Andrews," he'd said, touching the brim of his black Stetson.

She'd been so stunned, she'd simply stood there and hadn't uttered a word. They'd only met once before, the summer she had turned eighteen and worked at the doctor's office before going off to college. Clay had brought his grandfather in for an eye infection and an exam, but Paige was certain that Clay wouldn't have remembered her, even though she certainly remembered him.

"I heard your '57 Chevy is for sale," he'd said in a voice as thick and dark as molasses. "That right?"

Paige had blinked, then nodded. Her grandmother had bought the car new, but had barely put ten thousand miles on the engine driving it to the grocery store and back. It had been parked in the garage and covered for the past twenty years, and was in perfect condition. Paige had considered keeping the vintage car, but she had her own little blue sedan, and the reality was, she needed the money to help pay funeral and medical expenses. Paige had put the For Sale notice on the bulletin board at Peterson's Feed and Grain just that morning.

"What's your price?" he'd asked.

Price? She hadn't even thought about a price. And staring into Clay's rugged, handsome face had seemed to rob her of the ability to speak, let alone think. "I—I don't know. Whatever you think it's worth, I suppose."

He'd stared at her for a long moment, which had only flustered her all the more, then pulled a check out of the pocket of his blue chambray shirt and handed it to her. "That's a fair price," he'd said. "You can hold on to it if you want to think about it for a while or ask around to make sure I'm not taking advantage of you."

"I'm sure you wouldn't do that," Paige had said quickly, then felt herself blush when his gaze narrowed and met hers. "But wouldn't you like to drive it first?"

"Not necessary. I know I want it. I'll come back later and pick it up."

He touched the brim of his hat again, then turned and strode away. He'd already gotten into his truck and started his engine before Paige even looked at the check. Eleven thousand dollars! She gasped at the unbelievable figure. That would not only pay for the funeral, but the rest of her grandmother's medical expenses, as well.

The car couldn't possibly be worth that much. She'd tried to wave him back to tell him he'd made a mistake, but he'd already driven away. Who would pay that kind of money for an old car? Paige had thought in amazement.

But she found out later, after she'd gone on the Internet, that a lot of people would have paid around that price, though Clay had given her top dollar without so much as driving, or even looking at the car.

"Do you think the rumors about his ex-wife are true?"

Sheila's question to Daphne brought Paige back to the present. Clay still stood in front of the library, his hands on his hips as he glanced impatiently about. Cars slowed to stare at him. He glared back.

"What woman would leave a man who looks like that?" Daphne stared longingly at Clay. "Plus the man has more money than he knows what to do with. A woman would have to be crazy to leave a man like Clay Bodine. Besides," Daphne added, "no one knows for certain if he really was married or not. She never came to town once in the three months they were supposedly married, then suddenly she was gone."

"Judith Parcher insists that Clay did her in," Sheila whispered. "She says he buried her on his property somewhere and told everyone she'd run off."

"Judith Parcher's a lunatic and an old biddy," Daphne said defensively. "She also swears she saw Elvis bull riding at the rodeo last week."

Both Daphne and Sheila laughed at that, and even Paige found herself smiling at the absurdity. She'd lived in a small town long enough to know that most rumors were based on very little fact. *The Life of Clay Bodine,* as told by the people of Wolf River, would sit nicely on a library shelf next to all the other great works of fiction.

And if *she* wrote the book, Paige thought as she watched Clay glance at his wristwatch, it would sit on the erotica shelf. Since he'd bought her grandmother's car, Paige had had more than one fantasy about the sexy rancher, though she'd never tell that to a living soul—not even her best friend, Rebecca. Paige especially liked the one where he made love to her in a barn stall on fresh hay, and then there was the one in the meadow, beside a creek where Clay—

"He's coming this way!"

Sheila shrieked, then made a mad dash toward the cash register, then stood casually behind the counter. Daphne shot for the magazine rack and snatched up a magazine, pretending to be engrossed in the pages.

Not wanting to be caught standing at the window, Paige quickly stepped away, but stumbled over a display of bagged dog food. Her basket tumbled from her arm, and the contents scattered across the floor.

He hadn't time to stand around on street corners all day and be gawked at, Clay thought as he strode across the street. He had a mare that had already bagged up in preparation to foal, ten missing cows in the far east section of his ranch and a pile of paperwork that was quickly spilling over the sides of his desk.

He'd rather face a cornered, angry bull than that mountain of paperwork, but from the time he'd taken over the ranch after his grandfather had died, Clay had vowed never to trust anyone with his ledgers but himself. He'd kept that vow, but the cost had been burning the midnight oil on more nights than not—which had left him little time for other midnight activities of a much more pleasurable nature.

A situation he intended to remedy very soon, he thought, and walked into the drugstore. A bell tinkled over the door and Sheila Gordon, a woman he'd dated once in high school, looked up from behind the cash register, then placed a dramatic hand over her well-endowed chest.

"Why Clay Bodine—" Sheila's eyes were big and round behind her thick glasses "—what a surprise."

"Sheila." Clay knew that Sheila, along with Daphne Pringle, had been watching him from the window. He glanced over at Daphne—who was supposedly reading an issue of *Ranch and Farm Science*—and watched her lift her gaze with feigned surprise. Clay had never dated Daphne, but had known her from high school, too.

"Hi, Clay," Daphne purred. "Haven't seen you in ages around here. You're looking good."

"Thanks." He spared the blonde a nod. "You, too."

A sound from behind the magazine rack caught Clay's attention. He looked down and saw the soles of a pair of black leather loafers.

"Is there something I can help you with, Clay?" Sheila asked hopefully.

"No, thanks."

Daphne's smile widened as he moved closer, then faded when he moved past her. He stepped behind the magazine rack and saw Paige on her knees, reaching for a small, cloth mouse the same pale shade of gray as the long-sleeved, calf-length dress she wore. She'd obviously dropped her shopping basket and was occupied with picking up its spilled contents. Several long strands of wispy, sandy-brown hair had escaped from the tight knot at the base of her neck. "Ms. Andrews."

When he knelt beside her, she stiffened then looked up slowly. "Mr. Bodine."

Even her eyes were gray, he noted, with a tint of green around the iris, fringed by thick, dark brown lashes. He hadn't noticed her eyes when he'd come to her house a few months ago. Nor had he noticed her skin was pale as a baby's and appeared to be just as smooth and soft, too.

But he'd had no reason to look then, either.

He reached for a package of foot pads lying on the floor and handed it to her. Her cheeks colored bright pink as she snatched the package from him and threw it into her basket. "Thank you."

They both reached for the bag of red licorice at the same time and when their fingers brushed, she yanked her hand away as if she'd been burned.

Good Lord, but the woman was jumpy, Clay thought.

He tossed the bag of licorice into the basket, then—much to her distress—took hold of her elbow and helped her to her feet.

"Could I speak with you for a few moments?" He held on to her arm, had the distinct feeling she would have run if he hadn't.

She stilled at his question, then blinked slowly. "You want to speak…with me?"

Clay could practically feel Daphne and Sheila's eyes burning into his back. "Somewhere private?"

"I—" Page clutched her basket tightly to her "—is this about the car?"

With Daphne and Sheila hanging on every word, he could hardly tell Paige why he needed to speak with her. "Yes," he said loud enough so the other women wouldn't need to strain to hear. "I wanted to talk to you about the car."

"Is something wrong with it?" The distress in her gray-green eyes turned to worry. "If there's a mechanical problem, maybe I can have Wayne at the repair shop take a look at it and I'd be more than happy to—"

"It's more of a paperwork issue," he said. "If you'd just give me a few minutes, I'm sure we can clear it up."

"You can use the back office," Sheila offered eagerly. Both women had stopped trying to pretend they weren't listening. "Larry won't mind. He's out for the rest of the afternoon, anyway."

"Thanks." Clay moved toward the back of the drugstore toward the pharmacist's office, tugging Paige along with him. She held onto her basket as if it were a life preserver and she was drowning.

Inside the small, cluttered office, Clay closed the door behind them, then let go of Paige's arm. She stepped quickly away.

"I hope you haven't changed your mind, Mr. Bodine," she said nervously. "The car—"

"Just call me Clay," he said evenly. "And this isn't about the car."

"It's not?"

He shook his head. "I lied about the car so no one would know the real reason I wanted to speak with you."

She furrowed her brow. "The real reason?"

"Look, Paige, in about fifteen minutes, it's going to be all over this town that you came into the back office of the drugstore with me. Now that doesn't bother me in the slightest, but I suspect it might bother you."

As if to confirm his statement, she shifted awkwardly.

God, but this was going to be harder than he'd thought. He'd spent the past two days going over this moment in his mind. What he would say. How he would say it. But now that he was actually standing here, he couldn't remember one word. Something about this woman disarmed him. Maybe the expression of innocence shimmering in her eyes, or maybe the sound of absolute amazement in her voice.

Dammit, anyhow. He tugged his hat off and dragged a hand through his hair. "Paige—is it all right if I call you Paige?"

"All right."

"Why don't you put your basket down and sit?" He gestured toward the chair behind the pharmacist's desk.

"Thank you, but I'd rather stand."

"Please." He wasn't used to saying the word and it left a bitter taste in his mouth. "I promise this won't take long."

She hesitated, then sat, but still kept a death grip on the basket.

Clay walked to the office door and opened it. Daphne and Sheila jumped back, then quickly scurried off. Shaking his head, Clay closed the door again and faced Paige.

"How much do you know about me?" he asked.

His question obviously confused, as well as surprised her. "What do you mean?"

"I assume you've heard about me, about my family and all the other rumors that have circulated over the years."

"I—" She glanced away, then said quietly, "I've heard."

"So you know that my father embezzled a large sum of

money from the bank fifteen years ago, and that he went to prison?''

She brought her gaze back to his. ''Yes.''

''And you know that I paid the money back?'' he asked. ''Every penny, and interest, too?''

''Mr. Bodine—''

''Clay.''

''Clay,'' she said his name hesitantly. ''Why are you telling me all this?''

''You also probably heard that my mother left Wolf River right after my father was arrested,'' he went on without answering her question. ''She couldn't face the humiliation. I was fifteen at the time.''

Clay watched Page's face soften, saw the familiar expression of pity in her eyes. The knot in his gut tightened. He didn't want her pity, dammit. He didn't want anyone's pity.

He expected the typical ''I'm sorry'' from her, but when she set her basket down, then folded her hands over her knees and kept her gaze on his, quietly waiting, the knot in his gut loosened.

''I went to live with my grandfather on his ranch,'' he continued. ''The Rocking B. When he died four years later, I inherited twenty thousand acres and a small herd of cattle. In the past eleven years I've increased the herd tenfold and established myself as a reputable horse breeder.''

''Dutton's Disciple won the blue ribbon at the county fair last August,'' she said almost wistfully.

He lifted a brow at her comment, thought it odd that she would have known his top stud horse had won a prize almost a year ago. He wondered what other surprises the Wolf River librarian might have for him, then forced his attention back to the reason he was here.

"Almost six years ago," he went on, "I married the daughter of a wealthy businessman in California, but she—Nancy—left me after three months of living on the Rocking B and filed for divorce. In spite of the various rumors that have circulated, my ex-wife is not locked in my basement."

"I hadn't heard that one," Paige said, her eyes wide. "I heard—"

When she stopped herself, then bit her bottom lip and glanced away, Clay almost laughed. "She isn't buried on my property, either, if that's the one you heard."

Paige stared at him for a long moment, then shook her head. "I still don't understand why you're telling me all this."

"Just give me a minute and you will." He let out a long breath, then continued, "Nancy was killed in a boating accident in the Caribbean last month. Her parents contacted me to give me the news."

"I'm sorry," Paige said quietly.

While he'd certainly never wished Nancy any harm, it still surprised him that he felt nothing for his ex-wife. No grief. No sadness. Just…nothing. "I'm not here for sympathy."

"Then why are you here?" she asked. "What is it that I can possibly do for you?"

Clay leveled his gaze with Paige's. "You can marry me."

Chapter 2

Paige blinked.

You can marry me?

She blinked again.

Obviously, she hadn't heard him correctly, even though she was sitting no more than three feet away and he'd spoken quite clearly. She'd been a twisted bundle of nerves from the moment he'd asked to speak with her. She'd barely been able to breathe, let alone think clearly. In her anxious state, she must have had some kind of strange, momentary brain dysfunction.

What woman *wouldn't* be absolutely flustered by the man, Paige thought. His presence filled the small office. His blatant masculinity, his dark intensity, his rugged good looks. Heavens, he should carry smelling salts for all the swooning women he left in his wake.

"Excuse me?" she finally managed, though the words sounded like a tiny little squeak. She watched as he prowled to the door of the small office, then turned abruptly and faced her.

He dragged a hand through his thick, dark hair. "I didn't mean to blurt that out."

Of course he hadn't. Paige released the breath she'd been holding. *Thank God.*

"I'd intended to ask you to marry me *after* I'd explained everything," Clay said. "I just got a little ahead of myself."

A little ahead of himself? Paige felt her heart stop. That was the understatement of the century. Good Lord, he *had* really asked her to marry him. Too stunned to reply, or even react, she sat still as a stone.

"It wasn't just Nancy's death that the Barringtons called to tell me about." A muscle jumped in Clay's jaw. "It turns out that when Nancy left me, she was pregnant."

Paige managed to find her voice, but it was no more than a whisper. "You have a child?"

"She'll be five in August. Her name is Julia."

Clay's eyes softened as he spoke his child's name. For a moment, Paige saw the wonder there, and the longing. "She never told you?"

"No." The hard glint of anger returned. "I never saw, or even spoke to Nancy after she left. There was really no reason to. Our lawyers handled everything."

"But I don't understand." Paige shook her head. "Why would she keep your own child a secret from you?"

"It probably would have delayed the quick divorce she wanted. That we both wanted," he added. "Plus she knew me well enough to know that if I'd been aware of her having my child, I would have insisted on visitations and joint custody. She wouldn't have wanted that kind of inconvenience in her life."

What kind of a woman, what kind of a *mother,* could deprive her own child of a father because it might inconvenience her? Paige wondered. It was beyond her imagination. "What about Nancy's parents? Did they go along with their daughter keeping Julia from you?"

"They told me they didn't approve, but Nancy was insistent they keep quiet. Shortly after she had the baby, Nancy picked up with a musician in Los Angeles and started touring with his band. The Barringtons have practically raised Julia. They feel that she should stay with them."

"Why did they contact you at all, then?" Paige asked.

"Because my name is on the birth certificate," he said flatly. "Either Nancy wasn't thinking clearly when she filled out the paperwork, or she knew she'd always have an ace in the hole if she ever had a need for me or my money. In any event, with Nancy gone, the Barringtons needed my permission to gain legal guardianship. They contacted me two weeks ago and offered visitations."

Paige lifted her brows in disbelief. "Just visitations?"

He started to pace again. "I told them I'd settle for nothing less than full custody. We had one court hearing in California and the judge set up a visitation schedule to allow my daughter to get to know me. I managed to have the case transferred here to Wolf River and there's a hearing scheduled in a few weeks to determine custody.''

''You're her father.'' Paige frowned. ''Of course the court will award you custody.''

''The Barringtons will bring in the best lawyer to fight me.'' His mouth set into a hard line. ''My lawyer has already prepared me that they'll use the fact I'm a single father against me.''

''Nonsense,'' Paige said firmly and straightened her shoulders. ''Single fathers win custody disputes all the time.''

''Since they've raised her from infancy, the Barringtons will contest that they are better suited to meet Julia's needs.''

''But you have rights,'' Paige insisted. ''Surely the judge will take the entire situation into consideration.''

''My lawyer feels confident, but I can't assume anything.'' Clay looked directly at Paige. ''I need to do everything I can to stack the odds in my favor, and that means having a wife.''

The intensity of Clay's blue gaze made Paige swallow hard, but she did not look away. ''You're serious,'' she whispered hoarsely. ''You really do want me to marry you.''

''I'm dead serious.''

A mixture of alarm and excitement rippled through her. It was ridiculous. Preposterous. Unthinkable.

And yet thrilling at the same time.

"There are dozens of women in Wolf River you could ask," Paige said, shaking her head. "Women more attractive and more interesting than me. Women you'd have much more in common with. Why in the world would you ask *me?* You don't even know me."

"I know what I need to know." He moved closer to her. "I know you're twenty-six, that you graduated from Texas University and you've worked at the Wolf River Library for five years. I also know that your parents were killed in a car accident when you were twelve, that you lived with your grandmother until she passed away six months ago, that you aren't engaged, though you do spend Friday evenings with Bernie Pratt."

Stunned, she simply stared at him. Other than the fact he'd bought the car from her, Paige wouldn't have thought that Clay Bodine had known she existed. "How—how do you know any of those things about me?"

"This is Wolf River, Paige. You don't even have to ask to know most folks' business," he said evenly. "But it's not as if I picked your name out of a hat, either. I carefully considered several women, but you were—are—my first choice. I'm not looking for a trophy wife. I need a mother for my daughter, someone who's dependable and stable."

"You'd actually marry someone you don't even know?" Eyes wide, she stared at him. "You really think that a marriage without love would be the best environment for your daughter?"

"Mutual respect and consideration between two people is more important than love," he said dryly.

They were *all* important to a marriage, Paige thought, but clearly, based on the tight set of Clay's jaw, he wasn't looking for, or interested in, love.

"And since I would like more children," he went on, "ours would be a real marriage in every other way."

A *real* marriage? He meant *sex,* she realized. Her heart stopped, then began to race.

"Unless—" he lowered his voice when she did not respond "—you find the idea of sleeping with me repulsive."

"Of course you aren't repulsive," she blurted out, then felt her cheeks burn at her outburst. She quickly glanced down at her folded hands and wished the floor would open up and swallow her whole. "But...I don't even *know* you, we don't know each other. Like that, I mean."

He stepped closer to her, so close that denim brushed her knees. Even that tiny contact sent shivers coursing through her. "Do you want children?"

"Of course I do," she replied softly.

"Then marry me," he said firmly. "We'll have as many as you want."

She'd always dreamed of a large family, especially because she'd been an only child. But her dream had included a husband who loved her, and she loved back. Not an arranged marriage with a man she barely knew.

This entire conversation was absurd. Shaking her head, she stood, careful to avoid touching Clay. She reached for her basket, then stepped away and turned to face him squarely. "I wish you luck in finding the right woman, Mr. Bodine, but I'm sorry I can't help you."

His mouth thinned, then he nodded stiffly. "Thank you for your time, Ms. Andrews."

"Goodbye."

She turned and opened the office door, prayed that he wouldn't see how her hand was trembling or her legs were shaking.

She felt his eyes burn through her back as she walked away. At the front register, she somehow managed to face Sheila and Daphne and smile, then casually mentioned that Clay had needed additional paperwork for the car she'd sold him. Still, Paige knew it wouldn't be long before the entire town heard about the drugstore encounter between Clay and herself.

It didn't matter, she told herself. By the time the town heard, they'd have a bigger, better story to tell—that Clay Bodine had found himself a wife.

Page couldn't wait to hear who the lucky woman would be.

The twelve-by-fifteen foot glass-and-steel greenhouse behind the Rocking B barn had a twenty-four hour controlled temperature between seventy-eight and eighty-four degrees with a humidity level of eighty percent. Misters turned on every hour for five minutes. Overhead lights, ordered from a specialty nursery in Florida, glowed for exactly ten hours and twenty minutes per day. If any system were to fail, an alarm would sound inside Joe's apartment over the bunk house.

Growing exotic orchids in Texas was not what you would call easy.

Gravel crunched under Clay's boots as he stepped into the greenhouse. The air smelled of damp earth, and except for the soft sound of Beethoven's Moonlight Sonata drifting from an overhead speaker, it was like stepping into a wild jungle.

"You raised in a barn?" Joe grumbled from the other side of the greenhouse. "Close the damn door."

Joe Morgan had been foreman at the Rocking B for twenty-five years, and the older man's moods, like the tropical flowers he so loved to grow, were unpredictable.

"I *was* raised in a barn." Clay shut the door. "You ought to know."

Joe glanced up from the yellow cymbidium he was carefully pruning with a pair of clippers. His sun-weathered, sixty-two-year-old face softened around the eyes. "If you weren't mucking out a stall, you were sleeping in one. Can't remember how many times Rita Mae had to drag you back to town."

Even as a child, Clay had felt more at home here at the Rocking B than in his parents' big house at the edge of town. Every time he disappeared, which was often, his mother would send their housekeeper to the ranch to bring him back.

"Rita Mae didn't mind." Clay stopped to examine an odd spike of red and gold stripes sprouting from a pot.

"You being a widower with two young boys, she had hopes of being the next Mrs. Joseph Morgan. You shoulda married her while you still had a couple of good years left in you."

"One wife was enough." Joe snipped off a dying spike of yellow flowers from the plant. "I had a ranch to help your grandpa run and a family to raise. A woman takes time and patience. Two things I didn't have."

The truth, Clay knew, was that Joe had simply never stopped loving his first wife. It was the reason he'd taken over the care of her orchids, so he could keep not only her plants, but her spirit alive, as well. He groused constantly about the amount of attention the plants required, but it was a labor of love.

"So what brings you out here at this hour of the night, boy? Wait, let me guess." Joe reached for a spray bottle and gave the plant he was working on a fine misting. "Your librarian turned you down flat, didn't she?"

Clay folded his arms and frowned at Joe. "You mean *your* librarian, don't you? I seem to recall you're the one who suggested Ms. Andrews."

"After looking at the list of women you'd put together," Joe said dryly, "it was obvious your brain had followed your good sense right out the back door. Minnie Wellmer, for God's sake. The women sets off car alarms when she laughs."

"She was raised on a ranch and she likes kids," Clay defended.

Joe rolled his eyes. "And Marsha Carter? She's a sweet girl and nice to look at, but she's got the brain of an emu."

"So maybe I didn't think everything through," Clay agreed irritably. "And maybe you're right and this is a bad idea, but dammit, Joe, I need a wife and I need one now. I've got no choice but to go back to my list."

While Joe tended his plants, Clay paced. He had to admit, if only to himself, that after meeting Paige, he really hadn't the heart, or the stomach, to approach any of the other women on his list.

Joe had been right—Paige Andrews, in spite of the fact that she was a bit mousy and more than a little frumpy, was the best choice all around as a mother for his daughter. Clay knew she was educated and that she ran the reading program for children at the library where she worked. He also knew she'd been seeing Pratt at the bank for quite a while, but according to the gossip lines, Bernie had been dragging his feet, and the relationship didn't appear to be serious.

Paige wasn't a beauty queen, Clay thought, but she wasn't hard to look at, either. She had big, smoky-green eyes, skin that looked soft as rose petals and a mouth—when it wasn't pressed into a thin, firm line—that he'd found more than a little interesting. He remembered how those pretty lips of hers had parted into a small *o* when he'd told her that their marriage would be a real one. She'd blushed bright as a fire engine over that little bit of news.

As strange, and annoying, as it seemed, that straitlaced, Miss Prim manner of Paige's—and the fact that she'd turned his proposal down—had seemed to make him want her all the more.

Shaking his head in frustration, Clay turned his thoughts to the other candidates on his list. He needed a wife to help raise his daughter, and like it or not, tomorrow he was going to have to ask one of those women to marry him.

Paige had a routine. Monday through Thursday, she arrived home from work at precisely six-fifteen, boiled water for tea while she looked over her mail, set her teabag to steep while she changed her clothes, fed Eudora, then made herself dinner. After she ate, she read for one hour, quilted for one hour, then took a long, hot bath before she went to bed and read until ten o'clock. Fridays were different because she went to Bernie's. On the weekends she mostly gardened and cleaned her house, but for the most part, her days, and her nights, were pretty much the same.

Until today.

Since Clay had asked her to marry him, Paige had felt...disconnected. As if someone had pulled the plug on her brain. She'd finished off her shift at work, had gone through all the motions, but she really hadn't *been* there. She knew she'd walked home from work and picked up her mail, then she'd set her tea to boil and steep while she changed into tan slacks and a white sleeveless blouse. But now, as she sat at her cozy kitchen table and stared at the leftovers she'd reheated from the night before and the steaming mint tea she'd poured, she realized she had no precise recollection of doing any of those things.

It wasn't real, she told herself. It *couldn't* be. Men like Clay Bodine simply didn't ask women like herself to marry them.

But he *had* asked, she knew. She hadn't dreamed it, and she hadn't imagined it. Clay Bodine, the most eligible, the most desirable man in Wolf River had proposed to her.

And she'd turned him down.

Well, of course you turned him down, silly.

A woman shouldn't marry a man because he was handsome or sexy, or because he suddenly needed a wife. And there should definitely be love, Paige told herself, though Clay had made it clear that love was not a consideration for him. He wanted a dependable caretaker for his daughter, a wife to raise the child he'd never known.

Someone "dependable and stable," so he'd told her.

Paige straightened her back, then stabbed a green bean and popped it into her mouth. Had it been necessary to throw those qualities in her face, even if she did fit the bill? Now if he'd only added *boring* to his criteria, she'd have been perfect.

Considering all the women who would fight for the chance to be Mrs. Clay Bodine, Paige supposed she should be flattered that she had been his first choice. But his reasons for selecting her, though well-intentioned, were not exactly ego-boosting. What he really wanted was a nanny, she thought. One he could take to his bed at night.

That he'd actually wanted their marriage to be a "real one" as he'd put it, had shocked her more than the proposal itself. Paige knew she was no femme fatale. Men didn't turn their heads when she walked by, and other than her Friday nights with Bernie, she hadn't been asked out on a date in two years, though Rebecca had made numerous attempts to fix her up. The idea of marrying Clay, then sleeping with him, quite literally stole her breath away.

And sent a tingle of excitement rippling up her spine.

Even though she'd turned him down, she couldn't help but wonder what it would be like to be Clay's wife. What it would feel like to be in bed with him. For him to kiss her, to touch her, to slip her nightgown off and put his mouth on her breast—

Her fork slipped from her fingers and clattered to her plate, shaking Paige out of her fantasy. Heavens! Just thinking about the man made her pulse quicken and her skin hot. And, to her embarrassment, made her throb with a need she'd never experienced before. She pressed her thighs firmly together to ward the feeling off, but the dull ache between her legs persisted.

Needing a distraction, she picked up her plate and headed for the sink, turned on the faucet, then squirted dish soap under the spray. She was elbow deep in lemon-scented bubbles, doing her best to think about anything or anyone but Clay Bodine when she heard the knock at her front door.

Frowning, she reached for a dish towel. No one ever knocked on her door this late, except Rebecca, who wouldn't have knocked, anyway. She would have just walked in the back door. But Rebecca was on a buying trip in Austin for her antique store, Paige thought, so it couldn't be her, anyway.

Paige had nearly reached the door when she froze.

What if it was Clay?

Don't be ridiculous, she told herself. Of course it wasn't Clay. Unless he wanted to tell her that he realized he'd made a mistake and he wanted to apologize.

Still, she held her breath as she lifted her eye to the peephole. Her breath rushed out again when she saw who it was.

Bernie.

How absurd for her to be disappointed, she told herself and waited a moment for her nerves to steady. Of course it wasn't Clay.

When she opened the door, she smiled widely. He was still dressed in his dark-brown business suit and yellow-striped tie. "Bernie. What a nice surprise."

"Paige." He nodded stiffly. "May I come in?"

"Of course."

She stepped back, surprised not only by his visit, but by the fact that he was alone. Bernie rarely came to her house without his mother. Like Paige's grandmother, Mrs. Pratt didn't approve of them being completely alone together. Never mind her son was thirty years old, Bernie's mother ruled with an iron fist.

"Would you like some tea?" Paige offered.

"No, thank you. If you have a minute—" he slicked a hand over his short, blond hair, then shifted awkwardly "—I'd like to talk with you."

"Of course." Confused by his odd behavior, Paige finished wiping her hands dry, then led him to the sofa, where they both sat. While he adjusted his tie and suit jacket, she folded her hands and waited patiently for him to speak.

"Paige, I—" His voice broke. He cleared his throat, then turned on the sofa so their knees almost touched. "We've been dating for quite some time now, you know."

Paige had never seen Bernie so nervous before, except maybe the first time he'd kissed her. *He's going to dump me,* she thought.

"So, ah, you know that I have feelings for you," he went on. "Strong feelings."

Great, Paige thought. Here comes the, "but I think we should see other people for a while," part. She did her best to sit very still and let him finish, when she really wanted to just smack him with the wet towel in her hands.

She'd had a very long day, after all.

He cleared his throat again, then took her hand in both of his. "Paige, I think we should get married."

She stared at him for a long moment, letting his words sink in. *I think we should get married?*

This wasn't possible. *Two* proposals in *one* day? Had she suddenly slipped into some kind of alternate universe where every man she encountered asked her to marry him?

"Bernie, I—I don't know what to say."

"I have an excellent health plan at the bank," he said. "And since we'd have live-in child-care, you could keep working, which would help increase our retirement portfolio."

"Live-in child-care?" She stared down at his smooth, cool, manicured hands. "What are you talking about?"

"My mother," he said, gaining confidence. "You have three bedrooms here, more than we need. Now that she's getting on in years, I couldn't just leave her alone. She'll be wonderful company for you, another female in the house to talk to about girl things."

Of all the women in the world that Paige would talk "girl things" to, Bernie's mother was definitely not one of them.

"Let me get this straight," Paige said very carefully. "You want to get married, live in my house, with your mother, and I can keep working after we have children to 'increase our retirement portfolio.'"

He squeezed her hand and smiled. "If we're careful, we should be able to retire in thirty to thirty-five years."

Retire?

Live-in baby-sitter?

I have strong feelings for you?

Golly, Paige thought, a fantasy proposal come true. What girl wouldn't swoon at such a romantic, tempestuous proposal? And to think it was her second one today, too! How lucky could one girl get? Any more luck and she'd throw herself off the roof.

She resisted the urge to yank her hand from Bernie's damp palm. "This is all so sudden."

"We've been seeing each other for almost two years, Paige," he reminded her. "And if we set the date before the end of the year, our tax liability will decrease, as well."

Well, now, *that* was certainly a reason to accept his wildly passionless offer of marriage, Paige thought. They'd save money on their taxes. Whooppee.

"I—I don't know what to say." Get out, was her first thought, but she simply stood. "There's so much to consider, and my head is simply reeling at the moment. Perhaps we can have lunch together tomorrow and discuss this more then."

"Oh, well—" Clearly confused that Paige hadn't immediately said yes, Bernie stood and smoothed a hand down the front of his tie. "Lunch would be fine."

Emotions held carefully in check, she walked Bernie to the door, offered a cheek when he bent to kiss her. "Good night."

Paige closed the door behind him, then walked numbly back to the kitchen and sipped on the cup of mint tea she'd made before dinner. To say that she was having one heck of a strange day was the understatement of the century. Eudora, who'd been curled up on a kitchen chair cushion, glanced up with a bored expression and gave a halfhearted meow.

"My feelings exactly," Paige said through gritted teeth as she plopped her hands back into the still-warm, sudsy sink water.

How many times had Paige envisioned the man she loved, and who loved her back, professing his love and asking her to be his wife? There'd been red roses and a sparkling diamond ring in her dream. Candlelight. Soft music. Flames dancing in a fireplace.

Not in one of those fantasies had the issue of retirement or tax benefits been mentioned. Not once had her true love suggested that his mother come live with them.

Tears burned her eyes as she stared at the snow-white mounds of soap bubbles. Fantasies were simply that, she thought. Fantasies. They held as much substance as the bubbles in her sink.

She scooped up a handful of bubbles and blew on them, watched them scatter and float on the air. Maybe it was time for her to be more realistic about her future. She wanted children desperately. Bernie had offered that.

But then, so had Clay Bodine.

She picked up a glass tumbler and plunged a sponge inside. Not that it mattered what the rancher had offered, she told herself. Surely by now he'd found himself a wife and forgotten all about the colorless, insipid Paige Andrews. Clay and his new fiancée were probably out celebrating right now, having dinner, sharing a bottle of champagne.

Practicing for the wedding night.

Knowing that she could have been that woman if she'd accepted Clay's offer made her skin tighten and her breath catch in her throat. Right at this very moment, he might have been holding her in his arms, kissing her, sliding his hand up her stomach to cup her—

At the sound of her front doorbell, Paige jerked her hand to the side. The glass cracked against the sink, then broke into several large pieces and fell back into the water.

Groaning her annoyance out loud, she grabbed her dish towel again and headed back to the door.

Paige had never known Bernie to be persistent about anything, but she liked the idea that he'd returned. Maybe he'd realized his proposal had been a little too…limp, so to speak, and he'd come back to give it another go.

Only it wasn't Bernie, Paige realized as she opened the door.

It was Clay Bodine.

Chapter 3

For the second time that day, Clay made Paige's heart stumble, then race. Still dressed in the jeans and blue shirt he'd worn earlier in the day, he stood on her front porch, his expression somber as he leveled those incredible blue eyes on her.

"Paige." He nodded tightly. "May I come in?"

What was he doing here? she wondered, unless it was to tell her he'd found someone to marry him, and she needn't concern herself about his situation. Or that he'd come to his senses and realized how completely incompatible they would be together, then apologize for bothering her with his problem.

A strange disappointment flooded her at any of those prospects. How pathetic I am, Paige thought. That she would have preferred to let herself think that Clay hadn't regretted asking her to marry him, even if he had found someone else.

"Of course. Please come in." Still gripping the dish towel tightly in her hands, she stood to the side of the door, then closed it behind him when he moved past her.

He said nothing for a long moment, just looked around her living room. She lived simply, Paige knew, but she'd made the house she'd inherited from her grandmother more than comfortable. Hand-quilted pillows on a burgundy floral sofa, lace curtains on the windows, an antique cherry-wood hutch that held crystal glassware passed down from her great-grandmother. The patchwork quilt she'd been working on lay across the overstuffed arm of a side chair.

And in the middle of the distinctly feminine room stood Clay, looking all the more rugged because of it.

When he turned to face her, her pulse skipped. Around the tight set of his strong jaw, he bore the faint shadow of a beard. His eyes held a razor-sharp edge to them she hadn't noticed this afternoon. He had a dangerous, wild look about him tonight, she thought, and licked her lips nervously. When his gaze dropped to her mouth and held there, Paige felt a little dizzy.

She forced herself to focus, let the years of etiquette her grandmother had imposed upon her to take over. "May I offer you some tea?"

Though she was certain she saw him wince at the offer, he looked back into her eyes and nodded. "Thanks."

Grateful to have something to keep her hands busy, Paige took a step back toward the kitchen. "I'll just be a minute."

"Wait."

Clay moved across the room toward her, a frown darkening his face. Her breath caught when he took hold of her hand.

"You're bleeding."

She glanced down, saw the bright red circle of blood on the dish towel. She'd been so distracted since she'd opened the door, she hadn't realized she'd cut herself.

"I broke a glass in the kitchen sink." She tried to pull her hand back, but he held tight. "It's nothing."

"Relax." He turned her palm up and looked at the small gash just under the base of her thumb. "Let me have a look at it."

"Really, I'm fine."

But she wasn't fine. With Clay standing so close, holding her hand, she was anything *but* fine. He was just so...overwhelming. He was a powerfully built man, at least a foot taller than her, and she had to tilt her head to look up at him. His hands were large and callused, yet his touch was surprisingly gentle. When he lightly rubbed the center of her palm with his thumb, a shiver ran up her arm.

"It stopped bleeding." But he was still stroking her hand. "Shouldn't need any stitches."

"Clay." Paige had to pull herself back before she swayed into him. "What are you doing here?"

Clay realized he'd been so caught up in the smooth,

silky feel of Paige's skin, at the sight of her shiny, sandy-blond hair brushing the tops of her slender shoulders, that he'd forgotten, for just a moment, the purpose of his visit.

What was it about Paige that set him on edge? he wondered. She wasn't what most men would consider beautiful, but she was certainly pretty, he realized. Especially now, with her hair loosened from that tight bun she usually wore, and the blouse and slacks she had on definitely displayed the fact that she did indeed have a woman's curves. And why hadn't he noticed the light splattering of freckles across her straight little nose, or the upward tilt in the corners of her full lips?

Realizing that he'd been sidetracked, he forced his attention back to the reason he was here and released her hand. "I want to apologize for this afternoon."

"That's not necessary." Her tone turned crisp as an autumn night. "Your need to get married was an impulsive decision based on the fear of losing your daughter."

He furrowed his brow. "My decision wasn't impulsive."

"Not your proposal, perhaps. But now that you've had time to reconsider, I completely understand."

He was glad she understood, because he sure as hell didn't. "I didn't come here to tell you I had reconsidered. I came here to ask *you* to reconsider."

That seemed to get her attention.

"You...what?"

"I know I scared you this afternoon," he said evenly.

"I shouldn't have cornered you like I did. It wasn't fair to you."

"Are you telling me you still haven't found a wife?" She stared at him in disbelief. "That the other women on your list turned you down, too?"

Clay damned himself for ever mentioning he'd had a list. Lord, it was hard enough he'd done this once today. "Can we sit down?"

"I—I suppose we could sit in the kitchen while I make tea."

"Never mind the tea." He'd rather drink radiator fluid. He took her by the arm, then led her to the sofa and sat next to her. "I didn't ask anyone else to marry me. I want to marry you."

Her eyes widened, then she shook her head. "I don't understand."

"Look," he said on a heavy breath, "I know this is hardly conventional, but if you're worrying about the stigma of being married to the son of a convicted felon I can under—"

"I most certainly would not worry about such a thing!" she said indignantly. "And I resent your implication that I would have such a small mind to associate your father's crime with you."

Clay lifted a brow. It appeared that the little mouse could indeed roar when she was offended. He lifted one corner of his mouth and took her hand in his. "Paige, I'll treat you well. Give you a home, children. Respect. All I ask is that you be a good mother to Julia and a wife to me. Once we're married, I won't look to other women, but I do have physical needs. You said you didn't find me repulsive.''

"Of course I don't," she muttered.

"We can build on that," he told her. "You can set the pace for intimacy between us."

"What if I won't be able to—" her gaze dropped and another blush brightened her cheeks "—satisfy your needs? Maybe you won't even *like* me in that way."

He was silent for a moment, then cupped her chin in his hand and lifted her face to his. "Easy way to settle that question."

He felt her body stiffen, saw the fear flash in her eyes as he lowered his mouth to hers. She'd pressed her lips into a firm line, as if she was determined not to respond, to prove to him she would be the wrong choice for a wife.

Clay had always enjoyed a challenge.

Lightly he brushed his lips over hers, then moved to the corner of her mouth to nibble. When he caught her lower lip between his teeth, he felt the tremor move through her body.

A good sign, he thought, moving his mouth over hers with whisper-soft kisses. When her breath shuddered out, he slipped inside. She tasted like mint and smelled like lemon, he realized dimly. Her mouth softened under his; her tongue touched his tentatively, a sweet, shy movement that made his blood heat up. Sliding a hand over her shoulder, he cupped the back of her head and brought her closer.

She made a sound, a soft murmur of surprise. She leaned

into her, lifted a hand to his chest, then slid her fingers up to rest on his shoulder. He deepened the kiss, slid his other hand around her waist and up her back, bringing her upper body flush with his. Her breasts, soft and full, pressed against his chest, threatening to snap the control he carefully held in check.

Oh yeah, he thought. No doubt in his mind that he and Paige would be quite physically compatible in bed. He reined in the growing need inside him, concentrated on pleasing her, on seducing her into saying yes, if that's what it took. He wanted Paige more than ever now, and he was determined to have her.

From the moment Clay's lips had touched hers, Paige had lost the ability to think clearly. In her entire life, no man had ever kissed her this way. With such...intensity. With such tenderness, yet passion at the same time. Her blood warmed and a longing stirred inside her, made her heart beat wildly against her ribs.

Relentless, his mouth moved over hers, the taste of coffee and man arousing her more than she would have thought possible. She felt the heat of his muscular chest pressed so close to hers, felt her skin tighten and her nipples harden. Wave after wave of shining, silver-tipped pleasure coursed through her body.

The sound of her soft moan shocked her, but at the moment, she was too overwhelmed to even be embarrassed. And if his kiss wasn't a powerful enough assault on her senses, she wanted, *craved,* more. Her body ached to be touched, as well.

And to touch, she realized.

She curled her fingers into the soft cotton of his shirt, felt the ripple of muscle underneath her hands. She felt small against him, vulnerable, yet the idea of his large, strong body moving over her own did not frighten her, it excited. The pleasure she felt became a frustration she'd never experienced before. She moved against him, her breathing ragged, and pressed her aching breasts closer. The pressure between her legs became an unbearable, pounding throb.

And then he took her arms in his hands and pulled away. It was all she could do not to drag him back. Confused, disappointed, Paige slowly opened her eyes.

His hands tightened on her arms and for one, wonderful moment she thought he might kiss her again. His blue eyes glinted with desire, his jaw tightened and flexed. But he didn't kiss her. Instead, he dropped his hands and leaned away from her.

"Well, I'd say that answers any questions about our sexual compatibility," he said hoarsely.

She hadn't the voice to answer, but she had regained enough control to be embarrassed by her unbridled response to Clay's kiss. Good grief, she thought, she'd all but ripped his clothes off.

"We could get a license first thing in the morning," he said tightly. "Say yes, Paige."

First thing in the morning? Her head began to spin. "I— I have to work tomorrow."

"On your lunch hour, then. And that's the other thing

I need from you.'' He reached for her again, took hold of her shoulders and met her gaze with his. ''I need you to at least take the summer off to be home with Julia. She'll start school in the fall, so if you still want to work, you can go back then.''

''But I can't just take the summer off. I have a responsibility. Schedules to make, orders to place, shipments to catalogue, a computer system that—''

Without warning, he kissed her again, cut off her protests with his mouth and made every other thought fly out of her head.

The sneaky bastard.

By the time he raised his head again, she would have agreed to anything. Anything and everything.

''We can be married on Friday.''

''So soon?'' Her voice sounded small and far away.

''Judge Winters can marry us in his chambers.''

Judge Winters marry them in his chambers? The last of Paige's marriage fantasy—a church wedding—shattered into tiny pieces. Of course Clay wouldn't want a church wedding, she realized. He was in too much of a hurry for that. And like he'd said, this was hardly a conventional marriage.

She thought about Bernie, weighed his proposal against Clay's, and realized there wasn't much difference in the hearts and flowers department. Neither man had offered romance or love. Clay brought a child to their marriage, Bernie brought his retirement plan and mother. Paige shuddered at the thought.

But Bernie had never kissed her like that. Bernie had never made her heart slam in her chest or her toes curl. She'd never once considered ripping Bernie's clothes off.

Should she refuse both men and hold out for love? she wondered. Or should she face reality that a plain, dull librarian might never find her knight in shining armor?

She looked into Clay's somber gaze, believed that he would be a good husband and father. The lengths he was willing to go for his daughter were certainly admirable. She also believed that he would treat her well. If he didn't love her, Paige knew that he would at least respect her. All those things meant a great deal to her.

And maybe, just maybe, she thought, he might learn to love her, and she him. She knew the odds were against her, but as the saying went, all things were possible in love and war.

"Paige."

She looked at him, knew that he was waiting. The mantel clock over her fireplace loudly ticked off the seconds. "My house…"

"You can keep it or sell it, whatever you want," he said. "Just say yes."

"I—I suppose I could rent it. Rebecca's been looking for a place. I—" Her throat tightened and suddenly she couldn't speak.

She drew in a breath and nodded.

His hands loosened on her arms, then he let go of her and stood. "I'll meet you at the courthouse at noon tomorrow, by the county records desk."

"What—what will we tell people?" she asked through the haze surrounding her brain.

"It's easy enough to let it slip to a few people that we've been secretly dating for a few months," he said with a shrug. "I don't much give a damn what anyone thinks, but I realize a story like that might be easier for you."

She appreciated that he was considering her reputation in Wolf River and the kind of scrutiny and criticism she might be under for marrying him so unexpectedly. "Thank you."

She walked him to the door, then leaned back against it after he left, afraid her knees might buckle if she tried to walk back to her sofa.

"I'm getting married," she whispered in wonderment and touched her fingertips to her mouth. Her lips still tingled from his kiss. After several long minutes, she sighed, then pushed away from the door, making a mental note to call Bernie in the morning and cancel their lunch date.

A warm rain fell Friday morning. By Texas standards, barely a drizzle. But it was enough to wet the streets and raise puddles on the concrete steps of the courthouse. Enough to keep most people from walking idly along the sidewalks of town. More than likely, the weather would clear as quickly as it had come on, then the humidity would settle in like a hot, Turkish bath.

Inside the courthouse, in the corridor outside Judge Martin Winters's private chambers, Clay paced. He'd arrived with Joe twenty minutes ago and been informed by Helen

Talbot, Judge Winters's matronly secretary, that she would call him inside when Paige was ready.

For the tenth time in as many minutes, Clay glanced at his wristwatch, then muttered a curse and looked at his foreman. Arms folded casually while he leaned against the opposite wall, Joe wore a gray tweed blazer, white dress shirt and black string tie. He shifted a toothpick lazily from one side of his mouth to the other, a habit he'd picked up since he'd quit smoking five years ago.

Clay glanced at the closed office door, had to shove his hands into his suit pockets to keep from reaching for the doorknob. "What the hell is taking so long?"

"Afraid your bride will change her mind?" Joe's deep brown eyes crinkled with amusement.

Your bride. Clay felt his throat close up at the term, then wiped at the fine sheen of sweat on his brow.

The truth was—Clay started to pace again—he *was* afraid that Paige might change her mind. Though they'd spoken on the phone every day since they'd filed for the license and taken their blood tests, he hadn't actually seen her. She'd hinted that her best friend, Rebecca Montgomery, had been less than thrilled at the news, but assured Clay she would proceed with the ceremony as planned.

And it wasn't as if he hadn't had second or third or even fourth thoughts about getting married himself. Hell, even a man who *wanted* to get married felt his feet getting a little cold before the big day. But every time he considered backing out, he thought about his daughter, thought about all the years he'd lost out on already. After two visitations with Julia, both in the Barringtons' house, Clay wasn't about to let one more day go by that he wouldn't be a part of her life. She was *his* child, and he intended to raise her. And if getting married would help him gain full custody of his daughter, then so be it.

And after kissing Paige the other night, he thought, getting married certainly wouldn't be all bad. He'd lain awake every night since then, thinking about the way her body had fit against his, how soft her lips had been, how sweet she'd tasted. Over and over in his head, he'd heard that little sound she'd made, half moan, half whimper, and he'd become aroused all over again.

He was more than anxious to take her to his bed and relieve the frustration she'd provoked in him.

On an oath, he glanced at his watch again. He'd give her five more minutes, he told himself. Then, ready or not, he was coming in.

"So let him wait," Rebecca said irritably behind the oak-paneled door of the judge's antechamber. "It'll do him good to sweat a little. Besides, I'm not finished with your hair. Now sit still and stop fidgeting."

"Easy for you to say," Paige mumbled. "You're not the one getting married."

Paige lifted a fingernail to chew on, but promptly had her hand slapped away.

"You'll mess up your manicure and your lipstick," Rebecca reprimanded. "And no, I'm not the one getting married. I'm not the one who's completely taken leave of my senses and agreed to marry a complete stranger, either.''

As if Rebecca would have to, Paige thought. If Rebecca wanted a man, all she'd have to do was wiggle a finger at him. With her auburn hair, emerald-green eyes and stunning looks, she was the type of woman that had men tripping over their feet and tongues. But marriage was not in Rebecca's immediate plans right now. She was more interested in running her antique store and for the moment, seemed to be happy with her life just as it was.

''We've been through this already.'' Paige sat on her hands to resist temptation. ''Clay wasn't a complete stranger to me. I told you. We met when he bought my grandmother's car.''

''Oh, yeah, that's right, you'd met.'' Sarcasm dripped off Rebecca's voice. ''First he shows up and wants Grandma's '57 Chevy, then he shows up and wants you.''

''I know I'm not supermodel material,'' Paige said stiffly, ''but I'd appreciate it if you didn't compare me to the purchase of an antique car.''

''Oh, honey, I'm sorry. I didn't mean it that way.'' Rebecca knelt and took Paige's hands in her own. ''You're the most beautiful person I know, inside and out. Clay Bodine's the luckiest man in the world. Just wait until he gets a look at you. His eyes are gonna pop out. You're beautiful.''

Paige doubted that Clay's eyes would pop out. She also doubted he'd think she looked beautiful. But after spending yesterday morning in a beauty salon, letting the hairdresser, a makeup artist and a hovering Rebecca have their way with her, Paige had to admit she at least *felt* pretty. Other than lipstick, she'd never worn cosmetics before, and was amazed at the difference a light application of mascara and blush made. Between the makeup and her new haircut of wispy bangs and layered sides, Paige barely recognized herself in the mirror. Her eyes looked bigger, her face softer, her lips fuller.

Next had come the manicure and pedicure, then an afternoon shopping trip to find an appropriate dress and shoes to wear for the ceremony. After two hours of disagreeing on everything they looked at, Paige finally agreed with Rebecca that a white silk suit dress and two inch white satin heels was perfect.

Rebecca hadn't let it end there. She'd insisted that the bride's trousseau include lingerie, too. Bras and panties in lace and silk, all definitely more sexy and more colorful than the boring, everyday cotton underwear Paige normally wore. Just thinking about wearing the thigh-skimming, white satin negligee with lace edging that Rebecca had bought her as a wedding present made Paige blush. The idea of putting on such a provocative, revealing negligee for Clay, and the realization that he'd be taking it off, made her insides turn inside out.

He was waiting for her, she knew. Outside in the corridor.

The room started to spin.

"Whoa, Paige, you all right?" Rebecca's eyes narrowed. "My God, you're pale as a ghost and your hands are like ice."

"I—I'm all right." Paige closed her eyes and drew in a slow breath. "I'm just a little dizzy."

"Honey, you don't have to do this." Rebecca squeezed Paige's hands. "I'll go out there right now and tell Clay you've changed your mind. I'll take you home and we'll eat chocolate and watch old Doris Day movies."

Paige laughed, then shook her head. "I haven't changed my mind, I'm just scared to death."

"Every bride is scared to death, even under the best circumstances," Rebecca said gently. "But if you want to get really scared, just think about Bernie's mother living with you. That alone should eliminate any doubts you're marrying the right man."

Paige could still see Bernie's face when she'd gone to the bank three days ago and turned down his proposal, then told him she was marrying Clay Bodine. His face had turned chalk-white, then beet-red.

"Are you telling me that you'd marry a man you've barely met?" he had gasped. "A man whose father is a criminal, rather than marry me?"

"Clay's father paid his debt to society." Paige lifted her chin defensively. "And Clay worked hard and made a success out of his ranch so he could pay back every penny."

Bernie's face had gone from red to deep purple. "So you're marrying him because he's rich."

"I most certainly am not marrying him because he's rich!" Paige said loud enough to turn heads in the bank.

"Why else would you marry him?" Bernie whispered harshly.

"Because—" She had barely caught herself before telling Bernie about Clay's daughter. No one in town knew yet, and the bank was hardly the place to announce it. "I don't have to explain myself to you, Bernie Pratt."

"There's something going on here, Paige. Men like Clay Bodine don't marry women—" he stopped, smoothed a hand down his tie "—ah, women they don't know."

Paige stiffened. "You were going to say women like me, weren't you?"

He shifted awkwardly. "No, of course not."

Bernie was a terrible liar. Paige watched his gaze dart away as he nervously fiddled with a stack of papers on his desk.

"Yes, you were going to say that." She'd suddenly felt a deep sense of sadness. "And you're right, Bernie. Women like me marry men like you. Which doesn't say much for either one of us, does it?"

"Paige—"

"I'm sorry, Bernie," she said quietly. "I hope you'll find someone who deserves you."

She rose from her chair and offered her hand. Bernie just stared at her as if she'd gone mad. Maybe she had, she thought. Because marrying Clay Bodine had to be insane.

But she hadn't changed her mind. If anything, she was

determined. Determined to be more than she'd ever been before. Not necessarily better. Just more.

She'd left the bank then and hadn't looked back.

"Paige." Helen Talbot came into the room, looking a bit flustered. "Your groom is about to break down the door if I don't let him in soon. Are you ready, dear?"

Was she? Paige felt the low, deep drum of her heart.

"One word," Rebecca said soberly. "Just give me one word and we're gone."

Everything was in place. Rebecca was watching Eudora for the weekend, Paige had a leave of absence from the library for the summer, Clay was waiting outside…

But she could still stop this, Paige knew. She could say that one word and walk away.

Drawing in a long breath to steady her nerves, Paige stood and nodded.

"I'm ready."

"It's about damn time," Clay grumbled under his breath, then followed Helen Talbot into the inner office of Judge Winters's chambers. The office was spacious, with floor-to-ceiling oak bookshelves and a polished hardwood floor. Two brown leather armchairs faced a massive mahogany desk, where a bottle of champagne chilled in a silver bucket of ice.

Judge Winters, a white-haired, bushy-browed man with silver-rimmed glasses, entered through a side door.

"Clay."

"Judge."

Fifteen years ago, before he'd become a judge, Martin Winters had been the defense lawyer who'd represented Clay's father at the embezzlement trial. Even knowing that the Bodine family had no money to pay him, and that the case would hardly make him a popular man in Wolf River, Martin had nevertheless worked tirelessly to reduce Wesley Bodine's jail sentence. In the end, he'd managed to trim a five year sentence down to four, and even after the trial, after Clay's father had been sent away to prison, Martin had called and visited the Rocking B regularly to make sure that Clay was all right and offer any assistance he or his grandfather might need.

Other than Joe, Judge Winters was the only person in Wolf River who had seemed to give a damn. The only other man who Clay considered a friend. The judge was the first person Clay had called when he'd found out about Julia, the only person he'd asked for advice.

"You sure about this?" the judge asked him quietly.

Clay nodded. "I'm sure."

The judge sighed, then nodded at Mrs. Talbot when she stuck her head in from the anteroom.

Finally, Clay thought, adjusting the tie that felt much too tight around his neck. All he wanted to do was say what had to be said, sign what had to be signed, then get the hell out of here.

Rebecca walked into the room first, then Paige.

And Clay's mind went blank.

Paige?

Good Lord. He stared at the woman dressed in a white

silk suit, could hardly believe this was the same woman he'd asked to marry him. When her smoky green gaze met his, his throat suddenly felt dry, and he could hear his pulse pounding in his brain.

He had to remind himself to breathe.

"Clay?"

"Yes?" He dragged his eyes off Paige and stared blankly at the judge. "What?"

Judge Winters smiled. "You stand here. Joe, you stand to Clay's right. Paige, you look lovely."

"Thank you, Your Honor."

Carrying a small bouquet of white rosebuds and baby's breath, Paige took her place beside Clay. She held her back straight as a post, kept her eyes locked on Judge Winters as he performed the ceremony. When Clay took her ice-cold hand and slipped a diamond solitaire and band on her finger, she looked up at him in surprise. They repeated the marriage vows, then Judge Winters proclaimed them man and wife.

It took less than five minutes.

"You may now kiss the bride."

Clay took Paige by the arms, felt her tremble as he bent to kiss her. It was a light kiss, a mere brush of lips, then he straightened and shook the judge's hand. While Mrs. Talbot sniffled and hugged Paige, Joe opened the champagne and poured, then handed everyone a glass.

"To the groom and his beautiful bride."

Paige sipped her champagne. Clay downed his in one gulp.

He managed to endure the polite small talk for all of ten minutes. "Are you ready?" he finally asked Paige.

He saw the flash of fear in her eyes, the intake of breath. She nodded stiffly, then hugged Rebecca.

Clay wasn't certain whether to be amused or annoyed when Rebecca glared at him.

They said their goodbyes, then he took Paige by the arm. Outside, the rain had turned to a warm drizzle. When Paige hesitated in front of a large puddle, Clay scooped her up in his arms. Her eyes were wide, her body stiff as he carried her to the parking lot.

"My car and suitcase are back at my house," she said awkwardly.

"I've already asked Joe to get your suitcase, and you won't need your car today. If you need to drive into town before we pick it up, you can use your grandmother's car." He dumped her into the front cab of his truck, then came around and started the engine. "We aren't going directly to the ranch."

Paige narrowed her eyes in confusion. "Where are we going?"

"To The Four Winds Hotel."

Chapter 4

He was taking her to The Four Winds?

Paige had no idea what to say. Clay had never mentioned they'd be going to Wolf River's biggest, and most luxurious hotel. She had assumed they'd immediately go to the ranch after the ceremony, especially after he'd declined Rebecca's offer to prepare a luncheon for the wedding party.

The man continually surprised her. Not just because he'd asked her to marry him, but also the bridal bouquet he'd had delivered this morning to her house, the champagne he'd sent to Judge Winters's chambers, the stunning diamond ring he'd slipped on her finger. And now The Four Winds.

She realized he'd done everything for appearances, but

still, she was grateful that he'd taken the time and consideration to make this day special for her. As if she mattered to him.

Foolish thinking, of course. But it *was* her wedding day, whether it was the real thing or not. And she *had* finished her glass of champagne, so she felt a little warm and tingly inside. Had he reserved the bridal suite for them? she wondered as he pulled into valet parking. Her heart beat faster at the idea that Clay might be anxious to start the wedding night now, even though it wasn't noon yet.

She cast a sideways glance at him, couldn't help but think how handsome he looked. The tailored black suit he wore accentuated his broad shoulders, and the silk teal tie around his neck made his eyes appear a deeper blue. She'd stood shoulder to shoulder with this man in front of Judge Winters and repeated her vows, as Clay had repeated his, but she barely remembered the words.

Married, she thought. Clay Bodine was truly her husband, and she was truly his wife. She still couldn't believe any of this was happening.

She slid out of the truck when the valet opened her door, waited until Clay came around and joined her. Casually, he placed a hand on her back as they walked inside the hotel. Her pulse jumped at the contact.

In the center of the marble-floored lobby, a huge bouquet of sweet-smelling flowers greeted the guests. Lush green plants spilled from fire-glazed pots of varying sizes. Classical music drifted softly from unseen speakers.

Paige had been here once before. Three months ago, she had treated Rebecca to a birthday dinner at Adagios, the five-star restaurant inside the hotel. The food and service had been memorable.

And now she was here with Clay.

As they approached the reservation desk, her hands trembled and excitement shivered up her spine. Anticipation of making love with Clay—in the middle of the day, no less—made her knees go weak.

"Welcome to The Four Winds." A pretty brunette desk clerk smiled at Clay. "May I help you, sir?"

"Would you please ring Mr. and Mrs. Barrington's room and tell them Clay Bodine is here to see them?"

Paige stiffened at Clay's words, and it felt as if all the air had been suddenly sucked from her lungs.

Clay wasn't bringing her here to be with him, Paige realized. He'd come to see the Barringtons. He hadn't even said Mr. and Mrs. Clay Bodine were here to see the Barringtons. He'd simply said Clay Bodine.

How ridiculous she'd been to think he'd wanted to be alone with her, intimately, in such a romantic setting as The Four Winds. Quickly she blinked back the moisture burning her eyes. She'd be careful not to make that mistake again, she told herself resolutely. If she was going to survive being Clay's wife, she needed to be strong. Any expectations that this marriage might be more than Clay had told her it would be was foolish.

And stupid.

"You can go up now, Mr. Bodine," the clerk said brightly. "Suite 1215."

They rode up the elevator in silence. Tension radiated from Clay as he knocked on the door. When it opened, a man, probably in his sixties, wearing black slacks and a white polo shirt stood on the other side. His neat, brown hair was gray at the sides and he wore silver-framed glasses over eyes the color of steel.

Clay nodded stiffly. "Barrington."

"Bodine."

Clay placed a hand on Paige's back, but kept his gaze on the elder man. "This is Paige, my wife. Paige, this is Robert Barrington."

She held her breath when the man's gaze moved to her. Had Clay told his ex-in-laws that he was getting married? she wondered. And had he mentioned that he'd be bringing his new bride here today, or was she a complete surprise?

Robert Barrington nodded politely, his gaze neither dismissive or inviting, then he opened the door wider and stepped to the side. "Come in."

Paige released the breath she'd been holding.

Inside the parlor of the well-appointed suite, sitting on a white sofa across the room, was a tall, slender woman, also around sixty, wearing a blue linen dress. Her thick, blond hair was swept into a French roll and knots of gold glittered on her earlobes. A dark-haired little girl wearing a pale pink jumper sat beside the woman. The child's features were delicate, her skin like porcelain, her deep blue eyes wide with worry.

"Go say hello to your father, Julia," the woman coaxed.

Julia glanced nervously from her grandmother to Clay, then slowly stood and walked across the room. Smiling, Clay knelt and held out a hand. "Julia, this is Paige, the lady I told you about. Remember?"

The little girl nodded, then held her hand out to Paige. "How do you do."

Well, she'd certainly been taught manners, Paige thought as she took the child's small hand. "I've looked forward to meeting you, Julia," Paige said with a smile.

"I'm Linda Barrington," the woman introduced herself. "I believe congratulations are in order."

"I—" Paige glanced at Clay, not certain what to say.

"Thank you," Clay replied as he straightened.

"Perhaps we could have lunch together, Clay," Linda Barrington suggested. "It would make the transition easier for Julia."

"It's just for the weekend, Linda," Clay said quietly. "I'm sure Julia will be fine." He smiled down at his daughter. "I have a little colt at my ranch that was born two weeks ago. Would you like to see him?"

Julia's face lit. "Can I pet him?"

"Sure can. Soon as we get back to the ranch and change our clothes, we'll go out to the barn." Clay's smile faded as he looked at Robert. "I'll have her back Sunday evening."

While Clay picked up Julia's suitcase, Paige stepped back and watched his daughter hug and kiss her grandparents goodbye. It was apparent that the Barringtons adored their granddaughter and though they were smiling and pretending to be happy for Julia's sake, it was also clear they dreaded this first separation.

Ten minutes later, with Julia buckled in the front seat of the truck between Paige and Clay, busily chatting about the colt, they drove out of town.

In the side mirror, Paige watched the town, and her life as she'd known it, slowly disappear from view.

The Rocking B Ranch was ten thousand acres of prime land as far as the eye could see and beyond. Sleepy-eyed cattle grazed in meadows still green from a wet spring, then drank from wide streams and narrow creeks that bubbled through the lower valley. A grove of Spanish oak shaded a small pond behind the house. Wildflowers bloomed in nature's palette of blues, reds and yellows.

Clay's grandfather, and his great-grandfather, had worked this land for over a hundred years. Every post had been set, every road had been cleared, every well had been dug with Bodine hands. The hard, slow work had been a labor of love, for both the men and the women they'd married, as well. Their lives had been simple, but they'd been happy. Clay had hoped that he and Nancy might have that same happiness here.

What a fool he'd been.

Clay knew now that Nancy had married him not for

love, but for adventure. For the fantasy of an exciting life
on a Texas ranch. She'd been visiting a friend in Dallas
whose father had just purchased a two-year-old from the
Rocking B and Clay had personally delivered the horse.
He and Nancy had been introduced at dinner that night
and sparks had flown between them. Their courtship had
been tempestuous, their elopement impulsive. On their
week long, West Coast honeymoon, they'd actually been
happy.

And then he'd brought her home.

Nancy had hated the simplicity of the town of Wolf
River, the isolation on the ranch, the extremes and un-
predictability of the weather. She'd hated the dust and the
smell of the animals and the absence of Saks Fifth Ave-
nue.

And it wasn't long before she'd hated him, too.

He obviously hadn't been thinking when he'd made
Nancy his wife and brought her home to the Rocking B.
Not with his head, anyway.

This time his marriage would not be based on lust or
love, he thought as he pulled off the highway and turned
onto a gravel road leading to the ranch. This time both
he and Paige understood that this was a practical, logical
marriage for both of them. Based on the kiss they'd
shared the other night, a marriage that they would both
find pleasurable, as well.

He thought of his big bed, knew that Paige would be
sleeping there tonight, and he felt instantly aroused. It had
been a long time since he'd been with a woman. He was

anxious to consummate their marriage and relieve the frustration that had been building steadily this past week.

He still couldn't get over how different Paige looked today. As a man, he fully appreciated her new style, but as her husband, he wasn't quite certain he was comfortable with the change. It made him…uneasy.

He scoffed at the idea, then glanced over at his new wife. She'd spent the thirty minute ride from town asking Julia questions about herself. If she liked to read books and play games, if she had a favorite television show or a movie. Because he hadn't a clue what to say to his own daughter, Clay was grateful that Paige had made his first time with his daughter—without the Barringtons standing guard—much easier for him.

"There's a horse!" Julia cried with delight when she caught sight of a roan gelding munching grass in the pasture beside the road. She pointed through the windshield. "And there's another one!"

"We can go see them after we take your suitcase inside," Clay told his daughter.

Eyes wide, Julia looked at Paige. "Will you come, too?"

"Of course, I will." Paige squeezed Julia's small hand. "But we all need to change our clothes first, okay?"

"I can do that real fast," Julia said with all sincerity.

Paige smiled at the little girl, felt her own trepidation grow at the new life that was suddenly facing them all. How strange it seemed that they were an instant family, yet they all knew so little about each other. Paige realized she'd taken a risk marrying Clay, just as he'd taken a risk marrying her. Other than the four- and five-year-olds she read to at the library for story-time days, Paige had never been around children. And now she was suddenly faced with raising one. What if she failed? Paige worried. Being a good parent couldn't be learned from a book. She was bound to make mistakes.

The enormity of the responsibility made Paige's stomach knot. She looked at the beautiful, dark-haired child sitting beside her, then at Clay. Love had not brought them together, she knew, but she was nonetheless determined to be the best mother to Julia, and the best wife to Clay, that she possibly could.

While Julia pointed out other horses in the pasture, Clay drove his truck through two red brick pillars and an open, wrought iron gate that delineated where the gravel road ended and a brick-lined concrete driveway began. A freshly-mowed lawn the size of a football field sparkled from the early morning rain, and the surrounding rose gardens bloomed in a riot of pinks and yellows. Though the skies had cleared, raindrops still clung to all the plants and dampened the ground.

Paige felt her breath catch when she saw the two-story red brick house at the end of the driveway. She had no idea what she'd been expecting, but certainly nothing this grand.

''It's beautiful,'' she heard herself whisper.

''My grandparents built it after they were married,'' Clay said as he turned off the engine. ''They'd planned on having a large family, but my grandmother died two years after my father was born and my grandfather never remarried.''

''It looks brand-new.'' Paige noted the panels of leaded glass beside the oak, double-entry doors, the fresh, white paint on the eaves and shutters, the shiny brass lamp on top of a black wrought iron pole beside the porch steps.

''I've done a little refurbishing the past few months,'' Clay said with a shrug, then got out of the truck.

Paige waited while Clay came around to the passenger door and opened it. She took the hand he offered and slid out of the truck, then lifted her gaze to his. When their eyes met and held, she felt a tingle run up her spine. When his gaze dropped to her mouth, her heart skipped.

Something passed between them. It was sexual, to be sure. But there was more, Paige thought when Clay's hand tightened around hers. A momentary flicker of…oneness. And for that one instant, Paige felt as if she truly was a bride, that Clay truly was her husband.

The moment dissipated as quickly as it had risen, and once again, she was simply the woman Clay Bodine had married, chosen from a carefully predetermined list of prospective wives. If he hadn't married her, Paige knew, then another woman would be standing here at this very moment. Another woman would be mother to Julia.

Another woman would be sharing his bed tonight.

Deciding this was hardly the time to be thinking about that, Paige stepped away as Clay helped his daughter out of the truck.

"The house is open," he said, nodding at the front doors. "Go ahead inside while I get the suitcases."

Paige took the little girl's hand and together they walked into the house. The tiled entry opened directly into a spacious, open-beam living room. To the right, Paige noticed her suitcase sitting beside an oak staircase that curved upward to the second story. To the left, a sparkling crystal chandelier hung from the ceiling of the formal dining room. The smell of fresh paint and wood stain hung heavy in the air.

Paige stared in wonder at the beauty of the large house, but was confused by one rather conspicuous detail.

There was no furniture.

Not one chair. Not one sofa. Not even a painting or a lamp.

Nothing.

She silently asked the question when Clay stepped into the entry carrying Julia's suitcase.

He shrugged. "Nancy took everything with her when she left, and I haven't needed much."

Obviously, Paige thought and stared at the barren house.

"We can pick up whatever you might want to bring here from your house." Clay picked up Paige's suitcase in his free hand. "And I've got the name of a decorator from Dallas you can work with. She told me she can put a rush order for anything you want."

Anything I want? Paige looked at the blank walls and empty rooms and felt overwhelmed.

"There are beds and linens upstairs," he said. "Plus the kitchen is stocked with everything you'll need for now, including a dinette set. There's food in the refrigerator that should hold us for at least a couple of days. I've also placed an ad for a housekeeper. I've narrowed a list of applicants down to two women you can interview whenever you're ready."

"You—you want *me* to hire a housekeeper?" Paige shook her head in disbelief. "And decorate your house?"

"The house is your domain now," he said flatly.

"But I don't know what style you like or don't like," she protested.

"You can paint the walls purple and green if it makes you happy. All I care about is the ranch and the livestock."

His words stung, but what did she expect? She knew he'd married her only to prove to the courts his daughter would be well cared for. In Clay's eyes, Paige thought, she was on the same par as the rest of the domestic help he intended to hire.

"Can I change my clothes and see the horses now?" Julia tugged on Paige's hand.

"Of course, you can, sweetheart." Paige smiled. "Maybe if you ask your daddy, we can find a carrot or apple to feed them, too."

"Can we?" Julia looked at Clay. "Can we, Daddy?"

"I think I can arrange that," Clay said with a nod, then started up the stairs. "Let's go see where your room is first so you can change your clothes, okay?"

Bouncing with delight at the prospect of feeding the horses, Julia let go of Paige's hand and clambered up the stairs behind her father.

Paige waited a moment, then drew in a deep breath, and followed behind.

He couldn't concentrate. Clay had totaled the column of expenses in his ledger three different times and come up with three different numbers. Twice he'd mislabeled an account, and he couldn't count the times he'd transposed figures.

He'd bought new bookkeeping software for his computer, but he hadn't had time to install it, let alone learn how to run it, so he was still scribbling away in the ledger system he'd always used. He considered that Paige might be familiar with computers since she worked at the library, but he quickly discounted the idea of asking for her help. He'd managed to get along quite well up to now by himself, so he figured the new program could wait a few more weeks.

Tossing the pencil in his hand down on his cluttered desktop, he rubbed his hands over his face, then sat back in his chair. He'd been in his office for the past hour, working to balance his books while Paige helped Julia bathe and get ready for bed. He'd gotten nowhere fast. He'd never had this much trouble keeping his mind on his paperwork before, had certainly never used more eraser than lead.

But he'd never had a child in his home before, either.

His child, he thought, listening to the sound of laughter coming from Julia's bedroom down the hall. From the bits and pieces of conversation he'd managed to pick up, Clay knew that Paige had been acting out a bedtime story for his daughter. Something about a princess and a dragon and a forest filled with elves.

More than once, he'd been tempted to go stand in the hallway and listen himself. The sound of Paige's enthusiastic role-playing intrigued him, tugged at his curiosity. When she assumed her deepest dragon voice and warned all who approached to run away, he couldn't help but smile.

Paige had been terrific with Julia today, Clay mused. She'd helped his daughter feed carrots to the horses, even though Paige herself was obviously a little nervous around the large animals. Julia had been insistent on meeting every horse in the barn and learning their names, and she'd also picked up a friendship with Scooter, a stray border collie mix that Joe had brought home last year. Though Scooter had never given Clay the time of day, the dog had taken an instant fancy to Julia and had followed her around the entire afternoon.

The day had gone by quickly, then he and Julia had set the table while Paige made a salad to go with a tray of lasagna supplied by one of the ranch hands' wives. Julia, with her endless questions about the ranch and the horses, had kept their first dinner together from being awkward. Clay was used to eating by himself, but he was determined to be a good father to Julia, and that meant sharing meals. Once Paige hired a housekeeper, they could arrange a scheduled time for breakfast and dinner so that they would all eat together.

He could hear Paige now as she raised her voice and announced herself as Emlyn the Elf, king of all the woodland elves. The sound of Julia's laughter made his throat tighten. He'd lost out on almost five years of his daughter's life. He couldn't make up for that, but he'd be damned if he'd share her with the Barringtons, either. He would not settle for joint custody, and he sure as hell wouldn't settle for visitations.

Julia was *his* flesh and blood. *His* child. She belonged with him, dammit.

Without thinking, he pushed away from his desk and wandered down the hall, stopping just outside Julia's bedroom to listen as Paige finished her story.

"The elves gathered around the fallen knight," Paige said quite solemnly. "Afraid that their rescuer had succumbed to the dragon's fiery tongue, they wept over his still body. The dragon, with his green scales glistening in the morning light, lifted his great head and roared, 'I am the mightiest creature in the forest!'"

"But what happened to the princess?" Julia asked, her voice heavy with concern.

"The princess," Paige went on, "distraught over the loss of her knight, snatched the sword from his still hand, then lifted the weapon high and faced the fierce creature."

Amused, Clay stuck his head around the corner.

Dressed in pink-and-white striped pajamas, Julia sat transfixed on the edge of her bed, watching Paige as she lifted a hairbrush high to act out the scene of her story.

"What did she do?" Julia narrowed her eyes. "Did she kill the dragon?"

"Oh, no." Paige shook her head dramatically. "This dragon could not be killed by mortal man. The princess, with her wisdom and intelligence, knew there was only one way to conquer the mighty beast. A secret known only to a true princess."

"What is it?" Julia asked breathlessly. "What's the secret?"

"I can tell you." Paige glanced over her shoulder, then looked back at Julia and lowered her voice. "But you must never tell a dragon."

With her fingertip, Julia made the sign of an *X* over her heart, then pretended to zipper her lips closed.

Clay leaned forward, watched as Paige leaned close and whispered in Julia's ear. Julia's eyes went wide.

"Really?"

Paige nodded. "Really."

Damn, Clay frowned. He hadn't heard what Paige had said.

"And now it's time for you to go to sleep," Paige announced. "I'll go get your daddy to come tuck you in, okay?"

Not wanting to be caught eavesdropping, Clay strode back to his office, then sat at his desk and scribbled meaningless numbers in his ledger he knew he'd have to erase.

That was how Paige found him a moment later. Elbows on his desk, bent over his paperwork with a pencil in his hand. The light of a single desk lamp shone on the ledger in front of him. She knocked lightly on the open office door. "May I come in?"

"Sure." He did not look up, but kept his attention on his work. "Just give me a second."

Paige glanced around the room as she entered. Like the rest of the upstairs, Clay's office was wall-to-wall plush, beige carpeting. He had a computer on his cluttered desk, but it wasn't turned on. The room looked as if he were just moving in, or just moving out. Stacks of books leaned against one wall. Cardboard boxes served as file holders. A fax machine and telephone sat on the floor beside his desk.

Why did he live like this? she wondered. His house, his office. It certainly wasn't because he didn't have the money to buy things he needed. Everyone knew that the Rocking B ranch was extremely successful, and that Clay had invested wisely over the years, as well. No one knew exactly what Clay Bodine was worth, but Bernie had told her once that he'd heard Clay's portfolio with stocks alone was in the millions.

He didn't live this way because he was cheap, either. When he'd bought her grandmother's car, Paige remembered, he'd written a check for top dollar without any negotiations whatsoever. And then today, he'd also given her carte blanche to decorate the house and hire a housekeeper, too.

No, Clay Bodine was not cheap. Paige was absolutely certain of that. He lived this sparsely because none of those things had mattered to him before, because he'd had no use for them. Until he'd found out he was a father. That had changed his life, his thinking.

Good Lord, that was an understatement, Paige thought as she glanced down at the diamond ring on her finger. He suddenly had a child, and now a wife.

And she had a husband.

And tonight was her wedding night.

Her pulse jumped, but she forced the thought out of her mind and moved closer to the man who was now her husband. "I thought you might like to come say good-night to Julia. She's had a long day and she's ready for bed."

Rolling his shoulders, Clay leaned back in his chair and turned his deep blue gaze on Paige. He stared silently at her for a long moment, then said, "It's been quite a long day for you, too, I imagine. Go ahead and get ready for bed and I'll join you shortly."

"Clay—" she cleared her throat "—I think that I should, that we should talk about—"

"Let's save it until after I've said good-night to Julia, shall we?" he suggested. "Go ahead and get ready for bed and I'll be there in a few minutes."

Paige stared at Clay's back as he left the room. He'd told her straight out to get ready for bed and he'd join her. No innuendos there.

She swallowed hard.

I can do this, she told herself, then squared her shoulders and headed for the bedroom Clay had shown her to earlier. *Their* bedroom. She was a grown woman for heaven's sake. Even though she'd never actually *done it,* she knew perfectly well what happened between a man and woman. The act itself had always seemed as if it would be…awkward, but considering the amount of attention paid to sex, and all the hoopla about it, it must be something pretty good. Or at least tolerable.

Opening her suitcase, she pulled out the pretty white silk gown that Rebecca had bought for her. She and Clay were married. He'd been polite with her, had certainly never threatened her in any way. She had no reason to be afraid of him.

But the fact was, she was terrified.

She tossed the sexy gown back into her suitcase. She wasn't ready for it, she decided. Tonight she needed something she would feel more comfortable wearing. Like a pup tent.

Since a tent obviously wasn't an option, she pulled out one of her everyday, soft cotton gowns. The neckline was high, with scalloped edging in eyelet trim and a lacing of white satin ribbon. The sleeves were long and the hem skimmed her ankles. She realized she would look like a Victorian spinster, but at this moment, with her knees starting to shake and her palms turning damp, she didn't much care. He hadn't married her to be sexy or gorgeous, anyway.

She hurried into the large master bathroom, then took

the quickest shower on record. She pulled the gown over her head, brushed her teeth, then ran a comb through her hair. Because she thought she'd be too embarrassed to take her underwear off in front of Clay, or for him to take them off her, Paige decided not to wear any.

She then sat on the edge of the bed, hands folded in her lap, and waited.

Chapter 5

"**W**as the baby cow scared?" Julia, clutching a worn teddy bear tightly to her chest, stared wide-eyed at her father. "Did she cry?"

"She cried a little bit," Clay said. "But not for very long. She was happy to get out of the mud."

"Did she find her mommy?" Worry furrowed Julia's small brow.

"Yes, she did."

"And her daddy?"

Not certain how to explain about the bulls and the cows, Clay decided to deviate from the truth a bit. "Ah, yeah. She found her mommy and her daddy, too."

When Julia relaxed and smiled brightly, Clay decided he'd made the right choice. Hell, what did he know about telling bedtime stories? When his daughter had asked for one, he'd simply related the rescue of a calf stuck in a mudhole, a fairly common occurrence for cows on a ranch.

"Time for bed now." Clay held the blanket up. "In you go."

Julia climbed under the covers and laid her head on her pillow. "Can I see the horses again tomorrow?"

"Sure."

"And feed them carrots?"

"All right."

Clay felt a hitch in his chest as he looked at Julia. My daughter, he thought in amazement. He'd taken a paternity test for the courts and it had been positive, but from the first moment he'd seen her, there'd never been a question in his mind she was his. He could see his ex-wife's traits in the little girl, especially in the shape of her face and her slender build, but Julia's eyes and hair color were his. She even had the same widow's peak in her hairline as he did.

"Good night, Daddy."

"Good night."

"Paige kissed me good-night," Julia said, her voice already sounding sleepy. "Aren't you going to?"

"Oh. Sure."

Leaning down, he pressed a kiss to her brow, felt the warmth of her skin, smelled the fresh scent of soap from her bath. Julia smiled, then closed her eyes and turned on her side as she snuggled into the bed. He had to swallow the thickness in his throat as he flipped off the overhead light and stepped into the hallway.

Other than a few of his ranch hands' kids who'd shown up from time to time, Clay had never been around children. What kind of a father would he make? he wondered. He sure as hell didn't have much to fall back on. His father had worked long hours when Clay was growing up, and his mother had worked at spending all the money his father earned.

And all the money his father had stolen, as well.

Clay hadn't seen his mother since the day she'd left Wolf River. She'd called once several months later and tried to explain. Had told Clay that she'd been too humiliated to face the people of Wolf River, that she hadn't been able to handle the pressure. That was right before she'd dropped the bomb she'd divorced his father and was already remarried.

His mother hadn't called again after that day. Clay knew he was a reminder of a life she'd prefer to put behind her. She'd moved on, and so had he. His father obviously had, too, because after he'd been released from prison, he'd dropped out of sight. Clay rarely thought about his parents anymore, but now that he was a parent himself, he had to wonder, and worry, if he'd be able to make the cut.

He stared at the closed bedroom door where his daughter was sleeping. He would do everything in his power to make Julia happy. To provide for her, to protect her, to take care of her.

That's why he'd married Paige. He'd known instinctively she would be the best mother for Julia. After today, after seeing how terrific Paige had been with his daughter, Clay was certain he'd made the right decision.

With a sigh, he moved toward the closed master bedroom door at the end of the hall, then knocked lightly. At the sound of Paige's quiet response to enter, he turned the knob.

By most standards, the long, white gown she wore was much too conservative and covered too much skin to be considered sexy. Yet the sight of her sitting on the foot of the bed, her back straight as a fence post, her long, delicate hands intertwined in her lap, made his throat turn to dust. Her face was scrubbed clean; her shiny sandy-brown hair tumbled past her shoulders to her back.

When her gray-green gaze lifted to his, her cheeks flushed a deep pink.

"She's asleep," he said, closing the door behind him.

Paige nodded stiffly. "I'm not surprised. She had a lot of excitement today."

"I'd say we all have." Clay watched Paige's eyes widen, saw the intake of her breath when he moved across the room and sat beside her on the bed. "Wouldn't you?"

Her hands tightened in her lap. "I suppose we have."

"You were good with Julia today," he said, tugging one boot off, then the other.

"She's a wonderful child."

"I know it has to be a little scary for her, coming to a strange place, being separated from the Barringtons." He dropped his boots beside the bed. "You made a difficult situation easier for her. Thank you."

"You don't have to thank me," Paige said quietly. "She's a pleasure to be with, plus she's very well mannered and incredibly bright. Based on the books she brought with her, it appears she's already reading at a first-grade level."

When Clay tugged his shirt from his jeans, Paige quickly looked away.

"Her grandparents were going to send her to a fancy private school in Beverly Hills." Just thinking about his child going to one of those stuffy, pompous schools made Clay's eye twitch. "The same school that three generations of Barringtons had attended."

"I'm sure they only want what's best for Julia."

"I'm her father," he said irritably. "Being with me is what's best for Julia."

"I agree with you." She glanced back at him. "All I'm saying is that the Barringtons love her very much. I could see it in their eyes today. This has to be very hard for them."

"Finding out I was intentionally denied my own child for five years is a hell of a lot harder."

"It was a terrible thing she was kept from you," Paige said with nod. "And I absolutely believe you should raise her. But surely you must realize this is a big change in her life."

When Clay said nothing, just stared at her and slowly began unbuttoning his shirt, Paige felt her heart jump into her throat.

Terrific, she thought dismally. Her first night here, their *wedding* night, and already she'd made Clay angry.

For someone who was supposed to be smart, Paige thought, she was showing very little common sense. This was hardly the time to be expressing an opinion that opposed Clay's, especially considering the fact that they would be sleeping in the same bed, and that he would be making love to her. The thought made her pulse skip and her palms damp.

Nevertheless, what she said was true. The Barringtons would always be a part of Julia's life, and whether he liked it or not, Clay was going to have to face that fact.

Just maybe not tonight.

He rose from the bed and stared down at her, tugging his open shirt from his jeans. Her breath caught at the sight of his bare, muscular chest. Dark hair swirled on his broad, upper torso, then narrowed over his flat, hard stomach to a vee pointing downward. Before she could think, her eyes followed that arrow and dropped to the bulge underneath the zipper of his jeans.

She barely knew this man, had been married to him only this morning. Other than the understanding that they would have sex, they'd never actually discussed the subject. She had no idea what he expected from her in bed. And she certainly had no idea what to expect from him.

Realizing that she was blatantly staring at his crotch, Paige snapped her head up to meet his gaze. The anger she'd seen in his deep blue eyes only a moment before was gone. Now his look glinted with sexual hunger. No

man had ever looked at her that way before, with such
raw, open need. It frightened and excited her at the same
time.

"I—I haven't thanked you for the bouquet and the
champagne," she said, feeling like an idiot that she was
babbling, but too nervous to stop it. "And the ring is beautiful, too. I never expected anything so extravagant."

She practically jumped when he reached down and took
her hand in his. He stared at the ring. "Joe made the arrangements."

"Oh." When would she learn not to assume anything
when it came to Clay? she chastised herself. Soon, she
hoped. "Well, just the same, thank you."

His thumb brushed over her knuckles. "How's your
hand?"

"My hand?" she said, her voice breathless.

"You cut yourself the other night." He turned her hand
over, then ran a fingertip over the faint red scar on her
palm. "It looks much better."

"It was barely a scratch." The touch of his rough fingertip on the sensitive skin of her palm sent arrows of
electricity up her arm. Her hand felt so small in his, Paige
thought, and it fully occurred to her how large a man Clay
was. He could do whatever he chose to do with her,
whether she agreed or not, and there would be no way she
could stop him.

But he wasn't doing *anything*, she realized, except holding her hand. And just that simple act had her nerves tied
in knots of anticipation.

He released her hand.

"Paige," he said softly. "Stand up."

Though she wasn't certain her knees would hold her, she stood slowly, careful to keep her eyes straight ahead. She felt the heat of his gaze as it swept over her. Her heart hammered against her ribs.

"Clay," she whispered, careful to keep her eyes just below his chin. "I think we should probably...talk about a few things."

"What things?"

"I—" It was so embarrassing to say out loud. "I haven't, I'm..."

When she started to look away, he took her chin in his hand and brought her gaze back to his. "Paige, are you trying to tell me you've never had sex before?"

Her cheeks burned. "No."

"No, you haven't had sex before?" he murmured. "Or no, you aren't trying to tell me that?"

"I—" She furrowed her brow. Darn it! He was confusing her more than she already was. "I've never made— had sex before."

He didn't look the least bit surprised. As silly as it was, Paige felt slightly hurt by his casual acceptance of her admission. Why should he be surprised? she thought. The frumpy, plain librarian. The only thing that would make the stereotype more perfect would be if her name was Jane.

"Are you afraid of me?"

His question startled her out of her indignation. Was she afraid of him? Good Lord, *yes!*

"I'm just a little…nervous about…well—" She closed her eyes. "This is my first time and all."

His thumb lightly brushed her cheek. "But are you afraid of *me?*" he asked her again.

She drew in a slow breath and opened her eyes. "Maybe a little."

He lifted her chin until their eyes met. "I've never hurt a woman in my life, Paige. The first time we make love, I promise to make it as easy for you as I can."

He pressed his lips gently to hers, unleashing a cage of butterflies in her stomach. When he lightly swept his tongue over the seam of her lips, she felt the heat sweep through her body.

Then he dropped his hand from her chin and stepped away. "I'll just get my clothes and let you get some sleep now," he said, his voice rough and deep.

Paige's eyes fluttered open. "What?"

"I think it's best if I sleep in the bedroom at the other end of the hall."

Paige stared at Clay in confusion as he disappeared into the large master bedroom closet, then came back out carrying some clothes. "You—you aren't going to…"

He shook his head. "Not tonight."

Stunned, Paige watched Clay pick up his boots. He turned back to her, slowly slid his gaze from her feet back up to her face. She was certain she saw desire in his eyes, was certain she heard the hesitation in his voice. So why was he leaving her?

Julia, of course, Paige realized. It was Clay's daughter's

first night in his house, his first night to have his child with him. Paige understood Clay's reluctance.

But they *were* married, she thought and barely managed to bite back the protest threatening to erupt. How pathetic was she that she would have to *ask* her husband to make love to her on their wedding night? Clearly, even with a new haircut and clothes, she was still resistible. He was more than willing to wait until the time suited him.

She lifted her chin. "What time shall I have breakfast ready?"

"Don't worry about me for breakfast," he said, shaking his head. "Joe and I have to get out early to the east pasture to repair a water valve. I should be back by noon and we can have lunch together."

She nodded, but when he turned to leave, she called to stop him. When he glanced back at her, Paige was amazed at how calm she suddenly was.

"About the housekeeper and decorator."

"What about them?"

"You said I could do whatever I wanted with the house, that your main concern was the livestock and ranch. Do you mean that?"

He narrowed a look at her. "What are you getting at?"

"I'd like to take care of the house and decorate it myself."

One dark brow lifted. "This is a big house, Paige. Julia needs to be your first concern."

"Of course she will be," Paige insisted. "But I'm not used to other people cleaning up after me. If I'm not able to adequately meet your standards of housekeeping, then I'll hire someone."

A muscle jumped in his jaw. "Fine."

"And Rebecca can help me with the decorating," Paige went on. "She not only owns an antique store, she also has a degree in interior design. If you don't mind me using your computer, I can also save money by buying most everything on the Internet."

"I'm not worried about saving money," he said tightly. "Buy whatever you want. Just don't expect me to look at fabric or paint or ask me which wall to hang a picture on."

"All right," she said with nod.

He stared at her for several long seconds, and she almost thought he was going to step toward her again. Her breath held, waiting, but then the moment passed.

"Good night, Paige."

"Good night, Clay."

When the door closed behind him, Paige sank back down on the bed with a sigh.

She wasn't sure if she was relieved or disappointed the evening had ended this way. Probably both. But one thing was for certain, Paige thought. Being married to Clay Bodine was not going to be a walk in the park.

Between the repair on the water valve and discovering a section of downed fencing, Clay didn't make it back for lunch. He'd called Paige from his cell phone to let her know, then told her he'd be there for dinner. It frustrated him that he'd missed a meal with his daughter and Paige, especially considering they only had the weekend together, but he'd long ago accepted the fact that the Rocking B was a seven-day-a-week, round-the-clock responsibility.

He loved the ranch. Loved the freedom of being outdoors and working with the animals. Hard work had never bothered him. He'd enjoyed putting his back into a job, using his hands. He found great satisfaction in knowing the land where his cattle and horses grazed was his own. He'd taken risks and been lucky, but he'd managed to turn the Rocking B from an average, mediocre business into an extremely lucrative enterprise. Between the ranch and his investments, Clay had more money than he could have ever dreamed.

In the beginning, his ambition to succeed had simply been to repay his father's debt to the bank. Clay had always been good at the hands-on aspect of ranching, but he'd discovered that he was good at the business end, as well. Then he'd ventured into stocks and bonds, and gotten lucky there, too.

Still, it was the challenge of making money and being successful that appealed to him, not the money or success itself. Before he'd found out about Julia, he could have lost every penny he'd ever made and he wouldn't have blinked an eye.

Now that he had Julia, though, his perception of life and money was different. He'd already set up a trust fund for her, and had recently rolled his high-risk stocks into more stable, secure investments. If anything ever happened to

him, she would be well-cared for with *his* money, not the
Barrington's.

And Paige, of course.

He thought about his new wife as he parked his truck
in front of the barn. But then, he'd been thinking about
her most of the day.

And certainly all last night.

It had taken a will of iron not to take her to bed last
night. Lord knew, he'd desperately wanted to. He hadn't
been able to get her out of his mind, had tossed most of
the night, struggling with himself not to simply walk that
short distance down the hall, slip between the sheets, then
slide into her slender body and pleasure them both.

After he'd kissed her that first time in her house, he'd
suspected she was a virgin. He'd tasted the sweetness of
her innocence, but it hadn't diminished his desire for her
in the least.

His daughter sleeping across the hall had not been the
only reason he hadn't made love to Paige last night. She
was his wife, after all, even though they'd only been married that morning. He'd always had a healthy appetite for
sex, and he'd looked forward to having a woman in his
bed every night. But even as much as he'd needed a wife,
he wouldn't have gone through with a wedding if he hadn't
thought that he and Paige would be compatible in bed.

But when he'd walked in the bedroom last night, when
she'd looked at him with such shy, nervous anticipation,
he'd nearly lost it right there. He'd taken that look to bed
with him last night, had carried it with him all day.

He needed more time. Time to contain this unexpected *need* he felt for Paige. When they made love, he needed to be in control, for her sake, as much as his own. She'd admitted she was afraid of him, if only a little. He didn't want her to feel as if making love was her duty as his wife. He wanted her willing and eager. He wanted her to open to him, to rise up eagerly and take him inside her. To wrap her naked arms and legs around him and move her body in rhythm with his.

Scooter's bark from inside the barn snapped Clay out of his thoughts. *Good God.* He thumbed his Stetson back from his face and wiped at the sweat on his brow. He had to stop thinking about Paige like that, or he'd never make it through the weekend. Or when they did make love, he thought, it would be over much too quickly.

Stepping from the truck, he walked slowly toward the back door of the house, giving himself a few extra needed moments to let his blood cool. The air was warm and humid, a typical Texas summer evening. He hadn't even reached the back door before the scent of something wonderful drifted to him. When he stepped inside, the sound of Julia and Paige singing stopped him. He listened to the tune for a moment, smiled when he recognized it as the ''spoonful of sugar'' song from *Mary Poppins*.

They didn't see him when he entered the kitchen through the laundry area. Paige stood at the stove with her back to him, and Julia was placing forks beside the plates already on the table. A roast surrounded by quartered potatoes and carrots sat on a platter beside the stove, and it appeared that Paige was making gravy.

He'd assumed she'd hire a housekeeper to take care of the cooking and other mundane household chores. He could still see the proud upward tilt of her chin last night when she'd told him she would prefer to take care of the house herself. It didn't matter to him, but he had to admit, there was something very satisfying about walking into his house and seeing his family gathered in the kitchen, preparing a meal.

His family.

The thought caught him like a fist in the chest. It was going to take some getting used to, having a child and wife in the house. He'd been alone too long, and even with Nancy, this house had always been cold. And Nancy, who'd been a vegetarian and only ate salad and tofu, had never cooked him an edible meal once.

He hung his hat on a hook beside the back door and moved into the kitchen. "Smells good."

Paige turned at the movement and instantly stopped singing. When their eyes met, she blushed.

"Daddy!" Julia ran to him and threw her arms around his waist. "We made you dinner and baked you a cake, too!"

"A cake, too?" He bent to hug his daughter, felt that familiar tightening in his chest at her enthusiastic greeting. "This must be my lucky day."

"It is," Julia said, her face beaming. "We wanted to s'prise you."

"You did."

"Dinner's ready." Paige turned back to the stove. "Why don't you wash up while we put everything on the table?"

"All right." He moved to the sink and rolled up his sleeves, then turned the water on and glanced over at Paige. She was dressed in a calf-length navy skirt and pale blue sleeveless blouse, and the sight of her bare, slender arms and lower legs sent a rush of heat through him.

"Paige and me used your computer and bought me a new bedroom set today," Julia said. "She let me pick it out myself and Betty Ballerina sheets, too!"

"Really?" Clay had never heard of Betty Ballerina, but he figured he had a lot to learn when it came to little girls. While he soaped up his hands, he looked at his daughter and smiled. "I'll bet you'll have the prettiest bedroom in Texas."

"I will," she said with a serious nod. "And California, too!"

"The pictures we printed out are on your daddy's desk," Paige said. "Why don't you run up and get them?"

Julia ran out of the room and Clay heard her singing the Mary Poppins song again as she skipped up the stairs.

Reaching for a towel, Clay turned back to Paige. "Sounds like you've kept busy."

"You haven't heard the half of it." Paige smiled. "We spent the morning saying hello to all the horses again and feeding them carrots. I'm sure you'll hear all about it over dinner."

Leaning back against the counter while he dried his hands, Clay watched Paige pour gravy from the saucepan into a bowl. Her hands fascinated him, and he couldn't take his eyes off her long, slender fingers, couldn't help but wonder what they'd feel like on his skin.

He sighed mentally, heard the sound of his daughter skipping back down the stairs, and he knew that it was going to be another long night ahead of him.

Chapter 6

Clay offered to help with the dishes after dinner, but Paige shooed both him and Julia out of the kitchen while she cleaned up. She knew that Julia would have to return to California with her grandparents the next afternoon, and she wanted him to be able to spend as much time with his daughter this weekend as possible.

Paige had also wanted a few minutes alone to absorb everything that had happened since she'd exchanged wedding vows with Clay. She was a married woman now. A wife. A mother.

While she loaded the dishwasher, Paige listened to the sound of Julia's laughter from the other room. Considering the circumstances, it amazed her how happy and well-adjusted the little girl was. From what Clay had told her,

Paige knew that the Barringtons, not Nancy, had raised Julia. The idea was unimaginable to Paige.

Without thinking, she touched her own stomach, wondered what it would feel like to carry a child, to give birth, then hold the tiny infant in her arms. Just the thought of it made her insides feel soft and warm.

At least she knew that Clay wanted more children. He'd made that clear to her when he'd told her that he intended her to be a wife to him in every manner. She was fairly certain they wouldn't consummate their marriage tonight, but what about tomorrow evening, after they'd taken Julia back to her grandparents? Her pulse quickened at the thought.

Heavens, she was wound tight as a clockmaker's spring. The waiting, and not knowing when they'd make love, was making her crazy. And frustrated, she realized. All last night, she'd lain in that big bed, *his* bed, and wondered what it would be like to have Clay beside her. Wondered what those big, rough hands would feel like on her skin. He'd kissed her before, on the mouth, but would he kiss her other places, too? Her breasts tightened at the thought and her nipples hardened. Would he kiss her there?

Oh, Lord, she hoped so.

''Paige!'' Julia burst through the kitchen door, waving a sheet of paper. ''Look what Daddy drew—a cow with three heads!''

Thankful for the interruption of her wayward thoughts, Paige smiled at the little girl. So that's what they'd been doing in the other room, she realized as Clay strolled in behind his daughter. Wonders never ceased, she thought.

"See here?" Julia held the drawing up for Paige. "Right next to my picture of a horse. See?"

Paige looked at the drawing. "You're absolutely right. Do cows have three heads?"

"Of *course* not," Julia said with exasperation, then rolled her eyes. "He's just being funny. Don't you think he's funny?"

"I do think he's funny." Paige glanced up at Clay, though she couldn't imagine she'd have ever used that word to describe him. "Very funny."

"Hey, I like my cow." He had a twinkle of humor in his eyes, though his expression was quite serious. "Or should I say cows?"

Julia giggled at that, then looked back at Paige. "Can I put our picture on the refrigerator? My grandma always does. I have lots of pictures on my refrigerator at home."

Paige watched the humor disappear from Clay's eyes when Julia mentioned her grandmother. Clearly he didn't want to be reminded that, at least for the time being, he had to share his daughter, and that she didn't yet consider the ranch her home.

"Of course we can put your picture on the refrigerator." Paige dried her hands on a dish towel. "But first you have to sign your name in the corner. All artists sign their work."

"Okay." Julia handed the picture to her father. "We both have to sign it, 'cause it's both our pictures."

"Should I sign it three times?" he asked.

"No, silly." Julia giggled again. "I'm gonna go get my other pictures and sign them, too."

Paige watched Julia run out of the kitchen, then turned her attention back to Clay. "I'll take her upstairs now. We need to get her bath started and pack her suitcase."

"There's no rush." He dug through a drawer by the kitchen phone and pulled out a magnet advertising Peterson's Hay and Feed, then put the picture on the refrigerator. "You'll have plenty of time to pack her things in the morning."

"Not if we're going to make the ten o'clock service."

He glanced at her over his shoulder. "What are you talking about?"

"I'm talking about church service at ten o'clock. We'll need to leave the ranch no later than nine-thirty to make it in time."

Shaking his head, he turned to face her. "I don't go to church."

"Julia told me she goes every week with her grandparents." Paige folded the towel and laid it on the counter. "I go quite often myself, though I admit, not every week."

"So you and Julia go, then. I'll drive you."

Paige had known that Clay wasn't going to like the idea, but from the look on his face, she'd have thought she'd asked him to douse himself with fish oil and run naked through town.

"Clay, you were willing to marry me, a woman you barely knew, in order to prove to the courts that you could provide the best home for your daughter. In comparison, spending an hour in church once in a while can't be that difficult.''

He pressed his lips firmly together. ''They're completely different issues.''

''Are they?'' she asked. ''Or are they both about creating the illusion of being a family?''

''It's not an illusion.'' He narrowed his eyes. ''We *are* a family now.''

''Legally, yes,'' she agreed. ''But maybe the courts will want to see a little more than that.''

He stared at her for the longest ten seconds of her life, then said through gritted teeth, ''Fine.''

He turned and stomped out of the kitchen.

Stunned that she'd actually convinced him, Paige released the breath she'd been holding and leaned back against the counter.

Clearly, being married to Clay Bodine would be difficult, Paige thought, but it most certainly would not be boring.

Wolf River Grace Community Church hadn't changed much in twenty-two years. The clapboard exterior and tall steeple were still white, the steps leading through the wide double doors were still brick. Nothing had changed much inside, either, Clay thought as he stared at the cathedral ceiling and tall, stained glass windows behind the pulpit, though the church didn't appear quite as large as he'd thought it was when he was ten years old.

Especially the pews, Clay noted, shifting his legs so his knees wouldn't keep bumping the seat in front of him. On those few Sundays when he'd come to church with his grandmother, Clay had fit much easier into the long wooden bench.

Beside him, Julia and Paige joined in on the song that would finally end the crowded service. Paige might have managed to induce him into putting on a dress shirt and tie and coming here, but there was no way in hell he was going to sing. Arms folded, he skimmed his gaze over the congregation. Most of the faces were familiar to him, though there were several new ones, as well. He knew that Wolf River was growing by leaps and bounds, especially since The Four Winds Hotel had opened, bringing in more jobs along with tourists and businessmen. The last cattlemen's convention held at the hotel's newly built convention center had been filled to capacity.

Nothing stayed the same, he knew. Change was as certain as taxes and death. Lord knew *his* life had certainly changed just as dramatically, in a much shorter span of time.

He glanced at Julia, watched her fingers fiddle with the pink ribbon tie on the neck of her white dress. Though he hadn't spent as much time with his daughter as he would have liked this weekend, he knew that she'd be back in two weeks and they'd have two entire weeks together before the court hearing. After that, Clay thought, he was confident that Julia would be coming home with him to stay.

But the changes in his life had only begun with his daughter, he thought and lifted his gaze to Paige. The yellow skirt she wore was long and flowing, her simple blouse with eyelet collar a crisp white. She'd pulled her soft, golden brown hair back into a bun, but the style didn't look as severe as it had before she'd changed her hairstyle. If anything, it made her neck look longer and her face softer.

Before he started to fantasize about his own wife while he sat in church, Clay looked away and focused his gaze two aisles over on the bald spot in the back of Hugh Foderman's head.

When he'd walked into church with Paige and Julia by his side this morning, Clay hadn't missed the slack jaws and open stares. He figured that by now, most everyone in Wolf River knew he and Paige had been married. There'd already been plenty of talk about them, Clay knew, and the fact that he'd had a child from his previous marriage. He also knew that there would be plenty more talk for some time to come, at least until something bigger and better came along to gossip about. He'd never paid any mind to loose tongues before, and he had no intention to start now.

But along with the curious stares, Clay had also noticed several disapproving glances directed at Paige. He'd considered that Paige might be the object of some criticism, but the snide, judgmental looks that had come from Judith Parcher and Maude Fetalmeyer had set Clay's teeth on edge.

But Paige hadn't appeared to notice the cool stares from the women, Clay thought, any more than she'd noticed the stares of interest from the men. More than one man had made Clay's eyes narrow in warning, and if Brett Rivers hadn't looked away when he had, Clay might have had to have a talk with the neighboring rancher about his lack of manners.

It's about time, Clay thought when the song ended, and was ready to get up and walk out when Pastor Sherman stepped up to the pulpit again.

"Before we leave today—" the young pastor smiled at his congregation "—I'd like to personally congratulate Clay Bodine and Paige Andrews on their very recent marriage."

Clay froze, then looked at Paige, who stared at the pastor in stunned disbelief. Terrific, Clay thought with a silent groan. It wasn't enough he'd shown up here, he and Paige and Julia were now suddenly under a microscope. Silence echoed as every head turned and stared. Then the church broke out in applause, with a few whistles and cheers.

"We'd also like everyone to join us in a celebration," the pastor continued when the room quieted down. "Sandwiches, drinks and cake, compliments of Rebecca Montgomery and the staff at Wolf River Library, will be served in the church garden."

Dammit to hell.

Based on the horrified look on Paige's face, she hadn't known about this, Clay realized. As the people filed out,

Clay was met with a few slaps on the back and several well wishes.

Paige leaned across Julia and said quietly, "I—I didn't know. Rebecca asked me if we were coming to church and I told her yes, but I swear, I had no idea she was up to something."

"Can I have some cake at the party, too?" Julia asked hopefully.

Clay forced a smile as he looked at his daughter. "Sure you can."

With nowhere else to escape, Clay set his teeth, then followed Paige and Julia out of the church.

"I could tell something was up the minute he walked into the drugstore and looked at you." Sheila Gordon elbowed Paige and winked. "You sure had everyone in this town fooled. To think you and Clay had something going on all this time, right under all our noses."

Stuck between Sheila and Daphne Pringle on the crowded garden patio, Paige managed a stiff smile. She'd been cornered by the two women a few minutes ago and they'd been pumping her for details about Clay and their courtship. She'd managed to avoid or be vague with every answer so far, but Paige had the feeling Sheila and Daphne weren't going to leave her alone until she gave them something good to chew on.

The word had been spread by the women she'd worked with at the library that there would be a celebration in the church garden this morning, Paige realized, which would certainly explain why there'd been such a large turnout for today's service. She should have known something was up when she'd spotted Sheila and Daphne sitting two pews ahead of her. Paige couldn't remember seeing the two women at Sunday service since they were all little girls.

Paige looked around for Rebecca, who'd been serving punch a few minutes ago, but there was no sign of her friend. *Friend.* Ha. That was certainly a loose name for a traitor, Paige thought.

Holding her smile carefully in place while Sheila rattled on about how surprised everyone in town was, Paige glanced over Daphne's shoulder and spotted Clay standing by the garden's three-tiered fountain. He was talking with Lucas and Julianna Blackhawk. The couple owned a ranch several miles west of town. Julianna was currently holding the newest addition to the Blackhawk family, four-month-old R.J., while the twins, three-year-old Nathan and Nicole played with Julia on the lawn.

Paige knew that Clay was unhappy about this unexpected reception, but there was nothing she could do about it now. He would simply have to grin and bear it, she thought, just the same as she would. Given her druthers, though, Paige would take the Blackhawks over Sheila and Daphne any day.

"And here we thought you and Bernie would be tying the knot one day," Daphne said while she sipped on a glass of punch. "I was in the bank on Friday after you and Clay got married. Poor Bernie was dragging round like a coon dog's jaw. Judith Parcher told me you two got into a knock-down, drag-out fight right there at the bank when you told him you were marrying Clay. Is that true?''

Knock-down, drag-out? Oh, for heaven's sake, Paige thought in exasperation. She'd barely raised her voice. Paige opened her mouth to answer Daphne, but Sheila beat her to the punch.

"Why do you listen to anything that old bat says?" Sheila curled her lip. "Judith lives for gossip and repeats everything she hears, whether it's true or not. Do you know she told MaryAnne Johnson and Stephanie Roberts that I was dating a married man?"

"You *were* dating a married man," Daphne said.

"But I didn't *know* he was married." Sheila folded her arms indignantly. "There's a difference."

When the two women began to argue, Paige decided it was time to leave. She started to back away and bumped into someone, who took hold of her arms to steady her.

"I'm so sorry," she said, turning around. "Please—" She stopped when she saw who it was.

Oh, dear.

"Hello, Paige," Bernie said without smiling.

"Hello, Bernie."

The conversation between Sheila and Daphne immediately went dead. Several other people standing around quieted, as well.

"So you went through with it," he said stiffly.

Terrific, Paige thought with a sigh. The last thing she wanted to do at this moment was discuss her marriage with Bernie.

"I didn't really think you'd do it." His frown deepened.
"When I went to pick up my mother's prescription at the
drugstore and Sheila told me about you and Clay, that he'd
asked you to marry him, I thought it was a joke."

What? Paige swiveled a look at Sheila. "You were listening?"

Sheila at least had the decency to look embarrassed.
"Well, I wasn't really *listening,*" she said quickly. "I just
caught a word or two from the vent by the cash register.
Just enough to sort of catch the drift. It was just so romantic, the way he couldn't wait to propose to you."

Obviously Sheila hadn't caught enough of "the drift"
to realize that Clay's proposal wasn't based on romance at
all. If Sheila *had* heard everything, she'd have known the
real reason Clay had married her. And if Sheila had known
that little detail, then the entire town would have known,
also.

But it was a little late to worry what the good people of
Wolf River thought about her marriage to Clay Bodine. It
was the price of living in a small town—Paige glanced at
Sheila—with certain people who had small brains.

That's why Bernie had suddenly asked her to marry him,
Paige realized. Because he'd heard from Sheila that Clay
had proposed, and Bernie had been afraid he'd lose his
"retirement portfolio," which had included Paige's in-
come at the library.

At the beginning throb of a headache, Paige pressed her
fingers to her temple. For a day that was supposed to be
a celebration, she wasn't exactly having a stellar time.

Paige nearly jumped when Clay stepped behind her and slid his arms around her waist, then pulled her back against his chest.

"You all right, sweetheart?" he asked.

Sweetheart? Her insides stampeded at Clay's endearment, but she did her best to look relaxed and comfortable in his arms. "I—yes. I'm fine."

"Good. I'm worried you haven't had enough sleep," he said, his tone suggestive.

Paige watched Daphne and Sheila's eyes widen and their jaws go slack.

"Congratulations," the two women said in unison.

"Thanks, ladies." Clay pulled Paige closer, then glanced at Bernie. "Hey, Pratt."

"Bodine." Bernie sounded, and looked, like he'd just drank starch. "Congratulations."

"Thanks."

When Clay bent his head and nibbled on her ear, Paige felt the heat of her blush work its way up her neck. Bernie turned bright red, while Sheila and Daphne watched with longing.

"Rebecca wants us to come over for a toast." Clay glanced up and smiled. "If you all don't mind that I pull my wife away, that is."

"Of course not," Sheila squeaked and Daphne nodded enthusiastically.

Clay looked at Bernie, who shrugged. "Sure."

"By the way, Pratt," Clay said. "I'll give you a call next week. I have some bonds maturing at my brokerage that I thought I'd transfer to your bank. Think you can handle the account?''

The prospect of personally managing even a piece of Clay's sizeable funds visibly brightened Bernie. He straightened his shoulders and puffed up his chest. ''I'd be happy to help wherever I can, Clay.''

''Thanks.''

Without warning, right in front of Sheila, Daphne, Bernie and everyone gathered around, Clay turned Paige in his arms and kissed her soundly on the mouth. Startled, she simply stood there. She knew the kiss was for show, but that didn't seem to stop her from slowly melting against him. Or stop her body from reacting. Vaguely, through the haze of pleasure radiating through her blood, Paige heard several ''oohs'' and ''ahhs'' and ''isn't that sweet?''

When he finally pulled away and looked down into her eyes, Paige saw that same glint of desire she'd witnessed after the first time he'd kissed her. She shivered from the promise he held in his gaze, and knew that tonight they would truly be man and wife, at least physically.

It was going to be a long day, Paige thought as Clay took her hand and led her toward Rebecca.

And perhaps an even longer night.

Chapter 7

The ride back to the Rocking B that evening was tense. Clay drove silently, his gaze focused intently on the road, his large hands set firmly on the steering wheel. Paige glanced at him occasionally from the corner of her eye, but the tight set of his jaw and his obvious lack of desire to speak, kept Paige from even attempting to start a conversation.

She understood his dark mood, had felt a sense of loss herself when they'd had to return Julia to her grandparents after the wedding reception at the church. Clay had smiled at his daughter, then hugged her goodbye and told her that he'd see her in two weeks. His manner had been lighthearted and relaxed in front of the Barringtons, but Paige had seen the strain in his eyes when he'd watched his daughter drive off with her grandparents. Knew that his frustration and anger were simmering just beneath the surface, threatening to boil over at any moment.

He'd waited out in the truck when Paige had gone to pick up Eudora from Rebecca, and she was glad that her cat was now in its carrier, between them on the front seat of the cab. It helped somehow to keep a sort of barrier between them, something to create not only a physical space, but a mental one, as well. A distraction, of sorts, not only of what they'd left behind them in town, but what lay ahead at the ranch.

Not just in the days and weeks ahead of them, Paige thought, though that was certainly something to think about. But specifically, what lay ahead *tonight*.

It was the first time they'd be alone in the house, and though Paige was doing her best to relax, her insides were jumping like corn in a hot pan. Clay hadn't said anything to her, or made any innuendos about tonight, but she'd *felt* it. Knew instinctively that the tension between them wasn't just about Julia going back to California. It was about sharing a bed, and what would happen in that bed.

Though it had felt as if the ride to the ranch was taking a lifetime, when Clay finally pulled up in front of the house and stopped the engine, the journey suddenly felt too short. Without waiting for him, she quickly opened her door and slid out, then reached for the cat carrier and held it close. When Clay came around and offered to take the animal from her, she shook her head and told him she'd rather do it herself.

Thankfully, he didn't argue, just went ahead of her and opened the front door.

"Eudora's never been anywhere else," Paige said when they were inside. "She might be a little nervous for a while."

Clay looked at the cat carrier, then lifted his gaze to Paige. "The cat's not sleeping with us, Paige."

Us. Her heart slammed against her ribs. "No, of course not. She has a bed of her own she's used to. I've already set it up in one of the extra bathrooms for tonight."

He nodded. "I've got to go out to the barn. You do whatever you need to do. I'll be back in shortly."

She hurried upstairs to the bathroom and opened the door of the carrier, but Eudora simply glared at her and refused to come out. Paige sighed, then moved the cat's bed beside the carrier and left the bathroom, closing the door behind her, though she did leave a night-light on for the animal.

Eudora would be fine, Paige knew. Though it might take the animal a little time to adjust to her new surroundings, the cat had always been extremely independent. Right now, Paige had other, more pressing concerns on her mind.

She'd barely made it out of the shower and into her nightgown when she heard Clay come into the bedroom. She quickly pulled a brush through her hair, then stepped out of the bathroom. Her breath caught when she noticed the sheets had already been turned down. She glanced nervously at Clay, who stood in front of the large closet with his back to her. It surprised her that he'd apparently al-

ready showered, probably in the downstairs bathroom.
Though he'd pulled his slacks back on, he was shirtless, a
towel draped over one shoulder.

Her heart leaped at the sight of him. He'd slicked his
hair back, and water still dripped from the dark ends, then
beaded on his broad, bare back. Muscles rippled as he
reached to hang up the shirt he'd worn that day.

She made a small noise, and he turned.

Heavens. She knew it wasn't polite to stare, but she
couldn't take her eyes off him. The muscles in his shoulders and arms were well defined and appeared rock-hard.
From what she could see, there wasn't an ounce of fat on
the man.

Without taking his eyes off her, Clay snagged the towel
from his shoulder and dragged it over his head and shoulders, then tossed it on top of a hamper inside the closet.

When he moved toward her, she held her breath. He
stopped in front of her, then reached up to brush her hair
off her shoulder; her breath shuddered out.

"You—you'll have to tell me—" she felt her cheeks
burn as she dropped her gaze "—I mean, if there's something I should, or that you want me to—"

"What I want, Paige," he said softly, "is for you to
relax. And to look at me."

She was at least able to do one of those things. Lifting
her gaze, she saw a tenderness and patience in his eyes
that startled her. And though only slightly, she did relax.

"We've got two weeks alone to find out what each of

us likes and wants,'' he said. ''Let's just let it happen, all right?''

She nodded slowly, was amazed at the soothing timbre of his voice, the gentle touch of his hand on her shoulder. He slid his fingers up to cup the back of her neck and eased her closer, then covered her mouth with his.

The kiss was a mere whisper, the slightest brush of his mouth over hers, but it was enough to quicken her pulse and warm her blood. Instinctively she placed her hands on his bare chest, felt the coarse sprinkling of hair under her fingertips and the steady, solid beat of his heart. His skin was warm, and he smelled of soap and man and sex. Dizzy from the sensations swirling through her mind and her body, she swayed into him on a sigh.

His lips were firm, unrelenting, yet—to Paige's delight, as well as her distress—clearly in no hurry. He took his time tasting, nipping the corner of her mouth, teasing the seam of her lips with the tip of his tongue, then retreating. Waves of heat rippled through her; her skin tingled, her breasts felt heavy and swollen. Her nipples grew hard and achy.

His hands slid down her back, then around her waist to pull her more intimately against him. Paige felt his arousal press against the vee of her thighs, and when she softly gasped, he slipped his tongue inside her mouth. He tasted like peppermint, she thought through the haze of sensual pleasure engulfing her. And when he deepened the kiss, she could barely think at all.

She met the easy slide of his tongue with her own, heard

the sound of her own labored breathing. His hands tightened on her waist, then inched upward toward her rib cage. She felt as if she were on fire, and when his thumbs lightly brushed the undersides of her breasts, she trembled.

Lost in his kisses, Paige hadn't realized until now that he'd slowly inched her backwards toward the bed. For the past two nights, she'd lain in Clay's bed alone, wondering what it would be like when he finally made love to her. The moment was here, she knew.

She shivered in anticipation.

Clay slid his hands down her arms, then lifted his head. Slowly she opened her eyes and saw the raw need that burned in his gaze.

"I'm going to take this off you now," he said quietly, and began to bunch the fabric of her gown in his fingers.

She swallowed hard, felt her stomach lurch as he inched the gown higher and higher.

When he raised the hem of her gown up to her waist and hesitated, she held her breath, knowing that he'd just realized she had no underwear on. He muttered something, but her heart was slamming so hard against her ribs, she couldn't hear what he'd said. She raised her arms as he gently tugged the gown over her head and tossed it on the bed.

In spite of her fear and embarrassment, Paige lifted her chin and met Clay's narrowed gaze.

The fierce, primitive expression of pure lust in his eyes made her breath catch. Before they were even married, she had made a decision to be an active participant in making love with Clay. Even though her insides were shaking, even though her knees threatened to collapse, she was determined to stand firm.

His gaze slid slowly down her body, then lifted again. He said nothing, just stepped toward her, reached out and gently cupped her breasts in his large hands. She quivered at his touch, and when his callused thumbs rubbed back and forth over her hardened nipples, sharp arrows of pleasure shot to the juncture of her thighs.

Closing her eyes, Paige leaned into Clay's touch. She'd never experienced anything like this before, hadn't known she was capable of such intense feelings. She'd always thought there was something wrong with her, that she might even be frigid when it came to men. But she was quickly learning that she was far from frigid, and at the moment, she was actually burning up inside.

When Clay lowered his head to her breast and took her in his mouth, her eyes flew open again and she gasped in shock. She clutched at his head, arching back as he sucked lightly. The fire inside her spread; the ache became unbearable.

"Clay," she said between ragged breaths. "Please."

It seemed as though he hadn't heard her. He simply moved to her other breast, swirled his hot tongue over the bud of her nipple, then once again pulled her into his mouth. If he hadn't slipped one of his arms around her back, Paige was certain she would have crumbled to the floor.

And just when she thought she might have to beg, he

lifted his head, then slowly lowered her to the bed. The mattress was soft against her back, the sheets cool. Keeping his eyes on hers, he reached for the zipper of his slacks and pulled it down. Transfixed, Paige watched as he shed his trousers—the only article of clothing he'd bothered to put on after his shower.

Though Paige certainly knew what a man looked like without any clothes, she'd never actually *seen* one, not a living, breathing one, at least. And she'd absolutely never seen a naked, extremely aroused male before. She felt a mixture of fascination, fear and excitement as she looked at Clay.

How was this, this *joining,* possible? she wondered. Her confidence, and the burning desire she'd felt only a moment before, dipped slightly.

Clay sensed the hesitation in Paige and struggled to hold onto the last threads of his control. He'd nearly lost it when he'd taken off her nightgown and looked down at her naked body. She had a slender build, a narrow waist and long, curvy legs. Her breasts fit his hands perfectly, and her taste intoxicated him.

His need to be inside her consumed him, but this was her first time, and the last thing he wanted to do was spook her. If they were to share a bed, and a life together, he wanted her to trust him completely.

Strangely, her innocence did not take away from the pleasure, but aroused him all the more. It didn't seem to matter that this was the modern world, where relationships casually came and went. At a primitive level, Clay was pleased that his wife had belonged to no other man before him.

He stepped out of his slacks, then lay on the bed beside her, gently gathered her in his arms and kissed her, lingering over her sweet lips, then moving to the smooth column of her neck. Her skin was like silk, warm and soft and shimmering. When he slid his hand down her side and over her hip to caress her buttock, she made a small sound and pressed against him.

Clay wasn't certain how much more he could take himself, but he was determined to bring Paige every step of the way with him. Though his own body screamed for release, he concentrated on pleasuring the woman in his arms. He brought his mouth back to hers at the same time he slid his hand around to the triangle of soft curls between her legs. She jumped when he touched her there, then gasped against his lips when he slowly, intimately, slipped one finger inside her.

"Clay, I—"

"Shh." He gentled her with another kiss, slowly moved his finger over the most sensitive nub between her legs. She was moist, swollen. Tight. He slipped deeper inside her body, stroking her. Her hands clutched frantically at his shoulders. On a moan, she moved against his hand, wanting, needing more.

"*Please*," she whimpered, wrapping her arms around his neck and pulling him closer. "Please...*now*..."

"Yes," he murmured, his own breath ragged and hoarse. "Now."

He moved over her, spread her legs with his knee, then eased inside her. She opened to him, dug her fingernails into his back and muffled her cry against his shoulder. With an effort that brought sweat to his brow, he stilled, waited for her to adjust to him. His muscles shook from the struggle between mind and body, but he waited, poised over her.

When she'd finally taken him fully into her body, she said on a rush of breath, "Don't stop. Please don't stop."

He hesitated, but then she began to move her hips and his mind went blank. Nothing else existed but the need for completion, the need to satisfy the intense, throbbing ache in his loins.

He thrust himself deeper inside the tight, velvet glove of her body. She met him, lifting her hips to take him deeper still, writhing under him in her own swirling world of emotions.

Clay felt the shudder move through her body, saw the surprise in her glazed eyes as she cried out. As she peaked, he thrust again and again, faster. On a groan, he shuddered violently into her, his body convulsing with his climax.

His lungs burning, his chest heaving, Clay rolled to his side, wrapping his arms around Paige as he brought her with him.

Paige was certain she would never move again. She felt as if she were drifting through soft, warm clouds. Dimly she heard the sound of her own slowed breathing and the slight rustle of sheets. If I'm dreaming, she thought, I don't ever want to wake.

But she wasn't dreaming, of course. She felt the long, hard length of Clay's body pressed against her own, heard the steady beat of his heart against her ear, and knew that this was real.

Turning her head, she pressed her lips against his chest and tasted the salty dampness of his skin. His arms tightened around her and pulled her closer.

Oh, yes, she thought with a sigh. This is definitely real.

"Are you all right?" he asked, breaking the silence between them.

She nodded, then lifted her gaze to his. The glint of desire still shone in his eyes and a thrill skipped through her. "That was…"

She hesitated, struggling to find the right word. There simply wasn't one to describe what she was feeling.

"What?" he murmured, pressing his lips to her forehead.

"Wonderful," she breathed, though it was so much more than that. "And amazing."

Smiling, he rolled to his back, bringing her on top of him. She gasped at the sudden movement, laid her palms flat on his chest to steady herself.

"I'd definitely say that settles any question about how 'compatible' we might be," he said, then skimmed his hands down her back and cupped her buttocks.

Heavens, Paige thought. That was certainly an understatement. The rough feel of his palms on her bottom stirred the heat in her blood. The idea that she would feel the need again so quickly and—based on the hard press of his arousal between her legs—that he felt it, as well, stunned her.

One week ago, if anyone had told her that she'd be lying naked in Clay Bodine's bed, as his *wife,* she'd have told them they were insane.

It sobered her to think that if she'd refused Clay's offer, another woman would be lying here right now. Strangely, the idea bothered her more than a little. He might not have married her for love, she told herself, but the fact still remained that he had chosen her. She knew better than to expect more from him, but fool that she was, she couldn't stop the flicker of hope inside her that one day, in time, he might come to love her.

Because somewhere between the time they'd exchanged vows and this moment, she'd fallen in love with him.

Paige knew better than to tell him. Knew that it would spoil the moment, that he might even turn away from her if she did. She couldn't bear that. Not after what they'd just shared.

She wanted to cherish this night and the magic of the feelings he'd roused in her. Feelings that were building again as he caressed and stroked her backside.

And along with these feelings came a sense of power, she realized. A boldness she'd never experienced before.

Experimenting with this sudden bravado, she moved her hands over the hard planes and angles of Clay's chest. His muscles flexed underneath her fingertips and when she moved her hips ever so slightly against him, she heard his sharp intake of breath. She met his heated gaze, then lowered her mouth to his.

She kissed him as he'd kissed her before. A gentle tease, a soft nip, then finally tasting the firmness of his lips with her tongue. He moaned deeply, then cupped the back of her head and dragged her closer.

When she moved her hips against his, matching the rhythm of her tongue, she felt him harden again, felt the wild beating of his heart against her own.

She rose over him, then slowly lowered herself, taking him inside her.

And then she began to move.

His hands clutched frantically at her hips. When she arched upward, he lifted his head, then closed his mouth over her breast and ran his hot, moist tongue over the hardened nipple.

The pleasure was more than Paige could stand. The climax slammed into her, shattering her into tiny, shimmering pieces. When Clay groaned hoarsely, then shuddered inside her, she collapsed on top of him.

Pressing her lips against his neck, she closed her eyes.

And smiled.

Chapter 8

The week passed quickly. While Paige concentrated on decorating and furnishing the large house, Clay was busy at the west end of the ranch doctoring the freshly branded and marked cows. As the weather turned hot, screwworms were an ongoing problem for the cattle, and it was critical to find the affected cattle and treat them as soon as possible.

"Hold 'er tight, son." Joe jumped down from his horse and approached the cow Clay had just roped and tied down. "She's a bossy one and mad as a bottled bumblebee."

If he hadn't been so busy struggling to contain the angry animal, Clay might have responded to his foreman's uncanny knack to state the obvious.

Joe administered the medicine, then slapped the animal's rump and stepped back. Clay released the rope holding the cow's hind legs and jumped out of harm's way, too. Indignant, the cow rolled to its feet, glared at her tormentors, then turned and hurried back to the herd.

"Ingrate," Joe muttered, then climbed back on his horse.

Grinning, Clay coiled the rope in his hand, then tipped his Stetson back and wiped at the sweat on his brow with the handkerchief around his neck. It had been a long, hot day, but a productive one, and even though it was only midafternoon, Clay was itching to head back to the ranch.

In the past, Clay wouldn't have considered quitting work until it was dusk. There was always something to do, if not out on the range with the cattle, then back at the corral with the horses. Besides, there'd been no reason for him to hurry back home to an empty house and a frozen dinner.

But now that he'd married Paige, Clay found himself looking forward to the end of the day. Looking forward not only to the meal waiting for him, but the woman who'd prepared the meal, as well.

Not a day had gone by that she hadn't surprised him in one way or another. The downstairs bathroom she'd insisted on wallpapering herself. The arrangement of wildflowers she'd picked and placed on the kitchen table. Getting up at 5:00 a.m. every day to make coffee and breakfast for him.

And the nights. *Lord*. He wiped at the sweat on his forehead again. Just thinking about the nights made his blood heat.

Damn, but he was one hell of a lucky guy.

From the first time he'd kissed her, Clay had suspected that there was a sensuality simmering underneath Paige's prim, straitlaced facade. He couldn't help but feel both pleasure and pride that he'd been the one to bring that sensuality to fruition. It seemed that with every passing day she grew slightly more bold, more curious, and last night she had come out of the bathroom wearing a sexy, white silk negligee.

At the sight of her long, curvy legs and the soft rise of her breasts under the plunging neckline, he'd been hard instantly. She'd walked slowly toward him, her gaze hesitant, her smile shy, and it had been all he could do not to drag her down on the mattress with him and slip into the sweetness of her body. Through a will of iron, he'd waited for her to walk to him, waited for her to slip beside him on the bed, waited for her to touch him.

He'd let her make all the moves, let her set the pace, and they'd made love slowly, drawing the passion out, making it all the more powerful between them.

He was already thinking about tonight, wondering what other surprises his new wife might still have for him.

"You gonna kiss that rope or maybe just sing to it?"

Startled out of his thoughts, Clay glanced up at Joe. A grin tweaked one corner of his foreman's mouth.

"Keep it up," Clay said, pulling at the slip knot on the rope, "and it'll be around your neck."

Amusement wrinkled the corners of the older man's eyes. Leather creaked as he leaned back casually in his saddle. "The way you been roping today, I'd probably die an old man before you managed to get hold of me. Even then I'd have to stand still and grab hold."

Clay glared at Joe, but he knew what the man said was true. He'd been so distracted today with thoughts about Paige, anyone looking on would have thought him a greenhorn for sure. It was downright embarrassing.

"You already are an old man," Clay said tightly.

"Not so old I can't see you got the bug."

"What bug is that?" Clay asked, though he really didn't care to hear the answer. Dropping the rope over his saddlehorn, he swung up onto his horse.

"The love bug, son." Joe tipped his hat back. "It's bit you square on the butt."

The absurdity of Joe's comment actually made Clay laugh and relieved some of the tension in his shoulders. "For God's sake, we've been married a week."

"The right woman is the right woman," Joe said flatly. "I knew the second I laid eyes on my Dory she was the one."

Clay couldn't imagine what it was like to love that deeply. He'd thought he'd loved Nancy, and that had ended in disaster. If he wanted his marriage with Paige to work, then he needed to keep his head on straight and his emotions in check.

"Joe," Clay said quietly. "You, of all people, know how it is with Paige and me."

Joe nodded. "I know exactly how it is, boy. Trouble is, I don't think you do."

As if to agree, Clay's horse threw its head up with a snort. "Nothing's changed," Clay said firmly. "We respect each other and we get along just fine. That's all I want. I made that clear to Paige when I asked her to marry me. Love has nothing to do with our relationship."

Joe's grin widened. "So we'll see you at poker tonight?"

Poker. Damn. Clay hadn't gone last week because of Julia, and he'd completely forgotten about tonight. There'd been an ongoing game every Saturday night for years at Joe's place. Clay rarely missed, but if he cancelled tonight, he knew he'd be the brunt of "the little woman" jokes for weeks. Not only from Joe, but from the guys, as well.

"Of course I'll be there." His hands tightened on the reins. "Why wouldn't I?"

Joe shrugged. "No reason."

"Damn straight there's no reason," Clay snapped. "Now if this quilting circle is over, why don't we get back to work? We've got ten more head to check out before we ride back."

Clay didn't wait for Joe's response, just swung his horse around. He'd stay out all night and play poker if he damn well pleased, he told himself. He didn't have to spend every night at home.

The love bug, my ass, he thought, shaking his head. He

and Paige barely knew each other, for crying out loud. Too much sun had obviously fried his foreman's brain.

He had a ranch to run, and at the moment, cattle to take care of. The last thing he needed, the last thing he *wanted,* was a woman on his mind.

The bed was mahogany—1880s plantation, four-poster, with a carved, massive headboard. The deep, rich wood was decidedly masculine, yet just soft enough around the edges to appeal to a woman, as well. The frame, with its new mattress, sat high off the bedroom floor.

It was a bed that a man could put his boots under, Paige thought while she tucked pillows into shams.

When Rebecca had shown her pictures of the bed, night-stands and matching armoire, Paige had negotiated the purchase from a dealer in Austin herself, and had it delivered immediately. She'd found the bedding—a deep chocolate and forest green print, with a green striped dust ruffle—on the Internet, then had the linens shipped special delivery so she'd be able to set everything up the same day.

Fluffing the pillow in her hands, she laid it beside its mate, then drew in the scent of freshly laundered cotton.

She'd ordered several other pieces of furniture and items for the house, some from the Internet, some from pictures Rebecca had shown her, but the bed for the master suite had been the first to arrive. Somehow, that seemed appropriate, Paige thought, since it was here, in this bedroom, where her marriage had truly began.

She couldn't believe that a week had passed since she

and Clay had stood before Judge Winters and said their vows. Eight days, to be exact. It felt as if she'd been here forever, as if her entire life before had been a dream, and now, living here, was reality. Seeing her toothbrush beside Clay's, hanging her clothes in the same closet, using the same shower.

She smiled at that thought. Last night, when she'd gone in to shower before bed, Clay had shocked her when he'd stepped in and joined her. She'd been embarrassed at first, but when he'd pulled her into his arms and kissed her, she'd quickly forgotten her modesty. She'd spent most of today remembering the feel of his slick, muscular body against hers, the touch of his hands soaping her back, then her breasts, then moving down lower still.

With a sigh, Paige kicked off her flats and sat on the edge of the bed. She sank into the thick down comforter, then bounced to test the mattress underneath. It was firm and solid.

She couldn't wait to break it in.

Did all new brides feel this way? Paige wondered as she ran her fingertips over the soft cotton fabric. Tingly and excited and nervous, all at the same time? Every day was a beautiful day. Every task, no matter how menial or difficult, was a joy.

She especially enjoyed cooking, and tonight, to celebrate their new bed, she'd dragged out the cookbooks she'd brought with her and tried some new recipes. Wine-roasted chicken, garlic potatoes, fresh peas and a lemon-strawberry Bavarian cake for dessert. She knew that Clay worked a long, hard day, and he seemed to enjoy eating the food she set on the table each night as much as she enjoyed preparing the meal. Lord knew, he could certainly pack it away, but the physical labor of working on a ranch kept his muscular body rock hard.

She thought about that body, what it felt like on top of her own, how it felt when he slipped inside her, and she couldn't help but blush. She laid back on the bed, closed her eyes and ran her hand over the pillow, wishing it were Clay.

Would he make love to her slowly tonight, drawing out each exquisite moment with precalculated precision? Or would he take her fast, with wild, reckless abandon?

Or maybe both. Smiling, she burrowed her face into the soft mattress.

She certainly hoped so.

He found her like that several minutes later. Though he'd certainly noticed the four-poster bed, it was the woman lying on top of it that truly caught his attention. Her slender body was stretched out on the big bed, her soft brown hair spilling over her face while her fingers moved idly back and forth over the pillow beside her.

Clay's throat went dry at the sight of her lying there, her feet bare, the skirt of her lavender dress flowing over her long legs. His gaze feasted on the curve of her hip, the soft rise of her breasts above the scooped neckline of her dress, the smooth column of exposed neck. He knew the spot just below her earlobe that made her sigh, knew if he lingered there, she would moan. There were other places that made her moan, too. A soft bite on her shoulder, a brush of his lips on the inside of her elbow, a sweep of his tongue over the heart-shaped freckle beside her hip.

He loved that freckle.

There were other places, too. Intimate places where no man had been before him. Places that Paige hadn't known existed. He'd found great pleasure in exploring her body, committing to memory every sweet curve, every soft valley. She'd been an enthusiastic learner, as well. On more than one occasion, she'd pleasantly surprised him with her eagerness to explore new avenues—to enter into virgin territory, he thought with a wry smile.

He watched her now, felt himself harden when her hand slid to the vacant spot on the bed beside her. His blood raced, then pounded in his temples.

No woman had ever aroused him more. No woman had ever made him ache.

He swore at the need that overwhelmed him, then drew back into the hallway to rein in his emotions.

He could control this, he told himself firmly. Maybe he had gotten a little carried away with the domestic scene this past week, but it would pass. He was certain that the intense need would level off to simple lust. They could enjoy each other, as husband and wife, as man and woman, without further complicating an already complicated situation.

He just needed to hold off letting himself get too wrapped up in Paige. Stop wondering what she was doing while he was out working. Stop thinking about what she smelled like, how soft her skin was. That little sound she made deep in her throat when he touched the right spot.

A few more days and Julia would be back in the house with them. Having his daughter here would surely cool the heat between Paige and himself. In a few weeks, they would all naturally ease into a relaxed family routine.

But he had to get a handle on the situation, on his feelings, now. Had to contain the emotions threatening to disrupt his carefully structured life.

Careful not to disturb Paige, he quietly went back downstairs, faltered at the incredible smell of the dinner she'd prepared, then shook it off. Dammit, but he was getting soft when he couldn't make a decision and be firm about it.

He called out to her as if he'd just come in, then made his way slowly back up the stairs.

"I'm in the bedroom," she called back.

She was standing by the bed when he walked into the bedroom, her pretty face lit with a smile. Once again, his determination stumbled. Once again he recovered.

He glanced at the bed as if he were seeing it for the first time. "New bed," he said simply.

"Do you like it?"

He focused on the bed instead of the seductive way she was nibbling on her bottom lip. "It's fine."

"Just fine?" Her smile dimmed.

"It's a bed." He turned and headed for the closet. "By the way, I'm going to Joe's place."

"Tonight?"

"We have a standing poker game every Saturday night. I didn't think to mention it before."

"Oh."

The single word was filled with disappointment. Clay's hand tightened on the pair of jeans he'd pulled from a shelf in the closet. He didn't turn around to look at her.

"Will you eat before you go?" she asked hopefully. "It's ready, if you're hungry."

Dragging a clean shirt from a hanger, he shook his head. "You go ahead without me. I'll have pizza later with the guys."

If he stayed, even to eat dinner, there was no doubt in Clay's mind that he'd never leave this house tonight. He couldn't give that kind of control to Paige. To *anyone*.

"All right," she said evenly. "I'll leave a plate for you in case you're hungry when you come in."

She was certainly taking this well, Clay thought, then glanced over his shoulder at her. She stood beside the bed, her hands clasped primly in front of her. She smiled at him when their eyes met. She not only didn't seem angry, she was being pleasant, to boot.

Dammit, anyway.

Maybe he'd been wrong about their situation, he thought. Maybe Paige hadn't got as caught up in their relationship as he had. Clearly she had control of her emotions, and seemed completely unfazed that he was going out to a poker game this evening.

Good, he told himself. That was what he'd wanted,

hadn't he? What he and Paige had agreed on. A marriage without entanglements. He should be relieved, if not downright happy, that she wasn't upset.

"I'm going to take a shower," he said through clenched teeth, then turned and headed for the bathroom.

He stripped off his dirty clothes and stepped into the hot shower, determined not to think about Paige. But when the image of her lying on the big bed crept into his mind, he felt the need rise again.

Dammit, *dammit.*

Swearing under his breath, he stuck his head under the spray of water and turned the faucet to cold.

"It must seem strange to you." Rebecca sliced two pieces of cake and set them on gold-edged china plates. "Coming to your house and seeing someone else living here."

"For heaven's sake, Rebecca." Paige rolled her eyes. "You aren't exactly someone else, you're my best friend. I'm glad you're living here."

After Clay had left the house earlier, Paige couldn't face the empty house—or the empty bed upstairs—by herself. She'd called Rebecca to see if she was home, made up a plate of food for Clay like she'd promised, then packed up the rest in her grandmother's old Chevy and driven into town.

How she'd managed to hide her disappointment and hurt from Clay when he'd so coolly told her he was going out, Paige still didn't know. She'd let herself want, let herself hope, for too much in the short time they'd been together. Today was a wake-up call to get her head out of the clouds. Obviously, she was going to have to be much more careful in the future.

"I'm glad I'm living here, too." Rebecca slid a plate across the kitchen table, then sat across from Paige. "My apartment over the store was getting much too cramped, and with the shop doing so well, I'm considering expanding upstairs. Since I already have a kitchen up there, I even thought about opening a tea room for lunch and small, private parties."

"What a wonderful idea." Paige could already picture the small, Victorian-style antique store serving tea in pretty china cups, finger sandwiches and scones with cream. "If you have it open by Christmas, I'm sure the library would book you for their holiday luncheon."

Rebecca cut off a bite of cake with her fork. "What makes you so sure?"

"Because I'm in charge of finding a restaurant," Paige said with a grin.

Rebecca grinned back, closed her eyes on a moan when she took a bite of the Bavarian cake. "Ohmigod, I think I just died and went to heaven."

At least *someone* was enjoying the dessert, Paige thought.

"If I do open a tea room, I *have* to put this on my menu." Rebecca took another bite, sighed with pleasure, then leaned back in her chair and leveled a gaze at Paige.

"Now you want to tell me why you're here, sharing this amazing meal with me, instead of your new husband?"

Paige knew she'd have to tell Rebecca sooner or later, had actually been surprised that her friend hadn't pushed her for information when she'd shown up on her doorstep with all this food.

Paige casually took a bite of her own cake, though she barely tasted it. "He had a poker game."

"Oh." Rebecca pursed her lips. "And I take it you didn't know."

"He forgot to mention it."

"I see." Rebecca lifted a brow. "So you had your first fight."

Paige glanced up sharply. "Of course not. It certainly wasn't important enough to argue about. I wouldn't have even minded at all if—"

She stopped, felt embarrassed to even say it.

"If what?"

"If our bed hadn't arrived today," she mumbled, then looked away. "I know it's silly, but I'd sort of thought that we'd...well, celebrate."

"And then he goes off to play poker." Rebecca shook her head. "Men. God, they can be such idiots."

"I shouldn't have assumed," Paige said firmly. "It's just that he's been home every other night, and he's been very, I mean, well, based on the past week, I thought that we would...that he might want to—"

"Have sex?"

Paige nearly choked.

A Wolf River Summer

"For heaven's sake, Paige." Rebecca rolled her eyes. "You're a married woman. Married women have sex, and sometimes lucky single ones, too. Which I haven't been one of lately," she said with a sigh. "But enough about me. So is it hot?"

"Rebecca!"

Laughing, Rebecca leaned forward. "Details, sister. I want details."

Paige felt her cheeks burn. "I can't talk about that."

"Okay, you don't have to talk about it. Just tell me— is it hot?"

Paige pressed her lips together, determined not to respond. But as Rebecca leaned closer, her brow lifted in anticipation, Paige couldn't help the slow smile that curved her lips.

"I knew it!" Rebecca grinned widely. "When you walked out of the anteroom in Judge Winters's chambers and Clay looked at you, I was ready to call the fire department. A person could weld steel with that look."

Paige knew the look only too well. That hungry, intense need she'd seen in his gaze this past week. Just thinking about it now made her pulse quicken.

"Clay is very…" Paige searched for the right word "physical. Whoever he'd married, he would have looked at them the same way."

"That's horse puckey." Rebecca shook her head. "He wanted *you,* sweetheart."

"Only because I was dependable and stable." So dependable and stable, she thought, that he didn't have to mention when he wouldn't be home for dinner.

"More horse puckey." Rebecca shook her head. "He might have had that silly thought in the beginning, but I don't believe for a second he would have married you if he wasn't attracted to you physically. And if he hadn't gotten your juices flowing, you wouldn't have married him, either, my dear. You would have married Bernie Pratt," Rebecca said with a shudder, then leaned closer and leveled her I-know-you-better-than-you-know-yourself look at Paige. "Come on, Paige. Admit it."

What was the point in denying it? Paige knew that Rebecca would see right through her if she tried to lie. Rather than look her friend in the eye, Paige picked up her fork and played with the cake on the plate in front of her.

"So maybe I was physically attracted to Clay before I married him," Paige said quietly. "Name me one woman in this town—including yourself—who's under eighty that wouldn't look at the man and feel her insides go soft? One woman who didn't wonder, at least once, what it would be like to be with Clay Bodine?"

When Rebecca didn't answer, Paige glanced up and saw her friend staring wide-eyed at her.

"Well, for heaven's sake," Paige said irritably. "You tell me you want the truth, and when I give it to you, you stare at me as if I'd just told you I was a double-agent for the CIA. Why are you *looking* at me that way?"

"You're in love with him."

Paige went still, then her heart gave a sickening lurch.

Was she so transparent? And if Rebecca could see it, then would Clay be able to see it, too? Maybe he had, she thought. Maybe that was why he'd gone out tonight without telling her. To keep an emotional distance between them.

"You *are* in love with him," Rebecca said breathlessly.

"I'd be a fool to fall in love with a man who married me simply to be a mother to his child." So Rebecca wouldn't see her hand shake, Paige slowly laid her fork down on the plate. "A man who made it perfectly clear not only that he doesn't love me, but he doesn't *believe* in love."

"Honey," Rebecca said, shaking her head, "those are the ones who fall the hardest."

Not Clay, Paige sighed as she pushed her plate away. Tonight she'd made a mistake and let him slip through her defenses. From now on, she thought, she was determined to be much more careful.

Chapter 9

When Paige woke on Sunday morning, the bed beside her was already empty. She'd heard Clay come into the bedroom last night just before 1:00 a.m., though she'd pretended to be asleep when he'd quietly called her name, not once, but twice.

Paige had recognized the husky tone in Clay's voice, and she knew if she'd turned to him that they would have made love. Unwillingly, her own body had responded to his soft whisper. She'd felt her skin tingle and her pulse quicken. Her breasts had ached to be touched.

Even when the mattress dipped beside her, Paige had kept her back to him, squeezed her eyes tightly closed and forced her breathing to be steady and relaxed. When he slid under the covers, then pressed his broad chest to her back, she'd had proof of his desire to make love. She'd wanted desperately to lose herself in that pleasure, had nearly given in to the need pulsing through her.

But she hadn't. The hurt from Clay's behavior the night before was still too fresh. The sting was too sharp. There were no emotions involved for Clay when he wanted sex, Paige knew. But for herself, the physical and the emotional were intertwined. When they made love, she gave herself to him completely. And she couldn't have done that last night, not while she was still upset with him.

She'd set herself up for it, of course. She'd let her guard down, let him get into her heart. But this was still all so new to her. Having a husband, being a wife, running a household. And soon she'd be taking care of a child full-time, too. It was more than a little overwhelming.

Maybe she was just being too sensitive right now, she told herself. Maybe in a few days, or a few weeks even, she'd get used to her life with Clay and little things like new beds and uneaten meals wouldn't bother her so much.

The possibility didn't make her feel any better.

On a sigh, she rose from the bed and showered, then dressed for church. Though Clay had attended the service last week because of Julia, he obviously did not feel the same compunction when it came to his wife. She could live with that, she told herself. It was not her intention, and certainly not in her nature, to force Clay to do anything he didn't want to do.

As if she—or anyone—could, she thought, buttoning the front of the red floral dress she'd bought before she'd married Clay. She'd never worn red before, but Rebecca had insisted the color was perfect for her. Now that she had it on, Paige stared at her reflection in the mirror. With the new hairstyle and dress, she barely recognized herself.

All her life, Paige had been a dowdy, colorless bookworm. She'd read stories of mystery and intrigue, with courageous heroines and dashing heroes. She realized now that she'd lived life through the characters in all those wonderful books. And for the first time in her life, she had an opportunity to *experience* life, not just read about it.

When it came to Clay, Paige prayed she could be just half as brave as those characters.

She quickly made the bed, slipped on a pair of white strappy sandals and as a last minute thought, went back into the bathroom where she ran a tube of rose-colored lip gloss over her lips and a touch of mascara on her lashes. She still wasn't used to applying cosmetics, but she did like the subtle way the makeup brightened her face.

She was disappointed that Clay wouldn't be joining her, but she was determined to enjoy the day in spite of everything. Leaving a note on the kitchen table to tell him where she'd gone, Paige gathered up her purse and the car keys to the Chevy, then drove into town.

Clay stomped the dust off his boots, brushed off his jeans, then limped through the back door. His thigh hurt like a sonofabitch, and though he couldn't be angry with the horse who'd kicked him, he was definitely angry at himself. He'd known better than to come up behind that two-year-old filly like he had. She was a pretty little roan, but high-spirited and a little nervous.

It certainly wasn't the horse's fault, Clay thought, that he'd had his mind on another high-spirited, nervous female. But he was infinitely glad that the blow hadn't been six inches to the left. If it had, he'd be singing soprano and very worried about his ability to ever father any future children.

Of course, after the way he'd left the house last night, Clay figured his chances of fathering any more children were greatly diminished, anyway. Though Paige hadn't seemed to mind that he'd gone off to play poker, she certainly hadn't received him warmly when he'd wanted to make love with her last night, either. She'd pretended to be asleep, but he'd felt her stiffen when he'd touched her, and he realized that maybe she hadn't been as unaffected by his leaving last night as he'd first thought.

But what had really surprised—and annoyed—him, was the fact that he'd felt like a heel all night. He hadn't been able to concentrate on one single hand, had made three bets out of order, and forgotten what game they were playing twice. He'd been forced to listen to constant ribbing about separation anxiety from his wife and then laugh it off, when what he really felt like doing was reaching down someone—anyone's—throat and ripping out that person's liver.

So much for a friendly game of cards.

He wasn't used to feeling guilty, didn't like it one little bit. He'd make it up to her, he told himself as he closed the back door behind him and walked through the laundry area into the kitchen.

He could take her into town for dinner tonight, or maybe even offer to look at some of the paint chips or drapery samples she had laid out on the living room floor. He shuddered at the thought, but he knew women liked men to do that kind of stuff.

He realized how quiet the house was as he walked through the kitchen. Paige usually had classical music playing on the intercom system, but today, the house was absolutely still. He called out to her, but she didn't answer.

For one heart-stopping moment he thought she'd left him. That she'd packed up her cat and clothes and driven back to town. He hadn't thought she was upset enough to do anything like that, but who the hell could figure out what was going on in a female's head? Lord knew he'd never been good at it.

His eyes narrowed with anger. If she thought she could walk away that easy, she had another thing coming. Dammit, if he had to go to town and have it out with her in front of everyone, then that's what he'd do and if she—

Then he saw the cat. Eudora sat in the kitchen doorway, looking at him like he was an idiot. Clay released the breath he'd been holding. Paige wouldn't have left without taking her cat, he was sure of that.

He spotted the note on the table and snatched it up, then groaned.

Church. He'd forgotten all about that. He hadn't even

thought about it being Sunday. Shaking his head, he raked a hand through his hair, then looked at Eudora.

"So I jumped the gun a little," Clay said irritably. "What was I supposed to think when she wasn't here?"

The cat meowed.

"She should have reminded me about church last night," Clay said in his defense. "It's my Sunday to tend to the horses."

Eudora flicked her own tail at that little bit of information.

"Yeah, well, what do you suggest?" Clay scowled at the animal.

The tabby got up and walked away.

"Thanks for the help," Clay called after the retreating cat.

He glanced at the clock on the kitchen stove. If Paige had come home after the service, she would have been home an hour already. Obviously, she'd gone somewhere else and hadn't bothered to call him.

He knew she'd gone out last night, too, because the Chevy had been parked in a different spot. He'd assumed she'd gone to Rebecca's, but what if she hadn't? What if she'd gone to see Bernie to cry on her old boyfriend's shoulder? His eyes narrowed at the thought, then he shook his head.

No. Paige might not be predictable, but she was honest. As much as he could trust anyone, he trusted Paige.

Shaking his head, he limped upstairs to take a shower. When he stepped into the bedroom, he stared at the new furniture and decided he liked it. Especially the antique four-poster bed. It was large enough to easily accommodate his tall frame, the mattress was firm, but extremely comfortable.

His ex-wife's taste had been the complete opposite of Paige's. When Nancy had moved into the house, she'd carted away every piece of furniture Clay had owned, then retained a designer from Beverly Hills to fly out and furnish the house. Everything she'd bought had been ultra-contemporary. Sharp lines, bold colors, lots of white, glossy woods with steel trim. When she'd left him, she'd hired a moving company to pack up every last piece of furniture. Every lamp, every chair, every god-awful eye-straining painting that she'd considered ''art.''

And even though he'd paid exorbitant prices for everything, Clay had still appreciated the fact that Nancy had emptied the house. It had saved him the trouble of dragging everything off to the nearest charity organization.

For the past five years, he'd been comfortable with just a dining table, bed and office furniture. He hadn't needed anything else. He worked most of the time, and even when he had dated, he never brought women here, anyway.

His gaze traveled from the mahogany armoire to the nightstands, then finally back to the bed. He'd always liked the idea of a four-poster bed. It stimulated certain fantasies that would no doubt make his wife blush, but hey, he thought as he headed for the shower, a guy could only hope, couldn't he?

He had no idea what mood Paige would be in when she

got back from town. Nancy had always given him the silent treatment when she was mad at him—right after she'd yelled at him.

But Clay was already well aware of the fact that Paige was nothing like Nancy. Paige was not selfish or condescending, and she certainly wasn't lazy.

She also wasn't predictable, Clay thought as he quickly soaped up. And that, strangely enough, was the one thing that worried him the most.

Arms loaded with groceries, Paige shoved her way in through the back door, dumped the paper bags and her purse on the kitchen table, then began to unload the items that needed refrigeration first. She'd stopped at Bud and Joe's Market to pick up fresh produce and meats for the week, along with several spices that had been missing in the kitchen pantry, especially some of the more uncommon ones.

After last night, Paige had seriously considered serving Clay frozen dinners from now on. Or maybe slap some lunch meat and cheese between some bread and toss that down on the table for his dinner. She'd even seen meals from the shelf that could be microwaved and ready in under ten minutes. The hours she'd save could certainly be put to use painting Julia's bedroom that lovely pale shade of yellow she'd picked out from the samples.

But the fact was, she *liked* to cook. Because of her grandmother's sensitive stomach, Paige had mostly made bland soups and boiled chicken for the past few years.

Trying new and interesting recipes had been fun, and watching Clay enjoy her cooking had been extremely satisfying.

There was no point in staying upset with him, Paige told herself as she dropped a head of romaine lettuce inside the vegetable crisper. They'd both lose.

But at the same time, she thought as she pulled a bag of apples from a shopping bag, she had no intention of being a doormat, either. Clay might not love her, but if their marriage was going to succeed, he needed to respect her. Not only as his wife, but as a person. He'd caught her in a vulnerable moment last night. If it happened again, she'd be ready to stand up to him and speak her mind.

Why wait for there to be a next time? she asked herself boldly. She'd speak to him now. Tell him how she felt. While she stared at the bag of fruit in her hands, she ran through various scenarios.

I would appreciate prior notice…

No, that sounded too prudish.

Clay, maybe next time…

Absolutely not. Much too timid.

Unless you'd like to make your own meals, Clay Bodine, I suggest…

She shook her head. Too combative.

I'm your wife, Clay. My time is valuable, too, and I feel that I deserve respect and consideration in this marriage.

That was pretty good, she decided.

"So how do like *them* apples?" she said with a nod.

"They look pretty good."

Startled, Paige squeaked at the unexpected sound of Clay's voice behind her. She whirled around to see him leaning against the kitchen doorjamb, watching her.

"Clay," she gasped. "You scared me."

"Sorry."

The black T-shirt he wore fit snugly over his muscled chest and arms. His jeans were clean, as were his black boots, which meant he'd just showered and changed. She watched as he pushed away from the doorjamb and walked toward her, stopped a foot away and dropped his gaze to her mouth. Her heart started to beat like a drum. When he bent to lightly brush his lips over hers, the scent of man and apples assailed her senses.

"New dress?" he asked softly.

Between his closeness and his lips on hers, Paige could barely remember what she had on. Oh, right. The red one. "Yes."

"Pretty," he murmured and traced the seam of her lips with his tongue.

"Thank you." She held back the threatening moan, had to remind herself to breathe.

"Can I help with anything?" he murmured softly.

Yes! You certainly can, her body screamed. Her knees went weak as she thought about all the ways he could "help" her.

But as tempting as it was, she wasn't ready to fall into Clay's arms just yet. There were things they needed to discuss first, and she was determined to stay focused on those issues, not the feel of his lips on her own.

"There is something," she whispered against his lips.

"What?" he asked huskily.

She pulled her head back, then shoved the apples at him. "You can put these in the refrigerator."

She turned away from him and began to empty the contents of another shopping bag. She said nothing about church and he didn't ask. They worked side by side in awkward silence, the tension between them tightening with each passing minute. Paige knew it wouldn't be any easier later to discuss what had happened last night. Which meant there was no time like the present. She slid a box of raisins in the cupboard, drew in a breath to steady herself, then turned toward him.

A bottle of apple juice in his hand, he walked toward the refrigerator. That's when she noticed the limp.

"What's wrong with your leg?"

He opened the refrigerator door and put the juice on the top shelf. "Horse kicked me."

"A horse kicked you?" she repeated in alarm.

"Nothing's broke." He snagged one of the apples he'd put in the fridge a moment ago and rubbed it on his chest.

The impulse to touch him, to soothe and fuss, overwhelmed her. Concern narrowed her eyes as she stepped closer to him. "But you're limping."

"All in a day's work," he said with a shrug, then bit into the apple.

"Where did it kick you?"

"In the barn."

She rolled her eyes. "Don't be smart."

He rubbed his hand over the top of his thigh. "Here."

Paige sucked in a sharp breath as she noted the proximity of the kick to Clay's groin. Eyes wide, she quickly looked back up. "Are you all right?"

"I'm sure everything still works." He chewed slowly. "We could test it out, if you're worried."

The light tease in his words was heavy with sexual innuendo. Paige felt her body respond to the deep, low timbre of his voice, and the hungry, fierce look in his eyes. Her pulse skipped, and the heat of his stare warmed her insides.

She was torn between her mind and her body, but determined not to let him use sex to clear the air between them. She swallowed hard, then met his steady gaze. "Clay, I think we should talk about—"

"I was an ass."

Surprised at his interruption, she simply stared, her mouth still open. He set his apple on the counter, then stepped closer to her, cupped her chin in his hand and looked down at her.

"I can't promise I won't be an ass again," he said evenly, "but I will promise that I'll be more considerate."

It wasn't exactly an apology, but it was close enough that Paige was too stunned to reply. Had he really called himself an *ass?* When she just continued to stare at him, he frowned, then dropped his hand and stepped back.

"Look, this isn't easy for me," he said flatly. "I've always come and gone as I pleased. I never had to think about anyone else. Now suddenly I have a wife and a kid.

I'm bound to make some mistakes. For God's sake, you could at least *say* something.''

First he'd thrown her off with his almost-apology, now he was getting irritable because she hadn't replied to his outburst. Heavens. Living with Clay was obviously going to be like riding a roller coaster. But even as she opened her mouth to speak, he started up again.

''Dammit, Paige.'' Hands on his hips, he paced to the other side of the kitchen, then back again. ''What do you want from me?''

If he was trying to make her mad in a ridiculous attempt to ease his own guilty conscience, he was doing an excellent job, she thought. Folding her arms, Paige pointed her chin at him. ''I don't believe I've asked you for anything.''

That stopped him. He looked down at her, and the anger slowly drained from his eyes. ''No, you haven't,'' he said quietly. ''Maybe you should.''

''There's nothing I want.'' *Except for you to love me,* she thought, but she might as well wish for the moon.

On a sigh, he reached for her hand and ran his thumb over the diamond on her ring, then suddenly he was pulling her toward the back door.

''Clay!'' she gasped. ''What are you doing?''

''I want to show you something behind the barn.'' He dragged her down the back steps.

''I've heard that one before,'' she said, but he just chuckled and kept pulling her along.

She could barely keep up with his long strides. Scooter came out of the barn, barking with pleasure as he joined the game. The sun beat down hard, and the smell of hay and horses filled the hot midafternoon air.

Other than a trip to the barn with Julia the weekend she'd visited, Paige hadn't spent much time outside since she'd come to the Rocking B. She'd been too busy inside the house to truly explore the ranch yet, and wasn't sure if Clay would object to her wandering around where his men were working. For the past week she'd heard the low growl of tractors, the whistles and shouts as the ranch hands worked the horses in the corrals, the occasional snorts and whinnies from the horses or the deep moo of a cow. Life on the Rocking B was very different from her house and job in town, but she'd come to love the ranch and already felt at home.

Because it was Sunday and midafternoon, the corrals were thankfully empty of horses and men. Paige would have been embarrassed if any of the ranch hands could see the way Clay was dragging her across the yard, despite her protests.

When they rounded the side of the barn, Clay stopped abruptly and turned, causing Paige to collide with the hard wall of his chest. He steadied her with his arms, then looked down at her. "Close your eyes."

"Clay, for heaven's sake, what are you—"

"Just do it," he insisted.

She sighed heavily, then closed her eyes, felt the anticipation and thrill of waiting for him to kiss her.

But he didn't. Instead, he stepped away and took both

of her hands in his, then kept walking. "Don't open your eyes until I tell you."

She did as he asked, felt the dirt path under her shoes as he guided her. He continued to warn her to keep her eyes closed while he pulled her along several feet, then turned her to the left and kept walking.

When he finally stopped, she heard the sound of a door opening, then felt the warm, moist rush of sweetly scented air.

"Eyes closed," he reminded her and pulled her forward.

Paige furrowed her brow, resisted the temptation to open her eyes. The smell of damp earth filled her nostrils. She felt and heard the crunch of gravel under her feet. The quiet strains of Mozart played overhead.

Clay let go of her, and she heard the door close again, felt a fine mist fall on her cheeks and arms.

Where in the world had he brought her?

"Okay," he said from behind her. "Open your eyes."

She did, then gasped.

Orchids.

Hundreds of them. She was too stunned to speak, just turned in a slow circle, taking in the kaleidoscope of colors and shapes. From the palest lavender to the deepest purple, from creamy yellow to startling gold. Pinks and whites and reds. The shapes on the flowers were as individual and as varied as the designs. She felt as if she were in a rainforest somewhere. All she needed was the sound of rushing waterfalls and screeching, colorful macaws to complete the picture.

"It's so beautiful," she breathed.

"They're Joe's," Clay said. "It's a hobby, of sorts."

Joe's? It was hard to imagine Clay's foreman cultivating orchids. Cactus, maybe, Paige thought, but *orchids?*

"What do you mean, 'of sorts'?"

"It was actually his wife's hobby." Clay looked around the greenhouse. "Joe took over when she got too sick to care for them. After she died, he just kept them going. That was ten years ago."

"Ten years?" Paige examined the delicate stalk of a tiny yellow flower that looked like a lion's head. "That's a long time."

"There were only twenty plants or so back then. Somehow it just kept growing. We've expanded the greenhouse twice."

She stepped toward and lightly touched the thick, waxy leaf of a large, white orchid with purple stripes in the center of the bloom. "How long were they married?"

"Twenty-six years." Clay shoved his hands into his front pockets. "She was a nice lady."

Paige bent to smell the tropical scent of a creamy white flower. "Did they have children?"

"Two sons and a daughter," he replied. "All of them scattered across the country now. We all kind of grew up together, though they're all younger than me. Joe sees them mostly around the holidays, but they stay in touch."

"He obviously loved her very much," Paige said wistfully.

Clay didn't answer, but he didn't need to. Love shimmered in every plant, every bloom, every leaf. The kind of love that endured beyond the bounds of life. Paige *felt* it, in the air, in her heart. Not just Joe's love for his wife, Paige knew, but her own love for Clay.

Why had he brought her here today? she wondered. Was this his way of saying he was sorry, without actually saying the words?

She wasn't sure, but she did know that him bringing her here, sharing this place with her, was something special. Something to cherish.

She walked to him, placed her palms on his chest and smiled up at him. "Thank you," she said softly, then rose on her tiptoes and pressed her lips to his.

His arms came around her, and he deepened the kiss. Her breath quickened as his tongue met hers, her heart beat heavy. He tasted like apple and dark, sweet desire. His hands slid down to her waist, pulling her tightly against him. He wanted her, she felt his arousal press against the junction of her thighs. And she wanted him. In every way, but for now, she would take whatever he offered.

He pulled away from her, his breathing ragged, and stared down at her. "Why don't we go try out our new bed?" he said huskily. "See how it holds up."

Our new bed, he'd said, and that simple word sent joy shivering up her spine. She smiled at him. "I'm sure it will hold up just fine."

Grinning, he took her hand and they hurried back across the yard toward the house.

Chapter 10

The following Friday morning, Clay and Paige drove into town to pick Julia up from the Barringtons. The morning was pleasant and they rode along the highway with the truck windows rolled down and a Tim McGraw-Faith Hill duet on the radio. Knowing that Clay was tense over meeting with the Barringtons again, Paige did not try to make conversation, she simply sat back and enjoyed the passing countryside and the wind lifting the ends of her hair.

This past week had flown by for Paige. The furniture for the living room, guest room and Julia's bedroom had arrived and already been situated, plus she'd had shelves delivered for Clay's office. If there was one thing Paige felt completely comfortable with, it was arranging the piles of books he'd had stacked on the floor. She'd also ordered a bigger desk, chair and file cabinet that would be delivered in a few days.

The house was slowly evolving into a home, especially since Paige had found a large steamer trunk in the attic that had belonged to Clay's great-grandmother. It was like finding a treasure chest. She'd been giddy with delight as she'd pulled the items out. An entire set of china, two crystal vases, a patchwork quilt and a needlepoint that read HOME SWEET HOME. Old photographs, including several of Clay, that she couldn't wait to frame and put up on the walls. Small toys, some antique, some from Clay's childhood. Baby clothes.

Paige had felt a longing rise in her as she'd brushed her fingers over a hand-knitted baby blanket. She was anxious to give Clay another child, and Julia a sister or brother. Anxious to feel life inside her, to hold a baby in her arms and place it to her breast. She and Clay hadn't discussed when they would try for a baby, but she considered bringing the subject up in a day or two.

Instinctively, Paige laid a hand on her stomach, then glanced over at Clay. Soon, she hoped.

While he was absorbed in his own thoughts, she studied the profile of the man she loved. She'd thought him handsome before, but now, just looking at him made her insides take flight. His rugged looks and size didn't intimidate her any longer and she'd become accustomed to the strong lines of his face and jaw. The sharp cut of his chin, the straight angle of his cheekbones, the slight bend in his nose. When he smiled, the blue of his eyes softened to the color of worn denim, but when he looked at her with desire, his eyes darkened to the color of an ocean at sunset.

She remembered making love after he'd shown her the orchid greenhouse last week, and the memory shivered through her like an electrical current. Something special had happened between them that day, something that hadn't happened before or since. Though only for a little while, Clay had let his guard down. His lovemaking had been more tender, more gentle, than it ever had before. There'd been no rush, no sense of desperation or urgency, just long, slow kisses that built ever-so-slightly, until the pleasure spiraled to what felt like torture and she'd begged him to hurry.

She'd felt something from him that day, something he hadn't given her before. Paige was too cautious, too afraid to give it a name, but it was more than sex and more than pleasure.

When Clay pulled into town, the sound of a friendly honk from a passing pickup brought Paige out of her reverie. From the sidewalks, several people smiled and waved as she and Clay drove down Main Street toward The Four Winds. For the past fifteen years, Clay had kept to himself on the Rocking B. But it wasn't going to be so easy for him now, Paige realized. With a wife and a child, he wouldn't be able to keep that same cool distance. It was obvious he wasn't comfortable with the outward display of attention from the townspeople, but he'd get used to it, Paige told herself. When he wanted to, she knew firsthand how quickly her husband could turn on the charm.

When Linda Barrington opened the hotel room door, however, Clay's charm was definitely in the Off mode. He nodded stiffly at the woman.

"Linda."

"Clay, Paige, please, come in." Linda Barrington offered a weak smile as she stepped aside to allow them entrance to the suite.

The simple emerald-green suit dress Linda wore hung loosely on her slender frame and Paige thought that the woman looked thinner than the last time she'd seen her, her face more gaunt. It was apparent that the custody battle, and knowing that Clay would most likely win, was taking its toll on her.

Paige felt for the woman, could only imagine how difficult this situation must be for her. She wanted to comfort her, assure her that she wouldn't be cut out of her granddaughter's life, but based on the hard press of Clay's mouth, this wasn't the time.

"I've just ordered some coffee and pastries." Linda gestured toward a room service cart. "May I offer you something?"

"I'd love a cup of coffee," Paige said before Clay could answer. It was obvious that Julia's grandmother had something to say, and Paige understood it would be easier for the woman if she were able to keep her hands busy. "Cream, no sugar, please."

"Please have a seat," Linda said, gesturing to the sofa.

Clay watched Paige move to the sofa and he shot his wife a disapproving glance. What the hell was the matter with her? he thought irritably. She knew perfectly well that he wanted to get Julia and get out as quickly as possible, yet here she sat primly on the sofa, her hands folded in her lap, watching while Linda poured coffee from a silver pot into a cup on a saucer.

Reluctantly, Clay slipped his hat off his head and held it in his lap as he sat on a chair beside the sofa, only half listening while Paige politely asked Linda about their flight. All he wanted to do was gather up his daughter and take her home, not listen to a bunch of female chitchat.

So where was Julia?

He looked at both of the closed bedroom doors and realized how quiet it was. A knot formed in his stomach. He didn't think the Barringtons would try to oppose the court-ordered visit, but then, he really didn't know them very well. Nancy had told him that her parents had objected to her marrying him, but he'd only actually met Linda and Bob once before he and Nancy had eloped and then once after.

"Where's Julia?" he asked Linda.

"With her grandfather, at the park on the edge of town," Linda said while she added cream to Paige's coffee. "She saw the swings there yesterday and asked if she could go. I said it would be all right."

The knot loosened in Clay's gut. "We could have taken her."

"You'll have plenty of times to take her," Linda said, her voice strained. "I wanted a few moments to speak privately with you."

"Is everything all right with Julia?" He hated not knowing what was going on in his own daughter's life, that he had to be kept updated by Linda and Bob. But no longer, he told himself. Julia would come back to the ranch with him today, and in two weeks, after the court hearing, he was completely confident she would be coming home with him to stay.

"Yes, of course she's all right," Linda reassured Clay. "She's wonderful. You know how much we adore her."

This was exactly why he hadn't wanted to stay here, Clay thought. He'd known Linda would try to talk him into compromising on his decision for full custody. "Linda—"

"We're only asking for a few weeks a year, that's all. Maybe a holiday or two."

"We've been over this a hundred times," Clay said firmly. "I've told you and Bob that as long as you call me first and make arrangements, you can come and visit Julia as often as you want."

"Why is it so difficult for you to let her come and stay with us on an arranged schedule?" Moisture filled her eyes. "We've done a good job raising her, haven't we?"

"Dammit, Linda," Clay said under his breath. "Don't do this."

"Clay—" The woman drew in a slow breath to compose herself. "We know that Nancy wasn't a good wife or mother, but don't punish us for that. Julia's all we have. If you would just agree to—"

"You kept my daughter from me for almost five years."

He felt the heat of his temper rising and struggled to contain it. "Why should I trust you now? Why should I ever trust you?"

"We wanted to tell you about Julia. We told Nancy you had a right to know. That Julia had a right to know." Linda's hands were visibly shaking. "But she threatened to take Julia to Europe with her and that musician and never return if we told you. She would have done it, Clay. You know she would. How could we have taken that chance?"

"If you'd have come to me before, we would've worked something out." Clay stood, his hands tightly gripping his hat. "I will not sign papers that give you legal decisions of any kind over Julia."

"We aren't asking for that," Linda said, her voice desperate. "We just want to know that we'll be able to spend time with her in California." Linda glanced at Paige, then touched her knee. "Paige, you're a woman, surely you can—"

"This discussion is over." Clay jammed his hat back on his head. "Paige."

Paige looked up at him, and when he saw the indecision in her eyes, he thought for a moment that he was going to have to argue with her, too. But thankfully, she simply set her coffee cup down and stood.

"Thank you for the coffee, Mrs. Barrington," Paige said softly, and the sympathy in her voice set Clay's teeth on edge.

"Linda, please." Forcing a smile as she rose from the

sofa, Linda looked at Paige. "We bought her a new pair of shoes for casual wear, but we thought you'd know best what to buy her for wearing around the ranch. She might need a pair of jeans, too. She's growing so fast, we can barely keep up with her."

"We'll take care of it," Paige answered, her tone gentle. "You don't need to worry."

"I know." Linda swallowed hard and hugged her arms close. "I'll go get her suitcase."

Paige was quiet in the hallway after they left Linda, but when they stepped into the elevator, she looked up at him, her gray-green eyes somber. "Clay, there must be some kind of a compromise, something that you can work out."

"I don't want to talk about this." He punched the elevator button to the lobby. "I'd at least expect my own wife to be on my side."

"This isn't about sides, Clay," she insisted. "This is about Julia."

"*I* know what's best for my daughter," he said more sharply than he intended. "And that's the end of it."

Paige pressed her lips into a thin line and lifted her chin. She didn't say another word, not in the elevator or the lobby, or on the drive over to the park.

When Julia saw them pull into the parking lot at the park, she jumped off the swings.

"Daddy!"

His heart tripped at the sight of her running toward him. He stepped out of the truck and Julia jumped into the arms he held out to her. She laughed when he swung her around, and when he put her down again, she ran to Paige and hugged her, too.

Bob hugged and kissed his granddaughter goodbye, then looked at Clay and nodded stiffly. There'd been no arrogance in the man's demeanor today. If anything, Clay thought, Barrington had appeared humbled as he'd cast one last look at his granddaughter before he walked away.

He wouldn't feel guilty, dammit. He *wouldn't.* Shaking the feeling off, Clay turned his attention back to his daughter.

"Will you push me on the swings?" Julia asked Paige.

"Your daddy will." Paige smiled brightly at Julia. "I have some errands to run. Your daddy is going to take you to lunch and shopping for some new shoes and pants. I'll see you both back at the ranch later, okay?"

"Okay." Julia kissed Paige's cheek, then ran back to the swings and called out, "Come push me, Daddy."

"Be right there." Clay kept his gaze on Paige. "*I'm* taking her shopping? I don't know anything about girl stuff."

"All the more reason for you to learn," she said evenly. "I'm sure you'll do fine."

He frowned at her, knew she was doing this because he'd snapped at her in the elevator. Women were just too damn sensitive, he thought irritably, but he certainly wasn't going to argue with her in front of Julia. "Where shall I pick you up when we're done?"

"I still have my own car at my house," she reminded him. "I'm going to go look at some curtain samples at

Rebecca's shop now, then I'll drive myself back to the ranch.''

A muscle jumped in his cheek. "You could have lunch with us."

The smile she gave him didn't reach her eyes. "I'm not really hungry. Maybe I'll have something in a little while with Rebecca."

"I'll drive you," he said, knew that it sounded like a command, not a request.

She shook her head. "Rebecca's shop is half a block from here, Clay. It's a nice day and I could use the exercise. Enjoy the time alone with your daughter."

She turned from him and waved at Julia, who sat on a nearby swing, waiting to be pushed.

"Come on, Daddy," Julia called.

Clay watched Paige walk away, her back stiff and shoulders squared. He wanted to go after her, wanted to explain to her why he couldn't compromise when it came to Julia. But he wasn't sure he could explain, wasn't sure he understood himself why he felt so strongly against any kind of written agreement with the Barringtons. Julia's visits with her grandparents would be on *his* terms, not the courts.

"Daddy."

With a sigh, Clay turned and walked toward the swings, felt his mood lighten slightly when Julia smiled at him.

He could pick out a pair of shoes and jeans for his daughter, he told himself. She was just a little girl, for crying out loud. How difficult could it be?

*   *   *

Paige was in the kitchen chopping carrots when she heard the slam of the truck door from the backyard, then Julia's excited shriek. It was nearly five o'clock, and though Paige would never admit it to Clay, she'd been slightly worried.

She'd had mixed feelings this morning when she'd left Clay and Julia at the park. Part of her was upset at Clay for refusing to even listen to what she had to say regarding Julia's grandparents, part of her was hurt that he continually referred to Julia as *his* daughter and *he* knew what was best for her. Paige understood Clay's bitter feelings toward his ex-wife, keeping Julia from him was a despicable thing to do. But she didn't understand why that bitterness extended so strongly to the Barringtons.

If he wasn't so pigheaded, Paige thought as she dumped the cut-up carrots into a pan, he wouldn't think that she was taking sides because she wanted him to try and understand how Julia's grandparents felt. How terrified they were of losing their only grandchild.

For Julia's sake, Paige hoped that Clay would be able to set his own feelings aside long enough to realize that there was room in his daughter's life for *all* the people who loved her.

The back door flew open at that moment and Julia came running into the kitchen. ''Paige! Wait till you see what Daddy bought me!''

Wiping her hands on a towel, Paige turned. Good heavens! Julia was certainly not the same, neat little girl Paige had seen only that morning. Her ponytail was askew and her hair and face were covered with sparkling, iridescent glitter. Chocolate dotted both corners of her mouth and stained the front of her white tank top and green print shorts.

And on her feet, she wore a pair of brand-new, shiny black cowboy boots.

"Aren't they great?" Excitement danced in Julia's blue eyes. "I couldn't decide if I like the brown or the black, so Daddy bought me both!"

Based on the number of packages in Clay's arms as he came into the kitchen, he'd bought Julia a great deal more than two pairs of boots.

"They're beautiful, sweetheart." Paige smiled at Julia. "They look just like your daddy's."

"I got a new dress and some pretty shoes for church, too," Julia said brightly. "And a Betty Ballerina instant-bake oven, and a Patsy Poodle stuffed animal, and a really cool jewelry-making kit with five hundred thousand beads."

"My goodness, you've had a busy day shopping, haven't you?"

"I even got my own big person's hot fudge sundae," Julia said with a nod. "With extra whipped cream and sprinkles on top. Isn't he the best daddy in the whole world?"

Paige watched Clay dump the day's purchases on the table and lifted a brow. "The absolute best."

"I want to go make a bracelet." Julia rifled through the bags, then pulled out a bright pink box with dozens of pictures of bracelets and rings on the front. "I can't wait to tell my grandma all the stuff I got."

Tucking the box under her arm, Julia stomped out of the kitchen in her new cowboy boots, then stomped up the stairs toward her bedroom.

Paige turned her attention to Clay and met his sheepish gaze.

"I guess I got a little carried away," he said with a shrug.

"A *little?*"

"Yeah, well, I know we were just going for shoes and jeans, but—" He stopped, then swore. "Jeans."

Paige looked at him in disbelief, then glanced at all the bags. "You didn't get the jeans."

"I guess I forgot." He slipped his hat off his head and scratched the back of his neck. "I could take her—"

Shaking her head, Paige put up her hand. "I'll take her. You'll need a semi if you go shopping with her again."

He grinned, then reached into one of the bags and pulled out a small, black velvet box. "I bought you something, too."

Her heart tripped when he handed the box to her. She opened it, then gasped at the heart-shaped diamond necklace inside.

"You can take it back if you don't like it." He jammed his hat back on his head, then shoved his hands into the back pocket of his jeans. "Get something else, if you prefer."

"It's beautiful." Bernie had given her a subscription to

Time magazine, a Dustbuster and a desk calendar, but no man have ever given her a present this nice before. In awe, Paige stared at the sparkling diamonds.

"Try it on," he said, inclining his head.

Lifting the delicate gold chain from the box, Paige tried to open the clasp, but her shaking fingers refused to work. Clay stepped behind her, then took the chain out of her hands and settled it around her neck. He hooked the clasp, then gently ran his fingertip down the necklace to the diamond heart.

"Thank you," she whispered, shivering at his touch. "But you didn't have to buy me anything."

"Of course I didn't have to." He wrapped his arms around her, pulled her close against his chest and lowered his head. "I wanted to."

I wanted to. She felt herself melt against him, felt as if her bones had softened at his tender words. She thought she could stand like this forever, with his arms holding her close, his lips brushing her ear.

"I want to give you things, Paige." He nipped at the shell of her ear. "Anything you want, just name it."

She blinked back the moisture burning her eyes. "There's nothing I want, Clay," she said quietly, though it was a lie.

There was one thing she wanted, Paige thought. Only one thing. Something that didn't come in a box, and no amount of money could buy.

Chapter 11

' 'The water is too cold,' Mindy Marmot said to Rosie Raccoon. 'I'll wait here on the shore for you and Sydney.'

'"But Mindy,' Rosie said. 'You're going to miss all the fun. We want you to come swimming with us.'"

Paige held the book up high so all the four- and five-year-olds gathered around her could see the illustrations in *Picnic by the Pond.* The popular children's book was one in a series of adventure stories about three friends, Mindy Marmot, Rosie Raccoon and Sydney Squirrel.

Today, Mindy, the fraidy-cat of the three, refused to go swimming in the pond.

'"There might be octopuses out there,' Mindy said.

'"Octopuses don't live in ponds, silly,' Rosie said. 'They live in the ocean.' Rosie and Sydney both laughed, which made Mindy very mad and she made a face at her friends.''

Paige held the book up again for the children to see the funny face that Mindy had made and the youngsters all laughed.

Paige had brought Julia to the library today for Thursday morning story time, and Elissa, the scheduled storyteller, had asked Paige if she would mind reading instead. Since reading to the children had always been one of Paige's favorite tasks when she'd been working at the library, she'd been happy to take over for the head librarian.

Paige still hadn't made a decision whether she would be returning to work part-time after Julia started kindergarten in late summer. Lord knew that between caring for an energetic five-year-old and a big house, there was plenty to keep her busy. Since Julia had returned to the ranch nearly two weeks ago, the time had flown by.

The court hearing was scheduled for tomorrow morning at ten, and even though Clay's lawyer had reassured him that he would be awarded full custody, Clay had grown more tense as the day had approached. In fact, he'd been downright cranky, Paige thought as she held up a picture of Sydney and Rosie diving into the pond and splashing Mindy Marmot.

Paige knew that Clay was anxious something might go wrong tomorrow, but she was certain he would relax after the hearing. Once he knew he had full custody of his daughter, he would have no need to worry.

He'll have no need for you, either, a little voice whispered. *You'll have served your purpose.*

The thought had been niggling at her all week. She'd known from the beginning, of course, that was the only reason he'd asked her to be his wife, but she couldn't seem to get her heart to cooperate with her mind. She would simply have to accept that Clay had married her as a means to an end and that was all. That fact that she'd fallen in love with him was her problem, not Clay's.

Shaking her thoughts off, Paige turned her attention back to the storybook, which ended with Mindy Marmot overcoming her fear of the water and coming out to swim and play with her friends.

The children all clapped when Paige finished reading, then jumped up and ran to the table where one of the moms was serving punch and cookies. Paige watched Julia giggling with one of the other little girls while two little boys made funny faces at them. Paige was happy to see how well Julia fit in with the other children that she would soon be going to school with. After the custody hearing was settled, Paige intended to enroll her at Wolf River Elementary.

''Paige?''

Paige turned at the sound of a woman quietly calling her name and was surprised to see Linda Barrington standing by the row of childrens' history books.

''Mrs. Barrington?'' Paige returned the book in her hand to the shelf behind her, then walked over to the woman.

"I thought you and Mr. Barrington were flying in tomorrow morning."

"Please," Mrs. Barrington said with a tired smile. "Call me Linda."

"Of course." Paige returned the smile. "Linda."

"We changed our flight and flew in late last night instead," Linda said. "I was hoping I might have a few words with you privately before the hearing tomorrow."

"But how did you know we'd be in town today?"

"Julia told me on the phone yesterday that you were bringing her to the library this morning for story time." Linda's smile brightened as she glanced over at her granddaughter, who was busy playing with the other children. "She was very excited."

The sadness in Linda's eyes as she watched her granddaughter was evident. Once again, Paige wanted to comfort the woman, but wasn't sure what to do or say. She could only imagine the anguish Linda Barrington was going through.

"She looks happy." Linda clutched the small white purse in her hands to her stomach, then brought her gaze back to Paige's. "Have you any idea what it feels like to lose a child?"

"I can't imagine anything worse," Paige said quietly. Just the thought of it made her heart ache.

"There isn't anything worse." Linda blinked at the gathering moisture in her eyes. "I know our daughter wasn't perfect, but we miss our Nancy so."

Paige put her hand on the woman's arm. "I'm sorry for your loss."

Linda nodded sadly. "We know we don't stand a chance winning custody of Julia. The only reason we tried, was because we were hoping that Clay would compromise and let Julia come visit with us on a regular basis."

"You can come here and see her as often as you want." Paige covered Linda's icy hands with her own. "Clay told you that."

Linda shook her head. "It's not the same as having her come stay with us. Now that Bob is retired, we have lots of time to spend with her. Places we'd like to take her. Clay won't allow that. He hates us for keeping Julia from him."

"I'm sure he doesn't hate you," Paige reassured the woman.

"If we were in his shoes, I'd be angry, too." Linda closed her eyes on a sigh. "We're just so afraid that Julia will forget us. If we could just have some kind of reassurance that he won't try to keep her from us."

"He won't do that," Paige insisted. "I know he can be stubborn, but maybe if we just asked him—"

"Maybe if you just asked me what?"

Paige felt her breath catch at the sound of Clay's voice behind her. She and Linda had both been so intent on their conversation, neither one of them had seen Clay walk into the library.

And based on the tight set of his face, he wasn't at all

happy about finding her speaking with Julia's grand-mother.

"Clay." Paige dropped her hand from Linda's. "What are you doing here?"

"I was picking up an order at Peterson's." His voice was flat. He looked at Linda. "Linda."

"Clay, please don't be mad at Paige for talking to me." Linda's face had turned pale. "She didn't know I was coming here. I just thought that, as a woman, Paige might be able to—"

"Influence me?"

Linda shook her head. "Talk to you."

"Paige understands that I'm the one who makes the decisions when it comes to my daughter. There's nothing to talk about."

Paige felt her insides twist at the cold tone of his voice. When he turned his ice-blue gaze to her, a chill shivered up her spine.

"Grandma!" Julia suddenly spotted her grandmother and ran across the library. "Grandma, you're here!"

Linda knelt and Julia flew into her open arms. "How's my baby?"

"Where's Grandpa?" Julia hugged Linda.

"Back at the hotel." Linda smoothed a hand over Julia's head. "He told me to tell you he misses you."

"Can I come and see him?" Julia asked. "I want to tell him Paige got me a library card."

"You'll have to ask your daddy, sweetheart." Linda

looked at Clay, her eyes pleading. "Just for a little while?"

"I want to sleep at the hotel with you, too," Julia said insistently. "Just tonight. Can I, Daddy, please? I can sleep in one of Grandpa's T-shirts."

Paige couldn't bear the thought of separating Julia from her grandmother, especially considering the court hearing was tomorrow. She knew she would be stepping onto thin ice if she interfered, but it was impossible to stand back and say nothing.

"We could pick her up in the morning and bring her fresh clothes," Paige told Clay, refused to allow herself to flinch when he shot her a look.

"Please, Daddy," Julia begged. "Pleeaasee."

A muscle worked in Clay's jaw, then he nodded stiffly. "We'll pick her up at ten."

Julia flung herself at Clay's legs. "I love you, Daddy," she said brightly, then jumped into Paige's arms and hugged her, as well.

"I love you, too, Paige."

Holding her grandma's hand, Julia skipped out of the library. Clay watched them go, then turned back to Paige, his mouth set in a hard line. "I want to talk to you. Outside. Now."

Paige lifted her chin and met his steely gaze. "Fine."

She followed him to the back parking lot, managing to smile and wave goodbye to Elissa and several other people she knew as she left the library. He stood beside his truck, a grim expression on his face as he held the passenger door open for her. She didn't bother to thank him when she slid into the cab and folded her hands in her lap.

He slammed the door, then stormed around and climbed into the truck beside her. Hands gripping the steering wheel, he stared straight ahead. Determined to wait him out, Paige kept her attention on a crew of workmen repairing a pothole on the street behind the library.

"Why would you do this?" he said after several long, tense moments.

"Why would I do what?" she asked calmly, though her stomach had more knots than a fishing net.

His fingers tightened around the steering wheel. "Go behind my back and meet with Linda like that."

Paige swiveled her head to meet his dark gaze. "I did *not* go behind your back, Clay Bodine. Linda knew that Julia and I would be at the library today and she wanted to speak with me."

"Convince you to change my mind about the joint custody, you mean."

Paige prayed for patience. "Not about joint custody. She told me that she and Bob never expected joint custody. They were just hoping to work out an arrangement of scheduled visits in California."

"Dammit, Paige, we've been over this," he said, raising his voice. "How can they expect me to trust them? If I drop this custody battle and give them what they want, what am I left with legally? We'll constantly be arguing over who has Julia when and for how long."

"Clay, that's not true." Lowering her voice, she leaned

toward him and laid a hand on his arm. "They just want some kind of assurance that you won't keep Julia from them."

"How can you come into this and after a few weeks think you know what the Barringtons will or won't do?" He jerked his arm away. "I was married to their daughter, remember? More than once, they tried to stop the marriage, and afterwards, when Nancy came to Texas, the phone calls begging her to leave me were almost daily."

"Did you hear the phone calls?" Paige asked. "Or did Nancy *tell* you about them?"

His eyes narrowed at Paige's question. Clearly, he hadn't considered the possibility that Nancy might have lied. "Linda and Bob had made it clear before the wedding that they didn't think I was good enough for their precious daughter," he said tightly. "Why should I think their opinion of me now is any different?"

"Even if they did have their doubts about you marrying Nancy," Paige said, determined to get through to him, "that was nearly six years ago. They aren't the same people. They have Julia now, and they lost their only daughter. Things like that change a person."

"You're naive to think that people like the Barrington's can change. They will say and do anything to keep control of Julia's life."

"Isn't that what you've done, too?" she asked carefully.

His face turned to stone, then he snapped his gaze away and white-knuckled the steering wheel. "I won't do it and that's that."

Paige straightened her back. "So I have no say in this."

"I make the decisions when it comes to my daughter."

"I see."

He swore under his breath, then drew in a deep, impatient breath. "We had an understanding about Julia."

"Which understanding was that?" she asked calmly. "The one that I'm a glorified nanny to *your* daughter, or the one where I keep *your* house, and conveniently share *your* bed?"

His gaze shot back to her, dark and cold and angry. A muscle jumped in his jaw. "This is about Julia. Not about you and me."

"Maybe you can separate the two," she said quietly. "But I can't. Not anymore."

"What the hell is that supposed to mean?"

She knew what she had to do, knew that it was the right thing for everyone, but knowing that didn't make it any easier. A numbing cold settled over her as she looked into Clay's eyes.

"You're right, Clay." A knot of ice formed in her stomach. "We did have 'an understanding' as you put it. But things have changed since then, at least, for me, they have. It wouldn't be fair to Julia for me to stay and pretend to be a mother to her. She deserves honesty, not lies."

For a split second, fear replaced the anger in Clay's eyes, but then it was back again, as cold and dark as before. "You're leaving Julia and me now, the day before the court hearing?"

She realized how desperately she'd wanted him to say something, *anything* that might have given her a reason to stay. Her heart felt as if it were ripping apart.

"Don't worry, I'll be at the hearing tomorrow," she managed to say through the thickness in her throat. "I'll clear out my things this afternoon, and I'll call one of the housekeepers from the list you interviewed. I'm sure we can work out the details over the next few days. I realize you probably won't want me to see Julia, but I'm asking anyway. I can come to the ranch, or when you come to town, maybe she can spend some time with me."

"Dammit, Paige." Frustration rumbled in his voice. "You can't just walk away like this. Not now."

"When's a good time, Clay? Next week? The week after that? Like you said, people don't change. And for the record—" she opened the door and slid out of the cab, felt the warmth of the sun on her skin, even though she was chilled to the bone "—I'm not leaving Julia. I'm leaving you."

How she managed to stand when her knees felt like soggy noodles, Paige didn't know. But somehow she held her head up, her shoulders straight, then put one foot in front of the other and walked away.

Clay couldn't remember the last time he'd gotten stewed to the gills drunk. Though he drank a beer or two on poker nights, he'd never been one to consume hard liquor in vast quantities. Too much alcohol numbed the senses and dulled the brain, made a person act stupid and lose control.

Which was exactly why he was currently nursing his third whiskey. If he'd ever needed a reason to numb his senses and dull his brain, it was definitely tonight.

He sat at Joe's kitchen table, frustrated that the whiskey had not yet quieted the roar in his head or the ache in his chest. When he'd showed up at his foreman's back door an hour ago, Joe had taken one look at him, then turned around and broke open a new bottle of Jack Daniel's. Joe hadn't said one word, just poured the shots into two glasses, handed one to Clay, then sat down at the kitchen table with a book about orchids and started to read.

Clay had tossed back the first two shots, but he truly didn't want to get completely smashed. He had a court hearing in the morning, and the last thing he wanted to do was to walk into the courtroom looking as miserable as he felt.

Dammit to hell, anyway.

"She left me," he said, finally breaking the silence.

Joe looked up from his book.

"Just like that." He swept a hand up to emphasize his sense of futility. "Packed up her suitcases, took her cat and went back to town."

That's why he'd come here, Clay knew. Because he couldn't stand the empty house. Couldn't stand being there, knowing that Paige was gone, that she wasn't coming back. Even after their argument, he hadn't really thought she'd follow through on her threat to leave.

When he'd driven back to the ranch this afternoon and she was gone, he felt as if he'd been sucker punched. He'd known she was angry, he'd been angry, too. That's why he'd waited to cool off before he'd gone back home.

But in his heart, he truly hadn't believed that she would go. He'd been so certain she'd calm down and realize that Julia needed her.

That *he* needed her.

The thought rocked him to the core, had him tightening his hand around his glass. He'd never needed anyone before. Didn't *want* to need anyone.

Joe took his glasses off, then closed his book and reached for the bottle of whiskey. "Is that so?"

Clay frowned. "That's what I just said, didn't I?"

"Can't imagine why she'd leave, considering your congenial nature," Joe said and topped off Clay's glass.

"I warned her I wouldn't be easy to live with," Clay defended himself. "She knew how it was between us, why we got married."

"So I guess you should have married Minnie Wellman." Joe sipped on his own glass of whiskey. "She wouldn't have given you two licks of trouble. Bet you could boss her around all day without a peep of backtalk."

"Damn straight." Clay nodded in agreement, then winced and dropped his head in his hand. "Good God, no. It makes my brain hurt to even think about it."

And his heart, he realized. His heart hurt, too, dammit.

He didn't know how to handle these emotions. Even when Nancy had left, he hadn't felt this…empty. He had no idea what to do, which way to turn. After the way he'd treated her, the things he'd said, why would Paige come back to him now?

She wouldn't. Not without a good reason.

So he'd give her a reason, then. A very good one.

But first, he knew he'd have to get her attention.

The alarm startled Paige awake at seven the next morning. Though she wanted nothing more than to simply burrow back into the haven of her soft bed, she slipped out from under the covers, sighing heavily as she turned off the persistent beep coming from the bedside clock radio. Too tired to stand just yet, she sat on the edge of the bed, waiting for her mind to come into focus with her surroundings, was once again hit with the reality that she was back in her own house, in her bed.

Yesterday afternoon, not knowing where else to go after she'd left the ranch, Paige had shown up on Rebecca's doorstep.

"You're staying with me," Rebecca had said emphatically and Paige hadn't argued. After her showdown with Clay, she hadn't the strength to argue with anyone. She could barely remember packing her things and driving back to town. After calmly explaining her situation to Rebecca, who'd listened and offered solace, Paige had retreated to the quiet of her old bedroom and let the tears come. It had been like opening a floodgate, but even when she'd finally been too exhausted and spent to cry any longer, she'd still tossed and turned all night.

Closing her eyes against the oppressive darkness that filled her, Paige drew in a long, deep breath. Her body felt limp, her limbs heavy, her brain like cotton. She considered slipping back into bed, only for a few minutes, but knew that a few minutes or a few hours wouldn't make a difference. The pain wrapped around her heart was too tight to let her rest. She knew she needed every ounce of strength she had in her to face this day. To face Clay, to look into Julia's eyes and tell her that she wouldn't be living with her and her daddy anymore.

She'd spent the entire night worrying about the little girl, several times had nearly driven back to the ranch. And though her heart told her to go, her gut told her no. She loved Clay. She would always love him. But she knew her love alone would not sustain their marriage. Respect and trust between two people were vital to any relationship. What kind of home could they provide for Julia, if they didn't have those elements?

Paige loved Julia, too. But she couldn't lie to the child, couldn't pretend to be someone, or something, that she wasn't. Julia deserved better.

Combing her hands through her hair, Paige sighed, then rose from the bed and tugged on her robe. After barely three hours sleep, she could only imagine what she was going to look like in the courtroom today. Her eyes would still be red from crying, and there were certain to be dark circles under her eyes. She could only hope that all those cosmetics she'd bought worked as well as they promised in the ads. Today she was definitely going to need all the help she could get.

When Paige opened her bedroom door, Rebecca was waiting outside with a cup of steaming coffee.

"I heard the alarm." Rebecca pressed the warm mug into Paige's hand and guided her toward the bathroom. "You have a warm bath waiting for you. Have a nice long soak. I'll go find you some clothes and bring them in."

Paige opened her mouth to protest being waited on, but Rebecca shook her head and shoved her gently into the bathroom. "Not one word, Paige Andrews Bodine. In the tub."

Rebecca's use of Paige's married name tightened the pain around her heart, but she simply hadn't the energy to resist. After Rebecca closed the door, Paige combed her hair and clipped it on top of her head, brushed her teeth, then pulled off her robe and gown and stepped through a mound of lavender-scented bubbles. Tugging the white lace shower curtain closed, Paige eased her body into the tub, sighed as she sank neck-deep into the popping bubbles.

"Bless you, Rebecca," she murmured. A bath was just what she needed to revitalize and confront what was going to be the most difficult day of her life.

Slowly, the kinks in her neck and shoulders loosened and her brain began to clear. She reached around the closed shower curtain for the coffee she'd set beside the tub, took a long sip, then set the mug back down and closed her eyes.

Mentally she began to prepare herself for the day. She had more than enough time to kill before she had to be at the courthouse. Too much time, she thought. The waiting was going to be as difficult as actually sitting in the courtroom beside Clay, pretending that they were a happily married couple.

I can do this, she told herself firmly. For Clay and for Julia, she would pretend one last time.

She hadn't thought about divorce yet. Though she suspected that was inevitable, she supposed there wasn't any rush for at least a few months.

Her eyes popped open.

Unless Clay wanted to remarry.

Her breath caught at the possibility. She didn't think she could bear it if he married someone else. Couldn't imagine knowing another woman was in Clay's house.

In Clay's bed.

In *her* house, in *her* bed.

Just the thought was like a knife in Paige's heart.

Who was she kidding? she thought on a small whimper. Of course he would remarry.

Hoping to drown the painful idea, she closed her eyes tightly and sank deeper into the bubbles. She couldn't think about that now. She'd never get through this day if she did.

Through the bubbles popping in her ears, Paige heard the bathroom door open, then the sound of Rebecca bringing her clothes in. Paige wasn't ready to get out and get dressed yet, though she wasn't certain that she'd ever truly be ready.

"Thank you, Rebecca," she said through the bubbles rising over her chin.

"It's not Rebecca."

At the sound of Clay's deep voice, Paige opened her eyes on a small gasp. She sat abruptly, then realized the mistake and quickly slid back down in the water.

"Clay!" She was at least thankful that she had the shower curtain between them. "Get out of here!"

"We *are* married, sweetheart."

How dare he come in here like this and call her sweetheart! And how could her best friend—her *ex*-best friend—let him in? Paige was definitely going to have words with Rebecca over this.

"If you're coming to check up on me," she said, keeping herself discreetly covered with bubbles, "I told you I'd be at the courthouse and I will. Now please leave."

"I'm not coming to check up on you. I'm here to give something to you."

When he reached to open the shower curtain, Paige grabbed hold to keep it closed. "I don't want anything from you, Clay Bodine," she lied. "I just want you to leave me alone."

"I can't, sweetheart," he said with a sigh. "Now let go, or I'll come in there with you and we'll talk about it some more."

He meant it. Paige could hear the determination in his

voice. Fuming, she made sure the critical parts of her naked body were covered with bubbles, then let go of the
shower curtain.

When he opened it, her breath caught in her throat.

Orchids.

The bathroom was filled with them. On the floor, the
toilet lid, the counter. All wrapped in silver foil and tied
with pretty red bows. He'd managed to bring in at least
eight pots, all blooming, in purples and pinks and yellows.

"How did you…?" She leaned close to the side of the
tub, placed her hands on the rim as she stared at the beautiful plants. Confused, she lifted her gaze to his. "I don't
understand."

"Rebecca gave me a little assistance." He knelt beside
the tub, then reached out and touched her cheek with his
fingertip. "Though I admit, when I showed up on your
doorstep at six-thirty, it took me a while to convince her
to let me in."

"You've been here since six-thirty?" She hadn't heard
the door, but then, she'd been in such a deep sleep, a
tornado could have come through and she wouldn't have
known. "But the hearing isn't until ten."

"I cancelled the hearing."

"You cancelled it?" She furrowed her brow. "Why?"

"I went to see the Barringtons last night," he said quietly. "After Julia was asleep. We sat and talked, really
talked. We've never done that before."

Not certain what to say, Paige simply waited for Clay
to continue. He looked as tired as she felt, and he hadn't

shaved this morning, either. And yet he looked wonderful, she thought, doing her best to concentrate on anything other than the gentle touch of his finger on her cheek.

"I asked them if they had tried to convince Nancy to leave me. They admitted they had, but only because Nancy had told them I neglected her, and that I'd had an affair." He shook his head on a sigh. "I should have known, should have considered that we'd all been lied to."

He slid his fingertip under Paige's chin and pulled away a dollop of bubbles. "They're coming to the ranch later and I've asked them to stay for as long as they like."

"The Barringtons are staying at the ranch?" she asked incredulously. "For as long as they like?"

"Well, for at least two weeks."

Two weeks! Clay and the Barringtons under one roof? Her mind was reeling in disbelief.

Despite the fact that her heart had began to pump faster, she shivered from the cooling water. Clay reached for her robe, held it up for her. "Now will you come out of there?"

When she hesitated, he rolled his eyes, then closed them. She stood, quickly grabbed her robe and tugged it on, then stepped out of the tub.

Clay opened his eyes and it took a will of iron for him not to drag Paige into his arms and kiss her senseless. There were blue-gray circles under her eyes and though her cheeks were flushed, her skin looked pale. He thought she'd never looked more beautiful.

"Come home, Paige," he said quietly. "Please."

He saw the startled look in her eyes, but she only pulled her robe tighter.

"I can't, Clay."

"You're my wife," he said softly.

"You've worked out your problems with the Barringtons." She looked away, then whispered, "You don't need a wife now."

"That's true. I don't need a wife." He stepped closer, cupped her chin in his hand and lifted her face. "But I need you."

Her eyes widened, but then she pulled away from him and shook her head. "I know you're worried about Julia, but she'll be fine with a housekeeper. She's amazingly strong, and she knows you love her, plus she can come see me—"

He swooped down on her mouth, cutting off her words with a kiss. He felt her stiffen and thought for a moment she might pull away, but then she leaned into him, her lips softening against his as she kissed him back.

Blood pumped hot through his veins, his heart slammed against his chest. He wrapped his arms around her and breathed in the sweet lavender scent of her skin, knew that he could never be without this woman. *His* woman, he thought. His wife.

When he lifted his head, her eyes slowly fluttered open. "*I* need you," he repeated firmly. "I'm asking, no, *begging* you to come back not for Julia, but for me."

She blinked in confusion. "For you?"

Lightly he brushed her lips again with his own. "I love you, Paige."

"You love me?" she said, her voice breathless.

"I love you," he whispered against her lips. "I want you to be my wife. Not a 'glorified housekeeper,' as you put it. But a real wife."

"But yesterday—"

"Yesterday I was a jerk. Like I told you before, I can't promise I won't be one again. I also can't promise that I won't beat my chest and growl when I want my way, either." He kissed the tip of her nose. "But I will promise that we'll be equal partners in marriage and parenting, for *all* our children."

Longing filled her eyes as she met his gaze. "All our children?"

"As many as you say, sweetheart, though personally, I'd like to fill every bedroom." Sliding his hand up her back, he pulled her closer. "When I came home to that empty house last night, I knew I had to get you back. Tell me you love me, Paige. Tell me you'll come home with me."

"I love you," she said softly, laying her palm on his cheek. "I think I loved you the first time you showed up at my door to buy my grandmother's car. My knees nearly gave out when you smiled at me. Lord, my knees are weak now, too."

"I was so afraid I'd lost you." Relief poured through his body. "I didn't know if I would be able to tell you what I'm feeling," he said, kissing her lightly. "I thought the orchids might show you how I feel. That I'll always love you, no matter what happens.''

Tears glistened in her eyes. ''And I'll love you,'' she whispered. ''Always.''

He knew there would be many years ahead of them, years of happiness, of pleasure, and certainly some heartaches. He could handle whatever life threw at him, just as long as Paige was by his side.

He'd tell her later that he was taking her on the honeymoon he'd never given her, that after church on Sunday morning, they'd be on a plane for a two week stay in Paris.

For now, he was content to hold her close, to thank his lucky stars, and God, for giving him the woman in his arms.

* * * * *

Look for Name Your Price *in November 2006, Barbara McCauley's latest Silhouette Desire.*

HAWK'S WAY:
THE VIRGIN GROOM
Joan Johnston

This book is dedicated
to my son, Blake.

May you always strive
to be the best you can be.

Chapter 1

Sweat streaming from his temples, strong hands clenched tight on the parallel bars that supported him, Mac Macready put his full weight on his left leg. He felt a sharp pain, but the leg held. He gritted his teeth to keep from groaning. So far, so good.

Mac kept his eyes focused on the area between the bars in front of him, willing his leg to work. He took an easy step with his right leg, then called on the left again. The pain was less sharp the second time he put his weight on the restructured limb. He could handle the pain.

More important, the leg had stayed under him. He glanced across the room at his friend and agent, Andy Dennison, and grinned.

Mac Macready could walk again.

"You did it, Mac," Andy said, crossing the room to slap him on the back. "It's great to see you back on your feet."

"About time," Mac said. "I've spent the better part of two years trying to get this damned leg of mine back into shape." A sharp pain seared up his leg, but he refused to sit down, not now, when he had just made it back onto his feet. He took more of his weight on his arms and kept walking. A bead of sweat trickled between his shoulder blades before it caught on his sleeveless T-shirt. He summoned another smile. "Give me a couple of months, and I'll be ready to start catching passes again for the Tornadoes."

Mac caught the skeptical look on Andy's face before his agent said, "Sure, Mac. Whatever you say."

He understood Andy's skepticism. Mac had said the same thing after every operation. Who would have suspected a broken leg—all right, so maybe it had been shattered—would be so difficult to mend? But his body had rejected the pins they had used to put things back together again at ankle and hip. They had finally had to invent something especially for him.

Then the long bones in his leg hadn't grown straight and had needed to be broken and set again. He had fought complications caused by infection. Finally, when he had pushed too hard to get well, he had ended up back in a cast.

The football injury had been devastating, coming as it had at the end of Mac's first phenomenal season with the Texas Tornadoes. His future couldn't have been brighter. He was a star receiver, with more touchdown catches than any other rookie in the league. His team was headed for the Super Bowl. With one crushing tackle, everything had fallen apart. The sportscasters had called it a career-ending injury. Mac wasn't willing to concede the issue.

"Good work, Mac," the physical therapist said, reaching out to help him into the wheelchair waiting for him at the end of the parallel bars. "Put your arm around me."

He flashed the young woman a killer grin, inwardly cursing the fact that after six measly steps he was on the verge of collapse. "Better watch out, Hartwell. Now that I'm back on my feet, I'm going to give your fiancé some serious competition.''

Diane Hartwell blushed. Most women did when Mac turned on the charm. He had the kind of blond-haired, blue-eyed good looks that made female heads swivel to take a second look. Mac wondered what she would think if she knew the truth about him.

Diane answered wryly, ''I'm sure George would gladly trade me to you for an autographed football.''

''Done,'' Mac said brightly, biting back a grimace as Diane bent his injured leg and placed his foot on the wheelchair footrest.

''I was only kidding,'' Diane said.

''I wasn't,'' Mac said, smiling up at her. ''Tell your fiancé I'll be glad to autograph that football for him anytime.''

''Thanks, Mac,'' Diane said. ''I appreciate it.''

''Think nothing of it, Hartwell. And tell George to hang on to that ball. Someday it'll be worth something.''

Once Mac resumed his career, he would break every record in the book. He had that kind of determination. And he had been that good. Of course, that was before the accident. Everybody—except himself—questioned whether he would ever be that good again.

It had been touch and go for a while whether he would even walk. But Mac had known he would walk again, and without the aid of a brace. He had done it today. It seemed he was the only one who wasn't surprised.

He had known he would succeed, because he had beaten the odds before. When he was eight, he had suffered from acute myelocytic leukemia. It should have killed him. He had recovered from the childhood disease and gone on to win the Heisman Trophy and be drafted in the first round by the Texas Tornadoes. Mac had no intention of giving up his dreams of a future in football.

Andy wheeled him down the hospital corridor to his room. ''When do you get out of here?'' his agent asked.

''The doctor said once I could stand on my leg, he would release me. I guess that means I can get out of here anytime now.''

''The press will want a statement,'' Andy said as he stopped the wheelchair beside Mac's hospital bed. "Do you want to talk to them? Or do you want me to do it?"

Mac thought of facing a dozen TV cameras from a wheelchair. Or standing with crutches. Or wavering on his own two feet. "Tell them I'll be back next season."

"Maybe that's not such a good—"

"Tell them I'll be back," Mac said, staring Andy in the eye.

Andy had once been a defensive lineman and wore a coveted Super Bowl ring on his right hand. He understood what it meant to play football. And what it meant to stop. He straightened the tie at his bull neck, shrugged his broad shoulders and smoothed the tie over his burgeoning belly, before he said, "You got it, Mac."

"Thanks, Andy. I am coming back, you know."

"Sure, Mac," Andy said.

Mac could see his agent didn't believe him any more than the doctors and nurses who had treated him over the past two years. Even Hartwell, though she encouraged him, didn't believe he would achieve the kind of mobility he needed to play in the pros. Mac needed to get away somewhere and heal himself. He knew he could do it. After all, he had done it once before.

"Where can I get in touch with you?" Andy asked.

"I'm headed to a ranch in northwest Texas owned by some friends of mine. I have an open invitation to visit, and I'm going to take them up on it. I'll call you when I get there and give you a number where I can be reached."

"Good enough. Take care, Mac. Don't—"

"Don't finish that sentence, Andy. Not if you're going to warn me not to get my hopes up."

Andy shook his head. "I was going to say don't be a fool and kill yourself trying to get well too fast."

"I'm going to get my job back from the kid who took over for me," Mac said in a steely voice. "And I'm going to do it this year."

Andy didn't argue further, just shook Mac's hand and left him alone in the hospital room.

Mac looked around at the sterile walls, the white sheets, the chrome rails on the bed, listened to the muffled sounds that weren't quite silence and inhaled the overwhelming antiseptic smell that made him want to gag. He had spent too much of his life in hospital beds—more than any human being ought to have to. He wanted out of here, the sooner the better.

He could hardly wait to get to the wide open spaces of Zach and Rebecca Whitelaw's ranch, Hawk's Pride. More than Zach or Rebecca or the land, he had a yearning to see their daughter Jewel again. Jewel was the first of eight kids who had been adopted by the Whitelaws, and she had returned to Hawk's Pride after college to manage Camp LittleHawk, the camp for kids with cancer that Rebecca had started years ago.

Mac remembered his first impressions of Jewel—huge Mississippi-mud-brown eyes, shoulder-length dirt-brown hair and an even dirtier looking white T-shirt and jeans. She had been five years old to his eight, and she had been leaning against the corral at Camp LittleHawk watching him venture onto horseback for the first time.

"Don't be scared," Jewel had said.

"I'm not," he'd retorted, glancing around at the other five kids in the corral with him. The horses were stopped in a circle, and the wrangler was working with a little boy who was even more scared than he was.

"Buttercup wouldn't hurt a fly," Jewel reassured him.

He remembered feeling mortified at the thought of riding a horse named Buttercup. And terrified that Buttercup would throw him off her broad back and trample him underfoot. Even though he'd been dying of cancer, he'd been afraid of getting killed. Life, he had learned, was precious.

"I'm not scared," he lied. He wished he could reach up and tug his baseball cap down tighter over his bald head, but he was afraid to let go of his two-handed grip on the saddle horn.

Jewel scooted under the bottom rail of the corral on her hands and knees, which explained how she had gotten so dirty, and walked right up to the horse—all right, it was only a pony, but it was still big—without fear. He sat frozen as she patted Buttercup's graying jaw and crooned to her.

"What are you saying?" he demanded.

"I'm telling Buttercup to be good. I'm telling her you're sick and—"

"I'm dying," he blurted out. "I'll be dead by

Christmas.'' It was June. He was currently in remission, but the last time he'd been sick, he'd heard the doctors figuring he had about six months to live. He knew it was only a matter of time before the disease came back. It always did.

''My momma died and my daddy and my brother,'' Jewel said. ''I thought I was gonna die, too, but I didn't.'' She reached up and touched the crisscrossing pink scars on her face. ''I had to stay in the hospital till I got well.''

''Then you know it's a rotten place to be,'' he said.

She nodded. ''Zach and 'Becca came and took me away. I never want to go back.''

''Yeah, well I don't have much choice.''

''Why not?'' she asked.

''Because that's where you go when you're sick.''

''But you're well now,'' she said, looking up at him with serious brown eyes. ''Except you don't have any hair yet. But don't worry. 'Becca says it'll grow back.''

He flushed and risked letting go of the horn to tug the cap down. It was one of the many humiliations he had endured—losing his hair...along with his privacy...and his childhood. He had always wanted to go to camp like his sister, Sadie, but he had been too sick. Then some lady had opened this place. He had jumped at the chance to get away from home. Away from the hospital.

"Your hair doesn't grow back till you stop getting sick," he pointed out to the fearless kid standing with her cheek next to the pony's.

"So, don't get sick again," she said.

He snickered. "Yeah. Right. It doesn't work like that."

"Just believe you can stay well, and you will," she said.

The circle of horses began to move again, and she headed back toward the fence. It was then he noticed her limp. "Hey!" he shouted after her. "What happened to your leg?"

"It got broken," she said matter-of-factly.

Mac hadn't thought much about it then, but now he knew the pain she must have endured to walk again. Jewel would know what he was feeling as he got out of the hospital for what he hoped would be the last time. Jewel would understand.

After that first meeting, he and Jewel had encountered each other often over the next several

years. He had beaten the leukemia and returned
as a teenager to become a counselor at Camp
LittleHawk. That was when Jewel had become
his best friend. Not his *girlfriend*. His *best
friend*.

He already had a girlfriend back home in Dallas. Her name was Louise and he called her Lou
and was violently in love with her. He had met
Lou when she came to the junior-senior prom
with another guy. She had only been in the
eighth grade. By the time he was a senior and
Lou was a freshman, they were going steady.

He told Jewel all about the agonies of being
in love, and though she hadn't yet taken the
plunge, she was all sympathetic ears. Jewel was
the best buddy a guy could have, a confidante,
a pal. A soul mate. He could tell her anything
and, in fact, had told her some amazingly private
things.

Like how he had cried the first time he had
endured a procedure called a back-stick, where
they stuck a needle in your back to figure out
your blood count. How he had wet the bed once
in the hospital rather than ask for a bedpan. And
how humiliating it had been when the nurse

treated him like a baby and put the thermometer into an orifice other than his mouth.

It was astonishing to think he could have been so frank with Jewel. But Jewel didn't only listen to his woes, she shared her own. So he knew how jealous and angry she had been when Zach and Rebecca adopted another little girl two years older than her named Rolleen. And how she had learned to accept each new child a little more willingly, until the youngest, Colt, had come along, and he had felt like her own flesh-and-blood baby brother.

Mac had also been there at the worst moment of her life. He had lost a good friend that fateful Fourth of July. And Jewel... Jewel had lost much more. After that hot, horrible summer day, she had refused to see him again. So far, he had respected her wish to be left alone. But there was an empty place inside him she had once helped to fill.

He had received an invitation to her wedding the previous spring. It was hard to say what his feelings had been. Joy for her, because he knew how hard it must have been for her to move past what had happened to her. And sadness, too, because he knew the closeness they had enjoyed in the past would be transferred to her husband.

Then had come the announcement, a few weeks before the wedding, that it had been canceled. He had wondered what had gone wrong, wondered which of them had called it off and worried about what she must be feeling. He would never pry, but he was curious. After all, he and Jewel had once known everything there was to know about each other. He had picked up the phone to call her, but put it down. Too many years had passed.

Mac had never had another woman friend like Jewel. Sex always got in the way. Or rather, the woman's expectations. And his inability to fulfill them.

What kind of man is still a virgin at twenty-five? Mac mused.

An angry man. A onetime romantic fool who waited through college for his high school sweetheart to grow up, only to be left for another guy.

It hadn't seemed like such a terrible sacrifice remaining faithful to Louise all those years, turning down girls who showed up at his dorm room in T-shirts and not much else, girls who wanted to make it with a college football hero, girls who were attracted by his calendar-stud good looks. He had loved Lou and had his whole life with her ahead of him.

Until she had jilted him her senior year for Harry Warnecke, who had a bright future running his father's bowling alley.

Lou had been gentle but firm in her rejection of him. "I don't love you anymore, Mac. I love Harry. I'm pregnant, and we're going to be married."

Mac had been livid with fury. He had never touched her, had respected her wish to remain a virgin until she graduated from high school and they could marry, and she was pregnant with some guy named Harry's kid and wanted to marry him.

It had taken every ounce of self-control he had not to reach out and throttle her. "Have a nice life," he had managed to say.

His anger had prodded him to hunt up the first available woman and get laid. But his pain had sent him back to his dorm room to nurse his broken heart. How could he make love to another woman when he still loved Lou? If all he had wanted was to get screwed, he could have been doing that all along. His dad had always told him that sex felt good, but making love felt better. He had wanted it to be making love the first time.

His final year of college, after he broke up with Lou, he went through a lot of women. Dating them, that is. Kissing them and touching them and learning what made them respond to a man. But he never put himself inside one of them. He was looking for something more than sex in the relationship. What he found were women who admired his body, or his talent with a football, or his financial prospects. Not one of them wanted him.

It wasn't until he had been drafted by the pros and began traveling with the Tornadoes that he met Elizabeth Kale. She was a female TV sports commentator, a woman who felt comfortable with jocks and could banter with the best of them. She had taken his breath away. She had shiny brown hair and warm brown eyes and a smile that wouldn't quit. He had fallen faster than a wrestled steer in a rodeo.

She hadn't been impressed by his statistics— personal or football or financial. It had not been easy to get her to go out with him. She didn't want to get involved. She had her career, and marriage wasn't in the picture.

Mac didn't give up when he wanted something—and he'd wanted to marry Elizabeth. As the season progressed, they began to see each other when they were both in town. Elizabeth was a city girl, so they did city things—when they could both fit it into their busy schedules. Mac wooed her with every romantic gesture he could think of, and she responded. And when he proposed marriage, she accepted. Elizabeth made what time she could for him, and they exchanged a lot of passionate kisses at airports where their paths crossed.

He had carefully planned her seduction. He knew when and where it was going to happen. He was nervous and eager and restless. By a certain age—and Mac had already reached it— a woman expected a man to know all the right moves. Mac had been to the goal line plenty of times, but he had never scored a touchdown. He was ready and willing to take the plunge—figuratively speaking—but now that he had waited so long, the idea of making it with a woman for the first time was a little unnerving. Especially with Elizabeth, who meant so much to him.

What if he did it wrong? What if he couldn't please her? What if he left her unsatisfied? He read books. And planned. And postponed the moment.

Then he broke his leg. *Shattered his leg.*

Mac tasted bile in his throat, remembering what had happened next. Elizabeth had come to the hospital to see him, flashbulbs popping around her, as much in the news as his girlfriend as she was as a famous newscaster. She listened at his bedside to the prognosis.

His football career was over. He would be lucky if he ever walked again. He would always need a brace on his leg. Maybe he could manage with a cane.

He had seen it in her eyes before she spoke a word. The fear. And the determination. She said nothing until the doctors had left them alone.

"I can't—I won't—I can't do it, Mac."

"Do what, Elizabeth?" he asked in a bitter voice that revealed he knew exactly what she meant, though he pretended ignorance.

"I won't marry a man who can't walk." She slipped her widespread fingers slowly through the hair that fell forward on her face, carefully settling it back in place. He had always thought it a charming gesture, but now it only made her seem vain.

"I can't go through this with you," she said. "I mean, I...I hate hospitals and sick people and I can't...I can't be there for you, Mac."

He had known it was coming, but it hurt just the same. "Get out, Elizabeth."

She stood there waiting for...what?...for him to tell her it was all right? It wasn't, by God, all right! It was a hell of a thing to tell a man you couldn't stand by him in times of trouble. *For better or for worse.* It told him plenty about just how deep her feelings for him ran. Thin as sheet ice on a Texas pond.

"I said get out!" He was shouting by then, and she flinched and backed away. "Get out!"

She turned and ran.

His throat hurt from shouting and his leg throbbed and his eyes and nose burned with unshed tears. He shouted at the nurse when she tried to come in, but he couldn't even turn over and bury his head in a pillow because they had his leg so strapped up.

Mac forced his mind away from the painful memories. There had been no seductions during the past two years, though he had spent a great deal of time in bed. He had been too busy trying to get well. Now he was well. And he was going to have to face that zero on the scoreboard and do something about it.

He could find a woman who knew the ropes— there were certainly enough volunteers even now—and get it over with. But he found that a little cold and calculating. The first time ought to be with a special woman. Not that he would ever be stupid enough to fall in love again. After all, twice burned, thrice chary. But he wanted to like and respect and admire the woman he chose as his first sexual partner.

Lately his dreams had been unbelievably erotic. *Hot, sweat-slick bodies entwined in twisted sheets. Long female legs wrapped around his waist. A woman's hair draped across his chest. His mouth on her—* He shook off the vision. Now that he was finally healthy—meaning he could get out of bed as easily as he could fall into it—it was time he took care of unfinished business.

Jewel's face appeared in his mind's eye. He saw the faint, crisscrossing scars from the car accident that had left her an orphan which had never quite faded away. Her smile, winsome and mischievous. Heard the distressed sound of her voice when she admitted her breasts kept growing and growing like two balloons. And her laughter when he had offered to pop them for her.

With Jewel he wouldn't have to be afraid of making a fool of himself in bed. Jewel would understand his predicament. But she was the last person he could ever have sex with. Not after what had happened to her.

He was sure she would see the humor in the current situation. Jewel had a great sense of humor. At least, once upon a time she had. He could hardly believe six years had passed since they had last seen each other. They had both been through a great deal since then.

Mac hoped Jewel wouldn't mind him intruding on her this way. But he was coming, like it or not.

Chapter 2

Peter "Mac" Macready was the last person Jewel Whitelaw wanted to see back at Hawk's Pride, because he was the one person besides her counselor who knew her deepest, darkest secret. She should have told someone else long ago—her parents, one of her three sisters or four brothers, her fiancé—but she had never been able to admit the truth to anyone. Only Mac knew. And now he was coming back.

If she could have left home while he was visiting, she would have done so. But Camp Little-Hawk was scheduled to open in two weeks, and she had too much to do to get ready for the summer season to be able to pick up and leave. All she could do was avoid Mac as much as possible.

As she emerged from a steamy shower, draped herself in a floor-length white terry cloth robe and wrapped her long brown hair in a towel, she learned just how impossible that was going to be.

"Hi."

He was standing at the open bathroom door dressed in worn Levi's, a Tornadoes T-shirt and Nikes, leaning on a cane. He didn't even have the grace to look embarrassed. A grin split his face from ear to ear, creating two masculine dimples in his cheeks, while his vivid blue eyes gazed at her with the warmth of an August day in Texas.

"Hi," she said back. In spite of not wanting him here, she felt her lips curve in an answering smile. Her gaze skipped to the knotty-looking hickory cane he leaned on and back to his face. "I see you're standing on your own."

"Almost," he said. "Sorry about intruding. Your mom said to make myself comfortable." He gestured to the bedroom behind him, on the other side of the bathroom, where his suitcase sat on the double bed. "Looks like we'll be sharing a bath."

Jewel groaned inwardly. The new camp counselors' cottages had been built to match the single-story Spanish style of the main ranch house, with whitewashed adobe walls and a red barrel-tile roof. Each had two bedrooms, but shared a bath, living room and kitchen. As the camp manager, she should have had this cottage all to herself. "I thought you'd be staying at the house," she said.

"Your mom gave me a choice." He shrugged. "This seemed more private."

"I see." Her mother had asked her if she minded, since Jewel and Mac were such old friends, if she gave Mac a choice of staying at the cottage or in the house. Jewel hadn't objected, because she hadn't been able to think up a good reason to say no that wouldn't sound suspicious. As far as her parents knew, she and Mac still were good friends. And they were.

Only, Jewel had expected Mac to keep his distance, as he had for the past six years. And he had not.

Mac's brow furrowed in a way that was achingly familiar. "I can tell Rebecca I've changed my mind, if you don't want me here."

Jewel struggled between the desire to escape Mac's scrutiny and the yearning to have back the camaraderie they had once enjoyed. Maybe it would be all right. Maybe the subject wouldn't come up. *Yeah, and maybe horses come in green and pink.* "I..."

He started to turn away. "I'll get my bag."

"Wait."

He turned back. "I don't want to make you uncomfortable, Jewel. I won't talk about it. I won't even bring up the subject." His lips curled wryly. "Of course, I just brought up the subject to say I won't bring it up, but I promise it'll be off-limits. I need a place to rest and get better, and I thought you might not mind if I stayed here."

His eyes looked wounded, and her heart went out to him. She crossed to him, because that seemed easier than making him walk to her with the cane. His arms opened to her and she walked right into them and they hugged tightly.

"God, I've missed you," he said, his deep voice rumbling in her ear.

"This feels good," she admitted. "It's been too long, Mac."

There was nothing sexual in the embrace, just two old friends, two very good friends, reconnecting after a long separation. Except Jewel was aware of the strength in his arms, the way her breasts felt crushed against his muscular chest and the feel of his thighs pressed against her own. She stiffened, then forced herself to relax.

"You're taller than I remember," he said, tucking her towel-covered head under his chin.

"I've grown three inches since... I've grown," she said, realizing how difficult it was going to be avoiding the subject she wanted to avoid. "It's a good thing, or I'd get a crick in my neck looking up at you."

He had to be four inches over six feet. She remembered him being tall at nineteen, but he must have grown an inch or two since then, and of course his shoulders were broader, his angular features more mature. He was a man now, not a boy.

He was big. He was strong. He could physically overwhelm her. But she had known Mac forever. He would never hurt her. She reminded herself to relax.

The towel slipped off, and her hair cascaded to her waist.

"Good Lord," Mac said, his fingers tangling in the length of it. "Your hair was never this long, either."

"I like it long." She could drape it forward over her shoulders to help cover her Enormous Endowments.

"I think I'm going to like it, too," he said, smiling down at her with a teasing glint in his eyes.

She gave him an arch look. "Are you flirting with me, Mr. Macready?"

"Who, me? Naw. Wouldn't think of it, Ruby."

Jewel grinned. In the old days, he had often called her by the names of different precious gems—"Because you're a Jewel, get it?"—and the return to such familiarity made her feel even more comfortable with him. "Get out of here so I can get dressed," she said, stepping back from his embrace.

The robe gaped momentarily, and his glance slipped downward appreciatively. She self-consciously pulled the cloth over her breasts to cover them completely.

"Looks like they've grown, too," he quipped, leering at her comically.

She should have laughed. It was what she would have done six years ago, before disaster had struck. But she couldn't joke with him anymore about her overgenerous breasts. She blamed the size of them for what had happened to her. "Don't, Mac," she said quietly.

He sobered instantly. "I'm sorry, Jewel."

She managed a smile. "It's no big deal. Just get out of here and let me get dressed."

He backed up, and for the first time she saw how much he needed the cane. His face turned white around the mouth with pain, and he swore under his breath.

"Are you all right?" she asked.

"No problem," he said. "Leg's almost as good as new. Figure I'll start jogging tomorrow."

"Jogging?"

He gave her a sheepish look. "So maybe I'll start out walking. Want to go with me?"

She daintily pointed the toe of her once-injured leg in his direction. "Walking isn't my forte. How about a horseback ride?"

He shook his head. "Gotta walk. Need the exercise to get back into shape. Come with me. My limp is worse than yours, so you won't have any trouble keeping up. Besides, it would give us a chance to catch up on what we've both been doing the past six years. Please come."

She wrinkled her nose.

"Pretty please with sugar on it?"

It was something she had taught him to say if he really wanted a woman to do something. She gave in to the smile and let her lips curve with the delight she felt. "All right, you hopeless romantic. I'll walk with you, but it'll have to be early because I've got a lot of work to do tomorrow."

"Figured I'd go early to beat the heat," he said. "Six-thirty?"

"Make it six, and you've got a deal." She reached out a hand, and Mac shook it.

The electric shock that raced up her arm was disturbing. It took an effort to keep the frown from her face. This wasn't supposed to happen. She wasn't supposed to be physically attracted to Mac Macready. They were just good friends. *Yeah, and horses come in purple and orange.*

She closed the bathroom door and sank onto the edge of the tub. She had always thought Mac was cute, but he had matured into a genuine hunk. No problem. She would handle the attraction the way she had from the beginning, by thinking of him as a brother.

But he wasn't her brother. He was a very attractive, very available man. Who once had been—still was?—her best friend.

She clung to that thought, which made it easier to keep their relationship in perspective. It was much more important to have a friend like Mac than a boyfriend.

Jewel repeated that sentence like a litany the next morning at 5:55 when Mac showed up in the kitchen dressed in Nikes and black running shorts and nothing else. The kitchen door was open and through the screen she was aware of flies buzzing and the lowing of cattle. A steady, squeaking sound meant that her youngest brother, Colt, hadn't gotten around to oiling the windmill beside the stock pond. But those distractions weren't enough to keep her from ogling Mac's body.

A wedge of golden hair on his chest became a line of soft down as it reached his navel and disappeared beneath his shorts. She consciously forced her gaze upward.

Mac's tousled, collar-length hair was a sun-kissed blond, and his eyes were as bright as the morning sky. He hadn't shaved, and the overnight beard made him look both dangerous and sexy.

Without the concealing T-shirt and jeans, she could see the sinewy muscles in his shoulders and arms, the washboard belly and the horrible mishmash of scars on his left leg. He leaned heavily on the cane.

She poured him a bowl of cornflakes and doused them with milk. "Eat. You're running late."

"Oh, that I were running," he said. "I'm afraid walking is the best I can do." He hobbled across the redbrick tile floor to the small wooden table, settled himself in the ladderback chair opposite her and began consuming cereal at an alarming rate.

"What's that you're wearing?" he asked.

She tugged at her bulky, short-sleeved sweatshirt, dusted off her cutoff jeans and readjusted her hair over her shoulders. "Some old things."

"Gonna be hot in that," he said between bites.

But the sweatshirt disguised her Bountiful Bosom, which was more important than comfort. "Hungry?" she inquired, her chin resting on her hand as she watched him eat ravenously.

"I missed supper last night."

She had checked his bedroom and found him asleep at suppertime and hadn't disturbed him. He had slept all through the afternoon and evening. "You must have been tired."

"I was. Completely exhausted. Not that I'd admit that to anyone but you." He poured himself another bowl of cereal, doused it with the milk she had left on the table and began eating again.

"Nothing wrong with your appetite," she observed.

He made a sound, but his mouth was too full to answer.

She watched him eat four bowls of cereal. That was about right—two for dinner and two for breakfast. "Ready to go walking now?" she asked.

"Sure." He took his dish to the sink and reached back for hers, which she handed to him.

Seeing the difficulty he was having trying to do everything one-handed, so he could hang on to his cane, she said, "I can do that for you."

"I'm not a cripple!" When he turned to snap at her, he lost his one-handed grip on the dishes. His cane fell as he lurched to catch the bowls with both hands. Without the cane, his left leg crumpled under him.

"Look out!" Jewel cried.

The dishes crashed into the sink as Mac grabbed hold of the counter to keep from falling backward.

"Damn it all to hell!" he raged.

Jewel reached out to comfort him, but he snarled, "Don't touch me. Leave me alone."

Jewel had whirled to leave, when he bit out, "Don't go."

She stopped where she was, but she wanted to run. She didn't want to see his pain. It reminded her too much of her own.

He stared out the window over the sink at the endless reaches of Hawk's Pride, with its vast, grassy plains and the jagged outcroppings of rock that marked the entrance to the canyons in the distance.

"It must be awful," she whispered, "to lose so much."

His eyes slid closed, and she watched his Adam's apple bob as he swallowed hard. He slowly opened his eyes and turned to look at her over his shoulder. "This…the way I am… It's just temporary. I'll be back as good as new next season."

"Will you?"

He met her gaze steadily. "Bet on it."

She knew him too well. Well enough to hear the sheer bravado in his answer and to see the unspoken fear in his eyes that his football career was over. They had always been deeply attuned to one another. He was vulnerable again, in a way he once had been as a youth—this time not to death itself, but to the death of his dreams.

"What can I do, Mac?"

He managed a smile. "Hand me my cane, will you?"

It was easier to do as he asked than to probe the painful issues that he was refusing to address. She crossed to pick up his cane and watched as he eased his weight off his hands and onto his leg with the cane's support.

"Are you sure it isn't too soon to be doing so much?" she asked as he hissed in a breath.

He headed determinedly for the screen door. "The only way my leg can get stronger is if I walk on it."

She followed after him, as she had for nearly a dozen years in their youth. "All right, cowboy. Head 'em up, and move 'em out."

He flashed her his killer grin, and she smiled back, letting the screen door slam behind her.

It was easier to pretend nothing was wrong. But she could already see that things were different between them. They had both been through a great deal in the years since they had last seen each other. She knew as well as he did what it felt like to live with fear, and with disappointment.

She had worked hard to put behind her what had happened the summer she was sixteen and Harvey Barnes had attacked her at the Fourth of July picnic. But even now the memory of that day haunted her.

She had been excited when Harvey, a senior who ran with the in crowd, asked her to the an-

nual county-wide Fourth of July celebration.
She'd had a crush on him for a long time, but
he hadn't given her a second glance. During the
previous year, her breasts had blossomed and
given her a figure most movie stars would have
paid good dollars to have. A lot of boys stared,
including Harvey.

She had suspected why Harvey had asked her
out, but she hadn't cared. She had just been so
glad to be asked, she had accepted his invitation
on the spot.

"Why would you want to go out with a guy
who's so full of himself?" Mac asked after she
introduced him to Harvey. "I'd be glad to take
you." As he had previously, every year he'd
been at Hawk's Pride.

"I might as well go with one of my brothers
as go with you," she replied. "Harvey's cool.
He's a hunk. He's—"

"Yeah, yeah, yeah. I get the message," he
said, then teased in a singsong voice, "Pearl's
got a boyfriend, Pearl's got a boyfriend."

She aimed a playful fist at his stomach to shut
him up, but the truth was, she was hoping the
picnic date with Harvey, their first, would lead
to a steady relationship.

Mac caught her wrist to protect his belly and said, "All right, go with Harvey Barnes and have a good time. Forget all about me—"

Jewel laughed and said, "That mournful face isn't going to make any difference. I'm still going with Harvey. I'll see you at the picnic. We just won't spend as much time together."

Mac looked down at her, his brow furrowed. He opened his mouth to say something and shut it again.

"What is it?" she asked, seeing how troubled he looked.

"Just don't let him… If he does anything… If you think he's going to…"

"What?" she asked in exasperation.

He let go of her hands to shove both of his through his hair. "If you need help, just yell, and I'll be there."

He had already turned to walk away when she grabbed his arm and turned him back around. "What is it you think Harvey's going to do to me that's so terrible?"

"He's going to want to kiss you," Mac said.

"I want to kiss him back. So what's the problem?"

"Kissing's not the problem," Mac pointed

out. "It's what comes after that. The touching and…and the rest. Sometimes it's not easy for a guy to stop. Not that I'm saying he'd try anything on a first date, but some guys… And with a body like yours…"

Her face felt heated from all the blood rushing to it. Over the years they had managed not to talk seriously about such intimate subjects. Mac never brought them up except in fun, and until recently she hadn't been that interested in boys. She searched his face and found he looked as confused and awkward discussing the subject as she felt.

"How would you know?" she asked. "I mean, about it being hard to stop. Have you done it with Lou?"

His flush deepened. "You know I wouldn't tell you that, even if I had."

"Have you?" she persisted.

He tousled her hair like a brother and said, "Wouldn't you like to know!"

In the days before the picnic, Mac teased her mercilessly about her plan to wear a dress, since she only wore jeans and a T-shirt around the ranch.

Her eldest sister, Rolleen, had agreed to make

a pink gingham dress for her, copying a spa-
ghetti-strapped dress pattern that Jewel loved,
but which she couldn't wear because her large
breasts needed the support of a heavy-duty bra.
Rolleen created essentially the same fitted-
bodice, bare-shouldered, full-skirted dress, but
made the shoulder straps an inch wide so they
would hide her bra straps.

On the day of the picnic, Jewel donned the
dress and tied up her shoulder-length hair in a
ponytail with a pink gingham bow. Her newest
Whitelaw sibling, fifteen-year-old Cherry, insisted that she needed pink lipstick on her lips,
which Cherry applied for her with the expertise
of one who had been wearing lipstick since she
was twelve.

Then Jewel headed out the kitchen door to
find Mac, who was driving her to the picnic
grounds to meet Harvey.

"Wow!" Mac said when he saw her.
"Wow!"

Jewel found it hard to believe the admiration
she saw in Mac's eyes. She had long ago accepted the fact she wasn't pretty. She had sunstreaked brown hair and plain brown eyes and
extraordinarily ordinary features. Her body was

fit and healthy, but faint, crisscrossing scars laced her face, and she had a distinctive permanent limp.

The look in Mac's eyes made her feel radiantly beautiful.

She held out the gingham dress and twirled around for him. "Do you think Harvey will like it?"

"Harvey's gonna love it!" he assured her. "You look good enough to eat. I hope this Harvey character knows how lucky he is." The furrow reappeared on his brow. "He better not—"

She put a finger on the wrinkles in his forehead to smooth them out. "You worry too much, Mac. Nothing bad is going to happen."

Looking back now, Jewel wished she had listened to Mac. She wished she hadn't tried to look so pretty for Harvey Barnes. She wished...

Jewel had gotten counseling in college to help her deal with what had happened that day. The counselor had urged her to tell her parents, and when she had met Jerry Cain and fallen in love with him her junior year at Baylor, the counselor had urged her to tell Jerry, too.

She just couldn't.

Jerry had been a graduate student, years older

than she was, and more mature than the other college boys she had met. He had figured out right away that she was self-conscious about the size of her breasts, and it was his consideration for her feelings that had first attracted her to him. It had been easy to fall in love with him. It had been more difficult—impossible—to trust him with her secret.

Jerry had been more patient with her than she had any right to expect. She had loved kissing him. Been more anxious—but finally accepting—of his caresses. They were engaged before he pressed her to sleep with him. They had already sent out the wedding invitations by the time she did.

It had been a disaster.

They had called off the wedding.

That was a year ago. Jewel had decided that if she couldn't marry and have kids of her own, she could at least work with children who needed her.

So she had come back to Camp LittleHawk.

"Hey. You look like you're a million miles away."

Jewel glanced around and realized she could

hardly see the white adobe ranch buildings, they
had walked so far. "Oh. I was thinking."

"To tell you the truth, I enjoyed the quiet
company." Sweat beaded Mac's forehead and
his upper lip. He winced every time he took a
step.

"Haven't we gone far enough?" she asked.

"The doctor said I can do as much as I can
stand."

"You look like you're there already," she
said.

"Just a little bit farther."

That attitude explained why Mac had become
the best at what he did, but Jewel worried about
him all the same. "Just don't expect me to carry
you back," she joked.

Mac shot her one of his dimpled smiles and
said, "Tell me what you've been doing with
yourself lately."

"I've been figuring out the daily schedule for
Camp LittleHawk."

"Need any help?"

She gave him a surprised look. "I'd love
some. Do you have the time?"

He shrugged. "Don't have anything else

planned. What kinds of things are you having the kids do these days?''

She told him, unable to keep the excitement from her voice. ''Horseback riding, picnics and hayrides, of course. And handicrafts, naturally.

''But I've come up with something really exciting this year. We're going to have art sessions at the site of those primitive drawings on the canyon wall here at Hawk's Pride. Once the kids have copied down all the various symbols, we're going to send them off to an archaeologist at the state university for interpretation.

''When her findings are available, I'll forward a copy of them to the kids, wherever they are. It'll remind them what fun they had at camp even after they've gone.''

''And maybe take their minds off their illness, if they're back in the hospital,'' Mac noted quietly.

Jewel sat silently watching Mac stare into the distance and knew he was remembering how it had been in the beginning, how they had provided solace to each other, a needed word of encouragement and a shoulder to lean on. She knew he had come back because she was here, a friend when he needed one.

"I can remember being fascinated by those drawings myself as a kid," Mac mused.

"Didn't you want to be an archaeologist once upon a time?"

"Paleontologist," he corrected.

"What's the difference?"

"An archaeologist studies the past by looking at what people have left behind. A paleontologist studies fossils to recreate a picture of life in the past."

"What happened to those plans?" she asked.

"It got harder and harder to focus on the past when I realized I was going to have a future."

"What college degree did you finally end up getting?"

He laughed self-consciously. "Business. I figured I'd need to know how to handle all the money I'd make playing football."

But his career had been cut short.

He turned abruptly and headed back toward the ranch without another word to her.

Jewel figured the distance they had come at about a mile. She looked at her watch. Six-thirty. Not very far or very fast for a man who depended on his speed for a living.

About a quarter of a mile from the house, Mac

was using his hand to help move his left leg. Jewel stepped to his side and slipped her arm around his waist to help support his weight.

"Don't argue," she said, when he opened his mouth to protest. "If you want my company, you have to take the concern that comes along with it."

"Thanks, Opal," he said.

"Think nothing of it, Pete."

She hadn't called him Pete since he had started high school and acquired the nickname "Mac" from his football teammates. It brought back memories of better times for both of them. They were content to walk in silence the rest of the way back to the house.

Jewel had forgotten how good it felt to have a friend with whom you could communicate without saying a word. She knew what Mac was feeling right now as though he had spoken the words aloud. She understood his frustration. And his fear. She empathized with his drive to succeed, despite the obstacles he had to overcome. She understood his reluctance to accept her help and his willingness to do so.

It was as though the intervening years had never been.

Except, something else had been added to the mix between them. Something unexpected. Something as unwelcome as it was undeniable.

No *friend* should have felt the frisson of excitement Jewel had felt with her body snuggled up next to Mac's. No *friend* should have gotten the chill she got down her spine when Mac's warm breath feathered over her temple. No *friend's* heart would have started beating faster, as hers had, when Mac's arm circled her waist in return, his fingers closing on her flesh beneath the sweatshirt.

She would have to hide what she felt from him. Otherwise it would spoil everything. Friendship had always been enough in the past. Because of what had happened, because she was in no position to ask for—or accept—more, friendship was all they could ever have between them now.

As they reached the kitchen door, she smiled up at Mac, and he smiled back.

"Home again, home again, jiggety jog," she said.

"Same time tomorrow?"

She started to refuse. It would be easier if she kept her distance from him. But it was foolish to deny herself his friendship because she felt more than that for him.

She gave him a cheery smile and said, ''Sure. Same time tomorrow.'' She breathed a sigh of relief that she wouldn't have to face him again for twenty-four hours.

''As soon as I shower, we can go to work planning all those activities for the kids,'' he said.

Jewel gave him a startled look.

''Changed your mind about wanting my help?''

She had forgotten all about it. ''No. I...uh...''

He tousled her hair. ''You can make up your mind while I shower. I'll be here if you need me.''

A moment later he had disappeared into the house. It was only then she realized he was going to use up all the hot water.

''Hey!'' she yelled, yanking the screen door open to follow after him. ''I get the shower first!''

He leaned his head out of the bathroom door. She saw a length of naked flank and stopped in her tracks.

''You can have it first tomorrow,'' he said.

His eyes twinkled as he added, "Unless you'd like to share?"

She put her hand flat on his bare chest, feeling the crisp, sweat-dampened curls under her palm, and shoved him back inside. "Go get cleaned up, stinky," she said, wrinkling her nose. "We've got work to do."

He saluted her and stepped back inside.

It was the right response. Just enough teasing and playful camaraderie to disguise her shiver of delight—and the sudden quiver of fear—at being invited to share Mac's shower.

Chapter 3

"Wow! Mac Macready in the flesh!"

Mac felt embarrassed and humbled at the look of admiration—almost adulation—in Colt Whitelaw's eyes. Mac had just shoved open the kitchen screen door to admire the sunrise on his third day at Hawk's Pride when he encountered Jewel's fourteen-year-old brother on the back steps. He had known the boy since Colt came to the Whitelaw household as an infant, the only one of the eight Whitelaw kids who had known no other parents than Zach and Rebecca. "Hi there, kid."

Colt was wearing a white T-shirt cut off at the waist to expose his concave belly and ribs and with the arms ripped out to reveal sinewy biceps. Levi's covered his long, lanky legs. He was tossing a football from hand to hand as he shifted from foot to booted foot. With the soft black down of adolescence growing on his upper lip, he looked every bit the eager and excited teenager he was.

"Mom said you were coming, but I didn't really believe her. I mean, now that you're famous and all, I didn't think you'd ever come back here. I wanted to come over as soon as you got here, but Mom said you needed time to settle in without all of us bothering you, so I stayed away a whole extra day. I'm not bothering you, am I?"

Mac resisted the urge to ruffle Colt's shaggy, shoulder-length black hair. The kid wouldn't appreciate it. Mac knew from his own experience that a boy of fourteen considered himself pretty much grown up. Colt was six feet tall, but his shoulders were still almost as narrow as his hips. His blue eyes were filled with wonder and hope, without the cynicism and disappointment that appeared as you grew older and learned that life threw a lot of uncatchable balls your way.

"Sit down and tell me what you've been doing with yourself," Mac invited. He eased himself into one of the two slatted white wooden chairs situated on the flagstone patio at the back of the cottage. Colt perched on the wide arm of the other chair.

The patio was arbored, and purple bougainvillea woven within a white lattice framework provided shade to keep the early morning sun off their heads and a pleasant floral fragrance.

Mac was aware of Colt's scrutiny as he gently picked up his wounded leg and set the ankle on the opposite knee. When he was done, he laid his cane down on the flagstone and leaned back comfortably in the chair.

"I was watching the game on TV when your leg got busted," Colt said. "It looked pretty bad."

"It was," Mac agreed.

"I heard them say you'd never walk again," Colt blurted.

Mac managed a smile. "Looks like they were wrong."

"When you didn't come back after a whole year, they said you'd never play football again."

"It's taken me a while to get back on my feet,

but I expect to be back on the football field in the fall as good as new and better than ever.''

"Really?" Colt asked.

Mac was fresh out of the shower after his second morning of walking with Jewel, and wished now he had put on jeans and boots instead of shorts and Nikes. The kid was gawking at his scarred leg like he was a mutant from the latest horror movie.

Mac figured it was time to change the subject, or he'd end up crying his woes to the teenager. He gestured to the football in Colt's hands and said, "Are you on the football team at school?"

Colt made a disparaging face and mumbled, "Yeah. I'm the quarterback."

Most boys, especially in Texas, would have been ecstatic at the thought of being quarterback. "It sounds as if you don't care much for football."

"It's all right. It's just…" Colt slid off the arm backward into the slatted wooden chair, with his legs dangling over the arm, the football cradled in the notch of his elbow. "Did you always know what you wanted to do with your life?"

Mac nodded. He had always known he wanted to play football. He just hadn't been sure his body would give him the chance. "How about you?"

"I know exactly what I want to do," Colt said. "I just don't think I'm going to get the chance to do it."

"Why not?"

"Dad expects me to stay here and be a rancher."

"Is that so bad?"

"It is when I'd rather be doing something else."

Mac stared at Colt's troubled face. "Anything you'd like to talk about?"

Colt shrugged. "Naw. I guess not." He settled his feet on the ground and rose with an ease that Mac envied. "Guess I'd better get going. Now that school's out for the summer, I've got a lot of chores to do."

Mac turned his eyes in the direction of the squealing windmill.

Colt laughed. "I'll get to it right away. Hope it hasn't been keeping you awake."

"I've slept fine." Like the dead. He had slept straight through the afternoon and evening of his first day here, and yesterday he had been exhausted after a day spent mostly sitting down, working out a crafts program for the camp with

Jewel. He knew his body needed rest to heal, but he was tired of being tired. He wanted to be well again.

Colt began loping away, then suddenly turned and threw the football in Mac's direction. Instinctively, Mac reached out to catch it. His fingertips settled on the well-thrown ball with remembered ease, and he drew it in.

Colt came loping back, a wide grin splitting his face. "Guess you haven't lost your touch." He held out his hand for the ball.

Mac looked up at the kid, an idea forming in his head. "How would you like to throw a few to me over the next couple of weeks, after I get a little more mobile?"

Colt's eyes went wide with wonder. "You mean it? Really? Hot damn, that would be great! I mean, golly, that would be great!" he quickly corrected himself, looking over his shoulder to see if any of his family had heard him. "Just say when and where."

"Let's say two weeks from today," Mac said. "I'll come and find you."

Colt eyed Mac's injured leg. "Are you sure—"

"Two weeks," Mac said certainly.

Colt grinned. "You got it." He took the ball and sauntered off toward the barn.

Mac let out a deep sigh. He had given himself two weeks to get back enough mobility to be able to run for a pass, when it was taking him thirty minutes to walk a mile.

He turned as he heard the screen door slam and saw Jewel. She was just out of the shower, having been second again this morning, since she had gotten a phone call the instant they came back in the door from their walk. She must have blown her hair dry, because it looked shiny and soft enough for him to want to put his hands in it.

The only time he had ever touched her hair in the past was to tousle it like an older brother or tug on her ponytail. He couldn't help wondering what it would feel like to have all that long, silky hair draped over his body.

Mac turned away. *This is Jewel. Your best friend. You'd better get laid soon, old buddy. You're starting to have really weird fantasies.*

She was wearing jeans and boots and a long-sleeved man's button-down, oxford-cloth shirt turned up at the cuffs with the tails hanging out. He wondered if the shirt had belonged to her fiancé and felt jealous of the man. Which was stupid, because Mac and Jewel had never been lovers.

Would you like to be?

He forced his mind away from that insidious thought. It would mess up everything if he made a move on his best friend. He needed Jewel's friendship too much to spoil things that way.

The shirt was big and blousy on her, and she wore her hair pulled over her shoulders in front to hide whatever there might have been left to see of her figure, which wasn't much.

He started to say "You look great!" and bit his tongue. It sounded too much like something a man might say to a woman he wanted to impress. "Hi," he said instead. "Hope you had enough hot water."

"Barely. I made it a quick shower. I'm definitely first tomorrow." She took the seat next to him, leaned back and inhaled a breath of flower-scented air that made her breasts rise under the shirt. The sight took his breath away.

Whenever he had thought about Jewel in the years they had been apart, it was her laughter he had remembered. The way her eyes crinkled at the corners and her lips curved, revealing even white teeth, and how the sound would kind of bubble up out of her, as effervescent as sparkling water.

He couldn't imagine why he hadn't remembered her breasts. He could see why a man might stare. Had they been that large six years ago? They must have been, or close to it, because he had joked with her about them a lot, he remembered. And she had laughed in response, that effervescent, sparkling laugh.

He realized he hadn't heard her laugh once since he had arrived. She had smiled, but her eyes had never joined her mouth. A sadness lingered, memories of more than uncatchable balls. More like forfeited games.

"Who was that on the phone?" he asked.

"Mrs. Templeton. Her eight-year-old son, Brad, is supposed to be a camper during the first two-week session, but he was having second thoughts about coming."

"Why?"

"She's not really sure. He was excited at first when his parents suggested the camp. She wanted me to talk to him."

"Were you able to change his mind?"

Her lips curved. "Brad's an avid football fan. I mentioned you were here—"

"You shouldn't have done that," Mac said brusquely.

She looked as if he'd kicked her in the stomach. "I'm sorry," she said. "I didn't think you'd mind. You always seemed to like spending time with the kids."

He made a face. "It isn't that I mind spending time with them. It's just—" He didn't want them to see him hobbling around with a cane. He didn't want them feeling sorry for him. He didn't want to be asked a lot of questions for which he had no answers.

He would know in the next few weeks whether his leg was going to stand up to the rigors of running. He wanted time by himself to deal with his disappointment—if that was what it turned out to be. He wanted to be able to rage against fate without worrying about some sick kid's feelings.

"I'm sorry, Mac," Jewel said, reaching out to lay her hand on his forearm.

The hairs on his arms prickled at her touch, and his body responded in a way that both surprised and disturbed him. He resisted the urge to jerk his hand away. That would only hurt her again.

This is Jewel. My friend. There's nothing sexual intended by her touch.

Jewel might be his friend, but his body also recognized her as female. This sort of thing— unwanted arousal—had happened once or twice when they were teenagers, and she had touched him at an odd moment when he wasn't expecting it, but he had always attributed those incidents to randy teenage hormones. That excuse wouldn't work now.

All right, so she was an attractive woman.

That excuse wouldn't work either. Jewel wasn't pretty. Never had been. Her nose was straight and small, her chin was square, her mouth was a bit too big and her eyes were Mississippi-mud brown. Ordinary features all. She did have an extraordinary body. Her long legs, small waist and ample breasts were the stuff of male dreams. But Mac was offended on Jewel's behalf to think that any man could want her because of her body and not because of who she was inside.

So, it's her mind you find attractive?

As a teenager, he had liked her sense of humor, her enthusiasm for life and her willingness to reach out to others. He hadn't seen much of the first two traits this time around, and he wasn't sure whether it was a continued willingness to reach out to others that had made her return to Camp LittleHawk or, as he suspected, a desire to retreat from the world.

Mac had no explanation for his response to Jewel except that he had been celibate for too long. What had happened when Jewel touched him was merely the healthy response of a male animal to a female of the species. The problem would be solved when he found himself a woman and satisfied the simple physiological need that had been too long denied. Which meant he had better make a trip into town sometime soon and find a willing woman.

"Do you want me to call the Templetons back and tell them your plans have changed and you won't be here, after all?" Jewel asked.

He shook his head. "I guess it won't hurt me to be nice to one little boy."

"If you'd rather not—"

"I said I would." He slid his leg off his knee and reached for his cane. "It's not that big a deal, Jewel."

She rose and reached for his arm to help him up.

He jerked away. "I'm not an invalid. I wish you'd stop trying to help me."

He saw the hurt look on her face, but that was better than having her know the sharp sexual response her touch had provoked. That would ruin everything. Better to have her think he was in a lousy mood than find out that he wanted to suck on her breasts or put his hand between her legs and seek the damp heat there.

"I'm going in to town today," he said, realizing he'd better get away for a while and cool down.

"Perfect! I need some things from the hardware store. Could you give me a lift?"

Thank God she wasn't looking at him, or she would have known something was wrong. He opened his mouth to refuse and said, "Sure. Why not? Give me a chance to change into a shirt and jeans and some boots first."

She gave him a blazing smile that made his groin pull up tight. Hell. He'd better find himself a woman. And soon.

No doubt about it, Jewel thought. Mac had been acting strange all day. Every errand he had run had taken him to the opposite end of town from her. Although they had made plans to meet for lunch at the Stanton Hotel Café, he hadn't arrived until she was nearly finished eating. She was sitting on one of the 1950's chrome seats at the lunch counter when he finally showed up, grabbed a cup of coffee, said he wasn't hungry, remembered something else he had to do in town and took off again.

If Jewel hadn't known better, she would have said he didn't want to be anywhere near her. But that was silly. They were best friends.

They had agreed to meet in the parking lot near the bank at four o'clock where Mac had parked his extended cab Chevy pickup and head back to Hawk's Pride. Jewel was sitting on the fender of the truck when Mac finally returned.

"You could have sat inside," he said. "It wasn't locked."

"It was too hot with the windows rolled up, and I needed a key to get them down," she said, lifting the hair at her nape to catch the late afternoon breeze. She heard him suck in a breath and had turned in his direction when a female voice distracted them both.

"Peter? Is that you?"

Jewel rose and turned at the same time as Mac to find a red-headed, green-eyed woman standing beside the bed of the pickup.

"Eve?" Mac replied in tones of astonishment that rivaled the woman's.

She ran toward him, and Jewel watched in awe as Mac dropped his cane to surround the woman with his arms. Jewel hurried to pick it up, certain Mac would lose his balance and need it at any moment.

Only he didn't.

Either he was stronger on his feet than he had been two days ago, or the petite redhead was stronger than she looked.

"Peter. Peter," the woman said, her gaze searching his face.

"Eve. I can't believe it's you!" he replied, his eyes searching her face with equal delight.

He suddenly looked around for Jewel and reached out a hand to draw her closer. "Jewel, this is Evelyn Latham. Eve and I dated for a while in college. She's the only person I ever let get away with calling me Peter."

Eve simpered. "It's because you have such a big—"

"Yeah," Mac cut her off. "Eve, this is my friend, Jewel Whitelaw. I'm spending some time at her parents' ranch."

Jewel saw Eve take one look at her plain face and her unshapely clothes and dismiss her as no competition.

Eve then gave Mac a quick, but thorough, once-over. "You look *purrr*fectly fit to me."

Jewel cringed at the way the woman drew out the word with her Texas accent. Eve obviously appreciated Mac's assets—one of which she had apparently seen up close and personal—and the sexual invitation she extended was clear, at least to Jewel.

Mac must have heard it, too. "What are you doing with yourself these days, Eve? I haven't seen you since...when was it?"

"Graduation day from UT, two years ago."

He looked for a ring on her left hand, but didn't find one. "I thought you were going to marry Joe Bob Struthers."

"I only told you that because I was mad at you for dumping me after only three dates...just when we were getting to know each other so well."

He's probably slept with her, Jewel thought. She couldn't fault Mac's taste. The woman was gorgeous. She wore a clingy green St. John knit dress, with a fashionable gold chain draped across her flat stomach.

Mac gave Eve a look that suggested he would be happy to pick up where they had left off. "So you're not a married woman?"

"I'm free as a bird," Eve confirmed.

"I thought you were a Dallas girl, born and bred. What are you doing out here in the far reaches of northwest Texas?" Mac asked.

"My dad bought the bank here in town. I've been the assistant manager for the past year."

"I never expected any less of you," Mac said, "graduating the way you did at the top of the class."

Pretty *and* smart. That was a lethal combination, Jewel thought. Not that Jewel was competing in any way with Evelyn Latham for Mac's affection. She and Mac were just friends. But she couldn't help thinking that if Mac got involved with Eve, she would see a whole lot less of him, and she did enjoy his company.

"What are you doing here?" Eve asked Mac in return. "Aren't you supposed to be off playing football, or something like that?"

Jewel couldn't believe the woman had dated Mac but had no idea when the football season began and ended.

"It's the off-season," Mac said with an indulgent smile. For the first time it must have occurred to him that he didn't have his cane. He looked around for it, and Jewel handed it to him.

He took it and leaned on it. "I'm here visiting friends and recuperating from a football injury."

"You were hurt?" Eve asked.

Jewel rolled her eyes. Mac gave her a nudge with his hip, and she straightened up.

"You could say that," Mac said. "I guess you didn't hear about it."

Eve turned her mouth down in a delightful moue. "As you very well know I never cared much for football, only for the way you looked in those tight pants."

The sexual innuendo was even more blatant this time, and Jewel felt uncomfortable standing there listening to it. "Sorry we can't stay," she said. "Mac was just giving me ride home."

The pout that appeared on Eve's face would have looked right at home on a three-year-old. "Oh, Mac. I was hoping you'd have dinner with me."

"I still can," Mac said. "I'll take Jewel home and come back. What time and where?"

"How about eight o'clock? My house." She gave Mac an address in the newest condominium complex in town.

Mac grinned. "I'll be there."

"Don't dress up," Eve purred. "I want you to be comfortable."

"You got it," Mac said.

With Jewel standing right there, Eve went up on tiptoe and gave Mac a kiss right on the mouth. Jewel noticed Mac's arm went around her waist quick enough to draw her close, so the kiss wasn't unwelcome. It went on a long time, and from the way their mouths shifted, their tongues were involved.

Jewel stood frozen, unable to move. At last the kiss broke, and Mac shot her a quick, embarrassed look. It was too little, too late. He should have thought of her feelings before he practically made love to another woman right in front of her.

Only it shouldn't have mattered if he kissed somebody else. They were only friends.

"See you at eight," Mac said as he backed away from Eve.

"I'll be waiting," Eve said in a sultry voice.

Mac went around to his side of the truck without stopping to open Jewel's door. Not that she needed her door opened for her. She got in and sat near the edge of the seat, opening the window as soon as Mac started the truck and sticking her elbow out.

"Sorry about that," he said after a few

minutes. "I shouldn't have embarrassed you like that."

"I wasn't embarrassed," Jewel said. "Kiss all the girls you want. It doesn't make any difference to me."

"All right. If that's the way you feel. Just so you don't worry, I may not be back tonight."

"Thanks for telling me," Jewel said. "I won't wait up for you."

She really didn't care. He was just a friend. He'd had another girlfriend most of the time she had known him. This was no different. Except, the whole time she had watched Mac kissing Eve the most stunning thought had been running through her head.

I wish it were me.

Chapter 4

Mac went to Evelyn Latham's house with one purpose in mind: to get laid. Eve opened the door wearing a clingy red velour jumpsuit that sent a wake-up call to his body. He was sure all it would take was one kiss to get the old machinery back into action. So he pulled her into his arms and kissed her and…nothing. Not a damned thing happened.

He worried about the situation all through supper and all through the glass of merlot they enjoyed by the fire he started for her in the stone fireplace. When they ended up entwined on the

couch, he willed his body to react to the feel of
her lips against his, to the feel of her body beneath his hands. He felt the sweat pop out on
his forehead. But…nothing.

This wasn't supposed to happen. Just because
he hadn't made love with a woman didn't mean
that he didn't want to. He wanted to, all right.
His damned body just wasn't cooperating! He
made up some excuse for why he couldn't
stay—his aching leg had come in handy for
once—and bolted.

He drove around for two hours wondering if
he was going to spend the rest of his life a virgin. What the hell had gone wrong? He hadn't
been able to figure it out but had finally conceded that driving around all night wasn't going
to give him any answers.

Then he remembered he had told Jewel he
would probably be out all night. What was she
going to think if he came back early?

That you don't take your time.

Yeah. Probably she'd just think he'd gotten
his fill of Eve already. He couldn't imagine getting his fill of Jewel in bed. The thought of
touching her skin, the feel of her hair against his
body, the smell of her.

His body stirred in response.

It's too late, buddy. You already missed the party. You have to do that when there's a flesh-and-blood woman around.

And when it was some other woman besides Jewel. It wasn't going to do him any good getting aroused by thoughts of her, because she was the last person he could have sex with.

Hell, his leg *was* killing him. He had some exercises he was supposed to do at night that he hadn't done to relax the muscles. He needed to lay his leg flat in bed. He needed...he needed to know he could function as a man. The situation with Eve had been disturbing because it had never happened to him before. What if something was wrong with him? What if all those operations had done something to his libido?

You don't have any problem responding to Jewel.

He recalled his feelings for Jewel, the ones that had sent him off in search of another woman. They weren't as comforting as they should have been. He had felt the same sort of semi-arousal with Eve before he kissed her, but when it came time for action, his body had opted out.

Mac cut the pickup engine at the back door to the cottage. No lights. At least he'd be spared the ignominy of Jewel seeing him sneaking in àt two in the morning. He didn't want to have to make some explanation about why he was home early. He wasn't about to tell her the truth, and he hated like hell to lie.

He eased the kitchen door open—Western doors were rarely locked, even in this day and age—and slipped inside.

"Hi."

Mac nearly lost his balance and fell. "What the hell are you doing sitting here in the dark?"

He reached for the light switch, but Jewel said, "Don't."

The rough, raw sound of her voice, as though she had been crying, stayed his hand. He remained where he was, waiting for his eyes to adjust to the dark. He finally located her in the shadows. She was sitting with her elbows perched on the kitchen table, her face buried in her hands.

He limped over, scraped a chair closer and sat beside her. He felt her stiffen as he laid an arm across her shoulder. "Are you all right?

"I'm fine."

"You don't sound fine. You sound like you've been crying."

"I didn't think you'd be back tonight."

Which meant she had expected to have the privacy to cry without being disturbed. It didn't explain *why* she had been crying. She tried to rise, but he kept his arm around her and pressed her back down. "I'm here, Jewel."

"Why is that, Mac? I can't imagine any woman throwing you out. Which means you left on your own. What happened?"

This was exactly the scene Mac had been hoping to avoid. "She...uh...we...uh..."

"Don't tell me Eve didn't make a pass."

"She did," Mac conceded reluctantly.

"Then why aren't you spending the night with her?"

"I...uh...that sort of thing can give a woman ideas."

"I see."

"You do?"

"Sure. Spend the whole night in a woman's bed, and she tends to think you might be serious about her. Everyone knows you're a love'em and leave'em kind of guy."

"I am? I mean, I suppose I am. I haven't

found a woman I'd want to settle down with who'd have me.'' That was certainly no lie.

Eve had wanted him, all right. It should have been the easiest thing in the world to take her in his arms and make love to her. The situation had been perfect: willing woman, intelligent, not a total stranger, attractive—hell, absolutely beautiful. And it had been absolutely impossible.

Mac bit back the sound of frustration that sought voice.

''You should go to bed if you're going to get up early and walk tomorrow,'' Jewel said.

''I'd rather sit here with you,'' Mac replied.

''I'd rather be alone.''

''Are you sure?''

''I'll be fine.''

Mac leaned over to kiss her softly on the temple. Her hair smelled of lilacs. It reminded him of warm, lazy summer days they had spent lying on the banks of the pond that bordered the Stonecreek Ranch. He resisted the urge to thread his fingers through her hair. It might comfort her, but it would drive him damn near crazy.

''Just know I'm here if you need me,'' he said. ''You'd better get to bed, too, because I'm expecting you to walk with me tomorrow.''

"I don't think that's a good idea. It would be better if you go alone."

He stared at her, wishing he could see the expression on her face. Moonlight filtered in through the kitchen window but left her mostly in shadow. "What's going on, Jewel? Why are you shutting me out?"

"I got along fine without you for six years, Mac. What makes you think I need you now?"

Mac was stunned as much by the virulence in her voice as by what she had said. "If you want me out of here, I'm gone."

She clutched his forearm as he rose, rubbing at her eyes with the knuckles of her other hand. "Don't leave. Don't leave."

He pulled her up and into his arms, and she grabbed him tight around his neck and sobbed against his shoulder. He rubbed her back with his open palms, aware suddenly that she was wearing a thin, sleeveless cotton nightgown and nothing else.

His body turned hard as a rock in two seconds flat.

His equipment worked all right. At the wrong time. With the wrong woman.

"Damn it all to hell," he muttered.

Jewel needed his comfort, not some male animal lusting after her. He kept their hips apart, not wanting his physical response to frighten or distress her. "Tell me what's wrong, Jewel. Let me help," he crooned in her ear.

"It's too embarrassing," she said, her face pressed tight against the curve of his shoulder.

"Nothing's too embarrassing for us to talk about, my little carbuncle."

She hiccuped a laugh. "Carbuncle? Isn't that an ugly inflammation—"

"It's a red precious stone. I swear."

She relaxed, chuckling, and it took all the willpower he had to keep from pulling her tight against him.

"You always could make me laugh," she said. "Oh, Mac, I wish you'd come back a long time ago. I missed you."

"And I missed you. Now tell me what's so embarrassing that you don't want to talk about it?"

She sighed, and her breasts swelled against his chest, soft and warm. His heartbeat picked up. Lord, she was dangerous. Why couldn't this have happened with Eve? Why did it have to be Jewel?

Her fingers began to play in the hair at his nape. He wondered if she knew what she was doing to him and decided she couldn't possibly. She wouldn't purposely turn him on. What she wanted was comfort from a friend. And he intended to give it to her.

But he wasn't any more able to stop his body from responding than he had been capable of making it respond. All he could do was try to ignore the part of him that was insisting he do something. He focused his attention on Jewel. She needed his help.

"Tell me what's wrong," he urged.

"I wish things were different, that's all."

"Don't we all?" he said, thinking of his own situation. "But frankly, that doesn't sound embarrassing enough to keep to yourself. What is it? Got bucked off your horse? Happens to the best of us. Broke a dish? Do it all the time. If you broke a heart I might worry, but you can always buy another dish."

She laughed. The bubbly, effervescent sound he hadn't heard for six years. He pulled her close and rocked her in his arms in the old, familiar, brotherly way.

She stiffened, and he realized what he had

done. His hips, with the hard bulge in front, were pressed tight against hers. There was no way she could mistake his condition.

"Damn, Jewel," he said, backing away from her, putting her at arm's length and gripping her hands tightly in his.

He smiled, but she didn't smile back.

When she pulled free, he let her go. "We can still talk," he said, wanting her to stay, wanting to confess the truth to her. She was still his best friend. But somehow things had changed. He couldn't tell her everything, not the most private things. Not anymore.

Maybe he had been wrong to expect her to confide in him. Maybe she felt the same awkwardness he did, the distance that had never been there before. A distance he had put there, because he saw her not just as a friend, but as a woman he wanted to kiss and touch.

"I'm going to bed, Mac."

"Will you walk with me tomorrow?"

"I don't think—"

"Please, Jewel. You're my best friend. I'd really like the company."

She hesitated so long, he thought she was going to refuse. "All right, Mac. I suppose I owe

you that much.'' She turned and left without another word.

He waited until her bedroom door closed before he moved, afraid that if he did, he would
go after her.

He wondered what had been troubling her. He
wondered what she would have done if he had
lowered his head and sucked on her breasts
through the thin cotton. Blood pulsed through
his rock-hard body, and he swore under his
breath.

Mac went to bed, but he didn't sleep. He
tossed and turned, troubled by vivid erotic fantasies of himself and Jewel Whitelaw. *Their legs
entangled, their bodies entwined, his tongue
deep in her mouth, his shaft deep inside her. She
was calling to him, calling his name.*

Mac awoke tangled in the sheets, his body
hot, hard and ready, his heart racing. And all
alone.

He heard Jewel calling from outside the door.
''Mac. Are you awake?'' She knocked twice
quietly. ''It's time to walk.''

Mac groaned. ''I'll be with you in a minute.''
As soon as he was decent.

From the look of Jewel at the breakfast table,

she hadn't slept any better than he had. She was wearing something even less attractive than the sweatshirt and cutoffs she had worn previously. It didn't matter. He saw her naked.

Mac shook his head to clear it. The vision of her breasts, large and luscious as peaches, and her long, slim legs wrapped around his waist, remained as vivid as ever.

"Are you all right?" Jewel asked.

"Fine. Let's go."

She chattered the whole way to the canyon, but he would have been hard-pressed to remember a word of what she had said or his own responses.

Everything was different. Something was missing. And something had been added.

He wanted their old relationship back. He was determined to quench any desire he might feel for her, so things could get back to an even footing. He figured the best way to start was to bring the subject out into the open and deal with it. On the walk back to the house, he did.

"About what happened last night... It shouldn't have happened." His comment was vague, but he knew she understood exactly what he meant when pink roses blossomed on her cheekbones.

She shrugged. "I was just a woman in a skimpy nightgown."

"Jewel, I—"

She stopped and turned to him, looking into his eyes, her gaze earnest. "Please, Mac. Can we pretend it never happened?"

He gave a relieved sigh. "That's exactly what I'd like to do. It was an accident. I never intended for it to happen. I wish I could promise it won't happen again, but—" He shot her a chagrined look. "I'll be sure you're never embarrassed again. Am I forgiven?"

"There's no need—"

"Just say yes," he said.

"Yes."

She turned abruptly and started walking again, and he followed after her.

"I'm glad that's over with," he said. "I can't afford to lose a friend as good as you, Jewel."

"And I can't afford to lose a friend like you, Mac."

Jewel's eyes were as brown and sad as a motherless calf. Mac wished she had told him why she was crying last night. He wished she had let him comfort her. If she ever gave him another chance, he was going to do it right. He wasn't going to let his hormones get in the way of their friendship.

When they got back to the house, she hurried up the back steps ahead of him. "I get the shower first!"

"We could always share," he teased. He could have bitten his tongue out. That sort of sexual innuendo had to cease.

To his relief, Jewel gave him a wide smile and said, "In your dreams, Mac! I'll try to save you a little hot water."

Then she was gone.

Mac settled on the back stoop and rubbed the calf muscles of his injured leg. It was getting easier to walk. Practice was helping. And it would get easier to treat Jewel as merely a friend. All he had needed was a little more practice at that, too.

After he had showered, Mac made a point of seeking Jewel out, determined to work on reestablishing their friendship. He found her in the barn, cleaning stalls and shoveling in new hay for the dozen or so ponies Camp LittleHawk kept available for horseback rides. "Can I help?" he said.

"There's another pitchfork over by the door. Be my guest."

Mac noticed she didn't even look up from her work. Not a very promising sign. He grabbed the pitchfork and went to work in the stall next to the one she was working in. "I thought your mom usually hired someone to do this kind of heavy labor."

"I don't have anything better to do with my time," Jewel said.

"Why not?" Mac asked. "Pretty girl like you ought to be out enjoying herself."

Jewel stuck her pitchfork into the hay and turned to stare at him. "I enjoy my work."

"I'm sure you do," he said, throwing a pitchfork of manure into the nearby wheelbarrow. "But there's a time for work and a time for play. I don't see you doing enough playing."

"I'm a grown-up woman, Mac. Playing is for kids."

"You're never too old to play, Jewel." Mac filled his pitchfork with clean straw and threw it up over the stall so it landed on Jewel's head.

She came out of her stall sputtering and pick-

ing straw out of her mouth, mad as a peeled
rattler. She confronted him, hands on hips and
said, "That wasn't funny!"

He set his pitchfork against the stall and
laughed. "I think you look darned cute with
straw sticking out of your hair every whichaway." He headed toward her to help pull out
some of the straw.

When he got close enough, she gave him a
shove that sent him onto his behind. Only the
straw Mac landed in wasn't clean. He gave a
howl of outrage and struggled up out of the
muck, glaring at the stain on the back of his
jeans. "What'd you do that for?"

She grinned. "I think you look darned cute,
all covered with muck."

"You know this means war."

"No, Mac. We're even now. Don't—"

He lunged toward her, caught her by the waist
and threw her up over his shoulder in a fireman's
carry.

"Watch out for your leg!" Jewel cried.
"You're going to hurt yourself carrying me like
this."

"My leg is fine," Mac growled. "Good
enough to get you where I want you."

Mac headed for the short stack of hay at one end of the barn and when he got there, dropped Jewel into it. When she tried to jump free, he came down on top of her and pinned her hands on either side of her.

"Mac," she said breathlessly, laughing. "Get up."

"I want to play some more, Emerald, my dear," he said sprinkling her hair with hay.

"You're more green than I am," she taunted.

Mac took a look at the back of his jeans. "Yes, and I think you should pay a forfeit for that."

"You can have the shower first," she said with a bubbly laugh. "You need it!"

His laugh was cut off when he realized that what he really wanted was a kiss. He stared at her curving mouth, at the way her nose wrinkled when she laughed, at the teasing sparkle in her brown eyes. "I think I'll take something now."

He watched her face sober when she realized what he intended. He knew she must be able to feel his arousal, cradled as he was between her jean-clad thighs. He waited for her to tell him to let go, that the game was over. She stared up at him with luminous eyes and slicked her tongue quickly, nervously over her lips. But she didn't say get up or get off. And she didn't say no.

Friends, Mac. Not lovers. Friends.

Mac made himself kiss her eyelids closed before he kissed each cheek and then her nose and then…her forehead.

He rose abruptly and pulled her to her feet. She was dizzy, because her eyes had been closed, so he was forced to hold her in his arms until she was steady. She felt so good there, so very right. And so very wrong.

"I'm sorry, Jewel," he said. "That was totally out of line."

She took a deep breath and let it out. "Yes, I suppose it was. I think it's your turn to pay a forfeit, Mac."

He tensed. "What did you have in mind?"

She reached out, and for a moment he thought she was going to lay her hand on his chest and give him another shove. Instead, she grasped a nearby pitchfork and held it out to him. "You get to finish what I started. I'm going to get another shower and wash off all this itchy straw."

"Hey! That's not fair," he protested.

But she had already turned and stalked away.

"You and your bright ideas," Mac muttered

to himself as he pitched manure into the wheel-barrow. "What were you thinking? Maybe you could throw straw around when you were kids and it was funny, but there was nothing funny about what almost happened in that haystack. What if you'd kissed her lips? How would you have felt when she got upset?

How do you know she'd have been upset?

Mac mused over that question for the next hour as he finished cleaning stalls. Actually, Jewel had seemed more upset that he hadn't kissed her lips. Could she have feelings for him that weren't merely friendly?

Don't even think about it, Macready. The woman's off-limits. She's your friend, and she needs your friendship. Concentrate on somebody else's needs for a change and forget what you want.

Mac knew why he was having all these lurid thoughts about Jewel. He probably would be having such thoughts about any woman he came in close contact with at this stage in his life. It didn't help that Jewel turned him on so hard and fast.

Get over it, Mac.

"I intend to," Mac muttered as he set the

pitchfork back where it belonged and headed for the house. "Jewel is my friend. And that's the way it's going to stay."

At the end of two weeks Mac was walking the mile to the canyon without the aid of a cane and doing it in seven minutes flat. Jewel had difficulty keeping up with him when he broke into a jog. His leg was getting better; hers never would. She could picture him moving away from her, going on with his life, leaving her behind. She was going to miss him. She was going to miss playing with him.

The scene in the barn hadn't been repeated. Nor had Mac teased her or taunted her or done any of the playful things he might have done when they were teenagers. He had become a serious grown-up over the past two weeks. She hadn't realized how much she had needed him to play with her. To her surprise, she hadn't been intimidated or frightened by him in the barn. Not even when she had thought he might kiss her.

She had wanted that kiss, she realized, and been sorely disappointed when he kissed her forehead instead. Then she'd realized he had been carried away by their physical closeness, and when he'd realized it was her—his old friend, Jewel—he had backed off. He liked her, but not that way. They were just friends.

It should have been enough. But lately, Jewel was realizing she wanted more. She was going to have to control those feelings, or she would ruin everything. Mac would be leaving soon enough. She didn't want to drive him away by asking for things from him he wasn't willing to give.

"Hey," she called ahead to him. "How about taking a break at the bottom of the canyon."

"You got it." He dropped onto the warm, sandy ground with his back against the stone wall that bore the primitive Native American drawings and sifted the soil through his fingers. She sank down across from him, leaning back on her palms, her legs in front of her.

"You'll be running full out by this time next week," she said.

"I expect so."

"I won't be coming with you then."

"Why not?"

She sat up and rubbed at the sore muscles in her thigh. "I can't keep up with you, Mac." In more ways than one. He would be going places, while she stayed behind.

Mac dusted off his hands on his shorts, scooted around to her side and, as though it were the most natural thing in the world, began to massage her thigh. She hadn't let a man touch her like that since she had broken her engagement. Chill bumps rose on her skin at the feel of Mac's callused fingers on her flesh. It felt amazingly good. It dawned on her that she didn't feel the least bit afraid. But then, this was Mac. He would never hurt her.

The past two weeks of waiting for Mac to repeat his behavior in the barn had been wonderful and horrible. She loved being with Mac. And she dreaded it. Since the night he had come home early from Evelyn Latham's house, he had remained an avuncular friend. He had been a tremendous help planning activities for the children. He had made her laugh often. But with the exception of that brief, unfulfilled promise in the barn, there was nothing the least bit sexual in his behavior toward her.

She was unsure of what her feelings were for Mac, but there was no doubting her profound physical reaction to his touch. It was difficult not to look at him as a virile, attractive man, rather than merely as a friend. Even now, she couldn't keep her eyes off of him.

The Texas sun had turned him a warm bronze, but a white strip of flesh showed around the waist of his running shorts, confirming the hidden skin was lighter. She caught herself wondering what he would look like without the shorts.

"How does that feel?" he asked as he massaged her thigh. "Better?"

She nodded because she couldn't speak. *It feels wonderful.* She wanted his hands to move higher, between her legs. As though she had willed it, his fingertips moved upward on her thigh. She let him keep up the massage, because it felt good. Then stopped him because it felt too good.

"Wait." She gripped his wrist with her hand, afraid that he would read her mind and realize that the last thing she wanted him to do was stop.

"If you exercised more, maybe your limp wouldn't be so bad," he said.

She brushed his hand away from where it lingered on her flesh. "One leg is slightly shorter than the other, Mac. That isn't going to change with exercise."

"It might with surgery. They can do remarkable things these days. Have you thought about—"

"What's going on here, Mac?" she interrupted. "You never said a word to me in the past about my limp. You always told me to ignore it, to pretend it didn't exist, that it didn't keep me from being who I am. What's changed?"

Mac backed up against the wall again. His gaze was concentrated on the sand he began once more sifting through his fingers.

"Mac?" she persisted. "Answer me."

He looked up at her, his eyes searching her face. "How can you stand it—not being able to run?"

She shrugged. "I manage."

"I'd hate it if something like that happened to me."

"Something like that *has* happened to you."

He shook his head. "Uh-uh. I'm temporarily out of commission. I'm going to be as good as new."

Did he really believe that? Jewel wondered.

Yes, he had made astonishing progress in two weeks, but even she could see the effort it had taken. One look at his leg—at the scar tissue on his leg—suggested there was never going to be as much muscle to work with as there had been in the past. "What if you can never run again like you used to, Mac? What if you can't get back to where you were?"

"I will."

"What if you can't?"

"I'll be playing again in the fall. Count on it."

"You're purposely avoiding my question. *What if you can't?*"

He rose, but it took obvious effort to do so without the cane. She said nothing while he accomplished the feat—a minor miracle considering the condition he'd been in two weeks ago.

"Let's go," he said gruffly, reaching down to help her to her feet.

She shoved his hand out of the way. "I'm not a cripple, either, Mac," she said. "I can manage on my own."

"Damn it, Jewel! What do you want from me?"

"Honesty," she said, rising and standing toe

to toe with him, her eyes focused on his. "You never used to lie to me, Mac. Or to yourself."

"What is it you want to hear me say? I won't quit playing football! It's all I ever wanted to do."

"You wanted to be a paleontologist."

"That's what I said. But inside—" he thumped his bare chest with his fist "—all I ever dreamed about, all I ever wanted to do was run like the wind and catch footballs. It was just so impossible for so long, I never let myself hope for it too much. But I made it happen. And I'm not going to give it up!"

Jewel felt her heart skip a beat. She hadn't known. She hadn't realized. If what Mac said was true, then he was facing a much greater crisis than she had imagined.

"Avoiding reality isn't going to make it go away, Mac," she said gently. "You have to face your demons."

"Like you have?" Mac retorted.

Jewel's face blanched. She turned her back on him and headed up the trail toward the mouth of the canyon.

"Jewel, wait," Mac said as he hurried after her. He grabbed her arm to stop her. "If you're going to insist on honesty from me, how about a little from you?''

''What is it you want to know? You know everything,'' she said bitterly. ''You're the only one who does!''

He gave her an incredulous look. ''You never told anyone else? What about your fiancé?''

She shook her head violently.

''Why the hell not?''

''I couldn't tell Jerry. I just couldn't!''

In days gone by he would have put an arm around her to offer her comfort. But things had changed somehow in the two weeks since they had met again. His eyes offered emotional support, instead. ''God, Jewel. That's a heavy burden to be carrying around all by yourself.''

''I'm managing all right.''

''What happened to Jerry What's-his-name? Why did you call off the wedding?''

''I couldn't... I wasn't able... I could never...''

She saw the dawning comprehension in his eyes. ''I don't want or need your pity!'' She tried to run from him in awkward, hobbling strides, but he quickly caught up to her and pulled her into his arms.

''Don't run away,'' he said, his arms closing

tightly around her. "It doesn't matter, Jewel. It'll get better with time."

She made a keening sound in her throat. "It's been six years. I can't forget what happened, Mac. I can't get it out of my head. Jerry was so patient, but when he tried to make love to me, I couldn't let him do it. I couldn't!" Her throat ached. A hot tear spilled onto her cheek and a sob broke free.

She grasped Mac tight around the waist and pressed her face against his bare chest, sobbing as she never had on the day she had been attacked or at any time since then. She had been too numb with shock to cry six years ago. And she had been too full of guilt when she broke up with Jerry to allow herself the release of tears.

"Shh. Shh," Mac crooned as he rocked her in his arms. "It's all right. It doesn't matter. Everything will be all right."

She felt his lips against her hair, soothing, comforting, and then his hands on either side of her face as he raised it to kiss her tear-wet eyelids. He kissed her nose and her cheeks and finally her mouth. His lips were firm, yet gentle, against her own. She yielded to the insistent pressure of his mouth, her lips soft and damp beneath his. He kissed her again, his lips brushing across hers and sending a surprising frisson of desire skittering down her spine. *Oh, Mac...*

She pressed her lips back against his and heard a sharp intake of breath. She froze, then stepped back and stared up at him in confusion.

He opened his mouth to speak and shut it again, obviously upset and looking for a way to explain what had happened between them. She wondered if he had felt it, too, the wondrous stirring inside, the need to merge into one another. What if he did? Oh, God. It would ruin everything. She couldn't...and he would never... She took another step back from him.

"Wait, Jewel. Don't go," he said, reaching out a hand to her. "We have to talk about this."

"What is there to say?"

He took a step closer, and it took all her willpower not to run from him. She felt an equally driving need to press herself against him, which she resisted just as fiercely.

"I don't want what just happened to spoil things between us," he said, his voice anguished. "I could see you needed comfort, and I...I got a little carried away."

"All right, Mac. If that's the way you want it." She would ruin everything if she pressed for more. He obviously wanted things to stay the same between them. He wanted them to be friends. That was probably for the best. What if she tried loving him and failed, as she had with Jerry? She would lose everything. She couldn't bear that.

"What's wrong, Jewel?"

She mentally and physically squared her shoulders. "I shouldn't have fallen apart like that. I've spent a lot of time in counseling putting what happened six years ago behind me."

"Have you?"

"I'm as over it as I'm ever going to get," she conceded with a rueful twist of her mouth. "It doesn't matter, Mac, really. I have the kids at camp. I have friends. I have a full life."

"Without a man in it," he said flatly. "Or children."

She arched a brow. "Who says a woman needs a man in her life? And there are lots of children at Camp LittleHawk who need me."

He held up his hands in surrender. "You win. I'm not going to argue the point."

Jewel released a breath that became a sigh, glad the subject was closed. "We'd better get back to the house."

He looked as though he wanted to continue the discussion, but she knew that wouldn't help the situation. She decided levity was what was needed. "I hope you saved some energy, because I know for a fact Colt will be waiting for you when you get back to the house.''

Mac groaned. "I forgot. He's going to throw me some passes.''

"I can always send him away.''

"I suppose I can catch a few passes and keep him happy.''

"And keep who happy?''

Mac grinned. "So I'm looking forward to it. Think what that'll mean to you.''

She gave him a quizzical look. If Mac was up to catching passes, it meant he was getting well. If he was getting well, it meant he would be leaving soon. She wanted to hear him say it. Maybe then she could stop fantasizing about him. "What will it mean to me?'' she asked.

Twin dimples appeared in his cheeks. "You get the shower first.''

Jewel laughed. It beat the heck out of crying.

Chapter 5

If there was one thing Colt Whitelaw wanted more than he wanted to fly jets someday, it was to have Jennifer Wright look at him the way she looked at his best friend, Huckleberry Duncan. Jenny didn't even care that Huck had a stupid name. When Huck was around, Jenny wouldn't have noticed if Colt dropped dead at her feet. She only had eyes for Huck.

Which meant Colt got to spend a lot of time watching her when she wasn't looking. Jenny wasn't what most guys would have called pretty. She was short and skinny, her nose was too long and her teeth were slightly crooked. But she had the prettiest eyes he'd ever seen. Jenny's eyes were about the bluest blue eyes could get.

It wasn't just the color of them that he found attractive. When he looked into Jenny's eyes he saw the pledge of warmth, the promise of humor and depths of wisdom far beyond what a fourteen-year-old girl ought to possess.

Jenny might be the same age as him and Huck, but it seemed she had grown up faster—in more ways than one. For a couple of years she'd been taller than Huck. This past year Huck had caught up and passed her. Colt had always been taller than Jenny. Not that she'd noticed.

This past year something else had happened to Jenny. She had started becoming a woman. Colt felt like walloping Huck when Huck kidded her about the bumps she was sprouting up front, but when she bent over laughing and her shirt fell away, he had sneaked a peek at them. They were pure white and pink-tipped. He had turned away pretty quick because the whole time he was looking, he couldn't seem to breathe.

His body did strange things these days whenever she was around. His stomach turned upside down and his heart started to race and his body embarrassed him by doing other things that were still pretty new and felt amazingly good and grown-up. He had it bad for Jenny Wright. Not that he'd ever let her or Huck know about it. Because Huck felt about Jenny the way Jenny felt about Huck. It was true love both ways. When they got old enough, Colt figured they'd marry for sure.

He kept his feelings to himself. He liked Huck too much to give him up as a friend. And it would have killed him to stop seeing Jenny. Even if she was always going to be Huck's girl.

"Hey, Colt. I thought you were going to throw me some passes," Huck said, giving him a friendly chuck on the shoulder.

Colt watched as Jenny climbed up onto the top rail of the corral near the new counselors' cottages and shoved her long blond ponytail back over her shoulder. "You gonna be all right up there?" he asked.

She laughed. "I'm not one of your mom's campers, Colt. I'm healthy as a horse. I'll be fine."

Colt couldn't help it if he worried about her. He didn't want her to fall and get hurt. Not that she appreciated his concern. He turned the football in his hands, finding the laces and placing his hands where he knew they needed to be.

''Go long!'' he shouted to Huck, who had already started to run over the uneven terrain, which was dotted with clumps of buffalo grass and an occasional prickly pear cactus.

Colt threw the ball with ease and watched it fall perfectly, gently into Huck's outstretched hands. Huck did a victory dance and spiked the ball.

''We are the greatest!'' Huck shouted, holding his pointed fingers upward on either side of him in the referee's signal for a touchdown.

They made a pretty good team, Colt conceded. About the best in the state. Both of them would likely be offered athletic scholarships to college. Huck was so rich—his father was a U.S. senator from Texas—he didn't need a scholarship to pay for college. Colt's family could easily afford to send him to college, too, but he kept playing football because he had heard it might help him get into the Air Force Academy.

If Huck had wanted to go to the Academy, his dad, the senator, could write a letter and get him appointed. Colt didn't have that advantage. He would never presume on his friendship with Huck to ask for that kind of favor from Senator Duncan. So he had to find another way to make sure he got in.

Huck retrieved the ball and started walking back toward Colt and Jenny. Colt took advantage of the opportunity to have Jenny's full attention. "He's pretty good," he said, knowing Huck was the one thing Jenny was always willing to discuss.

"He is, isn't he," she said, a worried frown forming between her brows.

"Something wrong with that?" Colt asked, leaning his elbow casually on the top rail next to Jenny's thigh where her cutoffs ended and her flesh began. Casual. Right. His mouth was bone-dry.

"I don't want him to go away," she said.

He watched her face as she watched Huck. "You think football will take him away?"

"No. Huck loves football, but I think he'd be willing to attend a college somewhere close just so we could be together. Only..." Her head swiveled suddenly, and she looked him right in the eye. "You're going to take him away."

He swallowed hard, his hormones going into overdrive as she continued staring at him. He managed to say, "I am?"

She nodded solemnly. "He's going to want to follow wherever you go, Colt, and I know your plans don't include staying here in Texas. I don't want to get left behind.''

Jenny was dirt-poor, and even if she could have gotten a scholarship to a college some-where else—which, with her brains, she proba-bly could—she had to stay at the Double D Ranch to help take care of her sick mother and four younger brothers.

"Huck would never leave you behind,'' Colt said seriously.

"He might not have any choice. Not if he went off to fly jets somewhere with you."

Colt felt angry, vulnerable and exposed. "How did you know about that? About me wanting to fly jets?"

She shrugged and slipped down off the top rail of the corral. "Huck and I don't have any secrets."

"He shouldn't have told you,'' Colt said, feel-ing his heart begin to thud at the closeness of her. He wanted her to step back so he could breathe, so he could think straight. Didn't she see what she was doing to him? "That was pri-vate information,'' he snapped. "It doesn't con-cern you."

Her fisted hands found her hips. "It does when Huck is thinking about going with you."

"I never asked him to come along," he retorted.

"Hey, you two! What're my two favorite people arguing about?" Huck said, grinning as he stepped between them and slipped an arm around each of their shoulders. Colt stood rigid beneath his arm. Huck still had the football in one hand, and Colt knocked it to the ground.

"Ask your girlfriend," he said, bending to retrieve the ball and pulling free of Huck's arm. "I've got to go find Mac Macready. I'm supposed to throw some passes to him this morning."

Huck left Jenny standing where she was and headed after Colt. "Macready's really here? I mean, I heard rumors in town he was, but I wasn't sure. You're really going to throw some balls to him?"

"I said I was, didn't I?" Colt stopped where he was and looked back over Huck's shoulder to where Jenny stood abandoned. Her expression said it all.

See what I mean? You lead. Huck follows.

It wasn't his fault. It had always been that way. If Jenny didn't like it, she didn't have to hang around. Colt turned back to Huck.

Huck's sandy hair had fallen over his brow

and into his eyes. His rarely combed hair, combined with his ski-slope nose and freckled cheeks and broad smile, gave him an affable appearance he deserved. Huck didn't make enemies. He wouldn't have hurt a fly. Colt was sure he hadn't meant to hurt Jenny's feelings. Huck just forgot to be thoughtful sometimes.

"What about Jenny?" Colt asked.

"Hey, Jenny," Huck called. "You want to hang around and meet Mac Macready?"

Jenny shook her head.

"See? She's not interested," Huck said. "But I am."

Colt sighed. "You want to stay?" he asked Huck.

"Does a cowboy wear spurs?" Huck replied with a lopsided grin.

They headed for the counselor's cottage where Mac was staying, leaving Jenny behind at the corral. Colt glanced over his shoulder at her. It looked for a moment like she might follow them. Then she turned to where her horse was tied to the corral next to Huck's, mounted up and loped the gelding in the direction of her family's ranch.

"You shouldn't ignore Jenny like that," Colt said, turning back to Huck.

Huck seemed to notice suddenly that she had left. "What did I do?" He shook his head. "Women. They're mysterious creatures, old buddy. Don't ever try to understand them. It's a waste of time."

"Why did you tell her about me wanting to fly?" Colt asked.

Huck looked chagrined. "We were talking about the future and...it just came up."

"Make sure it doesn't come up again," Colt said. "That's my business, and I don't want the whole world knowing about it." Especially when he was afraid he wasn't going to be able to make his dream come true.

"Jenny isn't the whole world," Huck argued. "She's my girlfriend. I have to tell her things."

"Just don't tell her things about me," Colt insisted.

"That's hard to avoid when you're my best friend," Huck said. "Besides, if we're going to be jet pilots—"

"When did my plans become yours?" Colt asked.

Huck grinned and pulled an arm tight around Colt's neck in a wrestler's hold. "We're friends forever, pal. Where you go, I go. If you fly, I fly. Enough said?"

Colt wished it were that simple. He wished he could express his desire to be a jet fighter pilot and expect his parents to be happy about it. He had never said a word to them, because he knew they would hate the idea.

He might be one of eight adopted kids, but his mom and dad had made it pretty clear over the past couple of years that he was the one they expected to inherit Hawk's Pride. They already had his life planned for him. They expected him to come back home after college to manage the ranch.

He was grateful to have Zach and Rebecca Whitelaw for parents. He loved them enough to want to make them happy by fulfilling their expectations. It just wasn't what he wanted for himself. He wanted to fly.

So he made his plans surreptitiously, meanwhile letting his father teach him everything he would need to know to run the cattle and quarter horse end of the business. His father had told him his sister Jewel was taking over Camp LittleHawk, and that was fine with him. Although he kind of liked the ranching business, he wanted absolutely nothing to do with a camp for kids with cancer.

Not that he didn't have sympathy for the

plight of all those sick kids. But he had learned his lesson early. He had befriended a couple of them when he was old enough to make friends. It was only later, when he asked why they hadn't returned the following summer, that he learned the awful truth. Sometimes sick people died.

It was a sobering lesson: *Illness could rob you of people you loved.* He had found a child's solution to the problem that had stood him in good stead. He stayed away from sick people. Which was why he hadn't been to Jenny's house much, even though Huck went there a lot. Her mom was dying slowly but surely of breast cancer.

Colt might have argued further with Huck, except he caught sight of Mac Macready coming around the corner of the house with his sister, Jewel.

"Hey!" Colt called. "Ready to catch a few passes?"

"You bet," Mac called back.

Colt looked for signs of reluctance or resignation on Mac's face. After all, Colt was just a kid. He didn't see anything but delight.

"Just give me a minute," Mac said with a smile and a wave. "Be right with you." He turned and said something in Jewel's ear, then headed in Colt's direction.

* * *

Jewel heard the kitchen screen door open and called, "Is that you, Mac?"

"Jewel?"

"Colt?" At the sound of her brother's frightened voice, Jewel hurried from her bedroom wearing an oversized plaid Western shirt, jeans and boots, her hair still wet from her shower. She met Colt halfway to the kitchen. "What's wrong?"

Her brother stood white-faced before her. "It's Mac. He fell."

Oh, dear God. "Should I call an ambulance?"

"I don't know," Colt said, his hands visibly trembling. "I thought maybe you ought to come and see for yourself first. It was awful, Jewel. One minute Mac was fine, and then Huck tackled him and…he didn't get up."

"Huck *tackled* him? What on earth were you boys thinking, Colt? You know Mac's recovering from surgery!"

"We thought it would be more fun—"

"Did he hit his head when he fell?"

"I don't think so. I think—"

Before Jewel could make the decision whether to call 911, Mac appeared at the kitchen door, one arm around Huck's shoulder, the other pressed against the thigh of his scarred leg.

Colt had been pale, but Mac's face was completely drained of blood. His teeth were gritted against the pain, and he was leaning heavily on Huck Duncan's shoulder and favoring his leg. It took her a second to realize it wasn't his poor, wounded and scarred left leg he was favoring, it was the other one. Now both legs were injured!

"What happened?" she asked as she crossed quickly to hold the screen door open for him. As soon as she moved, Colt seemed to wake from his shocked trance and took a place on Mac's other side. The two boys helped him keep his weight off both legs as they eased him through the kitchen and onto the sofa in the living room.

While the boys stood awkwardly at her side, Jewel dropped to her knees and eased Mac's foot up onto a rawhide stool that Grandpa Garth had given her one Christmas, a relic of bygone days at his ranch, Hawk's Way. Then she started untying the laces of Mac's athletic shoe.

"I can do that," he said, trying to brush her hands away.

"Sure you can, but let me," she insisted. She eased off the shoe and the sock beneath it and immediately saw the problem. His ankle was swelling. "Can you move it?" she asked.

Slowly, hissing in a breath, he rotated the ankle. "Doesn't feel broken," he said. "I've had enough sprains to recognize one when I see it. Damn. This is all I needed."

"I'm sorry, Mr. Macready," Huck said in an anguished voice. "I didn't mean to hurt you."

Mac looked up at the boy and said, "Call me Mac. And it wasn't your fault, Huck. Your tackle wasn't what caused the problem. I just didn't see that gopher hole soon enough."

Jewel watched him smile at the boy, pretending it was no big deal, when she knew very well it was. This was a setback, no doubt about it.

"But your leg—" Huck protested, his eyes skipping from the awful scars on Mac's left leg to the swelling on his right ankle. "How're you gonna walk now?"

"One step at a time," Mac quipped with an easy grin. "Fortunately, I brought a cane with me. That should help matters some."

Jewel turned to Colt and said, "Wrap some ice in a towel and bring it here. You go help him, Huck."

When they were both gone, she gently moved the ankle. "Are you sure it isn't broken?"

He sighed. It was a sound of disgust. "It's a sprain, Jewel. Not even a bad one."

"I should have warned you about gopher holes," she said.

"I didn't step in a gopher hole," he said quietly, looking at the hands he held fisted against his thighs.

"Then what—" She saw the truth in the wary look he gave her. His leg—his *right* leg—must not have supported him. She reached out a hand, and he clutched it with one of his.

She didn't offer him words of comfort. She could see from the grim look on his face that words wouldn't change what had happened. She didn't point out the obvious—that his football career was over. He had to see that for himself.

But if she had thought this accident would make Mac quit, he quickly disabused her of the notion.

"This'll slow down my rehabilitation some," he said. "Will you mind if I hang around a little longer? I know camp's starting in a day or so—"

She rose to her feet, her hand coming free of his. "Of course you can stay!" she said, her voice unnaturally sharp. She didn't want him to go away. She liked having him here. But she couldn't believe he was ignoring the implications of this injury. How long was he going to go on batting his head against the wall? Couldn't he see the truth? Didn't he understand what this accident meant?

"Mac—"

He cut her off with a shake of his head. "Don't say it. Don't even suggest it."

"Suggest what?"

"This doesn't change my plans."

"But—"

His face turned hard, jaw jutting, shoulders braced in determination. She had seen that look before, but she had been too young and naive to recognize it for what it was.

"Be my friend, Jewel," he said. "Don't tell me why I can't do what I want to do. Just help me to do it."

She stared at him as though she had never seen him before. She knew now why Peter Macready had survived a form of cancer that killed most kids. Why he had become the best rookie receiver in the NFL, despite the fact he had never been the fastest athlete on the field. Mac didn't give up. Mac didn't see obstacles. He saw his goal and headed for it without worrying about whether it could be reached. And so he invariably reached it.

Jewel wished she had half his confidence. She might be a married woman now with a baby in her arms.

Maybe it wasn't too late for her. Maybe she could learn from him how it was done. Maybe she could take advantage of Mac's presence to give her the impetus to change her life. If Mac could recover from a shattered leg, why couldn't she recover from a shattered life?

The boys returned with two dish towels loaded with ice and fell all over each other arranging the cold compresses around Mac's ankle. Jewel saw Mac wince when their overenthusiasm rocked his ankle, but instead of snapping at them, he launched into a story about how he had played a whole football game with a taped-up sprained ankle, thanks to an injection of painkiller.

The teenage boys dropped to his feet in awe and admiration. Jewel started to leave, but Mac reached up and caught her hand. "Join us," he said.

"I have work—"

"Just for a few minutes."

She figured maybe he didn't want to be stuck

alone with the boys. She would stay with him
long enough to let them hear a story or two before shooing them away. She settled beside Mac
on the worn leather couch—another donation
from her grandfather's house at Hawk's Way.
Mac's arm slid around her as naturally as if he
did it every day.

She resisted the urge to lay her head on his
shoulder. Putting his arm around her had been a
friendly gesture, nothing more. But she was
aware of the way his hand cupped her shoulder,
massaging it as he regaled the three of them with
stories of life in the pro football arena.

As she sat listening to him, an insidious idea
took root.

*What if she came to Mac tonight and ex-
plained her problem and asked him to help her
out?*

She trusted Mac not to hurt her. She trusted
him to go slow, to be patient. He didn't love her,
and she didn't love him, so there wouldn't be
that particular pitfall complicating matters. It
would be just one friend helping out another.

She could even explain to him how she had
gotten the idea. That she had seen his determination to play football again and been inspired

to try to solve a problem that she had thought would never be resolved.

All she wanted him to do was teach her how to arouse a man and satisfy him...and be satisfied by him.

She tried to imagine how Mac might react to such a suggestion. He was obviously an experienced man of the world. Only... What if he wasn't attracted to her that way?

Her mind flashed back to the scene in the canyon earlier that afternoon, when she had felt Mac's arousal. But he had apologized for that. Maybe when push came to shove, he wouldn't want to get involved with her.

Jewel didn't hear much of what Mac said to Colt and Huck. She wasn't even aware when he sent them away. She was lost deep in her own thoughts. And fears.

She wished the idea hadn't come to her so early in the day. Now she would be stuck thinking about it until dark, worrying it like a dog worried a bone.

All she had to do was cross the hall tonight and knock on Mac's door and... She didn't let her imagination take her any farther than that. Oh, how she wished night were here already! It was so much easier to act on impulse than to do something like this with cold calculation.

Of course, she was far from cold when she thought about Mac. Her whole body felt warm at the thought of having him touch her, having him kiss and caress her. She just wanted to get through the entire sexual act once without cringing or falling apart. That's all she wanted Mac to do for her. Just get her through the moments of panic before he did it. Get in and get out, like a quick lube job on the truck.

The absurdity of that comparison made her chuckle.

"Are you going to let me in on the joke?" Mac said.

"Maybe." If she didn't lose her nerve before nightfall.

Chapter 6

Mac was lying in bed wondering what Jewel would do if he crossed the hall, knocked on her door and told her he wanted to make love to her. She would probably think he had lost his mind. He had to resist the urge to pursue her. Jewel didn't need a fumbling, first-time lover. He, of all people, knew how much she needed a kind, considerate, *knowledgeable* bed partner. Which, of course, he wasn't.

She needed a slow hand, an easy touch—wasn't that what the song said? He had a lot of pent-up passion, a lot of celibate years to make up for. He was afraid the first time for him was going to be fast and hard. Which might be fine for him. But not for her.

Mac wished he didn't have such vivid memories of what had happened to Jewel that day in July six years ago. Any man who had seen her after Harvey Barnes had attacked her... He made himself think the word. After Harvey Barnes had *raped* her...

He had never wanted to kill a man before or since. He had been there to come to her rescue because he had seen Harvey drinking too much and worried about her, like a brother might worry about his sister. Jewel would have pounded him flat if she'd known he had followed her and Harvey when they slipped off into the trees down by the river.

He had kept his distance, even considered turning around and heading back to the noise of the carnival rides at the picnic, which seemed a world away from the soothing rustle of leaves down by the river. He had heard her laugh and then...silence.

He figured Harvey must be kissing her. He was standing at the edge of the river skipping stones, thinking he'd been an idiot to follow her, when he heard her cry out. Even then, he hadn't been sure at first whether it was a cry of passion.

The second cry had chilled his blood and started him running toward the sound. He could remember the feeling of terror as he searched frantically for her amid the thick laurel bushes and the tangle of wild ivy at the river's edge, calling her name and getting no answer.

There were no more cries. He saw why when he finally found them. Harvey had his hand pressed tight over Jewel's mouth, and she was struggling vainly beneath him. He saw something white on the ground nearby and realized it was her underpants.

He might have killed Harvey, if Jewel hadn't stopped him. He hadn't even been aware of his hands clenched in the flesh at Harvey's throat. It was only Jewel's anguished voice in his ear, pleading with him, that made him stop before he strangled the life out of the boy.

Harvey was nearly unconscious by the time Mac finally let go and turned to Jewel. Seeing her torn, grass-stained dress and the trickle of blood coming from her lip enraged him all over again. Jewel whimpered with fear—of him, he realized suddenly—and the fight went out of him.

He started toward her to hold her, to comfort her, but she clutched her arms tight around herself, turned her back to him and cried, "Don't touch me! Don't look at me!"

His heart was thudding loudly in his chest. "Jewel," he said. "You need to go to the hospital. Let me find your parents—".

She whirled on him and rasped, "No! Please don't tell anybody."

"But you're hurt!"

"My father will kill him," she whispered.

He could understand that. He had almost killed Harvey Barnes himself. Then she gave the reason that persuaded him to keep his silence.

"Everyone will know," she said, her brown eyes stark. "I couldn't bear it, Mac. Please. Help me."

"We'll have to say something to explain that cut on your lip," he said tersely. "And the grass stains on your dress."

"My beautiful dress." The tears welled in her eyes as she pulled the skirt around to look at the grass stains on the back of it.

He realized it wasn't the dress she was crying for, but the other beautiful thing she had lost. Her innocence.

"We'll tell your father Harvey attacked you—"

"No. Please!"

He reached out to take her shoulders, and she shrank from him. His hands dropped to his sides. He realized they were trembling and curled them into tight fists. "We'll tell them Harvey attacked you, but you fought him off," he said in an urgent voice. "Unless you tell that much of the tale, they're liable to believe the worst."

He had never seen—never hoped to see again—a look as desolate as the one she gave him.

"All right," she said. "But tell them you came in time. Tell them...nothing happened."

"What if...what if you're pregnant?" he asked.

"I don't think...I don't think..."

He realized she was in too much shock to even contemplate the possibility.

She shook her head, looking dazed and confused. "I don't think..."

He thought concealing the truth was a bad idea. She needed medical attention. She needed the comfort her mother and father could give her. "Jewel, let me tell your parents," he pleaded quietly.

She shook her head and began to shiver.

"Give me your hand, Jewel," he said, afraid to put his arms around her, afraid she might scream or faint or something equally terrifying.

She kept her arms wrapped around herself and started walking in the opposite direction from the revelers at the picnic. "Take me home, Mac," she said. "Please, just take me home."

He snatched up her underpants, stuffed them in his Levi's pocket and followed her to his truck. But it was too much to hope they would escape unnoticed. Not with Jewel's seven brothers and sisters at the picnic.

It was Rolleen who caught them before they could escape. She insisted Mac find her parents, and he'd had no choice except to go hunting for Zach and Rebecca. He had found Zach first.

The older man's eyes had turned flinty as he listened to Mac's abbreviated—and edited—version of what had happened.

The dangerous, animal sound that erupted from Zach's throat when he saw Jewel's torn dress and her bruised face and swollen lip made Mac's neck hairs stand upright. He realized suddenly that Jewel had known her father better than he had. Zach became a lethal predator. Only the lack of a quarry contained his killing rage.

Jewel's family surrounded her protectively, unconsciously shutting him out. He was forced to stand aside as they led her away. It wasn't until he got back to his private room in the cottage he shared with a half-dozen boys aged eight to twelve and stripped off his jeans, that he realized he still had Jewel's underwear in his pocket.

The garment was white cotton, with a delicate lace trim. It was stained with blood.

A painful lump rose in his throat, and his eyes burned with tears he was too grown up to shed. He fought the sobs that bunched like a fist in his chest, afraid one of the campers would return and hear him through the wall that separated his room from theirs. He pressed his mouth against a pillow in the bedroom and held it there until the ache eased, and he thought the danger was over.

In the shower later, where no one could see or hear, he shed tears of frustration and rage and despair. He had known, even then, that Harvey Barnes had stolen something precious from him that day, as well.

Mac learned later that Zach had found Harvey Barnes and horsewhipped him within an inch of his life. And Zach hadn't even known the full extent of Harvey's crime against his daughter. It seemed Jewel had been right not to tell her father the truth. Zach would have killed the boy for sure. Harvey's parents had sent him away, and he hadn't been seen since.

Things weren't the same between him and Jewel after that. She smiled and pretended everything was all right in front of him and her family. But the smile on her lips never reached her eyes.

The end of the summer came too soon, before they had reconciled their friendship. He went to her the night before he left, seeking somehow to mend the breach between them, to say goodbye for the summer and to ask if she was all right.

"Harvey Barnes is gone," she said. "And tomorrow you will be, too. Then I can forget about what happened."

"I'll be back next year," he reminded her.

She had been looking at her knotted hands when she said, "I hope you won't come, Mac."

Something bunched up tight inside of him. "Not come? I come every summer, Jewel."

"Don't come back. As a favor to me, Mac. Please don't come back."

"But why? You're my best friend, Jewel. I—"

"You know," she said in a brittle voice. She raised her eyes and looked at him and let him see her pain. "You know the truth. It's in your eyes every time you look at me."

He felt like crying again and forced himself to swallow back the tickle in his throat. "Jewel—"

"I want to forget, Mac," she said. "I need to forget. Please, please don't come back."

A lump of grief caught in his throat and made it impossible to say more. When he left that summer, a part of himself—the lighthearted, teasing friend—had stayed behind.

Mac had honored Jewel's wishes and stayed away for six long years. The really sad thing was, it had all been for nothing. She wasn't over what had happened. The past had not been forgotten.

He had often wondered if he'd done the wrong thing. Should he have told her parents the truth, anyway? Should he have come back the following summer? Should he have tried harder to get in touch with her over the years, to talk to her about what had happened?

A soft knock on the door forced Mac from his reverie. Before he could reply, the door opened, and Jewel stood silhouetted in the light from the hall. She was wearing a sleeveless white night-gown with a square-cut neck. The gown only covered her to mid-thigh. He could see the shape of her through the thin garment, the slender legs and slim waist and bountiful bosom.

He sat up, dragging the sheets around him to cover his nakedness and to conceal the sudden arousal caused by the enticing sight of her in his bedroom doorway. ''Jewel? Is something wrong?''

She slipped inside and closed the door, so that momentarily he lost sight of her as his eyes adjusted to the dark. He heard the rustle of sheets and suddenly felt her body next to his beneath the covers.

''Jewel? What's going on?'' He hoped his voice didn't sound as shocked as he felt. He didn't know what she thought she was doing, but he intended to find out before things went much farther.

He had expected an answer. He hadn't counted on her laying her palm on his bare chest. She followed that with a scattering of kisses across his chest that led her to the sensitive flesh beneath his ear. His body was trembling with desire when she finally paused to speak.

''Nothing's wrong, Mac,'' she murmured in

his ear. "I came because…" She nibbled on his earlobe, and he groaned at the exquisite pleasure of it. "I need your help," she finished.

He put an arm around her shoulder, realized suddenly he was naked and clutched at the sheet again. "Anything, Jewel. You know I'd do anything for you. But—"

"I was hoping you'd say that. Because what I need you to do… It won't be easy."

He waited, his breath caught in his chest, for what she had to say. "Anything, Jewel," he repeated, his heart thundering so loud he figured she could probably hear it.

She pressed her breasts against his chest and said, "I want you to make love to me."

His heart pounded, and his shaft pulsed. In another moment, things would be out of hand. His eyes had adapted to the dark, and with the moonlight from the window he at last could see the feelings etched on her face. Not desire, but fear and vulnerability.

"I want to feel like a woman," she said in a halting voice. "I want to stop being afraid."

He couldn't keep the dismay from his voice. "Aw, Jewel."

A cry of despair issued from her throat, and

she made a frantic lurch toward the edge of the bed and escape.

He grabbed for her, knowing she had misinterpreted his words. It wasn't that he didn't want her. He wanted her something fierce. He just wasn't the experienced bed partner she thought he was. He caught her by the wrist and pulled her back into his arms and held her tight, biting back a groan at the exquisite feel of her breasts crushed against his chest with only the sheer cloth between them.

"It's all right, Mac," she said in a brittle voice. "I made a mistake. Let me go, and we'll forget this ever happened."

She held herself stiff and unyielding in his arms. "Jewel—"

"Don't try to make me feel better. I deserve to feel like an idiot, throwing myself at you like this. I just thought…with all your experience…"

This time he did groan.

She tried to pull away, and he said, "You don't understand."

"I understand you don't find me attractive. I'm sorry for forcing myself on you like this."

"No!" *Tell her the truth, Macready. She's your friend. She'll understand.*

But the words stuck in his throat. If he hadn't

cared for her, if he didn't want her so badly, if things hadn't changed between them like they had, maybe he could have confessed the truth.

"It's not that I'm not attracted to you," he said.

He saw the look on her face and realized she didn't believe him. How could she not see the truth when it was throbbing like mad beneath the thin sheet that separated them?

"Then why won't you make love to me?" she challenged.

"Because..."

He couldn't tell her the truth, and he saw she believed the worst—that she had imposed herself where she wasn't wanted, and he was rejecting her as kindly as he could.

"Aw, Jewel," he said again. His voice was tender, as gentle as he wished he could be with her.

She made a keening sound in her throat, a mournful sound that made him ache somewhere deep inside.

He realized he had no choice. He had to try to make love to her. He couldn't botch things much worse than he already had. He leaned over and pressed his mouth against hers, restraining the rush of passion he felt at the touch of her soft, damp lips.

She moaned and arched her body against his. Her mouth clung to his, and he felt her need and her desire.

Maybe it's going to be all right. Maybe I can get us both through this.

He tried to hold back, so he wouldn't scare her. Yet when his tongue slipped into her mouth it found an eager welcome. He thrust deep, mimicking the sex act, and she riposted with her tongue in his mouth.

He thought the top of his head was going to come off. He had never felt so out of control. His hands slid down her arms, feeling the goose bumps and her shiver of anticipation. She was as excited as he was. She wanted him, too.

His lips started down her slender throat, across the silky flesh that led to her breastbone and downward, giving her plenty of warning where he was headed. She could have stopped him anytime she wanted. He wasn't an animal. He had his desire on a firm leash.

She cried out when his mouth latched onto her nipple, and he sucked hard through the cotton. Mac knew it wasn't a cry of fear, because her hands grasped his hair and held him there.

Her moan of pleasure urged him on. He released her breast momentarily and kissed her mouth again, an accolade for her trust in him. "I won't hurt you, Jewel. I would never hurt you," he murmured against her lips.

"I know, Mac. I know," she replied in gasping breaths.

Their tongues dueled dangerously, inciting them both to greater passion. He clasped her shoulders, making himself go slow, telling himself *Go Slow*. He slid his hand across the damp cotton that covered her breasts all the way down to her belly, wishing the damned nightgown wasn't between his palm and her flesh, but feeling the heat of her even through the thin shift.

He grabbed the bottom edge of it, anxious to get it out of his way, and brushed her thigh with his fingertips. Just her thigh. She tensed slightly but didn't pull away. He managed not to heave a sigh of relief.

It's going to be all right. I'll be able to do this for her.

But he was overeager and excited, worried about whether he would be able to satisfy her, and a moment later his hand accidentally brushed against the soft mound between her legs.

She jerked away from him with a cry of alarm. But he still had hold of the nightgown, and the fragile material tore. He let go, but it was too late. She was already rolled up in a tight, fetal ball with her back to him.

"Jewel—"

"I can't!" she cried. "I can't."

He laid a hand on her shoulder, and she cringed away.

"Please don't touch me," she whispered.

He lay staring at her in shock. He should have known better than to try this. He should have known he didn't have the experience to do it right. "What can I do?"

She turned to him, her eyes awash in despair. "I'm sorry, Mac."

"Aw, Jewel."

"I thought it would be all right. Because it was you," she sobbed. "Because you're my friend."

He would have to confess the truth. He owed her that much. "It isn't you, Jewel, it's me," he said flatly.

"You're just saying that to make me feel better," she said.

"No. I'm not." He forced himself to continue as she stared up at him. "You mustn't be discouraged by what happened here tonight. I'm sure another man, a more experienced man, could have managed things better. I lost control and frightened you.''

"But I trust you," she protested.

"All the more reason I should have kept my hands off of you." He huffed out a breath of air and shoved a hand through his hair in agitation.

"When you find a man you love," he said earnestly, "a man who loves you enough to take his time and do things right, I'm sure you'll be able to get past what happened to you."

She sat up slowly, her chin sunk to her chest, her hands knotted in front of her knees, which were clutched to her chest. She swallowed hard. "What you're saying is that you're not that man."

"No. I'm not."

"I see."

Evidently not. Evidently he hadn't hinted broadly enough at his inexperience for her to realize the truth.

Now it was too late. In the heat of the moment he might have confessed his virginity. But as his passion cooled, he felt appalled at how close he had come to exposing himself to her laughter.

And she would laugh. It would be gentle

laughter, kind laughter, an effervescent bubble of disbelief. But he couldn't bear to hear it.

"If you won't do this for me, I don't know where to turn," she said at last.

"There are lots of men out there who'd be attracted to you, if you'd let them see your charms."

She shot him a twisted smile. "You mean my Enormous Endowments?"

"I wouldn't call them that," he protested with a startled laugh.

"What would you call them?" She thrust her chest out, and his mouth went dry.

He hesitated a heartbeat and said, "Astonishing Assets?"

She laughed, the bubbly, effervescent sound he remembered from long ago. "Oh, God, now I've got you doing it!" She grabbed a pillow and hugged it tight against her ribs, effectively hiding the Generous Giants.

"Look, Jewel, for a start, you're going to have to stop doing that."

"Doing what?"

"Hiding behind clothes, behind your hair, behind pillows." He tugged on the pillow, and she reluctantly gave it up. He was immediately sorry, because it was hard to keep his eyes off

her. He could see her brownish-pink nipples beneath the damp cloth.

"It was my breasts that got me into trouble
in the first place," she said. "Can you blame me
for wanting to hide them?"

"Maybe not," he conceded. "But hiding your
light behind a bushel is not the way to find your
Prince Charming. You're going to have to want
to attract a man to find the right one."

"I'm afraid, Mac."

He saw that in her shadowed eyes. In her
drawn features. From the instinctive way she circled her arms protectively around herself. But if
he couldn't help her out by making love to her,
the least he could do was help her find another
man to do it.

"You can start small—no pun intended—and
do this in baby steps. You've got to crawl before
you can walk."

"Meaning?"

"Go back to basics, to flirting, to wanting to
attract a man's attention."

"I can't do that."

"Can't? Or won't?"

"Won't."

"You can start with me," he coaxed. "I'll be
your lab rat."

She grinned wryly. "Hold that thought. Man as rat. I like it."

He gave her a crooked smile. "The idea is for you to start seeing men as *men*—get it?"

"All right," she conceded with a sigh. "I'll give it a try. Where do I start?"

"Wear some clothes that fit better. Something that shows off—"

"My Plentiful Peaches?"

He laughed. "Actually, yeah, that would do it."

She slid her legs over the edge of the bad and looked back over her shoulder at him. "I'm not so sure about this, Mac."

"Believe me, it'll work," he said, wrapping the sheet around his waist as he rose to follow her to the door. "You'll have the guys around here on their knees begging to take you out."

She arched a skeptical brow. "You really think so?"

"I guarantee it."

She paused at the door and put a hand on his naked chest. His heart thudded. His loins throbbed. She searched his face, and he hoped his lurid thoughts weren't apparent.

"What if I attract the wrong kind of attention?'' she asked. ''What if someone...some man...''

''Start here on the ranch. I'll keep an eye out for you. If any of the cowhands or counselors makes a wrong move, I'll be there. You can use me as your guinea pig.''

''Hmm. Man as pig. I like that even better.''

He laughed and tousled her hair. ''Cut it out.''

''You'll help me through this, won't you?'' she asked, her heart in her eyes.

''If you want to try out your seductive wiles on someone safe, I'm your man,'' he volunteered. He would keep his libido in check if it killed him.

''You don't know how much that means to me, Mac. You really think this will work?''

''It's sure as hell worth a try.''

''Thanks, Mac. Still friends?''

He wrapped his hand around her nape—to keep her at arm's distance—and said, ''You bet. And don't worry. Anybody makes the wrong kind of move, I'll cut him off at the pass.''

''My hero,'' she said, an impish grin forming on her lips.

''You bet.'' He knew he should shove her out the door and put temptation from his path, but he couldn't resist one last kiss.

He leaned down to her, keeping their bodies separated and pressed his mouth against hers with all the gentleness he could muster.

Her lips were pliant under his, soft and supple and incredibly sweet.

"Good night, Jewel. Go to bed and get some sleep."

"Good night, Mac. You, too."

He must have nodded, or grunted an assent, because she left the room and closed the door behind her. But he knew damned well he wasn't going to sleep.

Mac replayed the events of the evening in his head. If only he'd had more experience. If only his hand hadn't brushed against her and scared her. If only he'd known what to do to reassure her.

What was done was done. He'd had his chance and he'd blown it. The least he could do was help her find another guy to help her out, while keeping his own hormones in check. The last thing he wanted to do was scare her again. Which meant he'd better make sure she never found out her Beautiful Breasts turned him hard as a rock.

If she was going to start wearing clothes that fit, he'd better go shopping for some baggy jeans.

Chapter 7

Jewel decided the best way to avoid hiding behind her hair was to remove that option. She drove to the Stonecreek Ranch at the crack of dawn to have her sister Cherry whack it off. She had known Cherry would understand what she wanted to do and help her because, of all her adopted brothers and sisters, Cherry understood best what it meant to feel different.

Cherry was the last Whitelaw Brat to be adopted and had come to the family when she was fourteen, an extremely tall, redheaded, blue-eyed Irish girl—and an incorrigible juvenile delinquent. Jewel had been closest to her in age, only a year older. After a rocky start, during which Cherry did her best to break every rule— and offend every member—in the Whitelaw household, they had ended up becoming best friends.

The night Cherry was accused of spiking the punch bowl at the senior prom and expelled from high school, she had eloped with Billy Stonecreek to avoiding facing Zach and Rebecca. Cherry had become an instant mom to Billy's twin six-year-old daughters Raejean and Annie. Three years later, Cherry was six months pregnant, and as far as Jewel could tell, happy as a cat in a dairy.

Cherry had made the Stonecreek Ranch a comfortable place to live, substituting leather and wood furniture for the silks and satins bought by Billy's first wife, Laura, who had died in a car accident. Jewel was surprised, when she showed up at Cherry's back screen door unannounced, to catch her sister and brother-in-law kissing in the kitchen.

It wasn't the kiss that shocked her. It was the passion behind it. Billy's hands avidly cupped Cherry's breasts, and her hands clutched his buttocks. They were pressed together like flies on flypaper.

She cleared her throat noisily. "Excuse me."

Jewel imagined a ripping sound as they sprang apart.

"Jewel!" Cherry exclaimed, her voice revealing both relief and irritation. "What are you doing here?"

"Obviously interrupting something important," Jewel said with a teasing grin.

Her sister flushed a delightful pink, and Billy stuck his hands in his front pockets, a move that didn't do as much as he probably hoped to hide his state of arousal.

Jewel felt a little guilty for intruding, and if it hadn't been an emergency she might have turned and left. But she was afraid she would lose her nerve if she waited. She stepped into the kitchen, careful not to let the screen door slam behind her and wake the twins. "I need my hair cut. Could you do it for me?"

"Now?" Cherry asked, her brows rising practically to her hairline.

"Yes, now."

Jewel was wearing a sleeveless white knit shell and tight-fitting jeans that had been shut away in a drawer for six years. She watched as

Cherry perused her attire and exchanged a look with Billy, whose eyes had opened wide with astonishment once she stepped inside. Jewel resisted the urge to cross her arms over her chest. She was going to have to get used to men looking at her.

"Hi, Billy," she said.

"Hi, Jewel." It came out as a croak. He cleared his throat and tried again. "You look…" He searched for a word and came up with, "Nice. What's the occasion?"

He was clearly curious, as she suspected her family would be, about why she was suddenly exposing assets she had kept hidden for the past six years. "No occasion," she said. "I just want to get my hair cut. Can you help me out?" she asked Cherry.

"Sure," Cherry said. She turned to Billy. "You don't mind if we postpone breakfast for half an hour, do you?"

"I've got some chores I can do in the barn. Give a holler when you want me." Billy grabbed his Stetson from the antler rack on the wall and headed out the screen door. Cherry caught it before it could slam.

"All right," Cherry said once she had scissors in hand and Jewel was settled in a kitchen chair with a towel around her shoulders. "Spill the jelly beans. What's going on?"

"Nothing much."

"For the first time in six years I can see you have breasts," Cherry retorted tartly. "Believe me, anyone seeing your breasts for the first time wouldn't say they're 'nothing much.'"

Jewel laughed. That was why she liked Cherry so much. She didn't pull her punches. Cherry said exactly what she was thinking, even if it wasn't necessarily what you wanted to hear.

"I had a talk with Mac Macready last night," Jewel said. "He convinced me it's time to come out of my shell."

"I see," Cherry said.

Jewel realized Cherry was *seeing* a great deal more than she wished or intended. "It isn't like that."

"Like what?"

"It's not Mac I'm trying to attract."

"It isn't?"

"No. Not that I don't love him dearly. I do. As a friend."

"A *friend,*" Cherry repeated.

Jewel winced as nine-inch-long hanks of brown hair began falling to the kitchen floor.

There was no turning back now. "A friend," she confirmed.

"And this *friend* suggested you'd look better in skin-tight jeans and short hair?"

Jewel laughed. "Not exactly. He simply said I should dress to attract a man."

"What you're wearing ought to do it," Cherry confirmed.

"You think so? It's not too…enticing?"

"You're dressed fine, Jewel. Half the young women in this country are probably wearing similar outfits this morning. You can't help it if you have big breasts."

Jewel noticed Cherry said it without the capital B's. Jewel automatically thought Big Breasts, something she was going to have to get over if she was going to have any hope of surviving this metamorphosis.

"There," Cherry said, surveying her handiwork. "A few turns with my curling iron, and I think you'll be pleased with the result."

When Cherry was done, she held a mirror in front of Jewel's face. "Take a look."

Her hair swept along her chin in a shiny bob, with soft bangs across her brow. Jewel sighed. "Oh, Cherry, you're a marvel. I look—"

"Cute," Cherry said with an irreverent laugh. "No getting around it. You're darned cute."

"I'm twenty-two. That's too old for cute. Besides, my features are too ordinary to be—"

"Cute," Cherry persisted with a grin. "Let me call Billy, and he can confirm it." She called out the door for Billy, who bounded up the back steps and into the kitchen.

He paused in the acting of pulling off his leather work gloves as he looked Jewel up and down. "Who would've believed a haircut could make such a difference?"

"Isn't she cute?" Cherry asked.

"Sexy," Billy countered. When his wife nudged him in the ribs, he amended, "Sexy and cute."

Jewel's brow furrowed. She had never been pretty, and "cute" sounded like something you said about a one-year-old with a lollipop. One glance down explained the "sexy." Jewel felt the heat start in her throat and work its way up her neck to sit like red flags on her cheeks. "Good God," she said. "Have you got an extra shirt I can borrow?" she asked Billy.

"What for?" Billy said.

"She wants to go back into hiding," Cherry said scornfully. "Well, we're not going to help you do it. You turn right around and head out that door with your head held high. You've got nothing to be ashamed of. What happened to you six years ago wasn't your fault. It's about time you shoved Harvey Barnes out of your life and started enjoying it again.''

''That's pretty much what Mac said.''

''Good for Mac,'' Cherry said. ''Am I going to have to go with you to make sure you don't cover yourself up like a nun?''

''No,'' Jewel conceded with a chagrined look. ''I'll be all right.''

''Stand up straight and enjoy the looks you get. Because you darn sure deserve them!''

''Thanks, Cherry,'' Jewel said, giving her sister a quick hug. ''Thanks for everything.''

Her brother-in-law gave her a quick hug and teased, ''Definitely sexy. Go get 'em, Jewel.''

Cherry and Billy stood arm in arm on the back porch waving as she drove away. They were already kissing again as the dust rose behind her pickup.

It wasn't easy resisting the urge to slip a long-sleeved shirt over the figure-exposing knit shell the instant she returned home. It would have been easier if Mac had been there waiting, and

she could have gotten that first meeting over
with.

But he wasn't there.

She had left a note hanging on Mac's door
when she snuck out to get her hair cut. The note
she found stuck on her door when she got back
said that he had taped up his ankle and gone
walking despite the sprain. She left a third note
for Mac saying that she was eating breakfast
with her family and inviting him to join them,
then left the cottage before she lost her courage.

Jewel figured it couldn't hurt to have a buffer
between her and Mac when he saw her for the
first time in her new guise. Not that she thought
he wouldn't approve. After all, it had been his
idea for her to feature her assets more promi-
nently. But after last night...

In the bright light of day, Jewel found it hard
to believe she had crossed the hall to Mac's bedroom last night. Or that she had actually asked
him to make love to her. Or that he had refused.

She wished he had done it before kissing her.
Good Lord. Who would have thought a kiss
from Mac Macready could turn her to mush like
that? His lips had been soft and slightly damp,
and he had tasted...like Mac. Familiar and good.

If that was all she had felt, she would never

have gotten frightened the way she had. But there had also been something dark and dangerous about his kisses. A threat of leashed passion that once freed might... When Mac had accidentally touched her, that awful sense of powerlessness had returned, and the bad memories had all come crashing down on her.

She couldn't blame Mac for backing away like he had. What man wouldn't cut his losses? Mac had gently but firmly told her to find somebody else to make love to her. He wasn't available for the job.

She didn't want somebody else, she had realized. She wanted Mac. Which was why she was dressed like this. Cherry had seen right through her feeble protests. The only man she wanted to attract was Mac Macready. She would never have found the courage to shed her protective skin of clothing if she hadn't conceded this was one sure way of getting Mac's attention.

He had certainly seemed interested last night. That is, before she had gotten scared and scared him off. Before he had accidentally touched her below the waist, everything had been wonderful. Her knee-jerk reaction had come before her rational mind could tell her it was Mac.

That had been followed by the disturbing

thought that maybe even Mac couldn't make it all right. That maybe she would forever fear a man's touch in bed. She had kept herself curled up in a ball to avoid testing the truth. Because that possibility was too devastating to contemplate.

Jewel was determined to get over her fear. She was determined to give Mac another chance. And she wanted Mac to want another chance. She was understandably nervous about her next meeting with him. It made a lot of sense to diffuse the situation by including her family in the equation. Hence the unusual visit to her family's breakfast table. This morning she needed the support they had always given her. She wanted their reassurance that she looked all right, that she would not "stick out" in a crowd.

Jewel could smell biscuits and bacon through the screen door. She smiled and stepped inside, knowing she would find the warmth of hearth and home. She stopped just inside the door, enjoying the cacophony of seven voices—Rolleen was away at medical school—raised in excited chatter.

"Wow! You look different!"

Jewel smiled self-consciously at Colt as she settled into an empty chair at the breakfast table.

She was tempted to slump down, but forced herself to sit up straight. This was the new and improved Jewel Whitelaw.

Her mom gave her a bright smile and said, "You look lovely today, sweetheart."

"Why'd you cut off all your—"

Nineteen-year-old Jake elbowed fifteen-year-old Rabbit to shut him up. "You look real nice, Jewel," Jake said. He exchanged a knowing look with their father at the head of the table.

Jewel felt her cheeks heating. They had noticed the difference, all right, but so far had avoided commenting directly on it. She decided to keep their attention focused on her hair. "It's been so hot lately, I decided to get a trim," she said to appease the curious looks she was getting from sixteen-year-old Frannie and twenty-year-old Avery.

"Good idea," her father said, buttering a fluffy biscuit.

"I've got some time this morning if you need any last-minute help getting ready for the first drove of campers," her mother offered, as she set a bowl of scrambled eggs and a second platter of bacon in the center of the table.

"Everything's under control, Mom," Jewel said.

"When do you go to the airport?" her father asked.

"The flight from Dallas arrives at 9:30 this morning with about a half-dozen kids," she replied. "There's another half dozen and the two counselors arriving from Houston shortly afterward. Mac has volunteered to go with me in the van to pick them up. I invited him to join us for breakfast," she said. "I hope that's all right."

"Of course it's all right," her mother replied. "It'll be nice to visit with him. We've barely seen hide or hair of either of you. What have you been doing?"

"Mac's been walking in the mornings—"

"Is his ankle better?" Colt asked.

"What's wrong with his ankle?" her father asked.

Colt got busy scooping another spoonful of eggs on his plate and sent a pleading look toward Jewel not to betray him.

"He tripped and twisted it yesterday," Jewel said. "It seems to be all right this morning."

"It's fine," Mac said as he opened the screen door and stepped into the kitchen. "How's everyone this morning?"

He was greeted with a chorus of smiles and "hellos" and "hi's."

Jewel feasted her eyes on him. His blond hair was still damp from the shower, and the rugged planes of his face were shadowed by a day's growth of beard, so he hadn't even stopped to shave. He must have been afraid of missing breakfast. He was wearing a Western shirt tucked into beltless, butter-soft jeans and cowboy boots.

She looked up at him defiantly, daring him not to like what he saw. He was the one who had wanted change. She had provided it. He had better not complain.

Jewel saw nothing in his blue eyes but admiration. That flustered her as much, and perhaps more than the opposite reaction. She hadn't been ready for the blatant male appreciation of her figure that she found on his face.

"I hope I'm not too late for breakfast," he said as he slipped into the last empty chair, which happened to be across from Jewel.

"Just in time," Zach said.

Jewel could feel Mac's eyes on her but kept her gaze lowered as she ate her scrambled eggs. It was going to take some time for her to adjust to having men look at her with sexual interest. It was all right when Mac did it, because she did not feel frightened by him. But he was right. If she wanted to get over the past, this was a start in the right direction.

She heard Mac exchange comments with her father about the cattle and cutting horse businesses that supported Hawk's Pride, listened to him discuss football with Colt, smiled along with him as he teased Rabbit about his nickname, which dated from his childhood when he had loved carrots. Mac obviously knew her family well, and they apparently liked him as much as he liked them.

Jewel felt a rush of guilt at having deprived Mac of their company all these years. Having been Mac's friend, she knew how hard it was for his own family to treat him normally. His parents and older sister, Sadie, had hovered over him long after he was well, afraid to let him try things for fear he would get hurt and end up back in the hospital.

Zach and Rebecca loved Mac like a son, but they hadn't spent years with him in a hospital setting where he was fighting for his life against a disease that killed kids. They were willing to let him do a man's work. Jewel knew Mac had needed his summers as a counselor at Camp LittleHawk as much as Zach and Rebecca had needed his help with the kids.

"Right, Jewel?"

Jewel looked up at Mac, startled to realize he was speaking to her. "Excuse me. I wasn't listening. What was the question?"

Her family laughed.

"What's so funny?" she demanded, looking at them suspiciously.

"I said the reason the kids keep coming back year after year is that you're constantly making changes to keep things interesting," Mac said with a grin.

Jewel realized that this year she had made a huge change that was bound to be noticed—by the other counselors, if not the kids. One of the reasons she loved working with kids was that they never seemed to notice her ample bosom. "Change is good," she said, both chin and chest outthrust defiantly.

"Of course it is, darling," her mother said in a soothing voice.

"I wasn't complaining, Jewel," Mac said, his gaze staying level with hers.

She kept waiting for it to drop to her breasts. But it never did. There was nothing sexual in his gaze now. What she saw was approval and appreciation of her as a person. A thickness in her throat made it hard to speak. "We'd better get going," she said. "We don't want to be late to the airport."

"I'm ready when you are," Mac said, pushing back from the table. "Thanks for the breakfast, Rebecca. I don't know when I've enjoyed a meal so much. It's great to be back."

"It's great to have you back," Zach said, rising and putting a hand on Mac's shoulder as he walked him to the door." You're welcome anytime."

"Thanks, Zach," Mac said, shaking hands with the older man.

Jewel felt exposed once she and Mac emerged from the throng of hugging and backslapping brothers and sisters and parents and headed across the backyard toward the van.

She felt Mac's gaze trained on her again, intense, disturbing, because this time he was obviously looking at more than her face. She paused as soon as they were hidden by a large bougainvillea and turned to confront him.

She propped her balled hands on her hips, thrust her shoulders back and held her chin high. "All right, Mac. You were the one who asked for this. Look your fill and get it over with."

His lips curved. His eyes surveyed her intently. His voice turned whiskey rough as he said, ''You could stand there till doomsday, and I wouldn't get my fill of looking at you.''

Jewel would have scoffed, but the sound got caught in her throat. ''Mac...''

He stepped close enough to put them toe to toe.

She struggled not to give ground. ''Say what you think. Spit it out. I can take it.''

His thumb caressed the faint scars on her bared cheek, then edged into her hair. ''Your hair's so soft. So shiny. So sleek.'' His hand slid through her hair to capture her nape and hold her still as he lowered his head. ''I find you irresistible, Jewel.''

Jewel felt her heart thudding, had trouble catching her breath, then stopped breathing altogether as his mouth closed over hers.

He kept their bodies separated, touching her only with his mouth. The searing kiss was enough to curl her toes inside her boots.

He lifted his head and said, ''Welcome back, Jewel. I missed the old you.''

''Oh, Mac—'' She was on the verge of blurting out her strong feelings for him—the same feelings his kiss had suggested he had for her—when he interrupted.

''I don't think you're going to have any trou-

ble at all attracting the man of your dreams.''
He smile ruefully. ''You're going to have to remind me to keep my distance. I don't want any
good prospects to think I have any kind of claim
on you except as a friend.''

Jewel stared at him with stunned eyes, but
quickly recovered her composure. ''No sweat,
Mac,'' she said, turning and heading for the van.
''I'll make sure any men I meet know exactly
where you stand.''

She owed Mac too much to make him feel
uncomfortable by revealing her new feelings for
him before he was ready to hear them. But if
kissing her like this only reinforced the bonds of
friendship, she had her work cut out for her. The
changes in her hair and wardrobe had been useful in helping Mac to see her as a desirable female. All she had to do now was figure out how
to make him fall in love with her.

Chapter 8

Mac stared out the window of the van at the flat grassland that lined the road between Hawk's Pride and the airport, rather than at the woman behind the wheel. But he very much wanted to feast his eyes on Jewel.

He liked the bouncy new haircut that showed off the line of her chin and made her cheekbones more prominent. He liked the formfitting clothes that outlined a lush figure he yearned to hold close to his own. He was intrigued by the sparkle of wonder and delight—and unfulfilled promise—in her dark brown eyes.

Mac wished he had a Stetson to set on his lap.

He hadn't realized he would be so physically susceptible to the striking change in Jewel's appearance. A friend would have settled for giving her an approving pat on the back. His kiss had been a purely male impulse, an effort to stake his claim on an intensely desirable female.

Mac recognized his problem. He simply had no idea how to solve it. How did a man stop desiring a woman? Especially one he not only lusted after but also liked very much?

Jewel sat across from him behind the wheel not saying a word. But speaking volumes.

Tension radiated between them. Sexual tension.

He had told her to find another man, but now he wasn't so sure. She had certainly seemed to enjoy his kiss. Maybe if he seduced her in stages... If they took it slow and easy...

Who was he kidding? When it came down to the nitty-gritty, it was still going to be the first time for him. He was still going to be guessing at what he was doing. Besides, it wasn't fair to change his mind at this late date.

Who said life was fair?

''I appreciate you coming along to help today,'' Jewel said, interrupting his thoughts.

"My pleasure. How many people are we picking up?"

"Twelve kids, two counselors."

"Are you still hiring college kids?"

"Patty Freeburg is still in college. Gavin Talbot is in graduate school. I should warn you, this group of kids includes Brad Templeton."

"The kid who wanted to meet me?"

Jewel nodded. "His leukemia is in its second remission. You know how that works. You're afraid to get your hopes up that this remission will last, because you've already slipped out of remission once."

"You have to keep believing you can beat the disease," Mac said.

"Most kids aren't as lucky as you were."

"You think it was luck that I beat myelocytic leukemia?" he asked.

"Statistics say the chances of a kid surviving that kind of leukemia aren't good. What else could it have been?"

"Sheer determination. Willpower. It can move mountains. Recently it put me back on my own two feet when the doctors said I would never walk again without a brace."

"Granted, willpower is important. Determination counts for a lot. But are they enough to

get your leg back into shape for pro football?''
Jewel asked.

Mac felt a spurt of panic. "Sure. Why not?"

"Willpower can't replace the missing muscle
in your leg, Mac. Determination can't make the
scars disappear."

"I can compensate."

She nodded. "For your sake, I hope so."

"Why are you being so negative about this?"
Mac demanded, using anger to force back the
fear that had surfaced with her doubts.

"I'm not being negative, just realistic. You
learn to accept—"

"Don't accept anything that isn't exactly what
you want. Don't expect anything less than the
best for yourself or those sick kids, Jewel. You
deserve it. And so do they."

Jewel smiled ruefully. "To tell the truth, this
is an argument I don't want to win. I want to
believe in happily ever after for these kids and
for you. And I'm hoping desperately for it myself. I've taken the first steps toward a new me.
I have to admit it feels good, even though it is
a little scary."

He met her glance briefly and saw the fear,
before she returned her gaze to the road in front
of her. "Why scary?"

"Because I'm not sure how well I'll handle all the male attention once I have it."

"Encourage the men you're interested in, and discourage the ones you don't want."

She grunted her disgust. "You make it sound so easy. Encourage how? Discourage how?"

"Smiles. And frowns."

Jewel looked at him incredulously, then gave a bubbly laugh. "If it were only that simple!"

"It is," Mac assured her.

She eyed him doubtfully. "That's all there is to it?"

"Why not try an experiment? When this Gavin What's-his-name—"

"Talbot," Jewel provided.

"When Talbot gets off the plane, give him a 'You're the one!' smile, and see what kind of response you get."

They had arrived at the local airport just as the commuter plane from Dallas was landing. Jewel stopped the van close to the terminal and stepped out to wait for the plane door to open and the kids to come down the portable stairs to the tarmac.

The three girls and four boys on the Dallas flight all wore hats of some kind, a means of hiding the ravages of chemotherapy on their

hair. Baseball caps, berets, slouch hats, straw
hats, bandannas, Jewel had seen them all. Beneath the hats their eyes looked haunted, their
mouths grim. Jewel looked forward to easing
their worries for two weeks, to helping them forget for a short time that their lives were threatened with extinction.

A scuffle broke out between two of the boys
the instant they reached the tarmac. The other
kids spread out in a circle to watch.

"Hey!" Jewel cried, running to reach them.

Mac was there before her and picked up the
boy who had done the shoving, leaving the other
boy with no one to fight. "What's the problem?" Mac asked in a calm voice.

The boy on the tarmac was in tears. He
pointed to the boy in Mac's arms. "He said I'm
going to die."

"We're all going to die," Mac replied.
"Could get hit by a bus tomorrow."

The other kids smiled. It was an old joke for
them, but it still worked every time.

The crying boy was not amused. He pointed
to the kid in Mac's arms. "He said I can't beat
it. He said no one can. He said—"

Mac perused the thin, gangly boy held snug
against his side. "Doesn't look like a doctor to

me," he said. "Where do you suppose he got the information to make his diagnosis? You a doctor?" Mac asked the kid.

The boy clenched his teeth and said nothing.

"Guess that settles that," Mac said. "Any other questions?" he asked the crying boy.

The kid wiped his nose on the shoulder of his T-shirt and pulled his Harwell Grain and Feed cap snugly over his eyes. "Guess not."

Mac exchanged a look with Jewel, who began herding the children toward the terminal.

"Why don't you all come inside with me," she said. "We'll get a soda while we wait for the kids from Houston to arrive, along with your counselors."

As soon as they were gone, Mac set the boy down on his feet in front of him. Knowing the kid would likely run the instant he let go, Mac settled onto one knee, his hands trapping the kid's frail shoulders, and tried to see the boy's eyes under his baseball cap. The kid's chin was tucked so close to his chest, it was impossible.

"What's your name?" Mac asked.

"I want to go home."

"You sound pretty mad."

"I never wanted to come here in the first place. My mom made me!"

"Why'd you tell that boy he was going to die?"

"'Cause he is!"

"Who says?"

"He's got acute myelocytic leukemia, same as me. It kills you for sure!"

"I'm not dead."

The boy's chin jerked up, and his pale blue eyes focused on Mac's. "You're not sick."

"I was. Same as you."

The boy shook his head. "But you're—"

"I'm Mac Macready."

The blue eyes widened. "*You're* him? You look different from the picture on your trading card."

"I was younger then," Mac replied. *And twenty pounds heavier with muscle.*

"My mom said you'd be here, but I didn't believe her."

"You must be Brad Templeton." Mac let go of the kid's shoulders, rose and stuck out his hand. "Nice to meet you, Brad."

The boy stared at Mac's hand suspiciously before he laid his own tiny palm against it. Mac figured the kid for eleven or twelve, but he didn't look much more than eight or nine. The slight body, the gaunt cheeks, the hopeless look in his eyes, told how the disease had decimated him—body and soul.

"You ready to join the others?" Mac asked.

He watched as the boy looked toward the kids bunched in the front window of the terminal and made a face. "This is a waste of time."

"Why is that?"

"I mean, why bother pretending everything is all right, when it's not?"

Mac put a hand on the boy's back, and they began walking toward the terminal. "Why not pretend? Why not enjoy every moment you've got?"

The boy met his gaze, and Mac knew the answer without having to hear it. He had been through it all himself.

This was a child going through the stages that prepared him for death. The anger. The grieving. And finally, the acceptance. Brad Templeton had done it all before, when the first remission ended. Then death had given him a brief reprieve—a second remission. But having once accepted the fact he was going to die, it was awfully hard to start living all over again.

"Death doesn't always win," Mac said quietly.

Brad looked up at him. "How did you beat it?"

"Determination. Willpower."

Brad shook his head. "That isn't enough. If it was, I'd already be well."

"Don't give up."

"I have to," Brad said. "It hurts too bad to hope when you know it isn't going to make any difference."

They had reached the door to the terminal, but before going inside, Mac stooped down and turned the boy to face him. "Sometimes you have to forget about what the doctors say and believe in yourself."

Brad looked skeptical.

Mac didn't know who he was trying to convince, himself or the kid. Sometimes the doctors were right. Kids died. And football players got career-ending injuries.

He rose and said, "Come on, Brad. We can keep each other company this week and have some fun."

Brad snorted. "Fun. Yeah. Right."

Mac smiled. "If you're not smiling ear to ear when you get back on that plane in two weeks, I'll—"

"How are you two doing?" Jewel interrupted.

A whoosh of cold air escaped the terminal as she joined them in the Texas heat that was already rising from the tarmac.

"I was making a bet with Brad that he would be smiling by the end of next week."

Brad grimaced.

Jewel eyed Brad, then murmured to Mac, "Looks like you have your work cut out for you."

"Come on, Brad," Mac said, giving the boy a nudge toward the door. "Let's go inside and meet the other kids."

"I've already met them," Brad said sullenly. "They all hate me."

"We'll have to work on that, too," Mac said, sending Jewel a look that said "Help!" over his shoulder.

"I'd appreciate it if you'd keep an eye on everybody while I greet the folks on the plane from Houston," she said.

Mac realized the second commuter plane had arrived, Jewel was headed back out onto the tarmac. "Don't forget," he said. "Smile."

Jewel shot him a radiant smile. "How's this?"

Mac put an exaggerated hand to his heart. "Lord have mercy, girl, that's potent stuff!"

Jewel laughed and turned away, her hips swaying seductively in the tight jeans.

Mac was glad she'd turned away when she had. His hand was still on his heart, but it was keeping the damned thing from flying out of his chest. If she kept walking like that, he wasn't going to be able to go inside anytime soon.

He felt a tug on his shirtsleeve and looked down to see Brad staring up at him.

"You got the hots for her?"

Mac stared, agog. "The *hots?*"

"You know. Sexy chick like that—"

Mac put a hand over Brad's mouth. "Where did a kid your age learn—? Don't answer that. She's Miss Whitelaw to you."

The kid reached up to uncover his mouth. "I'm twelve. I was here when I was nine and Jewel said we can call her Jewel and she's a lot prettier now."

"And you're old enough to notice, is that it?"

Brad gave Mac a man-to-man shrug. "I haven't thought too much about girls 'cause… you know."

Mac put a hand on Brad's shoulder. "Yeah, I know how that is, too."

He ushered Brad inside thinking it was going to be a very long two weeks.

* * *

Jewel's heart was beating rapidly. Even kidding the way he was, Mac's admiring look had been enough to take her breath away. It was easy to keep the smile on her face long enough to greet the other five campers, Patty Freeburg and Gavin Talbot.

Patty was petite and pretty, with long blond hair she wore in a youthful ponytail, blue eyes and a wonderfully open smile. "Hello," she said. "I'm glad to be back."

"Good to have you back, Patty," Jewel said. "You know the drill. Would you mind helping the kids locate their luggage inside?"

"Sure," Patty said. "Come on, you guys, hup, two, three, four!"

The two boys marched, and the three girls giggled as they followed Patty toward the terminal.

Jewel turned to greet Gavin Talbot, who was hefting a duffel bag over his shoulder. She knew Gavin's credentials backward and forward. He was twenty-six and working on a Ph.D. in child psychology. Eventually he planned to become a clinical psychologist, and work with dying kids. He was spending time at Camp LittleHawk because it catered to children with cancer.

She knew Gavin would have to be an empathetic and caring man to choose such a career. She had not imagined he would also be stunningly handsome.

He was over six feet tall, with the sort of rangy body Jewel was used to seeing on cowhands, who led physically active lives. His sunstreaked, tobacco-brown hair suggested a lot of time out-of-doors, and the spray of tan lines around his dark brown eyes confirmed it. He was dressed in a white, oxford-cloth shirt, unbuttoned at the throat and turned up to his forearms, well-worn—though not ragged—jeans and cowboy boots.

"Hello, Miss Whitelaw," he said, reaching out to shake her hand as they followed Patty and the kids back to the terminal.

His large, callused hand engulfed hers, offering comfort, reassurance and something else…a spark of sexual interest.

Jewel didn't think she was imagining it. She felt a small frisson of pleasure merely from his firm handclasp. It was probably the way he looked into her eyes, as though seeking a connection, that made her insides jump a little.

"Call me Jewel, please, Gavin," she replied.

"Jewel," he repeated, the smile broadening, becoming more relaxed. "The name fits."

Jewel only had an instant to decide whether to frown or smile, as Mac had instructed. Jewel smiled.

She had only taken two steps when Gavin put a hand under her elbow and said, "You're hurt."

"It's an old injury that causes me to limp," she said, wondering if the interest she had previously seen would diminish, now that he knew she was considerably less than perfect.

Her opinion of him went up a notch when he said, "It doesn't seem to slow you down much."

She felt a spurt of anxiety when Gavin made eye contact with her again, because the sexual spark was still there. Well, she had wanted to attract him and she had. So now what did she do with him? She turned to find Mac staring at her through the terminal's front picture window.

Mac was safe. Mac was nonthreatening.

Mac also was not volunteering to help her get over the lingering fear that had kept her celibate all these years. Maybe seeing that someone else was interested in her would spur him to action.

She turned back to Gavin and forced another

smile onto her face. "You look like you spend
a lot of time outdoors."

"I own a cattle ranch south of Houston," he
said. "I spend my weekends there when I can."

"You should be right at home here," she said.
"We do a lot of trail rides in the early morning
and late afternoon for the children."

"What about moonlight rides for the grown-
ups?" he asked. "Ending with a romantic campfire and toasted marshmallows?"

Jewel was a little shocked at how fast Gavin
had made his move. She swallowed back the
knot of fear and shot him a calculated come-
hither glance. "I suppose that could be arranged."

"How about tonight?"

"How about what tonight?" Mac asked.

Jewel had been so busy staring back into
Gavin's brown eyes, she hadn't realized they
had reached the terminal. Mac's question caught
her unawares. "What?"

"Jewel and I were just setting up a moonlight
ride for tonight," Gavin said.

Jewel heard the warning in Gavin's voice.
*Stay clear. This one's mine. We don't want com-
pany.*

Mac ignored it. "Sounds like a fine idea," he

said. "Hey, Patty, you want to go for a moon-light ride tonight?"

Patty smiled. "Sure. Who all's going?"

"Everybody," Gavin said wryly, his gaze never leaving Mac's.

At least Gavin was a good sport, Jewel thought. She was grateful that Mac had realized how uncomfortable she would have been all alone with Gavin and had invited himself and Patty. With Mac along she would feel safer flirting with Gavin. And perhaps Mac would be moved to do a little flirting himself.

Jewel was amused to see how Gavin maneuvered to be in the front seat with her on the trip back, forcing Mac into the back with Patty and the kids. Gavin wasn't the least impressed by Mac's football hero status, because he wasn't a big football fan.

"I know that sounds like blasphemy in Texas," he said. "But I'd rather spend my Saturday and Sunday afternoons at the ranch, since I'm stuck indoors reading and writing the rest of the week."

"What's the name of your ranch?" Jewel asked as she started the van and headed back toward the ranch.

"Let's not talk about me," Gavin said, avoiding an answer. "Tell me about yourself."

Jewel watched Gavin stiffen as Mac suddenly leaned forward, bracing his arms on the back of the front seat, effectively interposing himself between Jewel and the counselor. "Mind if I listen?" Mac said. "Jewel and I haven't had much time to catch up on things since the last time we were together."

Jewel heard the insinuation in Mac's voice that suggested "together" meant more than sitting on a garden swing next to each other.

"You two are old friends?" Gavin asked, eyeing the two of them speculatively.

"We're rooming together," Mac said. "Didn't Jewel tell you?"

Jewel turned a fiery red at the knowing look Gavin gave her, even though the situation with Mac was perfectly innocent. She was a little perturbed at Mac. He seemed to be saying everything he could to keep Gavin at a distance. She appreciated his concern, but until he volunteered to take Gavin's place, she was determined to be brave enough to pursue the relationship.

She forced a laugh and said, "Mac has been like a big brother to me for years. He gets a little protective at times."

Gavin's brows rose, and the smile returned. "I see. Don't worry, Mac," he said, patting Mac's arm. "I'll take good care of her."

Mac grunted and shifted back into the back seat, his arms crossed over his chest.

Jewel shivered as she made brief eye contact with Gavin. It looked like she was going to get a chance to try out her feminine wiles tonight. Mac would be there, so she wouldn't have to worry about things getting out of hand. Toasting marshmallows over a campfire would be a marvelously romantic setting, perfect for establishing a friendly rapport with Gavin.

She wondered if Gavin would try to kiss her. She wondered if she should let him. She caught Mac's narrowed gaze in the rearview mirror and wondered, with a smile, if *Mac* would let him. She had better have a talk with Mac before the trail ride and let him know she welcomed Gavin's attentions for the practice they would provide.

Jewel shivered in anticipation. She only hoped that when the time came, and Gavin made advances, she would have the nerve to follow through.

Chapter 9

Mac stared through his horse's ears at Jewel, riding side by side with Gavin on the moonlit trail ahead of him. Patty had decided to stay at the ranch, so he had no riding partner. Mac watched Jewel lean close to hear what Gavin was saying. A trilling burble of laughter floated back to him on the wind. His neck hairs rose, and he gritted his teeth in frustration.

That could have been him riding beside Jewel. That could have been him making her laugh. Instead, he was reduced to the role of chaperon. And not enjoying it one bit.

Mac turned to see who was coming as another horse cantered up beside him bearing one of the three late additions to their trail ride. ''Hey, Colt. What's new?''

''You know anything about that Gavin guy?'' Colt asked, aiming his chin toward the couple ahead of them.

Mac stared at Gavin. ''He's as comfortable on a horse as any cowboy I've ever seen, he's educated, friendly, courteous and he appears to be interested in Jewel.''

''You think he'll try to hurt her?''

Mac saw the worry on Colt's young face. Six years ago the kid had been only eight, but obviously Jewel's trauma had left a lasting impression on her family. ''There's not much Gavin can do with me along,'' Mac reassured the teenager.

Colt heaved a sigh of relief. ''Thanks, Mac. Jewel is…well, she's pretty special.''

''I know.''

Colt glanced over his shoulder, frowned, then looked straight ahead again. ''I thought I might get to see a little more of Jenny if we came along tonight. I should have known she'd stick like glue to Huck.''

Mac arched a brow. "You have feelings for her yourself?"

Colt readjusted his Western straw hat, setting it lower over his eyes to hide his expression. "She's Huck's girl."

"You didn't answer my question."

"So what if I like her?" Colt retorted. "Nothing's gonna come of it. They'll probably get married as soon as Huck finishes college."

"College is a long way off. Maybe Huck will change his mind. Or Jenny will."

Colt snorted. "What difference would that make? She doesn't know I'm alive."

Mac wasn't sure what to say. He hadn't been too fortunate in the romance department himself. But he knew what he would do if he loved a woman. "Mind if I offer you some advice?"

Colt shrugged.

"If you get a chance to make Jenny your girl, grab it with both hands." He grinned at Colt. "It's awful hard for a woman to resist a man who loves her, heart and soul."

Colt eyed him sideways. "If you say so."

They had reached the ring of stones Camp LittleHawk used as a campfire site for barbecues. Mac watched as Gavin lifted Jewel from her horse, sliding her down the front of him as he settled her feet on the ground. He saw the stunned look on Jewel's face as she gazed up at Gavin. Was it fear or wonder she had felt at the intimate contact?

He kneed his horse into a lope to catch up to them. He was out of the saddle and at her side seconds later. "Hey, Jewel," he said, putting a hand on her shoulder. "Let's get the fire going for those marshmallows."

When she looked at him, he saw dazed pleasure in her eyes. Damn. She was definitely aroused. A quick glance at the front of her—at the pebbled nipples that showed through the knit top—confirmed his diagnosis.

So what was he supposed to do now? Disappear, so Gavin could get on with his seduction?

The hell he would.

He grabbed Jewel's hand. "Come on, Jewel. Let's get some firewood."

Jewel glanced at him in surprise, smiled and followed him to the box of firewood that was kept nearby. He loaded her arms with kindling and picked up a few logs to carry back himself. By the time they returned to the fire, Colt had unpacked the wire clothes hangers they had brought along and was unbending them to make marshmallow roasting sticks.

Mac and Jewel knelt together before the ring of stones that Jenny and Huck were straightening and began arranging the kindling and logs. Gavin arrived moments later with the bag of marshmallows, a thermos of hot chocolate and some paper cups from his saddlebag and a couple of blankets that had been tied behind Jewel's saddle.

"Up, you two," he said to Mac and Jewel. "Let me get this down under you."

Mac and Jewel scooted to the side, and Gavin spread the gray wool blanket where they had been, settling himself on the opposite side of Jewel from Mac and leaning close to whisper, "I think you've already started my fire."

Mac couldn't help overhearing. Or seeing Jewel stiffen slightly before she managed a smile and replied, "Give me a match, and I'll show you a real blaze."

Gavin, damn him, laughed and handed her a box of matches. Instead of letting her light the match by herself, Gavin held her hand as she drew the match along the edge of the box and lit the kindling. When the fire from the match had almost reached her fingers, Gavin lifted her hand to his mouth and blew it out.

Jewel made a mewling sound that had Mac's

insides clenching. His hands fisted unconsciously, and his body tensed to fight.

Until that moment, Mac had not realized the
extent of his feelings for Jewel. He had always
liked her and considered himself her friend. He
had missed talking to her in the years they had
been apart. He was more than a little attracted
to her. But the instinctual need to claim her, to
make her his and only his, rose unbidden from
somewhere deep inside him.

He resisted the strong urge to hit Gavin Talbot
in the nose and began straightening out a clothes
hanger to use as a roasting stick. Fighting the
metal was a better release for his tension than
starting an uncivilized brawl.

It was abundantly clear to him now, as it had
not been before, that he wanted to be the man
Jewel gave herself to for the first time. He
wanted to see her eyes when their bodies were
joined, hear her sighs as she learned the pleasure
to be found in loving each other.

But Gavin moved fast, and Mac wasn't sure
he was going to get a second chance with Jewel
if something didn't happen pretty quick to separate the two. It didn't take much of a fire to
toast marshmallows, and it wasn't long before
Colt opened the bag and began tossing marsh-

mallows around. Gavin was making Jewel laugh again, putting a marshmallow on the end of her roasting stick and whispering in her ear as it toasted on the fire.

"Jewel," Mac said quietly.

To his surprise, she looked immediately at him. "Yes, Mac?"

"Your marshmallow is on fire."

Because she was looking at him, she swung the burning marshmallow in his direction. Mac caught the coat hanger far enough back not to burn himself and blew out the fire. "Hope you like it charred," he said with a smile.

He blew on it to cool it, then pulled the gooey marshmallow off the end of the wire and held it out to her between thumb and forefinger. She leaned forward, her mouth open, and grabbed Mac's wrist as she bit into it. She held on to his wrist while she chewed, waving her hand at her mouth and making noises because the gooey marshmallow was both hot and deliciously sweet.

Then, as though it were the most natural thing in the world, she leaned over and sucked the rest of the marshmallow off of his thumb, licking it clean with her tongue.

Mac stared at her with avid eyes. She could

have no idea what she was doing. By the time she was done with his thumb and had started on his forefinger, his body was strung as tight as a bowstring.

Jewel looked up at him, his forefinger still in her mouth, and caught his gaze with hers. She might not have realized beforehand what effect she was having on him, but he saw she recognized immediately what she had done.

Ever so slowly, she withdrew his forefinger from her mouth, then let go of his wrist. She had to clear her throat to speak. "I forgot to bring along wet wipes," she said. "I figured that was the best way to get rid of the marshmallow."

Mac took the fingers that had been in her mouth and slowly licked off imaginary specks of sugar. "It seems to be all gone."

He watched Jewel swallow hard before Gavin distracted her attention.

"How about sharing this one with me?" Gavin said, putting a hand on her forearm to stake his claim and holding out a perfectly toasted marshmallow.

Mac saw the goose bumps rise on her flesh where Gavin's hand lay. Saw her tentative smile as she turned back to the other man.

"Sure, Gavin," she said. "I'd like that."

She pulled the gooey marshmallow from the wire and ate half of it before Gavin caught her wrist and, with a grin, turned the marshmallow toward himself. Mac watched in helpless fury as Gavin ate the rest of the marshmallow from her hand and licked her fingers clean.

When Gavin started kissing her fingertips, something inside Mac snapped. "That's it!"

"What?" Jewel said, turning bewildered eyes on him.

"Let's go, Jewel." Mac stood and grabbed Jewel's wrist to drag her to her feet. He was surprised when she resisted.

"What's wrong with you, Mac?" she said.

"I think this has gone far enough." He said the words to the counselor, who understand exactly what his problem was.

Gavin rose to his feet, his legs widespread. "I didn't hear the lady complaining about my attentions."

Gavin had a point. But Mac wasn't in a rational mood. "The lady is too polite to say anything."

Gavin raised a questioning brow and faced Jewel. "Is that true, Jewel?"

"I don't see... I mean, I think I may have encouraged... I just wanted to see..."

Gavin's lip curved wryly on one side. "Your point is taken," he said to Mac.

By then, Colt was on his feet on the other side of the fire. "You need any help, Mac?"

Jenny grabbed Colt's T-shirt where it hung out of his jeans and yanked on it. "Sit down, Colt. This doesn't concern you."

"She's my sister."

"Sit down, Colt," Jenny repeated.

Mac watched as Colt met Jenny's gaze and settled back onto the ground beside her.

By then, Jewel was up and standing nose to nose with Mac. "What's gotten into you?" she demanded in a harsh whisper. "You're the one who told me to flirt with him in the first place!"

"I didn't think it would go this far," Mac said stubbornly.

"Thanks to you," she hissed, "it's not likely to go much further!"

"That's fine by me," Mac retorted.

"I think I'll excuse myself and let you two settle this alone," Gavin said. "I can find my own way back."

"We'd better get going, too," Jenny said, rising and pulling Huck and Colt to their feet. "I don't want to be late getting home."

Within moments, everything had been picked

up and repacked, and the four of them were on
their way back to the ranch house, leaving Mac
and Jewel to put out the fire.

"All right, Mac," Jewel said. "I want to hear
from your own lips what possessed you to cause
such a scene."

Jewel was confused by Mac's strange behavior. "You're the one who told me to try out my
feminine wiles," she said. "The first time I do,
you act like a jealous lover."

She thought Mac flushed, but it was hard to
tell in the firelight.

"I thought you wanted me along to protect
you," he said.

"If I needed protection. Which I did not."

Mac kicked sand over the fire, creating a
cloud of smoke. "You *liked* the way he was
pawing you?"

"*Pawing* me?" she said. "Gavin's attentions
weren't at all unwelcome."

When Gavin had smiled at her, she had allowed herself to feel the pleasure of being attractive to—and attracted to—a handsome man.
When he had blown out the match, and his
warm, moist breath touched her hand, she had
not cut off the frisson of awareness that skittered

down her spine. When he had kissed her finger-tips, she had felt her heart beat more rapidly in response.

But none of those feelings in any way compared to the shock of awareness she felt when she had met Mac's gaze and discovered he had been aroused by the way she had sucked and licked his fingers clean.

It was the difference between a pinprick and being stabbed with a knife. While she was completely aware of both, one was slight and fleeting, while the other burned deep inside. One would disappear quickly; the other would not soon be forgotten.

She wasn't about to admit her vulnerability to Mac when he was behaving like a jealous idiot. Especially when he wasn't volunteering to take Gavin's place. "I liked what Gavin did," she said.

"I didn't," Mac said flatly.

"Why not?" Jewel demanded.

"He was moving too fast. You hardly know the guy."

"He didn't do anything I didn't allow."

"That's another thing," Mac said. "Just how far were you intending to go? Would you have let him kiss you?"

"Why not?" she said tartly.

Mac made a threatening, rumbly sound in his throat. "I can kiss you as well as some stranger can. If it's kisses you want, come to me."

"Last night you said—"

"Forget about last night. It never happened. We start new, here and now. You want to practice being a woman, practice with me."

Jewel eyed Mac in astonishment. She had exactly what she had thought she wanted. All she had to do was find the courage to follow through and take Mac up on his offer. She took a deep breath, let it out and said, "All right. I'll practice with you."

Mac heaved a sigh and knelt down to stir the ashes with a stick to make certain the fire was out. "Thank God that's settled."

"I want to be kissed, Mac."

She watched his shoulders tense, saw him drop the stick, then rise to face her.

"You want to be kissed now?"

"If you hadn't scared Gavin away, he'd be kissing me now," she pointed out.

It was hard to tell what Mac was feeling. His eyes were narrowed in—anger? His lips were twisted in a moue of—frustration? And his brow was furrowed deep with—apprehension? Which showed how good she was at reading men. What did Mac Macready have to be anxious about? He must have kissed a hundred women. She was the one who needed lessons.

''Come here, Jewel,'' Mac said in a voice that grated like an unoiled hinge.

It only took a couple of steps for her to reach him. His arms opened wide, and as she stepped between them, they folded around her. One hand caught at her nape, the other low on her spine, just above her buttocks. She was aware of goose bumps rising along her nape as his hand slid up and grasped a handful of her hair.

He did not pull her any closer, simply angled her head and lowered his mouth. His lips felt warm and full as he rubbed them against hers. ''Are you sure about this, Jewel?'' he breathed against her half-open mouth.

She made a sound in her throat which he must have taken as assent, because he kissed the left side of her mouth, then the right, before returning to the center. He slipped his tongue beneath her upper lip, then nipped at her lips with his teeth.

Jewel shivered. It was strange, standing upright, being held—but not held—in a man's arms. She leaned into the kiss, returning the gentle pressure of his mouth. She slid her tongue along the seam of his lips, and he opened for her. Jewel had never been the aggressor with a man. It felt wonderful to be able to taste and tease to her heart's content without being afraid.

Her arms roamed up Mac's back, feeling the corded sinew. One hand slid into the hair at his nape and played with it as she indulged herself kissing him, feeling the damp softness of his lips, tasting the inside of his mouth with soft, tentative thrusts that he returned. She felt him begin to tremble.

"Jewel," he murmured.

"Hmm." Her lips followed the line of his chin to a spot below his ear, and she heard him hiss in a breath.

"I think we'd better stop."

She leaned back and looked up into his hooded eyes, at lips rigid with passion. She smiled. "If I look anything like you do, perhaps you're right."

"You look beautiful," he said fervently.

"You don't have to say that," Jewel protested. "I know what I—"

He put his mouth on hers to silence her, pouring his feelings into a kiss that had her straining to be closer to him, closing the distance between them, until they were pressed close from breast to thigh. Jewel was so entranced by what Mac was doing with his mouth that it took her a moment to realize he had widened his stance enough to fit her between his legs.

He was aroused.

She squeezed her eyes shut and tried to concentrate on the kiss. It was so lovely. It felt so good. But her body below the waist had turned to stone.

Mac broke the kiss and looked down at her, his eyes worried. "Jewel?"

"Let me go, Mac."

"I won't hurt you, Jewel." He put one hand on her buttocks to keep her where she was. He smiled tenderly. "I'd very much like to put myself inside you."

Jewel felt the heat climbing up her throat at such plain speaking. "Mac—"

"But I'm not going to do anything until you're ready," he said, leaning down to give her a gentle kiss on the lips. "We have plenty of time."

"Your recuperation is almost complete," Jewel countered. "Look how far you've come in—"

He stopped her with another kiss. "We have

plenty of time for you to get used to me touching
you, wanting you.''

"It doesn't seem fair, Mac. I mean, for me to
use you like this.''

He smiled. "Believe me, I don't mind.''

His eyes seemed to be promising things she
knew he could not mean. She looked down and
said, "In a couple of weeks you'll be leaving
here, and I won't be seeing you again.''

He lifted her chin until she was looking into
his eyes. "You'll always be special to me,
Jewel. You have no idea how special.'' He
opened his mouth as though to say something
else and closed it again. "Look, let's just take
this one day at a time. You can start with simple
stuff like kisses and touches. Anytime you want
to practice, just let me know. How does that
sound?''

"Are you sure I won't be imposing?'' Jewel
asked.

"It'll be my pleasure,'' Mac said with a grin,
rocking his body against hers.

"Oh!''

His brow wrinkled in concern. "What's
wrong?''

"You're still...and I'm not... It's working!''
she said with delight. "I'm hardly affected at

all.'' Except that her pulse was throbbing, and she felt the strangest urge to push back against the hardness that rested between her legs.

Mac's smile looked a little forced. "See. You're already getting used to me."

He released her, and Jewel took a step back.

"I suppose we'd better get back," she said. "Camp starts tomorrow, and I'll be getting up early."

"I can help you after my workout."

Jewel smiled. "I'd like that."

"Don't forget. Anytime you feel like you want to practice, just let me know. There's no need to flirt with that Gavin character."

"I thought I might try my wings—"

"Try your wings on me!" He swung her back into his arms, kissed her hard on the lips, then stomped off toward his horse, leaving her standing there.

It took a minute for Jewel to catch her breath and steady her racing pulse. "I was just teasing!" she called after him, as she hurried to catch up.

Mac made a growling sound in his throat. "Let's go. It's late."

She stomped right over and stood in front of

him. "For heaven's sake! Where's your sense of humor?"

He grabbed her hand and placed it on the bulge in his jeans. "Right there. I'm not feeling too damn funny at the moment."

Even though he had immediately let go of her hand, Jewel was too shocked to jerk away. She left her hand where Mac had put it, feeling the length and hardness of him. This part of him didn't seem nearly so threatening through a layer of denim and cotton, warm and pulsing beneath her hand.

"Jewel," he said through gritted teeth. "What are you doing?"

"Learning."

He gave a choked laugh. "I think my sense of humor is—"

"In very fine shape," she said with a gamine grin. "Want to test it again?"

He caught her wrist and removed her hand. "I think I've had enough testing for one evening. Let's save this for another time."

"Anything you say, Mac," she answered cheerfully. "You're the teacher."

And Jewel was determined to be a very good pupil.

Chapter 10

Mac realized the dilemma he had put himself in. He was going to be kissing and touching Jewel over the next several weeks—and encouraging her to kiss and touch him—even though he had serious reservations about making love to her. Not because he didn't desire her, but because he was afraid if he did something wrong, he would mess things up for her even more. He decided he owed it to both of them to get some professional advice.

"Something's come up that I need to discuss with my agent," Mac said to Jewel at breakfast the next morning. "I've made reservations to fly to Dallas this afternoon."

"Couldn't you do it over the phone?" Jewel asked.

Mac shook his head and raised another spoonful of cornflakes. "Too sensitive. Requires face-to-face consultation."

"Why didn't you say something about this last night?" she asked suspiciously.

He grinned. "I was distracted last night."

Jewel blushed. Mac thought she had never looked lovelier. She was wearing a plaid Western shirt, tucked in at the waist of her jeans, that hinted at the fullness of her figure. Her brown hair looked sun kissed, and her brown eyes gleamed. As she turned toward him, the faded crisscross scars on her face took him back to a time when they were both much younger and someone had teased her about them.

Mac realized he must have cared a great deal for her even then. He could remember wiping away her tears with his thumbs, kissing her scarred cheek and saying, "These scars are as precious as any other part of you, Jewel, more facets to add texture to the diamond you are."

He had meant it then, and he could see it now.

Jewel laid her spoon in her cereal bowl and

said, "I'll miss you, Mac. When will you be back?"

Mac met her troubled gaze and said, "I don't know." He had no idea how long it would take to get an appointment with the one sex therapist he knew. Dr. Timothy Douglas might be too busy to fit him in for several days.

"You're not coming back, are you?" Jewel said flatly. "You've changed your mind about wanting to teach me, and you're leaving." The glow had left her face and the sparkle had faded from her eyes.

"What do I have to do to convince you I'm not going away?"

"Kiss me," she said. "That was the deal. I could ask anytime, and I'm asking now." She crossed her arms over her chest as though she thought he might refuse.

Silly woman. He wasn't about to refuse.

Mac crossed to Jewel in two steps, tipped her chin up and slanted his mouth over hers, kissing her with all the passion he felt, hoping to convince her he meant what he said. They were both breathing hard when he lifted his head. "I'm coming back," he said. "I just have some business to do in Dallas."

Tears filled her eyes as she looked up at him. "That was goodbye. I know it."

Mac shook his head in disbelief. He stood and put his hands on his hips. "Look, Jewel. Why would I make an offer like the one I made last night and leave the next day for good?"

"Because you had second thoughts," she said.

"No, I did not."

"Because you realized I might fall in love with you or something stupid like that, if you started kissing me all the time."

"That never crossed my mind!" The thought hadn't occurred to him, but he liked the idea now that she mentioned it.

"Probably you never thought of me falling in love, because kisses don't mean much to a man like you," she said, lips pouting.

How wrong she was! Mac thought. Her kisses, at least, made him feel a great deal, though he wasn't willing to go so far as to think in terms of love. A great deal of *like*. That was what he felt for Jewel Whitelaw.

But he couldn't resist kissing her again. He slipped his tongue inside her mouth and tasted her thoroughly. When he stood again, the revealing bulge was back in his jeans. He noticed that she noticed and felt his body tighten in expectation.

"I'll be back, Jewel. Trust me."

It was a lot to ask a woman who hadn't found much about men to trust.

She blinked back the tears and said, "All right, Mac."

He kissed her again, to thank her for trusting him, but when he felt the urge to pull her up and into his arms, he stepped back. "You've got campers to see to, and I've got a few things to do before I join you."

"You're still going to help me with the campers this morning?"

"Of course. Why wouldn't I?"

"I thought you might have to pack..."

"I'm only taking a few things."

She walked back to him and put her arms around him and hugged him tight. "I'm so glad you're coming back," she said. "I'll be waiting for you. I won't even flirt with Gavin while you're gone."

She was already halfway to the door by the time he realized what she had said. She turned back, winked and laughed, then headed out the door.

Mac watched her till she was gone, realizing

he had more problems to solve than just hers, if
they were to have any hope of a future together.
He had gotten a big signing bonus when he
joined the Tornadoes, but his five-year contract
had provided for a smaller salary in the first few
years. He had most of the signing bonus left, but
he had pretty much spent his first year's salary.

What if he didn't make it back onto the team?
Don't even think *that!*

Mac didn't believe in quitting or giving up or
giving in. But it was time for a reality check. He
had accomplished more than most men would
have. He was walking—hell, he was running
again—when the doctors said he'd be in a leg
brace the rest of his life. He should quit while
he was ahead. If he went back to playing football, chances were good he'd reinjure his leg.
Maybe next time his prognosis would be even
worse.

Mac called his agent's office and got Andy's
secretary. ''Tell Andy I'll be in his office about
four o'clock this afternoon. I'll fill him in on
everything when I see him.''

He headed out the door dressed in a starched
white oxford-cloth shirt belted into crisp new
jeans and almost new ostrich cowboy boots, so
he'd be ready if the media caught sight of him

in Dallas. Mac wanted to look confident and ready to go back to work for the Tornadoes on the outside, even if he didn't feel quite that way inside.

He stopped at the boys' bunkhouse to check on Brad Templeton, but apparently the kids had already headed over to the cookhouse for breakfast. He was about to leave when he heard something hit the tile floor in the communal bathroom. He stepped inside. ''Who's there?''

Nobody answered, but Mac knocked on the frame of the open bathroom doorway and said, ''Anybody here?''

Brad Templeton stepped out of one of the four shower-curtained stalls. ''How'd you know I was here?''

''I heard something drop.''

He made a face. ''My plastic cup.''

''Why aren't you at breakfast with the other kids?'' Mac asked, leaning casually against the bathroom doorway to put the kid at ease.

''I told Gavin I didn't feel well.''

Mac's easy pose evaporated. He took the few steps to bring him to Brad's side, whipped off the kid's New York Mets baseball cap and pressed his hand on Brad's forehead. It all happened so fast, Brad didn't have a chance to complain until Mac had already found out what he wanted to know. He replaced the cap. ''No fever,'' he said.

Brad tugged the ball cap back down over his nearly bald head. ''Naw. I'm okay.''

Fever was one of the first—and worst—signs that a remission was over, that the leukemia was back. It wasn't something to be ignored. ''Why'd you tell Gavin you were sick?'' Mac asked.

Brad shrugged, the kind of kid gesture that could have meant anything, but really meant, *I couldn't tell him the truth.*

''What's on the agenda this morning?'' Mac asked.

''Horseback riding,'' Brad mumbled.

''That sounds like fun. What's the problem?''

''I've never been on a horse before. I'd probably get bucked off and stomped to death. I don't want to die any sooner than I have to.''

Mac grinned.

''That's not funny!'' Brad said.

''You sound exactly like I did when I went riding the first time. Funny how being sick makes you want to live all the more, isn't it?''

Brad's brows rose almost to the brim of his ball cap. It was one thing for Mac to say he'd been sick, another for him to express a feeling that could only be had by someone who had personally faced death.

"Come on," Mac said, putting a hand on Brad's shoulder and ushering him toward the door. "Let's get you fed. I know just the pony for you. Gentle as a lamb."

"What's his name?" Brad asked.

Mac grinned. "Buttercup."

Mac paced the confines of Andy Dennison's office, from the bat signed by Ken Griffey, Jr., in one corner, to the football signed by Joe Montana in the other and back again. His agent had become his friend, and now he needed some friendly advice. But Andy was late.

He had too much time to think.

Andy must have leaked what time Mac was landing at Dallas/Fort Worth International Airport, because a bunch of photographers and reporters had been waiting for him when he exited the jetway. He had smiled for the cameras as he walked quickly toward the chauffeur-driven limousine waiting for him outside.

"It's great to see you walking so well, Mac," one reporter commented. "Will you be back with the Tornadoes this fall?"

"That's my plan," Mac said.

"You can walk. But can you run?" another reporter asked.

Mac smiled more broadly. "Does a Texas dog have fleas?"

Everybody laughed, but the reporter persisted. "What's your time for the forty?"

Mac's time for the forty-yard dash wasn't anywhere near the four-point-something-second range of most wide receivers, and nothing close to his own previous time. His hesitation in answering hinted at the problems he was having, and the reporters, smelling blood, attacked in earnest.

"Have you come to Dallas to announce your retirement?" one speculated.

"No," Mac said flatly.

"Are you here to see a doctor about your leg?"

"No."

"Are you negotiating with the Tornadoes to get your spot on the team back?"

"No comment."

That gave them more meat to chew on and distracted them from other lines of questioning. They asked a dozen more questions aimed at determining his exact status with the Tornadoes, before he reached the limousine and safety.

"Remind me to kill Andy when I see him," he muttered to Andy's driver.

The old man laughed. "He thought you could use the publicity."

"Why wasn't he here to keep the wolves off of me?"

"He's working on a big deal. Said he'd see you at the office at four, like you asked. You're all set up to stay at the Wyndham Hotel. I can take you there to freshen up, if you'd like."

"I need to make another stop first." Mac gave Andy's chauffeur the address of the sex therapist, who had agreed to see him today during a time someone else had canceled an appointment.

Dr. Timothy Douglas had first talked to Mac in the hospital after one of his operations, when Mac was scared to death that he would be impotent for life because nothing seemed to be working. The doctor had reassured Mac that the medication he was taking—and his state of agitation over the problem—had caused his lack of sex drive.

Douglas was not much older than Mac, but he was balding and wore spectacles, both of which made him look more distinguished. The good doctor had returned several times over the years to talk to Mac in the hospital, and it was during one of those discussions that Mac had admitted he was a virgin.

Douglas hadn't been able to control a smile. "Good for you," he'd said. "Too many men are indiscriminate these days."

"Sorry to burst your bubble, Doc, but I doubt I'd be able to say that if I'd been out of this bed more than a day at a time over the past couple of years."

Douglas patted his shoulder and said, "Wait for the right woman, Mac. You won't be sorry."

Douglas was the only person in the world who knew Mac's secret. And the only one he felt comfortable telling about Jewel's secret. Surely the good doctor could come up with some suggestions for how Mac could help Jewel without hurting her.

"This is a doctor's office," the chauffeur said when he stopped in front of the address Mac had given him.

"Sure is," Mac said. "Meet me back here in an hour."

Mac let himself out of the sleek black car and headed inside the office building.

The hour Mac spent with Timothy Douglas

had been well worth the time and trouble to get there. As he paced his agent's office, Mac worked through the various suggestions Douglas had made for how he could help Jewel.

"Patience is essential," Douglas said. "Thoughtfulness. Consideration. All the things you would normally expect in a loving relationship. Only, each step of the way, you need to check with Jewel to make sure she's still with you. Understand?"

Mac understood all right. The man was supposed to control himself while he attended to the woman first. "What if I can't wait?" he blurted, his face crimson with embarrassment.

"Do you care for this woman?" Douglas asked.

"Why the hell do you think I'm so worried?" Mac shot back. "What if I lose control and make things worse?"

"Be sure you're thinking of her at the crucial moment, instead of yourself, and everything will turn out fine."

"That's all there is to it?" Mac asked skeptically.

"Sex is a natural bodily function," Douglas said. "We're supposed to procreate. Your body will know what to do, even if you don't."

Mac took comfort in that last word of advice. But as he was very well aware, knowing technically what to do, and actually doing it, sometimes turned out to be two entirely different things.

On Mac's next lap across his agent's office, the door opened and Andy Dennison stepped inside.

"Hi there, Mac. What's new?"

"I can walk. And I can run."

Andy smiled and crossed to shake Mac's hand. "Congratulations. I should have known you would do what you promised. How about a cigar to celebrate?"

"No thanks," Mac said with a smile. "I'm in training."

"You don't mind if I have one." Andy crossed to his desk, took a cigar from a box on top of it, clipped the end with a sterling silver device, sniffed it and rolled the tobacco lovingly between his fingers. That was as far as he could go. No smoking was allowed in the building.

"When can I set up an appointment with the Tornadoes?" Andy asked.

"Not so fast," Mac said, seating himself in one of the two modern chrome and black leather chairs facing the desk. "What's the last date I could show up in training camp and still have a chance to make the team?''

"Depends on how fast you can run when you show up," Andy said bluntly.

"How fast is the new kid?"

Andy gave Mac a figure for the forty that made sweat bead on Mac's forehead. It was two seconds better than Mac's best time before he was injured.

"What about his hands?"

"Misses a few. Fumbles now and again."

Mac smiled. "Then I have a chance. Being fastest isn't everything. I proved that when I played."

"Yeah. But being slow will get you cut from the team," Andy pointed out.

"How slow is too slow?" Mac asked, leaning forward, his elbows on his knees.

Andy shrugged. "Hard to say. But if you aren't within a second or two of your best time…" Andy shrugged again.

Mac sighed and sat back, crossing his good ankle over his scarred knee. "I was afraid of that."

"Look, there's been some interest in using you as a sports commentator. Why not let me follow up and—"

"That isn't what I want to do with my life."

"What are you planning to do? I mean, if you don't make the team?"

Mac drew a complete blank. "I don't know. I haven't thought about it much."

"Maybe you should," Andy said. "Think about that sportscasting job. It's national television, lots of exposure, possibility of advertising bucks. Lot of dough in a job like that."

"Lots of travel, too," Mac said.

"Yeah, there's that."

"I want to settle down somewhere and have a family."

Andy cleared his throat. "Uh. I heard about that stop you made this afternoon. Anything I can do to help?"

Mac laughed. "It's taken care of, but thanks for the offer."

"Sure, Mac, just know I'm there if you need me. By the way, who's the girl?"

"Knowing your penchant for publicity I figure I'll keep that to myself for a while."

"Hey. Whatever you want," Andy said. "By the way, how long are you going to be in town?"

"Just overnight."

"Anxious to get back to your girl?" Andy said with a sly smile.

Mac thought about it, smiled and answered, "Yeah. I am."

"Look, I know some folks who'd like to have dinner with you. How about it?"

"Will it help you out?"

Andy grinned. "You're a great guy, Mac. I knew you'd come through. I'll have a tux delivered to your hotel room, and I'll have my limo pick you up at eight."

"A tux! What kind of shindig is this?"

"Charity ball in Forth Worth, complete with politicians and socialites. Won't hurt you to be seen there, Mac. You can use all the good press you can get. You'll be sitting at the mayor's table."

Mac shook his head. "How do I let you talk me into these things?"

Andy stuck the cigar between his teeth and grinned. "You like me?"

Instead of laughing, Mac looked Andy in the eye and said, "You stuck with me when a lot of other folks didn't. I'm not likely to forget that anytime soon." He left before Andy could form a response.

Chapter 11

Colt sat on the sagging back porch of Jenny's house waiting for Huck to come back out. He tugged at the frayed knee of his jeans, making the tear worse, then glanced up at the hot, noonday sun. He couldn't get what Mac had said about Huck and Jenny out of his mind.

College is a long way off. Maybe they'll change their minds about each other.

Colt would never do anything to separate the two of them—not that he believed anything could alter Jenny's devotion to Huck—but Mac had offered him a sort of hope he hadn't allowed himself to feel in a very long time.

Lately, Colt let his eyes linger on her more. He let his heart fall more completely under her spell. Even though his head said it was a stupid thing to do.

"Hey, Colt. You ready to go?"

Colt leapt up guiltily as the kitchen screen door slammed and stuck his hands deep into his back pockets. "Yeah. Sure." *Good thing Huck couldn't read his mind.*

"You're acting awful jumpy lately. What's your problem?" Huck asked as he crossed past Colt and down the creaking steps. "Some girl finally caught your eye?" he teased.

Maybe Huck could read minds, Colt thought uncomfortably.

"Who is it? Sarah Logan? Freda Barnett? I know—Betty Lou Tucker!"

Betty Lou Tucker was the prettiest—and most curvaceous—girl in school. Huck was way off the mark. The only girl Colt ever thought about was Jenny. And Jenny wasn't beautiful, she was just...Jenny. Colt thought of Jenny looking up at him with her bluer-than-blue eyes and felt the heat rising up his throat to make visible spots on his cheeks.

"Thought so," Huck said with a laugh. "Betty Lou's been looking at a lot of guys since she broke up with Bobby Ray.'' Huck unlooped the reins from the tie rail in front of the Double D ranch house and mounted his horse. ''You coming with me, or you gonna sit on Jenny's back porch all day?''

''I…uh…think I'll wait to talk to Jenny before I leave…about some stuff.''

Huck shook his head in disgust. ''Jenny's gotta feed the little ones before she can do anything. You might be waiting a while. She was asking me if I could help her out, but I've got better things to do with my time than housework. You're welcome to take my place.''

''Maybe I'll do that,'' Colt said, his heart thumping a little harder.

''See you tonight at the movies?'' Huck asked.

''Naw. My dad asked me to do some bookkeeping with him.''

''When are you gonna tell him you're not gonna stay on the ranch?'' Huck asked.

''Sometime,'' Colt said.

''Better be soon, or he'll be depending on you so much you'll never get out,'' Huck warned.

''I hear you,'' Colt said irritably.

Huck kicked his horse into a lope, raising a

choking cloud of dust from the dry, sunbaked dirt around the house.

Colt stepped back and waved away the worst of it so he could breathe, then turned and stared at the screen door. All he had to do was knock and offer his help. It was bound to seem a little odd to Jenny for him to volunteer, since he'd never been in her house before.

There was a reason for that. He stayed away from sick people, and her mother had been sick nearly the whole time he'd known her. Her mother's breast cancer had gone into remission for a long time, but after the youngest child was born, it had come back.

Now Mrs. Wright was dying of cancer. Colt knew what that meant. Hair falling out from chemotherapy. Frail limbs. Eyes dead long before the body was. He had seen too much of it at Camp LittleHawk. Enough to know that it hurt desperately to like—let alone love—someone who was ill and who might or might not survive another week, another month, another year.

The only thing that could make him go inside Jenny's house right now was the knowledge that he would get to spend time alone with her. They would probably talk and maybe laugh together.

That possibility was worth having to share Jenny's pain as she tended to her dying mother.

But Huck had said Jenny was feeding the little ones. Colt was the baby in his family, but he figured he could probably manage whatever Jenny asked of him.

Colt knocked on the door, said, "Jenny, I'm coming in," and let himself inside. He immediately took off his Western straw hat and stood still inside the screen door until his eyes adjusted to the darker room. When he could see, he found Jenny staring at him, her jaw hanging open.

"Colt. What are you doing in here?"

"Huck thought you might need some help." He clutched the hat against his chest feeling foolish, but said, "Here I am."

She smiled, and he knew it was going to be all right. He looked for a place to hang his hat, but didn't see anything.

"Put it on top of the refrigerator," she said. "That way Tyler and James can't get to it."

He looked at the baby sitting in the high chair before her and the older child sitting in a youth chair next to him. "They seem pretty well lassoed," he said, but he put the hat where she told him, anyway.

She gestured him toward her. "This is

Randy,'' she said, sticking another spoonful of something gross looking in the baby's mouth, ''and next to him is Sam. Tyler and James are playing in their room.

''Here. You can take my place.'' She rose and handed Colt the baby spoon and the open jar of baby food. ''Randy loves peas.''

Colt took one look at the contents of the jar and nearly gagged. ''This doesn't look edible.''

Jenny laughed, and he felt his whole body go still at the sound. ''Don't tell Randy. He eats it like it was green ice cream.''

Colt sat in the chair she had vacated and aimed a spoon of peas in Randy's direction. When his mouth opened, Colt shoved it in, and Randy cleaned it off. ''He's a human vacuum cleaner!''

''He'll probably end up as big and tall as my dad,'' Jenny said as she set a plate of more recognizable food in front of Sam. The music had gone out of her voice by the time she got to the end of her sentence.

''Where is your dad?''

''He left,'' she said, her eyes focused on Sam. ''Took off when Mom got sick the second time.''

''I'm sorry, Jenny. I didn't know.''

She tried to make light of it. "Can't really blame him. It isn't pretty to watch someone die. He loved her very much, you know."

Colt couldn't believe how matter-of-factly she was speaking about such a tragic situation. "It must be hard for you and your mom to get along on your own."

Her chin came up, and she looked at him with her incredible blue eyes. "We manage."

He heard her message loud and clear: *Don't feel sorry for me.* He admired her gumption. But what choice did she have? She wasn't old enough to leave home and get a job. Where would she go? He realized now why she had been so worried about being left behind by Huck.

"Good thing you have so much help around the house," he said. "All those brothers, I mean."

"I'm the eldest," she said. "Tyler is ten, James is nine, Sam is five and Randy will be one in a couple of months."

"Who takes care of them when you're in school?"

"Mom has a sister who takes care of her during the days and keeps an eye on the little ones.

I pick up the slack at night and give Aunt Lenore a rest.''

Colt caught her glance for a moment and saw a sort of desperation he had often felt himself. A yearning to be free to follow your own path, to see the world, to explore to your heart's content. And the knowledge that destiny—or your parents or family—had other plans for you.

He had thought Huck was the only impediment to having Jenny. He saw now what the future held for her as well as she probably saw it herself. Unless she ran away, and he did not see Jenny as the kind of person who ran away from anything, she would be tied to her family until the boys were grown.

Huck would leave her behind when she couldn't go with him, because Huck would never understand why she couldn't go. Colt understood, though. It was the same reason he might never fly jets. Because she couldn't bear to hurt her family to please herself. As he could never bear to hurt his.

Colt wanted to tell her that he understood. That he knew what she faced. That he would be there for her, even if Huck wasn't.

What if you get a chance to fly jets? an inner

voice asked. *Would you stay and work at Hawk's Pride just to be near Jenny?*

Colt was glad he didn't have to make that kind of decision for four years. He would be here for her now. Even though she was Huck's girl. And might always be.

Jewel, Patty and Gavin were sitting in the sand at the bottom of a canyon with eleven campers, pencils and notepads in hand, sketching the primitive art etched on the stone canyon wall that rose up on one side of them.

Some of the kids were sitting cross-legged, some lay on their stomachs. Only one child had not relaxed and made himself comfortable. The twelfth camper, Brad Templeton, stood directly in front of the wall, staring up at it intently.

"How are you doing?" Jewel asked the campers as she rose and began to walk among them to see what they had produced in the half hour they had been drawing.

"Okay."

"Pretty good."

"What's that thing there?" A girl's finger pointed to a stick horse etched on the stone wall.

"What does it look like?" Jewel asked.

"It's a horse, dummy," the boy sitting next to the girl said scornfully.

"Yes, it is, Louis," Jewel said. "But you can see why Nolie might not recognize it. It could be some other animal."

"It has a long tail and pointy ears like a horse," Louis said.

"True. But some dogs have long tails and pointy ears."

"Oh," Louis said thoughtfully. "It looked like a horse to me."

"That's why we're making these drawings," Jewel explained. "And writing down what we think they mean." She put a supportive hand on Patty's shoulder as she encouraged one of the campers and exchanged a thankful look with Gavin, who had one of the youngest—and most homesick—campers sitting in his lap.

"We'll send your drawings to an archaeologist at the university who studies primitive art. She can tell us what she thinks the drawing means. When I send you her findings later this summer, you can compare your conclusions with hers."

"Does the drawing really mean something?" another little girl asked, staring at the primitive figures.

Jewel shrugged and smiled. "I don't know. Maybe someone a long time ago was just having fun drawing."

The kids laughed.

Jewel had reached Brad's side and noticed his drawing pad was blank. "Is something wrong, Brad?" she asked quietly.

He kept his eyes on the stone wall and spoke in a voice that only she could hear. "I know what it means," he said.

"You do?" Jewel turned to stare at the wall of stick figures and arrows pointing in different directions with a sun above it all. "Tell me. I've always been curious."

"What does it matter? What does anything matter?"

Jewel's brow furrowed. "You can't give up, Brad," she said.

"Why not?" he shot back. "People give up on stuff all the time. They quit hobbies and they quit school and they quit jobs."

"They don't quit living," she said.

"Some do," he said stubbornly. "They just stop doing things. You know what I mean."

Jewel felt a chill run down her spine. *People like her. As afraid of living as Brad was of dying.* "Tell me about the drawings, Brad."

He turned to look up at the wall. "The man wants to go somewhere far away, to have an adventure. But he isn't sure which is the best way to go. So he doesn't go anywhere at all. He stays right where he is. Where it's safe."

Jewel stared at the wall. The sun shone brightly above a stick-figure man and his stick-figure horse. They were surrounded by arrows pointing in all different directions—some of them back at the man himself.

He doesn't go anywhere at all. He stays right where he is. Where it's safe.

Jewel's throat squeezed closed. Brad might have been describing her own life for the past six years. Recently she had begun to make changes, but even so, she had been relying on Mac to get her over the worst hurdles. That had to stop. She had to start thinking about moving forward on her own. Or she might end up stuck forever right where she was.

She had to stop letting the past control her present. She had to open herself to new relationships. She couldn't count on Mac to solve her problems. He wanted to be her friend, nothing more. That had become apparent when she discovered from reading the newspapers the real reason he had gone to Dallas three days ago.

She had died a little inside when she opened the Dallas newspaper the day after Mac had left and found a picture of Mac and Eve Latham smiling at each other at a Fort Worth charity function. If Eve was the woman Mac wanted, Jewel had to accept that and move on. She had to find the courage to start living again—without Mac's help.

The same way Brad had to keep on living, despite the fact he might be dying. "Do you think he ever took the trip?" Jewel asked softly.

Brad shook his head, and a tear spilled on his cheek. He knuckled it away with his fist. "He waited too late," Brad whispered.

Jewel took a step closer and enfolded Brad in her arms. Her chin quivered, and she gritted her teeth to keep from making any sound. How could she have been working here all these years and not have seen what Brad could see so clearly? How could she have let so many years go by not living life when it was so precious? How could she have given fear such a stranglehold on her future?

"It's never too late, Brad," she said fiercely. "All you have to do is take that first step, and then another, and another." She rubbed his shoulders soothingly, then pushed him back and tipped up his chin so she could see his eyes beneath the baseball cap. "Just one step, Brad. And the adventure begins."

"Everything all right here?" Gavin had brought the homesick child with him in his arms.

Jewel swallowed back the knot in her throat and turned to Gavin with a smile. "Sure. I think Brad is ready to do some drawing. Right, Brad?"

"Yeah," he mumbled.

"This one is about ready to go back," Gavin said, gesturing to the little girl with his chin. She looked happy and comfortable in Gavin's arms. He really was a great guy, Jewel thought, just not the guy for her.

"Tell you what," Jewel said. "Why don't you and Patty gather up everyone else and get them started back. I'll stay here a little while longer with Brad."

"You sure?" Gavin asked doubtfully. "It's pretty isolated out here."

Jewel laughed. "Hawk's Pride is safer than most big cities. Brad and I will be fine."

"Okay," Gavin said with a smile. "See you later."

"Thanks, Gavin."

"You're welcome, Boss," he said over his

shoulder. "Come on, guys. Let's get you all mounted up," he called to the campers. "Day's wastin'."

Jewel helped Gavin and Patty make sure all the campers were comfortable for the horseback ride up out of the canyon. Then she crossed back to where Brad was industriously working on his drawing.

"That's looking pretty good," Jewel said, admiring his sketch.

"I've had a lot of time to practice," Brad said, his lips curling wryly.

"What do you want to be when you grow up?" Jewel asked.

"I wanted to be a football player," Brad said, changing it to the past tense. "Like Mac Macready."

"Let's get some practice, then," Mac said.

Jewel and Brad both jerked their heads toward the sound of Mac's voice. He dismounted from his horse, a football tucked into his elbow.

Jewel was surprised Mac had returned, especially after seeing the photo of him with his arm around Eve Latham. Her first impulse was to rail at him, but she had no claims on Mac Macready. What "business" he did in his free time was up to him. She just wished he hadn't lied to her

about why he had gone to Dallas. That wasn't
something friends did to friends.

"What are you doing here?" Jewel said, her
voice sharp despite her wish to keep it level.

"I brought a football, figuring I'd throw a few
passes to the kids, but I passed them on the way
down, headed back for lunch. Gavin told me
you'd stayed behind with Brad, so I thought I'd
join you."

"Hi, Mac," Brad said shyly.

"Hi, Brad," Mac said, tossing him the football. "I need to talk with Jewel for a minute.
Why don't you go find us a place where you can
throw me a few?"

"You want me to throw to you?"

"You want to be a football player someday,
don't you? No time like the present to start practicing."

Brad shot Jewel a questioning look. *Should I
let myself hope? Should I take him up on his
offer?*

"One step, Brad," she said softly. "And the
adventure begins."

The boy smiled broadly and turned back to
Mac. "Okay, Mac. I'll go find us a good spot."
He turned and headed on the run toward a sandy

stretch that extended around a curve in the canyon wall.

Jewel compared the Mac in the newspaper photo to the Mac standing before her. He had looked impressively handsome in a tuxedo. But he was just as impressive dressed in a cutoff T-shirt that showed off a washboard midriff and rippling biceps. Cutoff jeans revealed his scarred leg, but emphasized his height. Tennis shoes and a Texas Rangers baseball cap with his blond hair sticking out every whichaway made him look like one of the kids.

She was quite aware he was not.

Jewel forced herself to stand still as Mac eyed her up and down in return. She was wearing a T-shirt with the neck cut out that was also cut off at midriff, exposing her narrow waist, and very short, fringed cutoffs that showed off her long legs. She might as well have been naked. The look in his eyes made her skin feel prickly all over.

Now that he was back, his gaze seemed to say, they could pick up where they had left off, kissing and touching.

But she could not forget the possessive look in Eve's eyes, or the way Mac's arm reached snugly around her. She was very well aware of how long he had been gone and who he had been with, but she couldn't very well confront him with Brad nearby.

"I missed you," he said softly.

"From the picture in the newspaper I wouldn't have said you were too lonely."

He frowned. "What picture?"

"The one of you with your arm around Eve Latham at a charity ball."

Mac groaned. "I can explain—"

"Later," she said, turning to walk away from him. "Brad is waiting for you."

He caught her arm. "I want this cleared up now. It was nothing, Jewel. Publicity my agent set up."

"With Eve Latham?" she said, raising a doubtful brow.

"With her father, actually. He's a big fan of the Tornadoes."

"I suppose Eve just happened to be there?"

"Believe me, I didn't set that up. In fact, I'd planned to come right back the next morning, but Eve's father arranged a golf game the next morning with the manager of the Tornadoes that I couldn't very well get out of, and my agent snuck a few more appearances into the mix. Believe me, I only wanted to get back here as quickly as I could.''

''Why?'' she said, staring him in the eye. ''So you could throw footballs to adoring campers?''

For the first time he looked angry. ''You know better,'' he said through clenched teeth.

''Do I? I have no claim on you, Mac. If you'd rather not follow through on what you promised, all you have to do is say so. It isn't necessary to make excuses.''

An instant later, he was kissing her hard on the mouth. It was as much a kiss of anger as of passion. Jewel felt both angry and passionate in return. Mac let her go abruptly, his breathing erratic, and said, ''I have no intention of backing out on my promise to you. It's up to you whether you choose to take advantage of my offer.''

Jewel stared at Mac, appalled at how easily he had aroused her, how easily he had made her want him. She was afraid to let Mac back in. ''I thought you'd lied to me about why you went to Dallas,'' she admitted.

''I would never lie to you, Jewel. That's not something friends do.''

She wanted to believe him. She wanted to go back to trusting him. Fear made her cautious. Fear made her reluctant to let him back into her life. Fear could keep her stuck in the same rut forever.

Jewel glanced at the etching on the stone wall. She took a deep breath and let it out. "All right, Mac. You've got yourself a deal."

She held out her hand for him to shake, and Mac raised it to his mouth, kissing it like a courtier of old. His grin reappeared, and she felt her insides flip-flop.

"Very well, my little hyacinth," he said.

"That's a flower."

"And a precious stone," he assured her. "See you in a little while." He let go of her and loped across the sand, calling out to Brad to throw him the ball.

Jewel stared at her hand where Mac had kissed it, then raised her fingertips to her recently kissed lips. Mac had plainly thrown down the gauntlet. She had a chance to grab for life with both hands. She had a chance to practice kissing and touching with him. And she had a chance to explore a relationship with him beyond the friendship they had shared for so many years. She could take it, or reject it. The choice was hers.

What she must not do was make no choice at all.

If she hadn't spent the past half hour in Brad Templeton's company, she might have chickened out. But Jewel couldn't very well demand Brad reach out for life, if she wasn't going to do it herself.

Brad threw Mac the ball and came racing back to her holding out his notepad and pencil.

Jewel exchanged a glance with Mac that was the closest she had ever come to flirting with him. It promised everything…later. She was rewarded with a look that made her body curl inside and her breasts feel achy and swollen.

Jewel felt a tug on her T-shirt and looked down at Brad, who stood beside her again, his eyes gleaming with delight. Oh, yes. Football. And hope.

"I'll take those things," she said, reaching out for Brad's notepad and pencil.

Brad turned and trotted right back to Mac. She saw the boy swallow hard as he reached out for the football Mac was handing him. Jewel thanked Mac with her eyes and got a wink that flustered her in return.

She knew better than to tell either male not to overdo it. But Jewel was concerned as the sun rose higher and Brad continued to throw the ball and Mac continued to run for it. They were both drenched with sweat. Brad looked flushed. And Mac was starting to limp.

"Hey, you two. How about a break?"

She caught Mac's eye and gave him a warning look. He glanced at Brad and said, "I'm whipped, partner. How about a tall, cold glass? Of water, that is," he said, slapping Brad on the shoulder as they started back toward where Jewel sat in the shade of the canyon wall.

Jewel stood up with the canteens ready and handed one to each of them. She lifted Brad's hat as though to rearrange it on his head and surreptitiously checked for a fever. He seemed warm, but the sun was hot. "How are you feeling?" she asked, unable to keep the concern from her voice.

"Fantastic," Brad said, grinning for the first time since he had arrived at camp. "That was fun, Mac. Thanks."

"Tell you what I'm going to do, partner. I'm going to autograph this football to you with thanks for a strong throwing arm, so you can take it home with you."

"Wow! That would be neat," Brad said, sounding more like a kid his age every minute. He flopped down onto the sand, looking exhausted but happy.

Jewel was aware of Mac's wince as he settled onto the ground beside Brad.

"I've got some snacks that'll keep us until we can get some lunch," she said, dropping to her knees and opening what was left of the graham crackers and peanut butter and celery she had brought for the campers. "That'll also give you two a chance to cool off before we make the ride home."

As they munched, Mac and Brad talked. Jewel watched them closely. Brad had a smile on his face and talked a mile a minute, as though someone had turned up the rpms on a record. Mac listened. He didn't look at her often, but often enough to remind her that he was ready and willing whenever she wanted to take that final leap of faith. "Are you ready to head back now?" Jewel asked, when Brad had wound down a little.

"I guess," Brad said. "Can we do this again?" he asked Mac as he shoved himself to his feet.

"As often as you want before you leave," Mac said.

Jewel noticed Mac wincing again as he straightened his scarred leg.

He caught her watching him and grinned, as

though he hadn't just been in pain. "Don't worry. Everything important is working just fine." He leered at her, making it clear exactly what he meant.

Jewel felt flustered and excited. And anxious. Mac looked exhausted. He was using humor—and sexual tension—to distract her and doing a pretty good job. She was also concerned about Brad. He seemed awfully red-faced even after his rest. "Are you sure you're both feeling all right?" she asked.

"I'm doing great!" Brad said.

"I'm just fine," Mac said.

Jewel pursed her lips. Typical males. Everything was fine until they keeled over. She decided to keep a close eye on both of them.

Mac was still grinning as he ushered Brad past her and headed for the horses, whispering for her ears only, "You look beautiful, Amethyst. And very, very desirable. I can't wait for...later."

Jewel's heart started to pound as she stared at Mac's back, wondering if she would have the courage to do this evening what she had been waiting six years to do. His calling her "Amethyst" reminded her that they had been friends for a very long time. That he would never hurt her. That she could trust him.

Surely Brad's admonition about postponing life had made a difference. Surely she would be able to let go of the fear and move forward with her life. All she had to do was take one step. And the adventure would begin.

Chapter 12

Brad was a different child when he entered the cookhouse for lunch—happy, talkative, showing off his football to the other kids and stuffing down a plateful of lasagna as though it was the best meal he had ever eaten. Jewel was proud of Brad for reaching out with both hands toward the future and grateful to Mac for putting an ear-to-ear smile on the boy's face.

However, Mac had not joined them for lunch, pleading the need for a shower. The entire time Jewel ate, she could not get the image of him naked in the shower out of her mind. She had the craziest urge to join him there which, of course, she did not indulge.

After lunch, when the campers took a rest break in their cottages, Jewel had no excuse to linger in the cookhouse. She drew herself up from the bench where she had been sitting and headed toward her cottage, not sure whether she wanted Mac to be out of the shower or not.

When she entered the cottage she felt disappointed not to hear the shower running. There was her answer. She had wanted an excuse to see all of Mac and had been thwarted. She headed for the bathroom anyway, thinking it would be nice to take a quick, cool shower herself while the campers were napping. The bathroom door was open on her side, so she assumed the room was empty.

It was not.

Mac sat in the tub covered with white bubbles—which she presumed had come from the glass-stoppered container of bubble bath she kept on the edge of the tub. He was leaning forward, his teeth gritted, his hands apparently gripping his scarred leg.

"Mac?"

He whipped his head around, swore, then

groaned. She saw his biceps ripple as he applied tremendous pressure to his leg.

"What is it?" she asked. "What's wrong?"

"Cramp," he gritted through his teeth.

She dropped to her knees on the fluffy bath mat beside the tub, her eyes focused on his straining face. "What can I do? How can I help?"

"I can't move...can't get out of the damned tub!"

"Do you want me to help you stand up?"

He shook his head violently and groaned again.

"How long has the muscle been cramped?" she asked.

"Too long," he snapped back.

His face was blanched with pain. The sweat on his brow and above his lip, which she at first thought had to be from the heat of the water, was apparently the result of fighting the cramp. For how long? Fifteen minutes? Twenty? "I'll call 911," she said, pushing off from the tub to stand up.

"Don't! I don't want news of this getting out."

"You need help, Mac," she said, angry because she was frightened.

"Then help me, damn it!"

"How?"

"Maybe two sets of hands working on the muscle will get it to uncramp more quickly."

She hesitated only a moment before dropping back down onto the bath mat. Before she could change her mind, she stuck her hands beneath the thin layer of bubbles into the water—which was merely lukewarm—and reached for his leg. Her hands tangled with his before she moved them upward, closer to his knee.

As she worked her fingers into the tightly clenched calf muscle she asked, "Has this happened before?"

He nodded. "Never this bad." His head rolled back and she watched his jaw muscles work as he struggled to endure the pain without making a sound.

"Please let me call someone, Mac."

"No," he grated out.

"Then let me run some more hot water. Wouldn't that help?"

He met her gaze, struggled with the decision, then nodded.

She tipped the lever to empty the tub, realizing after she did so, that the bubbles were going to run out with the water, leaving Mac exposed.

But she couldn't worry about his modesty—or hers—right now. She was too worried about his pain and the ramifications of Mac having such severe cramps in his leg after what would have been a very light workout if he had really been playing football.

The water drained quickly, and a slurping sound announced the tub was empty. Jewel shot the lever closed and turned on the water, making it as hot as she thought he could stand.

"Too hot?" she asked, turning to look at him for the first time since the tub had begun draining.

"No. It feels good."

Her breath caught at the sight of him covered here and there with bubbles. She quickly turned her head away, but the image of him, wet curls caught on his nape, water pearled on his shoulders, bubbles caught in the curls on his chest—and on other curls—stayed with her.

But not for long. For the first time, she took a good look at the leg she was massaging. "Mac, there's not much muscle left here. It's all scar tissue."

"I know," he said with a discouraged sigh. "That's the problem. What muscle there is left isn't enough to—" His hands gripped his ankle as an agonized cry tore from his throat. She moved her hands near his at the back of his ankle and felt the muscle spasming. The steaming hot water covered their hands as she held on tight with him for the sixty-five long seconds it took the spasm to pass. Suddenly, she felt the entire muscle ease.

Mac hissed out a breath and, after waiting to see if the tension would return, cautiously let go of his leg.

Jewel turned to look at him and saw his face was turned toward the tile wall. And that tears streamed from his eyes. "Oh, Mac."

"Go away, Jewel," he grated out.

She couldn't do that. Not with what she knew now.

Mac's football career was over. He knew it. And was grieving for it.

She didn't think about what she was doing, she just did it. Two seconds later she had her tennis shoes and socks off and had eased herself sideways into the tub on Mac's lap, her legs hanging over the side of the tub, her arms around his neck, her nose plastered against his throat. "I'm so sorry, Mac," she said, her nose burning, her eyes stinging with tears. "I'm so sorry."

At first she thought he was going to push her

away, but his arms closed tight around her and he pulled her close, pressing his cheek tight against hers. She could feel him trembling, feel him struggling to hold back the sobs, until at last they broke free.

She held him close, crooning words that made no sense, offering the comfort of her arms and her love. *Oh, my God. I love him.* It was a stunning realization. A frightening one when she knew his life, now that his future was so uncertain, might very well move in a different direction than hers. But that would not stop what she felt for him. He was another part of her, a part she needed to feel whole inside.

Jewel had no idea how much time had passed when Mac's heaving body finally quieted. He seemed completely relaxed, as though he had accepted the inevitable and was now ready to move beyond it.

"You'd better turn off the water," he said in a voice that was amazingly calm.

Jewel lifted her head and realized the water had reached the rim of the tub and was threatening to spill over. She reached around and shut it off, then turned shyly back to Mac. "I should get off of you and let you finish your bath."

"I wish you wouldn't."

She laughed uncertainly. "What did you have in mind?"

In answer, he lifted her at the waist and re-arranged her so she was facing him, her knees on either side of his hips. The extra weight of her legs caused the water to lap over the side of the tub, but Jewel had more important things to think about than a little water on the bathroom floor.

"Mac, do you think we should be doing this now? I mean, what if your leg—"

"Let me worry about my leg," he said.

When she opened her mouth to protest again, he covered it with his hand and said, "I'm fine. Really. Please, Jewel, don't leave me."

She kept her eyes focused on Mac's as he reached for the bottom of her soaked T-shirt and began to lift it up over her head. She raised her arms and let him remove it.

I love him. And I trust him, she realized.

Mac dropped the T-shirt onto the already soaked bath mat and reached behind her for the clasp of her bra. She gripped his shoulders and said nervously, "This is a first for me."

It was a warning and an offering and a prayer. *Please be careful. Please let my body please you. Please let me not be afraid.* She did not ask for what she wanted most. She did not say, *Please love me.* That was something Mac would have to offer on his own.

His eyes were intent on her face as he pulled her lacy, heavy-duty bra off and her Beautiful Breasts—with wonderful big B's, because Mac looked at them that way—fell free. The bra went the way of her T-shirt, and Mac reached out gently, reverently, to cup her breasts in his hands.

"Exquisite," he said, his thumbs flicking the nipples.

Jewel had to remind herself to breathe as sensation streaked from her nipples to a drawstring somewhere deep inside her womb and pulled it up tight. Her hands threaded into the damp hair at Mac's nape as he lowered his head to kiss each breast. His mouth latched onto a nipple and he sucked, gently at first, then more strongly.

Jewel's hips arched instinctively toward him.

"Easy," he said, his hands gripping her hips atop her cutoff jeans. "Slow and easy, Jewel. We have all the time in the world."

"I don't know what to do with my hands," she said anxiously. "Tell me what to do to please you."

He smiled. "You're doing fine."

"I'm not doing anything!" she replied pertly.

He lifted his hips, and she could feel his arousal.

"Oh. Well. I see."

Mac laughed, a rumbly sound, and kissed her quickly on the lips. "I love your innocence," he said, his eyes staring intently into hers. "I want to be the first, Jewel. I am so honored to be the first."

"But—"

He put his fingertips to her lips. "The first," he repeated.

In truth, this situation was so incredibly different from what had happened to her all those years ago, that the past didn't seem real anymore. Mac made her feel innocent, made her feel the joy and excitement—and normal fear—of an untouched woman.

He teased her and touched her and tasted her until they were both wrinkled from the water. And she did the same, enjoying the pleasure of rubbing her breasts against the crisp curls on his chest and returning the favor of kissing and caressing and sucking his nipples—which turned out to be surprisingly sensitive.

"We'd better get out of here," Mac said, "or we're going to turn into prunes."

Jewel felt a little shy standing up and stepping out of the tub. As much as she was tempted to look, she turned her back on Mac as he stood and stepped out of the tub behind her. She had already reached for a towel to cover her breasts, when he took it away from her.

He aligned his body with hers from behind, put his arms around her to cup her breasts and played with her nipples until they were aching and pointy. His mouth teased her throat beneath her ear with kisses, before he latched onto a particular spot and sucked hard enough to make her moan with pleasure.

"I'm only going to touch you," he said, explaining as his hands slid down the front of her, unsnapped her jeans, spread them wide and slid his hand beneath her panties. "To let you feel my hands on you."

She held her breath, expecting the fear to return. But it didn't. She felt only the warmth of his hand against her cooling flesh and the feel of his fingertips probing gently between her thighs. Slowly, carefully, he insinuated one finger inside her.

"Are you all right?" he asked.

"Uh-huh."

She felt his mouth curve into a smile against

her cheek. "I think maybe you'd better breathe," he said.

She exhaled and then gasped a breath of air as his finger slid deeper inside her. "Oh."

He paused. "Did I hurt you?"

"No. I feel..." She searched for the word. *Strange. Full. Achy.* Yes, but more than that. "I feel good," she said. "This feels so right."

"I'm glad." He used his other hand to encourage her to spread her legs, so he would have easier access to her. And slipped another finger inside her.

Her breath was coming in erratic spurts, and she reminded herself to keep breathing.

"Still okay?" he asked.

She nodded, then made a sound when his thumb found the tiny bud at the apex of her thighs and began to caress it. Her knees started to buckle, nature's way of getting her prone, and Mac compensated by putting a strong arm around her midriff and pulling her back tight against him. She could feel his arousal against her buttocks, hard and pulsing.

Instead of being afraid, she was aroused. She was sure she could make love to him this time without running away. She was ready to move forward. She wanted to feel him inside her. "Mac," she said. "I'm not afraid anymore."

"Good," he replied, his voice husky. "Just relax and let me make love to you."

Let me make love to you. It was what she had wanted for a very long time. Jewel let herself fully enjoy what Mac was doing to her—making love to her—without worrying about whether he was *in love* with her. He was as considerate a lover as she could ever have hoped for. He cared for her. That would have to be enough for now.

Mac had one hand inside her jeans, the other tantalizing her nipple, while his mouth teased the flesh at her throat. She writhed against him as her body experienced all the joy and pleasure she had not allowed herself to feel in the past.

As the tension built inside her, she reached out to the pleasure, indulged in it, delighted in it, until she felt herself losing control. "Mac," she said, the fright back in her voice. "What's happening to me?"

"Something wonderful. Let it happen, Jewel. Let me do this for you."

She trusted Mac. As he had trusted her to comfort him. More than that. She loved him.

Jewel gave her body into his hands and was rewarded moments later with a shattering climax, her body shuddering with wave after wave of intense pleasure. "Mac," she gasped. "Mac."

"I know," he said, his voice gentle, his breathing as erratic as hers. "I know."

Jewel felt totally enervated and was barely aware when Mac picked her up in his arms and carried her to her bedroom. He pulled the sheets down on her bed, stood her up long enough to strip the wet cutoffs and panties off her, then tucked her under the covers before she had time to feel embarrassed at being naked.

She expected him to join her. But the last thing she saw before her eyes slid closed was Mac's taut, untanned buttocks as he walked out of the room.

Mac knew that Jewel had expected him to join her in bed, and that he would have been welcome there. He could have eased the ache in his loins and gotten them both over hurdles that had stood in their way for years. He had learned from their recent lovemaking that he had not only the self-control—but the desire—to put Jewel's feelings and needs before his own.

Several things had stopped him from staying. Mac had realized, as he was making love to

Jewel, that he loved her. And not just as a friend, but as an inseparable part of himself. He wanted to spend his life with her. He wanted to plant his seed inside her and help her raise the children they would make together. He wanted to grow old with her.

Which raised a second problem. Mac Macready was another football has-been, who had no idea what he wanted to do with the rest of his life. After the horrific episode with his scarred leg in the tub, there was no denying the truth any longer. He would never play pro football again. Mac had not beaten the odds this time. He had lost.

It was a devastating realization.

If he had not had Jewel to hang on to, he didn't know what he would have done. She had understood his pain and his loss. She had offered comfort without platitudes. She obviously cared for him—even after seeing him at his most vulnerable.

None of the reasons he had for fearing commitment with a woman existed where Jewel was concerned. With her, Mac felt safe making that leap into the unknown, certain he could trust her to be there when he landed.

Which brought him to a third problem. Mac

had no idea whether Jewel loved him merely as a friend or the way he wanted to be loved. As a man. As her lover. As her future husband.

Mac had collected Jewel's clothes before he left the bedroom, wrung out all her wet things and hung them in the bathroom to dry. He had dressed himself in Levi's and a Western shirt, then laid himself down on his bed, his hands behind his head, to think.

On the way up out of the canyon at lunchtime, Jewel had encouraged Brad to tell Mac his interpretation of the primitive drawings on the canyon wall. Mac had listened attentively and heard in Brad's explanation an analogy of what life was like when it was lived in fear of reaching out for dreams. After all, dreams might never come true. You might end up disappointed, or in worse shape than if you had been satisfied with what you already had.

Mac had always believed in pursuing his dreams. He had never been indecisive. But clearly there were moments when old dreams had to be abandoned—and new dreams dreamed. Mac could no longer be a professional football player. So what else did he want to do with his life?

That wasn't an easy question to answer, because Mac had been so determined to regain the use of his scarred leg that he had refused to think about alternatives. Now he must. And he had to factor Jewel, and her commitment to Camp LittleHawk, into the equation.

The idea that rose immediately in his mind was such a simple solution—and yet so revolutionary in terms of how he had intended to spend his life—that Mac felt both excited and cautious about pursuing it. Maybe the best thing to do was to approach Jewel and see what she thought.

He was on his way back to her room when someone knocked hard and fast on the door to the cottage. He hurried to the door and opened it to find Gavin Talbot standing there.

"I think you better get Jewel and come to the boys' bunkhouse," he said. "Brad Templeton has a fever."

Chapter 13

Jewel blamed herself for not recognizing that Brad's flushed face at lunch was caused not only by excitement but also by the fever that signaled the return of his leukemia—and the end of his second remission.

She could barely manage to keep a smile on her face as she belted Brad into the seat of the chartered plane for the short flight back to Dallas Children's Hospital, which was waiting to readmit him. Brad was gripping Mac's football tightly in the crook of one arm. His eyes were feverishly bright, and he had a smile plastered on his face as phony as the one on hers.

Jewel felt Mac's presence at her side. She saw the muscles in his scarred leg as he knelt facing Brad. Mac knew what the end of Brad's remission meant as well as she did. The boy's chances of survival were considerably less now than they had been at the beginning of the week. Mac might very well be bidding Brad Templeton goodbye for the last time.

"Hey, tiger," Mac said, tugging the brim of Brad's cap down playfully. "How's it going?"

Brad readjusted the cap and said, "It's back."

"I know," Mac said. "Remember what I said."

"Yeah. Doctors don't know everything."

Mac nodded soberly. "You keep fighting," he said, his voice low and fierce. He spoke so softly Jewel could barely hear him. "Don't give up. I expect to see you back here next summer. In fact, I expect you to be a counselor someday at a sports camp I'm thinking about starting, where lots of football players like Troy Aikman and Dan Marino and Reggie White and Jerry Rice will come and spend a little time with kids like you."

Jewel wondered where Mac had come up with the idea of a sports camp to encourage Brad. The way Brad's face had lit up, it had certainly been a good idea. She was surprised by the other message Brad had heard in Mac's speech.

"Does that mean you're not gonna play football anymore?" Brad asked.

Mac shook his head. "My leg can't tolerate it."

"So sometimes the doctors *are* right," Brad said.

Jewel watched as Mac gripped Brad's free hand in his and said, "Believe in yourself, and you'll come through fine."

"Time for takeoff, folks," the pilot announced. The nurse who was traveling with Brad was already buckled into her seat.

Mac stood, but Brad held on to his hand and pulled him back down onto his knee. "Goodbye, Mac," he said, a farewell in case he never came back. His chin wobbled and tears welled in his eyes.

"See you soon, Brad," Mac replied. He hugged the boy, who dropped the football and reached up to grab Mac tight around the neck with both hands.

"I don't want to go back to the hospital," Brad said. "Please don't make me leave."

"You have to go. You need help to get well."

"I'm not going to get well. I'm going to die!" Brad cried.

"You'd better not," Mac said severely. "I'm counting on you to come through for me."

Jewel watched as Mac pulled Brad's hands free and reached down to retrieve the football from the floor of the plane and put it back in Mac's arms. "Remember, if I made it, you can make it, too," Mac said.

A tear spilled over as Brad glanced at Jewel for confirmation of Mac's promise.

Her throat was too swollen to speak. She whispered, "Come back soon, Brad," then backed away, keeping the smile on her face as long as she could. It was gone before she reached the door.

Once off the plane, Jewel ran all the way to the van. She had freely chosen to work with kids like Brad, knowing they didn't all make it. With some of them, it was especially hard to let go. Brad's life had seemed so full of possibilities, as Mac's had been all those years ago. Now Mac had lost his dream. And Brad might lose his life.

Jewel felt Mac's arms close around her from behind. He turned her to face the runway, which she saw through a haze of tears, and lifted her arm so she was waving at Brad as the chartered plane took off. Then Mac turned her to face him and closed his arms tightly around her, offering her a comforting shoulder to lay her head on.

"I can't bear it," she said. "First to see you so unhappy, and now Brad…" She couldn't say the word *dying*.

"Brad will make it," Mac said fervently.

"How can you be so sure?" she sobbed.

"I know these things," he said. "Besides, I'm going to need him when I start my sports camp for kids with cancer."

It took a moment for what he said to sink in. When it did, Jewel backed out of his arms and stared at him in shocked disbelief. "I thought you made that up for Brad's sake."

"Nope. It's for real." He opened the door of the van and hustled her inside, then got into the driver's seat and started up the vehicle.

"Why haven't I heard about this sports camp before?" Jewel asked, wiping the tears from her eyes.

He grinned at her. "Because I just thought it up this afternoon."

"Oh."

''I wanted to talk to you about it before I went much further with the idea. What do you think about it?''

Jewel's first thought was that it would take Mac away from Hawk's Pride. That was selfish. What Mac planned to do would help a great many children. ''I think what you're planning is one of the noblest, most considerate—''

The van veered to the berm and skidded to a halt. Before Jewel could say another word, Mac's arms were around her and his mouth had covered hers.

She had no time to think, only to feel. What she felt was overflowing love for this man who had so much strength, yet had let her see him when he was at his most vulnerable. She reached out to touch Mac's face tenderly, to thank him for being who he was.

He broke off the kiss abruptly, and she was caught by his gaze, which promised so much— hope, happiness and something else she was afraid to name, because she wanted it so much she feared she had merely wished it there.

''Look at me like that too long, love, and you're liable to get what you want right here and now, instead of when we get back to the cottage.''

Jewel stared into Mac's blue eyes, her heart pounding. Had he really called her *love?* Had he said they were going to be making love in a few minutes? He didn't repeat himself, merely started up the van and pulled back onto the road.

Jewel suddenly realized why Mac had reached out to her physically. Making love was an act to reaffirm life in the presence of death. *We can reach out for joy. We still have our lives ahead of us, whatever those lives may bring. This offer of lovemaking has nothing to do with Mac actually loving me. It's a reaction to Brad's illness.* She couldn't disagree with Mac's motive. Or with wanting to be held close, no matter what the reason. She wasn't going to deny him, or herself, the lovemaking he had promised.

''Tell me more about the camp,'' she said to break the strained silence.

''There isn't any more to tell,'' he replied. ''It's just an idea right now. Do you have any suggestions?''

''Where do you plan to locate it?''

He frowned. ''That's a problem. I probably have enough money left from my signing bonus with the Tornadoes to advertise the place and hire help for the first year. But I doubt whether I have enough to buy a piece of land and build buildings. Any suggestions?''

Jewel would have offered her facilities immediately, if she had thought he would accept. His explanation seemed to suggest he would be perfectly happy to open his camp right here.

The way he was looking at her, his heart in his eyes, gave her the courage to speak. ''Camp LittleHawk belongs to my mother, but she's said it can be mine whenever I want it. I think having a sports program here—with famous football players participating on occasion—would be a welcome addition.''

Mac smiled at her, and she felt her throat swell with emotion. ''Thanks, Jewel. Incorporating my idea with what you've already established at Camp LittleHawk would please me very much.''

They had arrived back at the cottage, and Mac quickly left the van and came around to help Jewel out. He took her hand and practically dragged her into the cottage. She realized why he was in such a hurry when, the instant they were inside with the door closed behind them,

he pulled her into his arms and pressed her to
him from breast to thigh. The evidence of his
desire was hard to miss.

"I love you, Jewel."

The way he blurted it out seemed to surprise
him as much as it surprised her. His eyes looked
wary, as though he wished he hadn't spoken.

She shoved back the hurt and said, "It's all
right, Mac. You don't have to say things like
that."

The wary look disappeared, and his jaw
firmed. "I don't *have* to say it. I *want* to say it.
I love you, Jewel. I think I have for a very long
time. I was afraid to do anything about it, afraid
even to admit it, I think, because of all the bad
things that happened when I loved someone in
the past.

"What's happened to Brad made me realize I
don't want to wait any longer. Life is too precious to waste a single day of it. I love you,"
he repeated. "And I want to make love with
you."

Jewel took a deep breath and let it out. If he
could find the courage to speak, so could she.
"I love you, too, Mac. I've been afraid to tell

you, afraid you wouldn't feel the same way. Afraid—''

She never got a chance to finish. His mouth captured hers at the same time he reached down to lift her up and carry her toward his bedroom.

Mac laid Jewel down on his bed as gently as he could and sat down beside her. He hadn't expected his courage to desert him, but it seemed for a moment that he wouldn't be able to go through with what he had planned.

It was late in the day, and the growing dusk gave everything in the room a soft, rosy glow. Jewel had never looked more beautiful to him. Or more trusting.

He had never been more nervous. Or frightened.

Think of her feelings, not your own.

"Are you all right?" he asked.

"More than all right," she said, a tender smile on her lips. "Kiss me please, Mac."

He had never been more gentle, more tender, more considerate of a woman. He brushed his mouth against hers, teased her lips, nipped at her and eased his tongue into her mouth to taste her. He felt her growing desire, her growing urgency to touch and taste in return.

He put his arms around her and pulled her close, feeling the tips of her breasts turn as pointy as pebbles when they made contact with his chest. "Would you like me to undress you?" he asked.

"I'd rather undress you," she said with a mischievous smile.

Mac was surprised, but when he thought about it, it seemed like a good idea. If he was undressed while she was still clothed, she would have the opportunity of escaping anytime she didn't feel comfortable. "Okay," he said. "Where would you like to start?"

She got off the bed and said, "Sit back on the bed, so I can take off your boots." She turned her back to him and tugged at each of his boot heels, while he gave her a shove with the opposite foot to help get the cowboy boots off. Then she pulled off his socks and said, "Stand up."

He stood barefoot on the wooden floor and watched as she slowly pulled his Western shirt out of his jeans and unsnapped the snaps, one at a time from the top downward. He wasn't wearing an undershirt, and she kissed her way down his chest. He was quivering by the time she reached the soft line of down that disappeared into his jeans.

When she ran her tongue around his navel, he nearly jumped out of his skin. "Good God," he muttered.

"You didn't like it?" she asked, looking up into his face.

He shoved both hands through his hair in agitation. "I'm about to explode because of it," he admitted.

Jewel smiled. "That's good, don't you think?"

Patience. Patience. Patience. He said it like a mantra, hoping he could endure her innocent exploration. He bit the inside of his cheek when she undid his belt, pulled it through the loops of his jeans and let it drop to the floor.

She unbuttoned the top button of his Levi's and began to lower the zipper. Her hand brushed against his tumescence, and he grabbed her wrist to avoid disaster. He wanted desperately to tell her it was the first time for him, but the words wouldn't come out. Instead he said, "It's been a while for me, Jewel. I don't want to disappoint you."

"What about Eve?" she asked.

He had forgotten all about Eve. "Nothing happened with her," he said.

"But you were gone so long that first night. And when you met her in Dallas, I thought—"

"She never turned me on," Mac blurted. "I couldn't… I didn't… Damn it, Jewel! You know what I'm trying to say." He could feel the heat rising on his throat. He couldn't believe what he had just confessed.

He waited for the laughter, and it came—a warm, happy sound that made his heart soar.

"Oh, Mac," Jewel said, her dark brown eyes bright with joy. "If you only knew how much I've wanted to hear you say those exact words— or something very like them."

"You have?"

"I've been terribly jealous," she admitted. Jewel rubbed her cheek against the curls on his chest, then kissed him, sending goose bumps skittering across his flesh. "I'm so glad," she said. "I've wanted you all to myself." The smile returned as she said, "And now I've got you."

She pushed his shirt off his shoulders until it caught at his wrists, effectively making him a prisoner. Instead of releasing the snaps, she shot him a grin and said, "You're my captive now. I can do whatever I want with you."

He leaned down to kiss her, and she stepped back and wagged her finger at him.

"Oh, no, you don't. I'm going to be doing the kissing and touching." She reached down and cupped him with her hand.

"You're going to kill me," Mac said through gritted teeth.

"You don't like it?" she teased.

"You know I like it," he retorted. "I like it so much I'm about to burst."

"Good," she said. "Now you stand right there while I undress."

Mac's eyes went wide when Jewel began a striptease in front of him. No woman had ever removed a T-shirt, bra, jeans and panties quite so seductively.

Don't think of yourself. Think of her.

Mac's pulse was pounding in his temples— and elsewhere. His whole body quivered with excitement.

"You're so beautiful," he said when she was naked at last.

She touched the crisscrossing scars on her face and the more visible scar on her thigh, where the operations to mend her leg had been performed. "You don't mind?"

He solved the problem of the imprisoning shirt by pulling his arms up over his head and using the shirt between his hands as a chain to encircle her and pull her close. "All I see is a beautiful, desirable woman."

She made a sound of pleasure when her breasts were finally pillowed against his naked chest. He spread his legs and urged her between them. Her hands curved around his waist and ventured up his back all the way to his nape. His blood raced as her hands caressed him.

He shuddered out a breath. *Think of her. Give her pleasure. Make it good for her. Don't think about yourself.*

He lowered his mouth to hers, sealing them together, mimicking the sex act with his tongue. The sounds she made in her throat caused his groin to tighten even more—if that was possible. He pushed against her and felt the heat of her through the denim as she rubbed her mound against him.

"I never knew it could feel so good," she whispered. "I never imagined how wonderful it would be."

He kissed her eyes and cheeks and nose before he reached her mouth again. She kissed him back eagerly, her tongue thrusting into his mouth, tasting him, dueling with him as he sought to return the favor.

Mac had forgotten about his jeans. She obviously had not. He felt her hands on the zipper again, and this time he let her lower it and reach inside.

"Okay?" she asked.

Think of her. Think of her. "Okay," he rasped.

But if she thought she was going to have it all her way, she was wrong. When Jewel reached for him, Mac got rid of his shirt and reached for her. He slipped two fingers inside her quickly, before she could protest, and settled his thumb on the tiny nub that was the source of so much delight.

"I can't...concentrate on you...when you're doing that...to me..." she panted.

His body was hard, pulsing in an agony of delight. It was a good thing she was not more experienced, although her innocence was likely to be his undoing.

He concentrated on bringing Jewel to a climax, focusing his attention on kissing her, touching her, pleasing her. Soon her hand was lax against him, her eyes closed, her jaw clenched as the pleasure overtook her. She leaned into him with her hips and arched her body toward him, making it easy for him to kiss her breasts, to suckle them and to tease them with his teeth and tongue.

Sweat beaded on his forehead, as he watched the play of expressions on her face. The rapture. The delight. The confusion as her body tightened more and more, as he pushed her higher and higher. The ecstasy as her body rippled with pleasure. And the love, as she looked up at him from hooded eyes and rose on tiptoe to find his mouth with hers and thank him with a kiss.

He picked her up, pulled down his bedcovers and laid her on the sheet. Her eyes had already slid closed before he pulled off his jeans and briefs and slid into bed beside her. He wrapped his arms around her and pulled her back into the hollow of his belly. He lay there bone hard and unsatisfied—but very pleased with himself.

He had brought Jewel to climax twice now and managed to control his own urgent need. Surely it would not be so difficult to put himself inside her and do it so she would not recognize his inexperience. She seemed to have put completely out of her mind what had happened six years ago.

He wished she were awake now. He wished he did not have to wait. If he could just make love to her this instant, he knew everything would be fine. But she seemed perfectly satisfied to lie beside him. She did not seem the least bit interested in any more touching or kissing.

Mac got the first hint of his error when he felt Jewel's hand sliding up his thigh, headed for the barely relaxed, unsatisfied part of him.

"Jewel? What's going on?"

She turned in his arms to face him. Her eyes were two shiny spots in the darkness. "I want to make love to you, Mac."

"We just—"

"I want you to put yourself inside me as deep as you can. I want to make you feel as wonderful as you've made me feel."

Mac swallowed hard. He felt like crying. "God, Jewel. Now?"

"Now." She touched him, and his body stood at rigid attention. She lay back and urged him over her.

She didn't have to urge him very hard.

For a moment she hesitated, and Mac realized she was remembering the past. This was the way he had found her with Harvey Barnes. Harvey was on top, and she was helpless beneath him. Like Harvey, Mac was stronger. He could do to her whatever he wanted.

Mac saw her rising fear and said, "It's me, Jewel."

Her whole body relaxed, and she smiled up at him sweetly. "I know, Mac. Love me, please. And let me love you."

Patience. Patience.

Patience went out the window the instant his body reached the entrance to hers. Mac tried to go slow, but she was wet and hot, and he wanted to be inside her so bad, that it took only three brief thrusts before he was buried deep inside her.

Mac paused, his weight on his elbows, his hips cradled in hers, and looked down, ashamed of his haste and afraid of what he would see on her face. "Jewel?"

"I'm fine," she said, her eyes glowing, her fingertips caressing his cheeks. "I'm wonderful."

It was all right. She couldn't tell it was his first time…because it was also the first time for her, he realized.

It was easy then, to think of her and not himself. "I don't want to hurt you," he said.

In response, she lifted her knees on either side of him, then wrapped her legs around his buttocks, seating him even more deeply inside her.

"My God," he muttered. "Jewel, I…" He withdrew and thrust as slowly and gently as he could, but the inevitable urge to mate, to put his seed inside her, drove him to move faster. When she lifted her hips and pushed back, the friction created unbelievably exquisite sensations.

Go slow. Slow down. Wait for her.

He saw Jewel's face through a haze of desire, heard her guttural sounds of pleasure and finally felt her body, slick and wet beneath him, begin to convulse.

Her body squeezed him, wringing pleasure beyond anything he could have imagined. He arched his head backward in an agony of joy as he spilled his seed inside her. His body pulsed, emptying itself in powerful thrusts before he lowered himself to lie beside her and wrapped her in his arms.

His breathing was ragged, his blood still pumping so hard it throbbed in his veins. He could not find breath for words, and would not have known what to say if he could have spoken.

"Thank you, Mac," Jewel whispered, snuggling close. "No man could have made me feel more lovely…or more loved."

Mac kissed her on the temple, a wordless thanks for saying what he had not been able to find words to express. The pleasure of this first time for him was all the sweeter, knowing she was happy.

Mac thought of all the women he could have made love to and had not. All the sex he had turned down in those early years, which had put him in the position of making love for the first time to the very woman he hoped to marry. As far as Mac was concerned, that meant Jewel was the only woman he would ever make love with.

Maybe he should have felt deprived. He did not.

Intuitively Mac knew that sex with a stranger—or even an acquaintance, would not have been as earth-shattering, or as bone-melting, as his experience with Jewel. Without the love he felt for her—and the love she felt for him in return—the sex act would not have brought him nearly so much joy.

"What are you thinking?" Jewel murmured.

"How much I enjoyed making love to you," he replied with a smile.

She kept her eyes lowered, and she was obviously struggling to speak as she said, "Considering the experience of the other women you must have slept with, I can't imagine my first efforts were much to shout about."

"Will you marry me?"

Mac had meant to distract her from a discussion of his sexual experience, and the proposal worked. But not in the way he had hoped.

"Does that mean you were satisfied?" she said, arching a brow. "I don't want to spend my life wondering how I stack up against the competition," she said wryly.

"I'm never going to be comparing you to anyone else," he muttered.

"Why don't I believe you?"

"Believe me."

"How can I believe you?" she said, rising to her elbow and staring down at him. "Are you telling me you never found a single other woman who was more appealing to you in bed than me?''

''That's exactly what I'm saying,'' he retorted, sitting up abruptly. ''Because there were no other women.''

She sat up just as quickly to face him, and the sheet dropped to her waist, exposing her breasts. ''You're kidding, right?''

The sight of her nipples, full and rosy, set his pulse to galloping. ''No man would kid about something like that. Until a few minutes ago I was a virgin. Now damn it, will you or won't you marry me?''

He had known she would laugh if she ever found out the truth. But he had never expected such gentle laughter. Such joyful laughter. Such loving laughter.

Jewel pushed him onto his back and straddled him with only the sheet between them. She leaned down, her lips close to his and said, ''Oh, yes, my darling. I will most definitely marry you.''

''It doesn't bother you that I don't have more experience in bed?'' he demanded.

She chuckled. ''Why should it? This way we can both learn exactly what pleases us. For instance, do you like it when I bite your earlobe like this?''

He shivered at the searing sensation of pleasure.

''Or would you rather I kissed this spot below your ear?''

Mac groaned. He had switched their positions and had her beneath him in two seconds flat. ''I like it all,'' he said, nipping her earlobe and then kissing her below the ear, feeling the frisson of pleasure that rippled through her. ''Just so long as I'm doing it with you.''

''Well, then,'' she said, smiling up at him, ''why don't we practice making a baby?''

Mac laughed, then cheerfully indulged the future mother of his children.

Epilogue

Jewel sat in a rocker on the covered porch of the two-story Victorian house Mac had built for them. It stood on Hawk's Pride land her father had given them as a wedding present four years ago. Jewel had wanted a white house with lots of gingerbread trim with morning glories entwined in it, and that was exactly what she had.

She sighed with pleasure every time she looked around her. This was her favorite place to be these days. She was nursing her second son, while the first, blond-haired, blue-eyed, three-year-old Evan, played with a football at her feet.

"Daddy!" Evan cried, leaping up as Mac appeared around the corner of the house.

Mac opened his arms when he reached the foot of the steps that led up to the front door, and Evan launched himself into his father's arms. The two looked very much alike, down to the twin dimples in their cheeks.

"Welcome home," Jewel said with a smile.

"It's good to be home," Mac replied, settling into the rocker beside her with Evan on his lap. "How's Dustin?"

"Hungry, as always."

"I can see why he enjoys dinner so much," Mac said with a teasing smile, as he eyed the breast that provided his son's nourishment.

Jewel blushed. Even after four years of marriage, Mac talked about her breasts as though they were the best gift he had ever been given. "How did your trip go?" she asked.

"I got two Pro-Bowl quarterbacks, a former Heisman Trophy winner and a record-setting kicker to commit to a week each at Camp Little-Hawk."

"Fabulous!" Jewel said. "I knew you could do it! What about the fund-raiser?"

Jewel had been as surprised as Mac when

Andy Dennison suggested they raise money for Mac's sports camp from the public. The Camp LittleHawk fund-raiser had become a highlight on the sports calendar and football players from around the league were delighted to be invited to participate.

"Everything is in place," Mac said. "Andy says he thinks we can double what we made last year."

"That'll mean we can build another couple of bunkhouses," Jewel said. "And hire the help we'll need to staff them."

Mac nodded and set his rocker to moving. "How were things around here while I was gone?"

"The high school-age summer counselors arrived yesterday for their week of training."

"Did he come?"

Jewel smiled. "He came."

Mac leaned his head back and turned his face away, but Jewel had already seen the tears that leaped to his eyes.

"He's been in remission for three years, Mac. Don't you think it's safe now to admit how much you like the kid?"

Mac turned back to her and reached out to take her hand in his. ''I suppose it is.''

''I thought so. That's why I asked him over for dinner tonight.''

''What?''

''You can come out now, Brad,'' Jewel said.

The screen door opened, and Brad Templeton stepped onto the front porch. ''Hi, Mac.''

Mac rose and set Evan down.

It was questionable which of the two men moved first, but the instant they met, they wrapped their arms around each other and hugged tight.

Neither of them said anything, but if they were as moved as Jewel was, they were both too emotional to speak.

Mac recovered first, pushed Brad an arm's length away and said, ''Let me look at you. How old are you now?''

''Sixteen,'' Brad said.

''You've gotten taller.''

''You look the same.''

Mac pulled off the New York Mets baseball cap and tousled Brad's dark hair. ''Looks like you need a trim.''

Brad grabbed the ball cap and tugged it down.

"Now that I've got a little hair, I'm not about to cut it off. Besides, the chicks like it like this."

Mac laughed as he put an arm around Brad's shoulder and headed back toward Jewel. "Just remember," he said, pointing his thumb at Jewel, "this one's taken."

"I thought you had the hots for her," Brad said, winking at Jewel. "Guess I was right."

Mac laughed, then sobered. "I'm so glad you made it back here," he said, his voice breaking with emotion.

"I owe it all to you. I kept on fighting, like you said. And here I am."

The screen door slammed again and Jewel's brother Colt appeared on the front porch, tossing a football from hand to hand. At eighteen, his shoulders had broadened, and he had grown a few more inches. His hair was too long, and his face held a perpetual look of defiance. "If the reunion is over, I promised to throw Brad a few passes."

"Sure," Mac said, giving Brad a nudge in Colt's direction. "Let's see what kind of speed you have, Brad."

Mac returned to the rocker and settled down,

picking up Evan again and holding him in his lap.

"Football," Evan said, pointing to Colt and Brad.

"Yep. Someday you're going to be playing, sport. But right now we're going to watch your uncle Colt and my friend Brad."

As the two of them watched Brad run in a zigzagging pattern, Jewel said, "Colt finally told Dad he's been accepted to the Air Force Academy."

Mac missed seeing Colt throw the football, because his attention had switched to Jewel. "What did Zach say?"

"He was angry that Colt hadn't said anything to him before now about wanting to go into the Air Force."

"And?"

"They're not speaking at the moment."

"What did Rebecca say?" Mac asked, his eyes back on Colt.

"Mom was hurt by all the secrecy. And she's afraid for Colt, because what he wants to do will put him in the path of danger."

Mac's mouth turned up wryly. "That shouldn't surprise her. Colt has led a pretty reckless life the past four years. It's a wonder he got through high school alive."

"I can't help thinking how unhappy Colt must have been all these years, knowing he was going to disappoint Dad and hurt Mom when he finally told them the truth about what he wanted to do with his life."

"Who'd have thought it," Mac said, watching the perfect spiraling pass Colt had thrown land gently in Brad's outstretched arms. "He would have made one hell of a pro quarterback."

"Apparently he'll play football for the Air Force Academy," Jewel said. "When he's done, he plans to fly jets."

Mac brushed his thumb across Jewel's knuckles, sending a frisson of pleasure streaking up her arm. "Do you think Colt would talk to me?"

"I'm sure he could use an ear to listen," Jewel said. "I've invited him for dinner, too."

Mac smiled. "Have I told you lately how much I love you?"

"It's been twenty-four hours, at least."

"I love you, Jewel." Mac raised her hand and kissed her palm.

Jewel found herself breathless as she met his avid gaze. "It's time for another lesson in the bedroom," she said.

"Oh? What are we learning this time?"

"How to make a baby *girl*," Jewel said.

"Sounds interesting," Mac said. "When does class start?"

"Right after the dinner dishes are done," Jewel said, "and you talk to Colt and he drives Brad back to Camp LittleHawk and we get these two into bed."

"I'll be there," Mac promised with a grin. "This is a lesson I don't want to miss."

Jewel laughed. "Just get it right this time, or you're liable to find yourself with a whole football team before we're through."

"I wouldn't mind," Mac said softly. "As long as we get at least one girl who looks just like you."

Before Jewel could answer, a football came flying onto the porch, and Mac and Evan abandoned her to play football with the two teenagers.

Jewel fingered the soft curls at Dustin's nape and brushed her hand across his baby-soft cheek. She was looking forward to Mac's inventive lovemaking tonight. Knowing his determination to do everything to the best of his ability, it was bound to be a delightful adventure, full of fun and laughter.

Only this time, she would have the last laugh. Jewel's smile grew as she imagined the look on

Mac's face when she told him—after the lesson, of course—that his daughter was already on the way.

*   *   *   *   *

THE LONG HOT SUMMER
Wendy Rosnau

This book is dedicated to my husband, Jerry, the hero in my life and partner in all things. To Tyler and Jenni, for their love and bright smiles. And to Lettie Lee, for her instincts, support and always taking my call.

Chapter 1

Angola State Penitentiary

The hell of it was, the parole deal stunk. But if Johnny agreed to the terms, he'd be breathing fresh air within the hour. It should have been an easy choice to make—he'd been rotting in Louisiana's maximum-security prison for six months. Yeah, it should have been easy—if only the terms of his parole weren't so ridiculous.

A buzzer sounded and the iron door electronically unlocked. "Come on, Bernard, put a wiggle in it," the guard ordered. "The warden wants to see you, pronto."

Contrary to the direct order, Johnny slowly got to his feet. Reaching into his shirt pocket, he pulled out his half-used pack of Camels, and passed the cigarettes to his cell mate, who lay sprawled on the top bunk. They exchanged a look; it said, Good luck, but don't bet too high on the odds. Then, in a lazy gait that had been a Bernard trademark for over half a century, Johnny sauntered through the open door and into the corridor of Cell Block C.

When Johnny entered the warden's office moments later, Pete Lasky looked up from the mound of paperwork scattered on his cheap metal desk. Lasky owned a pair of uncharitable blue eyes, and a false grin that exposed a row of coffee-stained teeth—an occupational hazard created by the monotony of ten-hour days sandwiched between a desk and a window overlooking a bleak, prisoner-filled courtyard. "So, Bernard, you wanna be cut loose today?"

The stupid question deserved a stupid answer, but Johnny didn't plan on getting cute; the sixty-year-old warden didn't own a sense of humor. "No chance for a fat fine and public service?"

"Sure would make life easier for you, wouldn't it?" Pete grinned. "Well, it ain't gonna happen. *Easy,* I mean. Never did like that word. *Easy* ain't gonna teach you when to keep your mouth shut or your fist out of some poor devil's face. And those are two lessons that would do you some good."

Johnny had heard it all before, and in most cases what was said about him was true. Only, in this particular instance—the one the warden was referring to—he hadn't been shooting off his mouth, or taking the first swing. Yeah, he'd retaliated, but only after Farrel had come at him.

"I've had two phone conversations with your hometown sheriff," the warden continued. "Looks like Sheriff Tucker's not any happier about these parole terms than you are. The way he tells it, you're about as popular in Common as a copper-belly at a Fourth of July picnic. But like I told him, I'm not in the 'happy' business." The warden opened his top drawer, then took out the paperwork for Johnny's release and laid it on his desk. "By the way, if you agree to this deal, that man—the one you damn near killed—is off-limits. Any criminal conduct will nullify your parole. Carrying a weapon will do the same. Failure to comply will earn you another six months inside. So what's it gonna be?''

Johnny jammed his hands in the back pockets of his faded jeans, and the image of Belle Bayou suddenly surfaced. With it came a treasured memory from his youth—his father teaching him how to fish cane-pole style at sunrise.

The truth was, if he agreed to the warden's parole deal, he would be waking up to that sunrise every morning for the next four months. He hadn't been back home in years—not until six months ago, anyway—but he'd never been able to forget the bond he'd formed with the bayou.

He knew the bayou as well as any of the old-timers. He knew where the best fishing spots were. Where the shy blue herons nested, and where every hidden channel in the bayou ended up. He also knew what a stir he'd cause by showing up in town again.

''Well?''

''I'll take the deal,'' Johnny said, glancing out the window behind Pete Lasky's desk. The sky was tauntingly clear, and maybe that's what had suddenly been the deciding factor. Or maybe it was remembering Belle. Either way, he heard himself say, ''Four months working for Mae Chapman at Oakhaven won't kill me, but staying in here another six just might.''

An hour later, Johnny walked out of Angola's front gate and into hell's kitchen. That's what his mama had always called the month of August in Louisiana. It was just after ten, and already the temperature threatened one-hundred. He headed north, his plan to catch the bus out of Tunica. A mile down the road, he pulled off his white T-shirt and ran the sleeve through an empty belt loop on his jeans.

He'd never intended to go back to Common when he'd

left fifteen years ago—both of his parents were dead and he had no other family—but after receiving that damn letter six months ago from Griffin Black, curiosity had overridden common sense. The letter had offered to pay him top dollar for his land. *His land?*

Now, everyone knew that Johnny didn't own any land in Common. True, his father had owned land years ago— a run-down sugarcane farm that had never earned him more than a sore back and a pile of headaches. But all things considered, delinquent taxes should have relieved him of the farm years ago. Only a week later, after strolling into Common city hall and telling the clerk what he was there for, Johnny had promptly learned that he did, in fact, own his daddy's old farm. But just how and why remained a mystery.

The truth was, there were only two people in town who cared enough to invest any time or money in him. Only Virgil didn't have any extra cash to speak of, so that left Mae Chapman. The question was, why would she do it?

Johnny left city hall with the intention of confronting the old lady with what he'd learned. But the day's heat was powerful, and he'd made a quick decision to stop by the local bar for one cold beer before showing up at Oakhaven. A bad decision, he realized, the moment he opened the door to Pepper's Bar and Grill and walked straight into his childhood enemy.

He hadn't been trying to kill Farrel Craig the way they had accused him of doing, as much as it had looked that way when Sheriff Tucker had shown up. Yes, he'd drawn his knife, but only after Farrel had come at him with a broken beer bottle.

It had looked bad, he couldn't deny that—but he hadn't been willing to roll over and let Farrel carve him up like a steak. Only, the authorities didn't see it that way. He'd been arrested and convicted for assault with intent to do bodily harm—the sentence: a year in Angola State Penitentiary.

So now here he was, six months later, faced with going back home to serve a lousy four-month parole sentence. And he would serve it. Only, by summer's end he intended to sell the farm and sever his ties to Common for good.

The sun was just setting as the bus rolled into Common and stopped on the corner of Cooper and Main. As Johnny stepped off the bus he glanced around the bare-bones town were he'd spent the first fifteen years of his life. The streets were nearly deserted. He supposed the sultry heat had driven most of the locals inside, or maybe they'd heard he was coming. He suddenly realized he could have been happy here if only the townsfolk would have given him a chance.

Gran would never willingly have agreed to hire such a disreputable man if she had seen the rap sheet that went along with him. Disgusted, Nicole tossed the paper on the Pendleton desk. She snapped off the old-fashioned floor fan sitting next to her, then picked up the phone and dialed the Pass-By Motel.

On the third ring Virgil Diehl answered in his thick cajun accent. "Motel. De coffee's black and dere's vacancies."

"Hello, Mr. Diehl, this is Nicole Chapman calling."

"Little Nicki! *Oui!* I heard yo' was back from de big city. Bet Mae's tickled pink, *ma petite.* Me, too. Yo' is de perdiest angel in all of St. James Parish. *Mais yeah.*"

"*Merci,* Mr. Diehl. You're kind to say so."

"Dat's me." Virgil chuckled. "Kind is good for business. But yo' kin't be wantin' a room, *ma petite,* so what yo' after?" He paused. "Maybe I already knows."

He no doubt did. By now the news of Jonathan Bernard's return and his newly acquired position at Oakhaven had most likely raced through the supermarket, the bakery, the corner drug, and both bars. "Sheriff Tucker told me Mr. Bernard is staying in one of your rooms," Nicole explained. "Is he registered?"

"Johnny? Yah, he's here. Fact be, he's jes' comin' through de door now."

"Could I speak to him, please?"

"Yah—sure t'ing, *ma petite*."

While Nicole waited, she turned the fan back on. A native of California, she was used to hot weather, but Louisiana's sultry heat was a new kind of hot. One that would surely kill her if she didn't acclimate soon—she had never perspired so much in all her twenty-five years.

She took another quick glance at the paperwork Sheriff Tucker had dropped by an hour ago. She hadn't read every word, but she really didn't need to. The gist was that Jonathan Bernard had been granted parole because of job security—thanks to Gran—and good behavior.

Good behavior. Nicole sniffed, taking another quick glance at the list of offenses the man had accumulated in the past thirty years. True, most of Jonathan Bernard's offenses dated back to when he was a teenager. And there was even a span of time—seven years, to be exact—when it appeared he had reformed. But when she'd mentioned that hopeful tidbit to Sheriff Tucker, he had assured her that Common's black sheep didn't know the meaning of the word *reform*.

That's why she intended to intervene. True, they did need someone to work a miracle on Oakhaven over the summer—the place was falling apart—but not Jonathan Bernard.

"This here's me. If it ain't free, I don't want it."

His phone manners spoke mountains for his character. The black-bayou drawl, however, sent an unexpected chill racing the length of Nicole's spine. She paused a moment, and in the process lost her train of thought. Scrambling to get it back, she settled for "Is 'me' Jonathan Bernard?"

"You got who you wanted. Only, folks call me Johnny. What you selling, *cherie?*"

A one-way bus ticket north, Nicole wanted to say. Instead, she said, "I'm not selling anything, Mr. Bernard. This is Oakhaven calling about your so-called job. The point is, the job is no longer available."

Silence.

"Mr. Bernard?"

"Let me talk to the old lady."

Nicole hadn't been ready for that. "I—ah, she's taking a nap in the garden." It was the truth.

"And she asked you to call me and say she's changed her mind, is that it?"

Nicole had hoped to settle this without involving her seventy-six-year-old grandmother. "I don't think—"

"The job is a condition of my parole," he drawled thickly. "The old lady signed papers agreeing to supply me with an eight-to-five job, five days a week for the summer. It's already been settled."

He was lying. Gran was too smart to sign anything without legal advice.

"I guess what I'm saying, *cherie,* is I'm nonrefundable."

Nonrefundable. Something in his voice suggested he was smiling. Narrowing her blue eyes, Nicole switched off the fan, then quickly flipped through the papers Sheriff Tucker had left. Sure enough, there it was, a copy of a legal agreement with her grandmother's signature on it. *Damn!*

"You still there?"

"I think there's been a misunderstanding." Nicole tried to keep her voice strong and confident.

"Is this where I get one of those sticky apologies over the phone?"

Nicole bristled, but she kept her mouth shut.

"I guess not. Well, I'll be moving into the boathouse sometime around four."

That bit of news was too alarming for Nicole to keep quiet a moment longer. "You're moving into the boathouse?" She nearly choked on the words. "I don't think so, Mr. Bernard! In fact, I—"

But it was too late for thinking or talking. Jonathan Bernard had already hung up the phone.

Chapter 2

Gran's garden was a blue-ribbon winner. Every kind of flower, in every color imaginable, from azaleas to camellias the size of grapefruits, flourished in the tropical heat. The old plantation-style house looked tired and desperate, the surrounding fields overgrown and empty of sugarcane, but the flower garden was breathtaking, the beauty so grand that Nicole couldn't help but sigh in wonder as she slipped through the wrought-iron gate.

She found her grandmother asleep beneath a hundred-year-old oak and knelt in the grass beside her wheelchair. Reaching up to brush a stray, snow-white strand of hair from Mae's wrinkled cheek, she whispered, "Do you plan on sleeping the entire afternoon away?"

The gentle touch and softly spoken words roused Mae, and she blinked open her blue eyes—eyes identical to her granddaughter's. "It must be getting late if you've ventured outside to wake me," she rasped, her solid voice a contradiction to her petite size. "Since your arrival two weeks ago I haven't seen you out much in the heat of the day. So what is it that has lured you away from that poor tired fan you've attached to your hip?''

Trouble, Nicole wanted to say, but she thought better of simply blurting out what she'd done. She glanced at Mae's ankle—a week ago the porch rail had given way and her grandmother had tumbled into the flower bed. She'd received a minor cut on her cheek, a few bruises and a sprained left ankle. "How's the ankle?" she asked. "It doesn't seem as swollen today."

"No, it doesn't. Thank the Lord, I didn't break it, or I would be in this chair longer than a month." She looked Nicole up and down. "So, what brings you outside? We blow an electrical fuse?"

"Very funny." Nicole made a face.

Mae made an effort to simulate Nicole's cross-eyed contortion.

Nicole laughed. "Okay, I've been a might excessive," she conceded.

"Clair and I have been trying to come up with a way for you to strap the fan on your back."

"I didn't know you two were so ingenious."

"There's a lot of things we haven't let you in on," Mae teased.

"Like hiring an ex-con for the summer?"

"So you've heard? Gossip, or from someone credible who hasn't twisted the entire story?"

"I assume Sheriff Tucker would be considered credible."

"He certainly would not. He's always disliked Johnny."

"If you took the time to read his rap sheet, you'd know why."

"Are you upset with me?"

"Can you blame me? I'm the last to know about this."

"It wasn't intentional. But honestly, I just forgot to

mention Johnny coming to work for us. I guess in all the excitement of your moving in, it slipped my mind.''

That might have been true of someone else, Nicole thought. But not of her grandmother. In her advancing years Mae Chapman might be losing a little of her agility, but nothing would slip her mind, which was as sharp as a razor blade and twice as quick.

''I would have remembered today, since this is—''

''The day he's moving in.'' Nicole stood and nailed her grandmother with a peeved look. ''So the truth is, you've hired an ex-con for the summer, and planned to tell me the day he arrived, is that it? Why so soon?''

''Now, Nicki, don't give yourself another headache. We old people get feebleminded from time to time.''

''You're about as feebleminded as I am,'' Nicole snapped, jamming her hands on her slender hips and narrowing her cool blue eyes. ''And don't you dare give me that sad, one-foot-in-the-grave slump. I'm serious. This man has an arrest record longer than a month-old grocery list. Sheriff Tucker says he's the dark side of trouble.''

''Bah! That's ridiculous. He's harmless.''

''Harmless? Sheriff Tucker says he nearly killed Farrel Craig at Pepper's Bar six months ago. I'd say he's about as harmless as a sunburned cottonmouth with a belly rash and a sore tooth.''

Mae chuckled. ''That was very good, Nicki. I must remember that one. Tell it to me again so—''

''Gran, I'm not trying to be funny.''

''I agree it was careless of Johnny to get caught fighting, but you see—''

''Caught? You condone his fighting. It's getting *caught* that you—''

''Don't put words in my mouth, dear. Farrel and Johnny were always going at it, but it wasn't all one-sided. None of us is perfect.''

one was perfect. Nicole had certainly made her shar... mistakes. Still, she needed to understand the reason behind what Gran had done. "So convince me we need him. Not just any carpenter, but Johnny Bernard."

"That's easy. Johnny's my friend and he needed out of that wretched place. In the bargain, we get a carpenter to restore Oakhaven."

"Friend?" Nicole felt her pulse quicken. "How good a friend?"

"Good enough to know it's time he stopped running and came home. There, I've said it. Said exactly what I've been feeling for years, and it's liberating to finally say it."

"Would he agree?"

"That he's been running?" Mae shrugged. "Probably not. I'll be honest with you, Nicki. You're going to hear a lot of gossip, most of it bad. But don't settle on an opinion until you've met him. I guarantee there is more to Johnny Bernard than what's in those reports. And far more than people in this town are willing to see, if they would just open their eyes."

Nicole could tell her grandmother believed wholeheartedly what she was saying. The question was, why would Gran feel so strongly about this man? What *wasn't* she saying?

"Actually, you and Johnny have more in common than you think, Nicki. He's not the only one the townsfolk have been gossiping about lately."

Her grandmother eyed Nicole's short cutoffs, then her hair. Self-consciously, Nicki tried to tame her shaggy blond hair into some semblance of order. "I'm from California, Gran. You know I'm—"

"A free spirit. Yes, I know."

Nicole smiled, not sure that was the word she would use. Or maybe it was, but in the past year she'd been reeducated on how dangerous being your own person could be. In fact, she'd lived through a nightmare and a half, and wasn't ashamed to admit her spirit had been broken. Snapped in half, actually.

Three months had passed since the miscarriage, but sometimes it felt like only yesterday. She still didn't sleep through an entire night, and she continued to experience depression—a condition the doctor believed would pass in time. Only, it wouldn't; Nicole was sure of it. Time could never wash away the guilt a woman felt over losing her child. Especially in this case, when Nicole hadn't been so sure she'd even wanted Chad's child. Not until after the baby was gone.

No, time would never erase her guilt, and she had told the doctor as much. She had told him she wasn't expecting miracles because, frankly, she didn't deserve any.

"The good news, Nicki, is that Johnny's an experienced carpenter. He'll be the perfect solution for our growing list of house repairs. Unless you've suddenly decided to buck up under the heat and learn how to pound nails and replace shingles. If not, I'd say we're in desperate need of a man around here. Someone who can swing a hammer and isn't afraid to sweat."

"And you're sure he's not afraid of hard work?"

"Johnny grew up hard, Nicki. There's no doubt in my mind he'll give us our dollars' worth. For the past two years he's been working in Lafayette for a construction outfit. The foreman told me he would hire Johnny back in a minute, no questions asked. He's that good. And he's a military man, too. An ex-marine. I suspect he's got hidden talents we don't even know about."

Nicole arched a brow. "And just how do you suppose we can utilize an ex-con who is an expert at warfare to his fullest potential?" She paused as if thinking. Finally, she said, "Funny, but I thought we were discussing restoring Oakhaven, not blowing it up."

"A regular funny-girl today, aren't you?" Mae shook her head. "I think you'll be surprised, my dear. Pleasantly surprised, that is."

Nicole didn't like surprises. Especially surprises that involved men. She said grimly, "He's arriving around four."

"You've talked to him? Wonderful!" Mae's excitement sent two birds nesting overhead into flight.

"I called the Pass-By Motel," Nicole admitted. "Sheriff Tucker said that's where I could find him." She purposely left out the part about trying to fire him over the phone. "He said he'll be staying at the boathouse."

"Yes, that was our agreement. Do you suppose, Nicki, you could send Bick down there to open the windows and air the place out? I'll scribble a message for Johnny. Bick can leave it on the table, since I can't get down there to meet him myself."

Mae's gaze traveled across the driveway to where a trail led to the boathouse. The trail was a quarter-mile through dense woods—a shortcut to Belle Bayou. "I haven't seen Johnny in fifteen years," she offered wistfully. "I intended to visit him in prison, but my lawyer advised against it."

Judging by the look in her grandmother's aging eyes, she was sorry she hadn't. Nicole found herself growing curious. She asked, "Is there some way I can help?"

Her grandmother reached out and patted Nicole's arm. "You already have—by coming home. First you and now Johnny. It's perfect." She paused. "When he left I had no idea it would be years before he came home. I wonder how he turned out in the looks department? If he ended up anything like his father or grandpa, watch out, dear. Gracious, but those Bernard men were handsome."

Nicole didn't need to see him to know how he'd turned out. The report on the desk in the study confirmed that Johnny Bernard had gotten his reputation the old-fashioned way: he'd earned every bit of it. And as far as his looks went, she didn't really care how handsome he'd turned out. They weren't shopping for a lawn ornament, just a simple carpenter. How he looked on a ladder was of no importance, as long as he could climb one.

She bent forward and kissed her grandmother's cheek. "When you get your note written, I'll see that Bick takes it with him. What do you say we have some lemonade? I'm dying."

"You're always dying," Mae teased. "Where should we have our lemonade? On the front porch?"

Nicole positioned herself behind Mae's wheelchair. "I've got an original idea. Why not relax in front of the fan in the study?"

An hour later, Nicole learned that Bick had taken himself off to town. Forced to run her grandmother's errand, she hurried along the wooded trail toward the boathouse. She checked her watch, glad to see that she still had an hour before Johnny Bernard would descend on them. She wasn't sure how she was going to face him after trying to get rid of him over the phone, but with any luck she wouldn't have to think about that until later. She would open the windows, leave Gran's note on the table and be gone before he even set foot on Oakhaven soil.

Within a matter of ten minutes, Nicole was through the woods, standing in a small clearing just west of Belle Bayou. All things considered, she was more intrigued by the moody swamp than frightened by it. It had a certain allure, a quality she had tried many times to capture on canvas.

It was an artist's paradise, she admitted. The colorful vegetation that grew out of the muck along the banks fascinated her as much as did the huge cypress trees with their gnarly roots and distorted branches. The branches dripping with Spanish moss along the water's edge reminded her of a travel brochure she'd once seen advertising scenic Louisiana.

Her gaze followed the grassy bank to the old wood and stone boathouse, this being the first time she'd come down to the bayou since she'd arrived from L.A. From an artist's point of view the place had immense possibilities. It was dark and eerie, straight out of a gothic novel, and when she decided to paint it, she would do so with that in mind.

She started down the overgrown path through the clearing, approaching the aging structure from the north side. She reached for the door's rusty latch, and as she pulled it open, it groaned loudly in protest. Inside, she ran her hand along the cool brick in search of the light switch. Relieved that it still worked, that she hadn't been greeted by any creepy-crawly surprises, Nicole followed the ray of light past the clutter and ascended the stairs to the second story.

To her surprise, what once had housed old tools and fishing gear now resembled a modest apartment. She recognized a few pieces of furniture from the house: a rocker, a bureau, a square table and two chairs. The dark red sofa, she remembered from the attic. An iron bed made up with a blue bedspread had been arranged in such a manner that one could lie down and still gaze out the window and enjoy the bayou's beauty at night. A partition wall cut the room in half. On one side, a small kitchen; on the other, an even smaller bathroom.

The window facing the woods, as well as the one overlooking the moody, black bayou, was already open. Puzzled, Nicole concluded Bick had second-guessed Gran's request and had opened the windows that morning. Not giving it any more thought, she placed Gran's note on the table and walked to the nearest window to gaze outside. She scanned the shoreline, noting the boat tied to the sagging dock, the cane pole resting across the seat.

Cane pole? Bick never fished with a cane pole.

She made the mental observation just as she heard something. A moment later, she identified the noise as footsteps—footsteps that had reached the stairs and were now steadily climbing.

She glanced at her watch. It was a little past three. *He* had said four. Nicole made a quick swipe at her blond bangs, swore silently at her bad luck, then forced herself to turn. Her first thought was that the black-bayou voice on the phone was a perfect fit for the dark and dangerous man who had suddenly filled the doorway.

Nicole's gaze drifted over Common's rebel, deciding that he was everything she had expected him to be, and more. A couple of inches over six feet, he stood shirtless, his long legs encased in ragged jeans. His broad shoulders looked hard as iron, his torso and stomach a series of layered muscles and corrugated definition. It was obvious he was in top physical condition. But then, what else did a jailed criminal have to do all day but get bigger and more dangerous by pumping iron in the prison gym? Hadn't she read a controversial article about that somewhere?

She had taken a few self-defense classes—living in L.A., it had been the smart thing to do. Even so, it would be almost funny trying to use what she'd learned against a marine who could add Angola State Penitentiary to his bio.

To be sure, he was a survivor. Of that, Nicole had no doubt—as she stared into a pair of rich amber, see-to-the-soul eyes that promised Johnny Bernard had seen it all, and possibly done it all, too.

She watched as he reached behind his back and closed the door. The movement shifted him slightly sideways, sending a stream of sunlight from the window into his straight, black hair. Loose, it would have touched his shoulders, but to combat the heat he had pulled it back from his face and secured it low at the nape of his neck.

If not for a straight high-bridged nose and a sensual mouth softening his otherwise hard features, he would have been almost too rugged to be referred to as handsome. Those two features, combined with a reckless thin scar trailing from his right eye to his temple, softened him and made him human, thus dangerously good-looking.

Clearing her throat, Nicole wrapped herself in false confidence—something she did often these days—and forced herself to speak. "I thought you said you were arriving at four o'clock."

"Did I?" He relaxed against the door and loosely folded his arms over his broad chest. The smile Nicole imagined him wearing earlier throughout their phone conversation appeared. He spared a quick glance at the plain silver watch on his wrist, then made eye contact with her once more. "Looks like you're early, too. Anxious to meet me, Nicki?"

She hadn't expected him to know her name, Johnny could tell by the surprise in her blue eyes. But he did know her name, and a whole lot more. He had pumped Virgil before he'd left the motel, and the old man had been eager to talk. In fact, he had claimed Nicki Chapman the "perdiest *femme*" he'd ever seen. And Johnny had to agree, she was the best thing he'd seen in a helluva long time.

Somewhere in her twenties, she was a little above average height, her body curvy and delicate. The delicate part warned him off right away—he avoided fragile women like they had the plague. They reminded him of glass figurines, and, frankly, they made him nervous. He did like looking at her, though. Liked her sexy long bangs and the way she let them play an intentional game of hide-and-seek with her eyes. Her honey-blond hair was shoulder-length and shiny. Her cutoffs, mid-thigh, flashed long, slender legs and sexy knees. Her short T-shirt was a distinct shade of blue, a perfect match for her eyes.

She'd been born in L.A. Her parents had died two years ago in a plane crash. This came from Virgil. She was an only child like Johnny, Virgil had said, but he couldn't remember what she did for a living. Apparently, she'd moved in with the old lady a few weeks ago with the intention of making Oakhaven her permanent home.

"I came to drop off a note from Gran." She gestured to the piece of paper on the table. "I had planned to open windows, too, but I see you already opened them." She thrust her hand out. "Ah, I'm Nicole Chapman. Mae's granddaughter. We met on the phone."

Johnny was surprised that she offered her hand. Most people were reluctant to get that friendly with him. Too bad he was going to have to decline the gesture. He wasn't sure what he had on his hands, but they were filthy. He unfolded his arms and showed her that both of his hands weren't even the same color. "I was catching supper, among other things," he explained. "Catfish."

Her gaze drifted to his dirty hands, then she promptly dropped the one she'd offered. "Since you're here and you'll be working for Oakhaven, I—"

"Will I, *cherie?* No new plan to fire me before I get started?"

"You made it clear over the phone that the choice wasn't mine, remember? I believe the word you used was *nonrefundable.* I checked with Gran and that seems to be the case." She broke eye contact with him and glanced around the room. "Gran took a lot of time to fix this place up. I guess that means something." She brought her gaze back to his. "You're a carpenter, isn't that right, Mr. Bernard?"

"Johnny. The name's Johnny. And, yeah, I'm a carpenter."

"Well, Oakhaven is in need of major repairs, *Johnny,* so it looks like there will be plenty to keep you busy."

Her concession to use his name amused him, and Johnny grinned. "So I've noticed."

She arched one delicate eyebrow, but didn't argue with him.

He gestured to the rocker, then shoved away from the door and strolled past her to the couch. Once she'd slipped into the chair, he dropped down on the couch and let his long legs sprawl apart. The day's heat had flushed her face, and he noted she looked miserably hot. He, on the other hand, had never felt better. He loved the Louisiana heat; it was in his blood, the hotter the better. He'd run away from Common years ago. Only he hadn't left the state. He'd been calling Lafayette home for almost two years.

"Will the job take the entire summer?" she asked.

"That depends on what's on the old lady's list."

A bead of sweat slipped past her left temple and down her cheek. She made a swipe at it, then lifted her right leg a fraction of an inch, then the other one. It didn't dawn on Johnny until he saw her go through the motion a second time that her bare legs were sticking to the wooden chair.

"Do you have a glass of water with ice?" she suddenly asked.

"Sure." Johnny stood and walked into the small kitchen. He scrubbed his hands, then retrieved a glass from the cupboard, filled it with water and dropped in a couple of ice cubes from the space-saving fridge. He returned and handed it to her. "One glass of water, served with ice."

She peered into the glass, then glanced at his clean hands. "Thank you. I haven't adjusted to the humidity yet," she quietly explained, "but I will eventually."

Johnny wasn't convinced—she looked about as miserable as she could get. He returned to the couch and watched her use the glass to cool her warm cheek. "Carpenters don't come cheap," he drawled, watching her slide the glass down her neck, then back up. She had a pretty neck, long and pale.

"No, they don't. But I imagine carpenters on parole are just happy to be working at all."

Johnny laughed out loud, liking her honesty. "So I'm supposed to work cheap, is that it? Or am I donating my time?"

She moved the glass to her opposite cheek and closed her eyes for a moment. "That's something you'll have to work out with Gran. She sprained her ankle a week ago and she's in a wheelchair. I imagine we can get our supplies at Craig Lumber, don't you think?"

"If they don't carry it, I'm sure they'll order it."

"Good, I'll call them tomorrow and make sure Gran's account is in order."

"Jasper Craig still own the lumberyard?"

"Yes, but I'm told Farrel— Ah, his son runs the business now that his father's retired."

By the look on her face, Johnny was sure she knew about the bar fight that had landed him in jail—at least, Sheriff Tucker's version. "My parole states no physical confrontations. What that means, *cherie,* is I'm not supposed to engage in any violent behavior. I don't plan on killing Farrel Craig the next time I see him."

"Should that make me feel better?"

Johnny shrugged. "For the record, I didn't start that fight at Pepper's. Even though I'm sure that's what you've heard. The truth is, if I had wanted Farrel dead, I would have killed him years ago. Leastwise, that's what I told the judge. Now, maybe after I've been in town awhile I'll feel different—Farrel being the number-one jackass that he is."

"So you're saying the bar incident wasn't your fault?"

"I'm saying, maybe I defended myself a little too good." Johnny paused. "Now about those repairs. The place looks like hell. Where do we start?"

For the next half hour, they discussed what Johnny would tackle first. The rotten roof and porch were the most urgent. But there was more: inside jobs for a rainy day, a dead tree in the front yard, painting, window repair.

After a while, Nicole stood, peeling her legs away from the chair one at a time. "If you could figure out some kind of a supply list, I would appreciate it. That's really not something I understand. If you can't—"

"I can." Johnny stood.

She looked nervous suddenly, and as she attempted to step around the chair she stumbled. Before she landed on the floor, Johnny took one long stride and reached out to grip her upper arm, quickly bringing her back to her feet. She was as lightweight as a hollow-legged bird, he noted, letting her go as quickly as he had rescued her.

Hastily she handed him the empty water glass then pulled herself together without delay, impressing him once more with how cool and collected she could be.

She crossed to the door, surprising him when she suddenly turned around in the doorway. "Gran called you her friend. I'm curious to know if it works both ways. Do you consider my grandmother your friend, Johnny Bernard?"

Johnny stayed where he was, his hands shoved into his back pockets. "I really don't think that's what you want to know, *cherie*. What you really want to know is if she'll be safe around me? The answer is, yes. I wouldn't hurt the old lady, or anyone she cares about. Good enough?"

"If you mean it," she said bluntly, and left.

Johnny listened to her light footsteps descending the stairs. And once the outside door creaked, he moved to the window to watch her cross the clearing.

Part of the reason the heat was eating her up so badly was that she moved too fast, he decided. In Louisiana, things were best done at half speed. She needed to learn that, if she was ever going to appreciate the tropical heat. He should mention it, but right now wouldn't do much good—she'd be too busy second-guessing his motives to take a suggestion from him.

The afternoon passed quickly. Before Johnny knew it, the sun had melted into the bayou and he'd spent four hours repairing the dilapidated dock that had been ready to float away in the next windstorm. Now as he walked along the trail in the dark, his thoughts turned to the old lady. He couldn't put off seeing her any longer, though that's just what he'd been doing. Why, he didn't know. Maybe because she was going to look at him long and hard with those knowing blue eyes of hers, and she was going to make him start feeling guilty for leaving fifteen years ago without saying goodbye.

The minute he emerged from the wooded trail and glanced across the driveway, he knew he'd put off seeing her too long. The two-story house was completely dark except for one lone light shining in the left wing. Relieved in a crazy way that made him feel like a vulnerable kid again, he crossed the driveway and ambled toward the big house. He could see the improvements Henry had made over the years. Mae's late husband had been a handy devil. The courtyard had been enlarged, and there was a swing in the backyard he didn't remember from when he was a kid. Two more sheds had been built west of the big field. The carport had been extended, and now accommodated not only Mae's '79 Buick, but a sleek-looking white Skylark.

Henry had died of a heart attack five years ago. Virgil had written the news to Johnny in the Marines. Johnny hadn't kept in contact with anyone else in town, but Virgil

was a persistent old bird and he had tracked Johnny down
years earlier. He had written faithfully over the years.
Johnny had never been much of a letter writer, but he'd
managed one or two a year, which had suited Virgil just
fine.

More than once, Johnny had thought about writing to
Mae. But he hadn't known what to say, so he'd just told
Virgil to let her know he was alive. The day he'd received
the letter of Henry's death, for one crazy second he'd
wanted to come back for the funeral. But then he'd remembered how hard it had been burying his father, and a
few years later his mother, and he had chickened out.

In the sheds, Johnny found old lumber and Henry's car-
pentry tools. In the older shed, he found Henry's tan '59
Dodge pickup. The memories the pickup resurrected were
unexpected. Johnny tucked them away after circling the
pickup twice, then wandered back to the house and found
a sturdy oak in the front yard to settle against.

While lighting a cigarette, he saw someone pace by the
French doors in the left wing of the house. Johnny knew
immediately who it was—the blue-eyed bird with the
shapely legs and long bangs was easy to spot. Smiling, he
slid down the tree to the ground and rested his back against
the sturdy oak. He ignored the steady hum of mosquitoes
overhead and the distant rumble of thunder. An hour
passed, and still he watched her pace the room anxious
about something, or someone. Was his arrival keeping her
up? It made sense; she must have heard some pretty wild
stories about him by now.

By the time she turned out the light and went to bed, it
was after midnight, and Johnny had smoked a half-pack
of cigarettes. He got to his feet and strolled out the yard
and down the driveway. Since leaving Angola he couldn't
get enough fresh air, and, although it was late, he decided
to walk to his parents' old farm.

The thunder continued as he reached Bayou Road and headed east. His pace, however, slowed steadily, his surroundings triggering memories from the past.

Johnny tried to shake them off, but in a matter of seconds he was a kid again, running so fast his lungs felt as if they would explode inside his chest, his bare feet pounding the dirt while Farrel chased after him waving a stick. He could hear Clete Gilmore hollering, calling him ugly names and encouraging Farrel to *"Get him!"*

As he ran, he could see Jack Oden out of the corner of his eye, could see him gaining on him. More than once Johnny had wished that the gangly kid they all called Stretch had been his friend instead of Farrel's.

Johnny stopped abruptly. He was breathing fast, as if he'd actually been running. He shook his head, forced the image back into the black hole where it belonged. He started down the road again, this time noticing that the potholes had gotten deeper, the ditches still waterlogged and ripe with decay.

A rusted-out mailbox signaled the farmhouse was just up ahead. He stepped over the rubble that had once claimed to be a sturdy gate, and walked steadily on. His heart rate picked up again, making his chest feel miserably tight. He didn't want to feel anything, he told himself. Least of all, vulnerable and scared. Lonely. Yet of all the feelings tugging at his insides, those inescapable emotions dominated.

He scaled the porch steps and stopped, his hand poised on the doorknob. He turned the knob—surprisingly it wasn't locked. He took a deep breath, preparing himself for whatever bleak remains still haunted the old house. Then, after fifteen long years, Johnny opened the door and stepped inside.

The floor creaked just the way it used to, the sharp smell of rotten wood swelling his nostrils in protest. He lit a match and glanced around the empty living room. The place had been ransacked, which couldn't have taken more than ten minutes—poverty keeping them from owning so much as a picture to hang on the wall.

He turned to his right and held the match toward the kitchen, and when he did, something scurried across the bare wood floor. He shifted his gaze to the shredded curtains at the window, then to the crude set of cupboards, the warped doors all standing open.

He walked past the kitchen and into the little room his parents had designated his. It was barely big enough to fit a mattress on the floor, and to his surprise the old ragged remains were still there, molding in the corner.

Despair overwhelmed him, and Johnny's stomach knotted. He hadn't expected to feel this way, hadn't wanted any part of the past to intrude on the present. But he was a fool to think that it wouldn't—there was just too much he had run away from.

The depth of poverty that had kept his family in a choke-hold continued to gnaw at Johnny once he returned to the boathouse. He stood at the window overlooking Belle Bayou, a cigarette cornered in his mouth, and closed his eyes. Not liking his melancholy mood, he willed himself to think of something else. The vision that popped into his head had silky blond hair and sexy blue eyes. Johnny took his time, treated himself to the perfect fantasy.

It was all too wicked and perfect to come true, of course. But a man could dream. And so he did.

Chapter 3

The dream was nasty, and *he* was in it.

Disgusted with herself, Nicole jerked awake and sat up in bed. A quick glance at the clock on the nightstand told her it was barely six. She'd grown used to functioning on five hours or less these past few months, tormented by the nightmare she'd left behind in L.A. Last night, however, her thoughts had shifted to the man with the river-bottom drawl and see-to-the-soul eyes.

She told herself it was because of Gran and the unusual situation surrounding Johnny Bernard's return. But was it? The man had taken her completely by surprise yesterday. He had looked dark and dangerous, yes—but not entirely in the way she had envisioned.

Disgusted that she was giving so much thought to the subject, Nicole wrestled with the rose-colored satin sheets and climbed out of bed. The sticky, warm air inside the room settled against her, and she sighed with the knowledge that she would have to find some way to cope with the heat again today. Her gaze fell on the fan near the end of the bed, and she almost reached out and turned it on. No, if she was ever going to adjust she would have to stop relying on that damn fan.

She swept her blue satin robe off the foot of the bed, slipped it on and tied the sash around her trim waist. A quick glance outside had her wondering if the late-night rain had left a breeze behind. Relief an open door away, she moved to the French doors that led on to the front porch and flung them wide in a sudden burst of hopeful energy.

At the very least, she had expected to hear a chorus of morning songbirds, but instead she felt a *clunk* and heard a string of colorful cursing, half of it in French. In an instant she knew who owned that distinctive drawl. Dreading her next move, Nicole forced herself to peer around the door.

He was leaning against the house wearing beat-up jeans and scuffed brown western boots. His hair was tied back the same as yesterday, too. One of his hands was rubbing his hip and the other was pinching his nose to stem the flow of blood.

Blood. Oh, God!

Nicole ducked back inside, grabbed a handful of tissues from the box on the nightstand and dashed back outside. "Here," she said, shoving the pink tissues in his face.

He took the offering without saying a word and pressed the tissues to his nose. Within a few minutes the blood had stopped flowing, and he balled up the tissues and jammed them into his back pocket. Giving her his full attention now, he said, "You carry accident insurance, *cherie?* It looks like working for you could be dangerous."

Instead of anger, Nicole saw amusement dancing in his dark eyes. He rubbed at his hipbone again, then flashed her a crooked smile, which Nicole rejected with a stubborn lift of her chin. "If you're looking for fringe benefits, Mr. Bernard, you won't find them here."

His grin turned wicked. "Oh, I don't know. Insurance ain't everything." He gave her a thorough once-over. "And the name's Johnny. Remember?"

Nicole didn't care one bit for his sexist ogling. "Since you're in one piece, I'll leave you to whatever it was you were doing." She turned to go back inside, then hesitated. "Which was…?"

"Checking out the condition of the porch. You did say it was top priority, right?"

"Yes, I did. But this early?"

"I couldn't sleep. You, too?" He frowned. "Funny, I had you pegged for a snoozer 'til noon."

How he did it, Nicole didn't know. But as she turned to leave, he slipped in front of her and blocked the door with one of his long arms. It brought them in close contact, forcing Nicole to acknowledge his hairy, bare chest covered in a sheen of sweat. He had powerful biceps, too, all muscled and honed impossibly hard.

"I could use a glass of water. Got one?"

"Water?" Nicole was suspicious, and yet she couldn't very well deny him after asking for the same courtesy yesterday at the boathouse. "Wait here."

He dropped his arm. "I'll pass on the ice," he told her.

She hurried past him, through her bedroom and into the private bathroom, where she filled a glass quickly. But as she stepped back into her bedroom, she was brought up short—Johnny Bernard stood only a few feet from her bed.

He turned, saw her surprise, and said, "Red Smote just pulled in the front yard. Hanging around outside your open door looked worse than just coming in. Should I leave?"

"I think that would look worse, don't you?" Nicole glanced at the clock. It was barely six. "If Red sees you leaving at this hour…" She didn't need to go on.

"Red's the biggest gossip in town," he agreed. "At least, he used to be. We wouldn't want the town speculating on something that never happened." He relaxed his stance and shoved one hand into his left front pocket. "Hell, if a guy's gonna be accused of something memorable, he should at least have the pleasure of doing it first."

He was teasing her, his knowing eyes full of mischief. But just for the record, to let him know she wasn't a pushover, she said, "I know where to kick you to make it hurt the most, so if you've got any ideas, I suggest you forget them."

He laughed. "You won't get any work out of me if I can't walk, *cherie.*"

He had a point. Nicole took the necessary steps to close the distance between them, and handed over the glass of water. Then, to make sure Red was truly in the yard, she chanced a quick glance out the door. Sure enough, he was leaning on the hood of his run-down, red Ford pickup, talking to Gran's handyman, Bickford Arden, the husband to their loyal housekeeper. Several mornings a week the two elderly men went fishing before breakfast. Hoping that was the plan and that they would head to the bayou soon, Nicole turned around to assure Johnny that he could leave shortly, only to find he'd moved closer to her bed and had become very interested in the rumpled satin sheets where she'd tossed and turned half the night.

Color swept into Nicole's cheeks, and Johnny turned just in time to witness it. "Restless night?"

"The heat," she responded.

He glanced around the room. Nicole was sure he had no interest in floral wallpaper in Wedgwood-green and gypsy-rose, but his eyes seemed to miss nothing. She doubted that he would be able to quote what the massive bed, bureau and matching vanity were worth on the antique collectors' market, but, still, his interest was keen as his hand brushed over each piece in obvious appreciation. Finally, he stopped in front of her vanity, his dark eyes finding her in the generous mirror. "Heard you're staying."

"Yes, I am," Nicole assured.

"And the heat?"

"I'll learn to love it."

He grinned. "You move too fast. Slow down some. That'll help." He emptied his water glass, set it on the vanity, then turned his attention to her lacquered jewelry box. With a flick of his wrist, he flipped the top open and looked inside.

Surprised by his boldness, Nicole stared speechless as he rummaged through her personal items, a piece at a time. Finally, his head came up to capture her reflection once more in the mirror. A minute dragged into two before he let his gaze drop back to her modest assortment of baubles, and he pulled out an inexpensive bracelet. "No shiny rocks, *cherie*." He looked at her in the mirror again as if waiting for her to say something. When she didn't, he returned the bracelet to the box and closed it. "So what's important to you, Nicki Chapman? It's obviously not a box full of gold and silver."

No it wasn't, Nicole admitted to herself. To some women, expensive jewelry was important, but not to her. Oh, she liked nice things, but she was more a simple pleasures kind of woman. She enjoyed painting a breathtaking sunrise. Walking in a warm summer rain. She thought a bona fide laugh, a beautiful smile, priceless. But those were her private thoughts and she didn't intend to share them with a stranger.

"Look, Mr. Ber—Johnny, what's important to me is my business. Yours is doing the job you were hired to do, not asking questions."

"Does that work both ways? You don't have any questions for me?"

"It's not the same thing," Nicole argued. "I'm not on parole. And I haven't earned a reputation in this town as a troublemaker."

Instead of being offended his dark eyes softened and he wagged a finger at her. "Shame on you for listening to the gossip, *cherie*. You know what they say. Half of it usually isn't true."

"And the other half?"

"Sometimes fighting back is the only way you can survive."

It was clear that he was a man ripened by experience and polished by a predatory edge. Still, was he saying all that was just a false front? That he'd reacted instead of acted? Nicole had done much the same thing, only not in such a grand fashion. She'd donned her L.A.-cool facade to survive the pain she'd left behind, and even before she'd lost her baby, when Chad had walked out on them, she'd pasted a smile of indifference on her face.

She didn't want to dismiss his offenses so easily, but if she was right, she couldn't help wondering who or what had prompted his less-than-sterling reputation. Surely not just bad blood between him and Farrel Craig.

She asked, "Why did you ignore Gran's message to stop by the house yesterday?"

"I didn't ignore it. I came by."

"You certainly did not."

"Yes, I did. I started to fix the dock at the boathouse and lost track of time, but I showed up about nine." He shrugged. "The place was dark, except for this room. I didn't knock at the front door because I figured the old lady had gone to bed already."

Was he telling the truth? Nicole didn't know, but then, why would he lie? "She waited all afternoon and into the evening. That was inconsiderate. Let's hope today you find the time. After all, she is the one responsible for getting you out of prison early, Mr. Bernard.''

''Johnny. My friends call me Johnny.''

''Friends?'' Nicole arched a brow in a mocking fashion that she knew wouldn't go unnoticed. ''So far, the only friend you have in this town—the only one I'm aware of, anyway—is my grandmother. And I'm still confused as to why she's so willing, when you don't appear to appreciate her kindness with even the simplest thank-you.''

Her chastising seemed to amuse him. He said, ''Actually I have two friends in this town. Maybe in time I could add you to the list and make it three. What do you say, *cherie?* Think you could stop disliking me long enough to cut me some slack?''

''Cut you some slack?'' Nicole sniffed. ''And then what?''

''Then we get on with the reason I'm here.''

''Whether I'm your friend or not, Mr. Bernard, you will do the job Gran expects of you. A full day's work, plus room and board, for the taste of freedom.''

''Yeah, that was the deal we made. But what about *our* deal?''

''I don't understand.''

He gave her another head-to-toe. ''You're not exactly ugly, *cherie*. If you can get past the gossip and give me a fair shake, I'll see that I keep my hands in my pockets and my dirty thoughts to myself.'' He made a show of stuffing his hands in his back pockets.

Well, that was certainly blunt enough, Nicole thought. ''Dirty thoughts are dirty thoughts, Johnny. Maybe the deal should be not having them at all.''

His laugh bounced off the walls. ''*Cherie,* I've been in prison six months. My dirty thoughts are what kept me sane.''

There was no way she could respond to that without wading into dangerous water, so Nicole kept silent.

A moment later, he rounded the bed to gaze at the painting hanging on the wall. She had painted the picture of Oakhaven's private swimming hole three years ago when she and her parents had come for a two-week visit. It was the summer before her parents had been killed in a plane crash.

"Nice picture. Someone local paint it?"

"No." In L.A. Nicole had been a rising star on the gallery circuit. Or at least, she had been until a few months ago. Lately, painting had become as difficult as sleeping.

He turned around, reached into his back pocket and pulled out a wrinkled slip of paper. "I've got a supply list started." He circled the bed, stopped less than a foot away from her and handed her the list. "They might have to order some of this, so get on it right away."

Nicole accepted the paper, but when she glanced at it and none of it made sense, she turned and laid it on the nightstand. "I'll call today."

"The shingles come in different colors and styles. They'll have some samples at the yard you can look at." He glanced outside. "The coast is clear."

Nicole walked to the French doors. Sure enough, Bick and Red had left for the bayou. She felt him come up behind her, brush past. She said, "Will you see Gran today? She really was in a mood last night when she finally gave up on you."

He turned around, waited as if expecting her to say more.

Finally Nicole gave in and said, "Please?"

A lazy smile parted his lips. "Yeah, as soon as she gets her hair combed and her teeth in, I'll come by." He started to leave again, then hesitated. "See how easy it is, *cherie?*

A simple 'please,' and already you've got me eating out of your hand.''

He cut down the dead tree in the front yard before noon. Officially, he had two days before he started work, but the tree was an eyesore, and, anyway, it felt good to do some physical labor.

Sweat-soaked from the day's heat, Johnny took a good whiff of himself and wrinkled up his nose. A sour fungus growing on something rotten smelled better than he did right now. He glanced at the sky and decided it had to be around one o'clock. He hoisted the chain saw and axe and returned them to one of the sheds, then headed back to the house.

He found the old lady in the garden. He stopped just outside the gate, his chest tightening awkwardly as he assessed her asleep in her wheelchair beneath the old oak. She had always affected him strangely, touching that vulnerable part of him, that little-boy part that was attracted to someone who treated him like they cared. He still didn't know why she had bothered with him; he'd been a wild little bastard. But if he had any good in him at all, Mae Chapman could take credit for it.

She blinked awake as if sensing he was there, her blue eyes cloudy and content as they fastened on him. Her thinning wisps of white hair were pulled back in an attempt to make a small bun at her nape. She was thinner than he remembered, her frail body lost in the fabric of her simple yellow cotton dress.

"I expected to see you yesterday—this morning at the latest," she called out, her voice strong and lucid. "You got a reason to avoid me?"

She spoke bluntly, but without rancor. Her raspy voice sent another burst of emotion through him as Johnny swung the gate open and strolled through. He noticed the bandage on her right ankle, smiled when on further inspection, he saw her small feet tucked into a pair of modern-looking tennis shoes meant for a woman half her age. "Heard you were laid up." He gestured to her injury. "Didn't see any need to bother you too early."

"My ankle's got nothing to do with my ability to get out of bed. And it hasn't affected my speech, either." She spun the wheelchair around to face him.

"No, it doesn't appear so." Johnny grinned. "Then again, you were never short on words, as I recall."

His teasing brought a smile to her gaunt face, exposing a row of perfect-fitting dentures. "Land sakes, look at you." She gave him a prideful once-over. "You still got your daddy's eyes. Kept his shiny hair, too. Delmar would have liked that."

At the mention of his father, Johnny's thoughts turned to the events that had lured him back to town six months ago, and what had happened since. "Are you the one?" he asked. "Have you been paying the taxes on the old farm?"

Her reaction to his question was a slow lifting of one thin white brow. "Now, why would I want to do that?"

"Beats the hell out of me," Johnny countered, still feeling far more emotion than he liked.

"I never invest in anything that isn't a sure thing."

"Oh? Then why did you waste your time on me all those years ago? Or have your lawyer hammer out a deal with the parole board? If you got a reason for dragging me back here, old lady, I want to hear it."

"Your manners are still gut rot, *boy.*"

"Answer the question!" Johnny demanded, his patience stretched. "I got a letter from Griffin Black six months ago wanting to buy me out. Now I was sure he was crazy, that is until I came back here and found out I still owned the farm. Don't pretend you don't know what I'm talking about."

She looked crestfallen. "I had no idea this would cause so much trouble. I'm sorry."

She looked suddenly old and vulnerable. Ashamed of himself, Johnny said, "I was coming to see you that day. After I left city hall and I'd found out about that trustee business, I stopped for a quick beer and—I guess you know what happened after that."

"What always happens when you and Farrel get within ten feet of each other." She shook her head. "But I'm to blame this time. If I had let you know about the farm, none of this would have happened." She narrowed her eyes. "I would have told you if you had bothered to write, that is."

Johnny swore. "Keeping that land for me was a foolish mistake."

"I suppose me caring about you is foolish, too?"

Johnny ignored the question. "Virgil says you're going to be in a financial squeeze if you don't sell off your fields or start making a profit from them. You should be putting your money to better use than wasting it on that worthless farm on the hill."

"Virgil's got a big mouth. And speaking of old Big Mouth, how come you wrote to him and not me? It wouldn't have hurt you to write me a few lines every other year, would it?" She looked him squarely in his eyes. "You didn't have to leave, you know. Henry and me were prepared to take you in when your mother died. You could have lived here with us instead of run off like you did."

Yes, he knew she would have taken him in. And that's what had scared him the most. The people who had cared about him had never stayed very long in his life. It wasn't rational thinking, but he'd been scared to death to depend on Mae and Henry after his mother had died. It had been easier just to run away. To leave all his problems behind and start over where no one looked at him twice because his name happened to be Bernard.

"What did you tell Griffin?" she asked.

"He's offering a fair price. Besides, what do I need with a piece of land when I'll be gone in four months?"

"Do me a favor. Wait to make your decision until the end of the summer."

"It won't make any difference," Johnny insisted. "As soon as my parole is up, I'll be going back to Lafayette."

When she didn't argue with him, Johnny leaned against a nearby oak and turned his attention on the house. Ready to discuss the repairs on the porch, the sight of Nicole crossing the front yard in a black skimpy top distracted him. He let his gaze wander, his eyes fastening on her cutoff jeans, noticing once more how they hugged her backside like an overcharged magnet. "How come I never knew about *that?*" he asked without thinking the question through, a moment later wishing he had.

The old lady followed his line of interest. "Nicki? That would be Alice's fault. She was a stingy woman, my daughter-in-law. She didn't like sharing my son Nicholas, or my granddaughter. Henry and I were visited a few holidays a year, and we got Nicki one week each summer. It wasn't enough, but it was better than nothing."

Johnny heard the bitterness in the old lady's voice. "She says she's staying. That her idea or yours?" He glanced back just in time to catch the old lady arch both white eyebrows.

"It was my suggestion, but Nicki's decision."

Johnny followed Nicole's progress as she crossed the road. "So what's her story?"

"If and when she thinks you should know, I'm sure she'll tell you."

Johnny had hoped the old lady would feel generous and

offer a little free information. But it looked like she wasn't going to. Instead, for the next half hour they talked about how hot the summer was expected to be, the repairs on the house, and who had died since he'd been away.

Johnny didn't mention Nicole again, or the fact that he'd been in her bedroom that morning. It might be perverse, but he liked knowing something the old lady didn't. Liked keeping the memory of the slender blonde in her robe all to himself.

After a time, the conversation waned, and he shoved away from the gnarly oak. "I'll see you later." He took a step toward the gate.

"Not so fast. Will the boathouse do? You could never get enough of the bayou."

"Still can't," he admitted. "I fixed the dock yesterday. That's why I was late making it up to the house last night. You'd gone to bed. Guess I forgot you old people turn in early," he teased.

When he turned around to give her one last look, he caught her smiling. "You always had a smart mouth. But it's a good-looking one, to be sure," she conceded. "Join me for supper?"

Somehow, arriving on the back doorstep like a stray dog looking for a handout didn't sit too well. Johnny shook his head. "I don't think so."

She grunted, and she, too, shook her head, which sent the loose skin on her cheek into a slight tremor. "The more things change, the more things stay the same. Supper's at seven. Come through the front door, and put on a shirt."

A bar of soap jammed in his back pocket, Johnny left the boathouse and headed for Oakhaven's swimming hole. He didn't have to think twice how to find his way. He hung a left off the trail, ducked under a familiar leafy hickory, and the swimming hole came into plain view.

Small and secluded, the pond still looked like a well-kept secret in the middle of nowhere.

Johnny pulled off his boots, stripped his socks and unzipped his jeans. He was just seconds away from sending them to the ground when he heard a loud *splash*. He gave his jeans a tug back to his hips, yanked his zipper upward, then moved to the water's edge.

So this is where she'd gone.

Johnny watched as Nicole surfaced, then rolled onto her back and began kicking her way to the middle of the pond. Something blue caught his eyes along the shore. He slipped through the foliage and found her towel and cutoffs draped over a downed hickory limb. A pair of canvas sling-back shoes were perched on a stump.

She had no idea someone was there, and he could have sat and watched her all afternoon—something he would have enjoyed doing if he weren't so annoyed by the fact that she was so unobservant. He scanned the bank until he found two flat stones. Then, gauging the distance, he dropped down on one knee and let the first rock fly. It entered the water like a shot out of a gun, sailing past Nicole's pretty nose with deadly accuracy. By the time he'd sent the second rock zooming on its way, her feet had found the bottom of the pond, and she was searching the bank with alarm in her wide eyes.

When she spied him, her alarm turned to anger. "Are you crazy! You missed me by less than an inch." Her voice was shrill, irritation evident in the straining pitch.

"No, it was more like four," Johnny quipped.

She waded toward him, her breasts swaying gently in her swimsuit. She left the pond behind and kept coming up the grassy bank. "One inch or four—I don't see much difference, Mr. Bernard. It was too close and—"

"Johnny."

She stopped a few feet away and met his eyes disparagingly. "What?"

"You keep forgetting my name."

She glared down at him where he still knelt in the grass. "We've been all through that," she snapped.

"Yes, we have." He glanced around as if looking for something, or someone. "You haven't seen old One Eye around, have you?"

"One Eye?" She tipped her head to one side and began squeezing the water from the ends of her hair. "What's a 'one eye'?"

Johnny stood and hung his hands loosely on his hips. "One Eye's a gator. He used to take his afternoon nap in this here swimming hole years ago."

Her hands stilled. "An alligator? Here?"

Johnny told the lie easily. One Eye had always favored the privacy of the black bog deeper in the swamp. And he might still be there. But more than likely, the aging gator had been turned into a purse or a sturdy pair of boots by now.

He let his gaze travel the length of her delicate curves. Outlined in the skimpy, two-piece swimsuit, she was definitely hot. He wanted to stay in control of the situation, but his imagination was working overtime, and right now he would have liked nothing better than to run his hands over her satin-smooth skin, lick the water beads from her bare shoulders, lower her to the grassy bank for some serious one-on-one.

"You always run around half-dressed, or is this a sign my luck's changing? Twice in one day. I'd say that's—"

"Is there something you wanted besides stopping by to give me a hard time?"

Now there was a phrase. Johnny shifted his stance hoping to ease his discomfort, then reached for her towel and tossed it to her. She caught it, and after drying herself off, she picked up her cutoffs and slipped them on.

"Next time you think about swimming, it would be smart to tell somebody where you're going." Johnny glanced over Nicole's shoulder to where a snake hung camouflaged in the branches. It was a harmless variety, and yet it could just as easily have been poisonous. She was completely unaware of her surroundings, and, again, it angered him. "This isn't L.A., *cherie.* You got more to worry about here than rush-hour traffic and parking tickets. Here, you never know what might fall out of the sky."

She looked thoroughly annoyed with him. She said, "If that's all you came by to say, it's getting late. Gran will be—"

"Glad I came along to make sure you didn't drown, or worse."

"I'm a good swimmer."

With lightning-quick reflexes, Johnny shot his arm out past her head and yanked the snake out of the tree. As it dangled from his outstretched hand, thrashing to free itself, he drawled, "And just how good are you with curious snakes?"

To his surprise, she didn't go crazy on him and start screaming the way he'd expected she would. She did, however, take several steps back. "I didn't see it," she admitted.

"I know." He gave the mottled brown snake a mighty heave into the woods. "It's just a harmless milk snake, but until you see it, how would you know? By then, it could be too late." Lesson over, he changed the subject. "You call Craig about those supplies we need? Talk to him about ordering shingles?"

"I tried."

"What do you mean, tried?"

"Farrel Craig wasn't in his office when I called this

morning. It'll have to wait until Monday. I've decided to go into town, that way then I can order the shingles.''

His bar of soap must have slipped out of his pocket. She bent to pick it up and tossed it to him. ''When you decide to wash, don't forget to use it.''

She was past him before he had a chance for a comeback. Johnny watched her go, her hips swaying slowly. Each step she took appeared innocent enough, and maybe that was the turn-on. There was something erotic and very inviting about a woman who had no idea how completely she affected a man, inside and out. And there was no doubt Nicole Chapman affected him. He'd spent half the night thinking about her, and most of the morning.

Once she was gone, Johnny unzipped his jeans and shoved them to his knees. He was just stepping out of them when he saw her shoes sitting on the stump.

Nicole stopped to examine her injury. The inch-long cut on the bottom of her foot wasn't deep, but it hurt like the devil. Angry with herself for forgetting her shoes, she started back to the pond, limping like a lame bird. She wouldn't have forgotten the damn shoes if it hadn't been for that blasted snake. It had taken all the composure she owned to keep from screaming and acting foolish.

If she'd returned to the pond a second sooner, Nicole was sure, she would have caught Johnny Bernard buck naked. He looked as surprised as she did when she reappeared—his hair loose and hanging free to his shoulders, his jeans riding low on his hips, the zipper at half-mast.

She motioned toward the stump where her shoes sat. ''I—I forgot them.'' She took a step to retrieve them, and winced when a sharp pain shot into the bottom of her foot.

''What happened?''

''Just a scratch.'' Nicole tried to downplay her injury and the pain it was causing. Johnny Bernard hadn't come right out and said what he thought of a city girl moving to the country, but she sensed he didn't think she would last long.

His gaze sharpened. "You didn't step on something you shouldn't have, did you?"

Was he trying to be funny or was he serious? She had thought it was a stick that she'd stepped on, but now suddenly worried, Nicole hobbled to the nearest tree. Leaning against it, she raised her foot to examine the injury. The blood covering the bottom of her foot made it difficult. She wiped it away, trying to pinpoint the pain.

"Here, let me have a look."

Nicole glanced up and found him standing over her. "No, really, I'm fine."

"Let's make sure."

She slid down the tree and sat. "Just don't make it hurt worse."

He crouched in front of her and took hold of her foot. His hands were big and warm, rough from the kind of work he did. He wiped away the blood on his jeans, then carefully examined the cut. Finally he said, "You'll live, but you need surgery."

"What!"

Nicole tried to jerk her foot back, but he hung on. In fact, he tightened his grip. "Easy. There's a sliver in there, and you could drive it deeper if you're not careful."

"A sliver?" Relieved, Nicole sighed and relaxed against the tree.

"A good-size sliver," he corrected. "It needs to come out."

"And it will," Nicole assured. "Gran can—"

"I don't think you should wait." His dark eyes found hers. "If you put your weight on it, you could break it off or force it deeper. 'Course, I could carry you to the house…"

"Carry me? No. I—"

"Yeah, that's what I figured." He worked his hand into the front pocket of his ragged jeans and came up with a long sleek knife that unfolded into something that looked like it came straight out of a Rambo movie. That he owned such a knife was bad enough, but to think he was going to use it to probe the bottom of her foot was worse.

"Wait!"

He looked up. "You change your mind, *cherie?* You want a ride to the house?"

Damn him, but he almost looked as if he were enjoying this, Nicole thought.

When she didn't answer, he settled more comfortably in the grass, tucked his hair behind his ears, then took hold of her foot again. She wasn't expecting him to be gentle, but as she leaned her head against the tree and braced herself for what was to come next, she had to give him more than a little credit; he treated her foot like a piece of fragile glass.

She closed her eyes at the first prick of pain. "Talk to me," she insisted. "Say anything. Gran said you were a marine," she began, sucking in her breath as the pain began to build.

"For five years."

"Ouch!" Nicole bit her lip.

"Easy. This damn thing's twice as long as it is deep. Just breathe slow and even."

He sounded sincere. Nicole braced herself and tried to do as she was told. "Why did you quit the military?"

"I didn't quit. I was medically discharged." His hand stilled, and he glanced up. He offered her a smile before he lowered his head and went back to work. Quietly, he drawled, "I won't cut your toes off, *cherie.* I promise."

"I didn't mean to—"

"I spent some time in Kuwait." He looked up, laid the

knife in the grass. "This isn't working, *cherie,* but I know what will."

Before Nicole could ask him what he had in mind, he lifted her foot upward and pulled. The movement dragged her away from the tree, and, to keep her balance, she arched her back and rested on her elbows for support. He took in her sprawled position and said, "Now, don't move, no matter what. Okay?"

Nicole hesitated, then nodded warily.

He lowered his head, and a moment later his warm breath touched the bottom of her foot. Nicole had no idea what he meant to do until she felt his tongue slide over the cut. She clutched the grass at her sides in tight fists and craned her neck to see what was going on. He'd said don't move, but my God, he was licking the bottom of her foot!

She tried to sit up while at the same time pulling her foot away. He looked up. "I said, don't move. Trust me. I know what I'm doing."

He went back to work, and Nicole felt his tongue glide slowly over her foot once more. She decided to give him exactly one minute, and if he didn't—

"Ou-ouch!" Nicole jerked her foot away from him with such force that it sent her falling onto her back. She closed her eyes for a second, the pain momentarily stealing her breath. It had felt as if he'd sent the sliver clean through the top of her foot.

"You all right?"

Nicole slowly opened her eyes. Johnny was kneeling over her, the ends of his black hair almost tickling her face, those unnerving eyes smiling down at her. He opened his mouth and stuck out his tongue. And there it was—the wicked-looking sliver.

"It's huge," Nicole gasped.

He turned his head away from her and spit the splinter

into the thick brush, then sat back on his heels. "When I was a kid, my mama used to take slivers out that way. We never owned a pair of tweezers." He reached for his knife and slipped it back into his pocket, then stood and held out his hand to help her up.

Nicole took his offered hand, and he easily pulled her up. She tested out her foot, the pain only slight now. "Thank you," she said softly.

"You're welcome."

Now that her crisis was past, Nicole once again became fully aware of Johnny Bernard. They were standing close, his chest gleaming and hard, his half-zipped fly exposing an appealing dark navel. Yes, she'd noticed his attributes yesterday and again this morning in her bedroom, but that didn't mean she wanted anything from him, because she most definitely did not.

"I need to get back," she announced quickly.

"Yeah, me, too. I've been invited to supper."

Nicole reached for her shoes and slipped them on. "I thought you said you didn't have many friends."

"That's right. Just so you know, *cherie,* the old lady invited me to join the two of you for supper. See you at seven."

Chapter 4

"A little warning would have been nice," Nicole insisted.

"Warning? Why would you need to be warned?" Mae asked. "You don't have to do any cooking. Clair will take care of that like she always does. All you have to do is show up. You don't even have to change your clothes or comb your hair if you don't want to. You look fine."

Gran had completely missed the point. She wasn't talking about her clothes, for heaven's sake, or the menu. She simply saw no reason for Johnny Bernard to share meals with them. He had a kitchen in his apartment above the boathouse. Wasn't that good enough?

"I still can't believe how much he's changed," Mae mused. "I tell you, Nicki, when Johnny stepped into the garden today, and I got my first look at him after fifteen years, I couldn't believe it was the same scrawny youngster. Oh, I knew it was him—he's got his daddy's eyes and his grandpa Carl's mouth." Mae plucked another wilted blossom off the azalea in the corner and dropped it into her lap, then focused her attention on Nicole once more. "Did you say it was at the swimming hole you ran into him?"

Nicole sat a little straighter in the white wicker chair on the front porch. "Yes. I went to cool off."

"Ninety-eight in the shade today," Mae confirmed. "Tomorrow is supposed to be even hotter."

"Oh, goodie."

Mae chuckled. "You'll get used to it, dear. Now then, down to business. Over supper, I think we should discuss our remodeling ideas with Johnny—the first being the attic. I know there are other things that seem more important, but it would make such a lovely studio for you, Nicki."

"I know you think so." Nicole did, too. It was a wonderful idea; that is, it would have been if she felt at all creative and focused these days. Only, she hadn't been able to do much of anything but feel sorry for herself the past three months. She wanted to return to work, she really did—but just thinking about painting caused her palms to sweat.

She stood and crossed to the porch railing, unwilling to let her grandmother see her anxiety. "I've been thinking about taking the summer off," she said, struggling to keep the emotion out of her voice. "I haven't had a vacation away from my career since I sold my first painting four years ago. I'm tired and—"

"The entire summer?" Mae gave a hollow whistle. "Do you think that's smart? You love your work, and the galleries...won't they be anxious to get something new on their walls?"

"I've taken that into consideration," Nicole assured, leaning against the support post. But she wasn't worried about the galleries; what she wanted most of all was the fever back. She wanted to wake up tomorrow morning with a driving need to create something alive and beautiful. But what if she never felt the fever again? What if she had lost her talent? What if it had vanished along with everything else? She couldn't begin to describe the fear that daily clawed at her insides. And if she tried to explain it to Gran, she would have to reveal everything. And right now she simply couldn't do that.

She closed her eyes and willed herself to think of something else. She was successful in putting it out of her mind, but, in the trade-off, the topic circled back to another unpleasant topic. Her grandmother asked, "Did you see Johnny got rid of that old dead tree in the yard?"

Nicole concentrated on growing a nasty headache, the kind that drained your complexion and dulled your eyes. The kind that would excuse her from the supper table.

"Nicki, did you hear? The tree's gone."

Nicole opened her eyes and glanced out into the front yard. "Yes, I noticed," she said without emotion.

"Make sure you comment on it at supper. Say he's done a fine job, or something to that effect. A little praise is what he needs to hear right now. It will boost his confidence."

"I think I'm coming down with a headache," she primed.

"Well, take something before it gets out of hand, dear. You wouldn't want it to spoil supper."

"No," she agreed, "that would be unfortunate."

A stingy breeze, slow and barely evident, drifted onto the porch. Like a greedy beggar, Nicole raised her chin in an attempt to cool her warm cheeks. She could smell the potted azalea in the corner, the fried chicken Clair Arden was preparing for supper. "Will it rain tonight?"

"No, but maybe tomorrow. So did we decide on green or gray shingles, Nicki? I think you said green, right?"

Nicole felt a tug on the uneven hem of her orange tank

top. She glanced down to see that Gran had wheeled up close.

"The shingles, Nicki. What color? I can't remember what we agreed on."

"We didn't, did we?"

"We certainly did." Mae arched a thin brow. "This drifting in and out that you do—is it a creative thing, or is there something on your mind I should know about?"

"What?"

"I keep telling myself it isn't that I'm a boring old woman, but that you're simply creating upstairs."

"Upstairs?"

"In the mind, Nicki. Honestly, one minute we're having a conversation, and the next you're lunching with the fairies."

"I was thinking about how to remodel the attic," Nicole lied.

Mae pointed at Nicole's splattered tank top. "Is this another one of those fashion statements? What do they call this one? Homeless, or the rag of the month?"

Nicole didn't feel like smiling, but Gran's comments were always amusing. The dress code in Common was definitely not as liberal as in L.A. "Have the ladies at the garden club been talking?"

"Of course," Mae admitted honestly, her eyes reflecting not a bit of censure. "No one moves to Common without getting a head-to-toe and a couple dozen opinions for free. Pearl Lavel tells me her son saw you last week at the post office and he's been talking about you ever since. Sounds to me like you made quite an impression on Woodrow. If you're wondering, he's single and twenty-seven. I don't believe he's a strong enough personality for you, though, and Clair agrees."

They'd had a similar discussion earlier in the week. Only, it had been in reference to Gordon Tisdale's son,

Norman. He was single, too. A thirty-six-year-old teacher
at the grade school. Gran and Clair's assessment of Norman, however, was that he didn't have a sense of humor—
a vital component for a lasting marriage.

Nicole rubbed her temple, the headache she'd been hoping for was going to be a reality very soon if they started
talking about eligible bachelors, marriage and babies.

Mae glanced at her watch. "It's almost seven. Johnny
should be coming soon."

The comment prompted Nicole to look across the road
to the wooded trail. The sun was sinking, causing shadows
to grow between the trees. Soon the mosquitoes would
come, and like a gray cloud of doom they would chase
anyone with half a brain inside. "Did you know his family
well?"

"Yes. Delmar and Madie were good people, honest and
likable. Madie was the prettiest girl in town, I always said.
And the men agreed. They were all after her." Mae returned to the azalea bush and began plucking dead blossoms. "That old farm was a curse, though. Nothing ever
grew in those fields, no matter how hard Delmar tried.
Finally, he gave up and took himself off to town. Got a
job at the lumberyard working for Jasper Craig. No one
else in town would hire him, but Jasper surprised everyone
and took Delmar on. It lasted a few months, then the accident happened."

"What accident?"

"Delmar was run over."

"Run over? Was he killed?"

"I'm afraid so. The driver of the car must not have seen
him. It happened down the road about a mile. They never
did learn who was behind the wheel. Henry found him
early that morning. We called Sheriff Tucker, and he came
out. Delmar was so badly mangled, they didn't show him
at the funeral. Poor Madie cried her eyes out for months.

Johnny…well, after that, things just got harder for him. Then Madie got sick a few years later and died from cancer. Day after we buried her, Johnny ran off.''

Nicole turned to face her grandmother. ''You wanted him to stay, didn't you.''

Mae's eyes turned warm with affection. ''The first time I saw that boy something inside me melted. He was barefoot and so skinny he was all ribs and legs. He had a smart mouth and language like nothing I'd ever heard. 'Course his orneriness was just a front, you see, a way to cover up being scared. The kids in town were awfully mean to him. It's why I know that fight at Pepper's wasn't all Johnny's doing. I'm not saying he didn't participate, but I know in my heart he didn't start it.''

''And how can you be so sure?''

''Farrel Craig was on the other end of that fight. Anytime that boy got near Johnny, there was trouble. Farrel and those two puppets of his, Clete Gilmore and Jack Oden, used to chase Johnny home after school everyday. It started way back in grade school.'' A honeybee buzzed around Mae's head. She paid no attention as she went on. ''I've never told this to a soul, but Henry and I would have adopted Johnny if he hadn't run off. Yes, Nicki, I wanted him to stay, and I would be lying if I denied I want him to stay now. Running away from your problems isn't the answer. Deal with the demon, I always say. Or the demon will chase you all your life.''

Nicole gazed across the yard, not knowing what to say. The summer oak leaves began to rustle, and she angled her face to catch the elusive evening breeze. She closed her eyes and concentrated on the night sounds coming alive in the distant bayou.

Suddenly the feeling of being watched intruded on her, and she opened her eyes just as a shadowy figure broke through the oak grove and started across the road. She fixed her gaze on Johnny Bernard's slow, ambling gait, on the quiet strength he exuded with each step. No one else walked quite like he did, she decided. There was something mesmerizing about the unhurried way he moved. Something raw and earthy. Primal.

He wore a white T-shirt stretched over his iron chest. He'd even taken the time to tuck it into a pair of jeans that were in better condition than she'd seen him in so far, but even at this distance, she could see they weren't hole-free. He was crossing the yard now, his shiny black hair moving slightly in answer to the sultry summer breeze. She hadn't wanted to think about their afternoon meeting at the pond, but suddenly she could think of nothing else. The memory of how easily he'd handled the snake, the way he'd gotten her attention by skipping rocks practically under her nose. The way his silky tongue had slid over the bottom of her foot.

Aware that her heart had begun to race, Nicole quickly spun away from the railing.

"Nicki! Nicki, where are you going?"

"He's coming." Nicole headed for the open French doors that led into the study, her voice straining to sound normal. "I'll tell Clair supper will be on time."

Mae arrowed her wheelchair in front of the open French doors leading into the study. "You don't mind wheeling an old lady in, do you? Nicki went to tell Clair we're on our way."

Johnny had seen Nicole shoot inside like someone had lit a fire under her. Instead of commenting on it, though, he sauntered up the steps and positioned himself behind the old lady's chair. "You trust me to keep it under the speed limit?"

"Trusting you was never a problem, dear boy." She reached back to pat his arm.

Johnny felt her warm fingers, and it brought back a mountain of memories. He'd never liked being touched as a boy. But that had never stopped Mae Chapman. She was one of those affectionate types, always patting him and tousling his hair. Once or twice she'd even hugged him. He had tried to figure her out, had at first been suspicious of her motives. Finally, he'd given up, and no matter how crazy it sounded, decided that she just liked him. Still, it humbled him. No one in Common liked the Bernards.

He pushed the wheelchair through the study and into the oak-paneled hall. Even though he'd lived only a few miles from Oakhaven, he'd never been inside the twelve-room house. Not until today, anyway, when he'd slipped into Nicki's bedroom uninvited. Oh, he'd been asked as a boy, or maybe *coaxed* was a better word. The old lady used to tempt him with cookies and apples. He never liked taking charity, though, and had preferred a trade if it was something he wanted badly enough. Most of the time he'd bartered for food. But one time it had been for a pair of shoes Mae's son, Nicholas, had outgrown.

Nicholas had been tall and blond like Henry and big-hearted like Mae. Virgil said he'd become a lawyer. It must have damn near killed the old lady to lose him in a plane crash only three years after losing Henry, Johnny thought. And Nicole—it must have devastated her to lose both her parents at one time.

They passed a small parlor and entered a dining room with high ceilings and papered walls in a light shade of green. The house was just as he'd imagined it would be, full of antiques and pictures. Spit-polished until even the floors shined. The oak table in the middle of the room could seat ten people, easily. Johnny noticed an end chair was missing so he steered Mae to the open space. Then he sat in the vacant chair to her left, leaving him a clear view of the open door.

"I was glad you tackled that dead oak," Mae said. "I was just telling Nicki on the porch about this idea I have for the atti—"

"Green. We've decided on green shingles."

Johnny glanced toward the door, as Nicole stepped into the room. She was wearing a yellow sleeveless shift, short enough to see her bare knees and just straight enough to accent her narrow waist and shapely backside. She'd twisted her hair into a messy knot on top of her head, and her exposed neck drew his attention to a small mole just below her left ear.

Usually he preferred his women dark and sturdy enough to go the distance. Nicole was fair, and curvy in a delicate way that would make a man want to take his time. The image of slow and easy lovemaking sent a shudder ripping through him, and Johnny tore his gaze away from her. Even though he knew he shouldn't be thinking what he was thinking, he'd been thinking it all day. And after what happened at the swimming hole, he'd been thinking about more places to put his tongue than the bottom of her foot.

"Water, anyone?"

"Yes, please," Mae said.

Johnny nodded in agreement with the old lady. Clair Arden hurried in and deposited a platter of fried chicken and dumplings in the middle of the table. The compact housekeeper, who was in her late fifties, barely stood five feet tall. She had round cheeks and warm brown eyes. She smiled at Johnny, and it was one of those smiles that hinted she knew something he didn't. He pondered that, while she made two more trips, leaving a basket of corn bread, coffee and a dish she called *maque choux*—corn served with tomatoes, green peppers and onions.

Mae's heavy sigh drew Johnny's attention, and he turned just in time to see her sway forward.

"Mae?" It was Clair's voice. "What is it?"

"I feel light-headed all of a sudden," she complained.

"Gran!" Water forgotten, Nicole hurried back to the table. "What's wrong?"

"I'm sure it's nothing. Oh, my." She placed her hands on the table to keep from tipping out of her chair.

"Gran! Is it the heat? It is, isn't it?"

"Now, Nicki, don't blame the weather," Mae scolded gently.

"Maybe you should go lie down," Johnny suggested.

Mae waved a hand in rejection of the idea. "I'll be fine in a minute."

But one minute slipped into two, then three. Nicole said, "I'm phoning Dr. Jefferies."

"Nonsense," Mae protested. "I don't intend to bother that busy man with something so foolish as a little dizzy spell."

Nicole exchanged a look with Johnny. He could see she was worried. Not sure what to do, he finally stood, pulled the wheelchair away from the table and hunkered down in front of it. He was just about to insist that she let Nicki call the doc when he noticed the old lady's eyes—they were as sharp and clear as a blue sky, certainly not the eyes of a woman suffering from a dizzy spell. Her skin was its normal color, too. Was she faking being sick? It sure as hell looked that way.

Johnny thought for a minute, then made a show of examining her face. "Yeah, you really don't look good," he said. "I thought I noticed it earlier in the garden. Only, it's worse now. You remind me of a catfish dangling on a hook just before it goes belly-up."

Nicole gasped from somewhere behind him. He didn't have to look to know her eyes would be wide with stark surprise. Mae gave him a suspect look, and he countered it with one of his own. They were reading each other perfectly, and neither needed to elaborate on the message.

Suddenly he felt Nicole's hand on his shoulder, shoving him out of the way to plant herself in front of Mae's chair. "Don't listen to him, Gran. He doesn't know what he's talking about. I'll take you to your room and get a cool cloth for your head. You'll be fine," she assured. She turned and shot Johnny a frosty glare. "In the future, don't try to help. Obviously, you don't know the first thing about it."

"That's not how you felt this afternoon. As I recall, you even said 'thank you.'"

"Thank you? What did she say 'thank you' for?" Mae asked.

"It was nothing," Nicole insisted, glaring at Johnny.

"Now children, don't fight," Mae intervened. She gave Nicole a weak smile, followed by a long sigh. "Oh, you win. I'll rest in my room if you promise to sit down and eat with Johnny. Clair, go get Bick. I'll have him take me to my room so the children can have a nice, quiet supper."

"I'll take you," Nicole insisted. "I'm not hungry."

"Nonsense," Clair piped up. "You can't afford to miss a meal if I'm going to win my bet with Mae and put five pounds on you by the end of the month. You're much too skinny, honey."

Johnny watched the two old women exchange a look. It was obvious the housekeeper was in cahoots with Mae and that they had anticipated Nicole's argument and rehearsed their lines. He watched Clair hustle out the door, and return a moment later with Bick.

Bickford Arden was as tall as Clair was short. He strolled into the room wearing baggy tan pants, a blue cotton shirt and a beat-up blue baseball cap. He smiled at Nicole, nodded in Johnny's direction, then grasped Mae's wheelchair and spun her toward the door. Clair said, "I'll make you a cool lemonade and bring it to your room, Mae."

The entourage left, with Nicole following. Johnny returned to his seat to wait and see if she would join him. A few minutes later, she came back through the door wearing a thin-lipped scowl that clearly warned she wasn't too happy with the way things had turned out.

At the sideboard, she retrieved their water glasses and brought them to the table. Without a word she plopped his down, splashing water onto his plate. While Johnny reached for his napkin and mopped up the spill, she seated herself.

"A hooked catfish going belly-up?" she said. "Why don't you just get the shovel out and start digging a grave in the backyard?"

"I had my reason for saying that. Would you like to hear what it was?"

Instead of letting him vindicate himself, she said, "She's an elderly woman. A sweet, sensitive—"

"Sneaky."

"Sneaky?" She glared at him. "Gran is the most good-hearted person I know."

Good-hearted had nothing to do with it, Johnny thought. A woman who could con a man back into town when he had promised himself never to return was sure capable of staging a little dizzy spell. It made him wonder what was coming next. Discarding his manners, he reached for the chicken and dumplings. After serving himself, he passed Nicole the platter.

She dished up a small helping, set the platter down and reached for her napkin. Johnny watched her snap it open and lay it in her lap. It prompted him to look for the wet ball he'd laid beside his plate. He decide to forgo it, and left it where it was.

While she cut her chicken into small pieces, Johnny devoured his first piece using his fingers. He was on the second when he glanced up and caught her watching him.

He wasn't eating like a well-mannered gentleman, but he wasn't exactly foaming at the mouth, either. "Something wrong?"

"No."

Johnny grabbed up the wet ball and made a quick swipe around his mouth. When she became preoccupied once more with her own food, he forked a healthy helping of dumplings into his mouth, then reached for another piece of corn bread. The bread was addicting, but he curbed his desire to make a pig of himself.

He noticed she was eating more slowly than he was, and he tried to pace himself. Maybe if he said something… "Does Henry's old Dodge run?"

She looked up. "Why do you want to know?"

"I sold my wheels from inside prison. Thought I could use the pickup while I'm here. I could drive you into town Monday morning and pick up those supplies we need."

She stopped her fork on its way to her mouth, set it back down. "You want the two of us to go to town together? To Craig Lumber? Why?"

"Why not? You afraid to be seen with me, *cherie?*" Johnny reached for another piece of chicken.

"Of course not."

"Afraid I'll start trouble or something?"

"Or something."

Johnny leaned back in his chair and rested his arms on either side of his plate. "I don't plan on making trouble."

"It sounds like you don't really have to, it just follows you." She speared a small piece of chicken and brought the fork to her mouth.

"What if I promised to stay in the pickup?" Johnny offered.

She left half her food and slid the plate back an inch.

A moment later, Clair came through the door with two slices of pecan pie. She frowned at Nicole's plate, but removed it anyway, replacing it with a large piece of pie. "My husband wanted to know if you're a card player," she asked, giving Johnny her full attention.

The question caught Johnny by surprise. Still, the idea of a few hands of cards on a hot summer night had a certain appeal. "I can hold my own," he said.

"Red don't play so good," Clair confessed. "Bick usually heads into the kitchen around nine-thirty for a cup of coffee. If it suits you, you're welcome. The coffeepot's always on." She turned to Nicole. "Mae's feeling better, honey. It must have been a touch of the heat, just like you said. Be a good girl and eat your pie, now. I've only got two weeks left to win my bet."

They finished dessert in silence. Nicole left her crust; Johnny was tempted to lick the plate. When she laid her napkin beside her plate and stood, Johnny had just sucked the last of his coffee down. She said, "If I don't see you tomorrow, I'll meet you Monday morning on the front porch at ten o'clock. You can drive me to town, but when it comes to the lumberyard, I'll handle the order. Deal?"

Johnny hadn't expected her to give in so easily. "You've got a deal." He stood when she did. She was halfway to the door when he said, "The old lady faked it."

She stopped, one hand on the door frame, and turned slightly. "What did you say?"

"The dizzy spell was all an act." He closed the distance between them. "It's the truth. She faked it, and Clair Arden was in on it."

"That's ridiculous. Why would they do that?"

Johnny hooked a thumb into the waistband of his jeans and relaxed his broad shoulder against the doorjamb. It brought them within a foot of each other, and he caught a whiff of her light, spicy perfume. "I got my own theory, but maybe you should ask her."

"And just what is yours?"

"I'd rather not say until you've had a chance to discuss it with her."

She stared at him for a minute, then took a step closer to the door. To leave she would have to brush past him, or get him to move. Johnny wasn't surprised when she said, "You're blocking the door."

"Is it just me, or do you hate all men, *cherie?*"

"Get out of my way," she insisted.

"As soon as you answer the question. Do you always pace the floor half the night, or is it just since I moved in? Is it because my name is Bernard?"

Her eyes went wide. "You admit to spying on me?"

"Not intentionally. I was out walking and noticed your light."

"So you stopped and watched!" Her voice had turned accusing.

"That's not the way it was."

"I'll just bet it wasn't."

Her eyes had turned a stormy shade of blue-gray. She was more than simply angry. "You still haven't answered my question. What's keeping you up nights?"

"None of your damn business."

"Were you trying to think of another way to get rid of me?"

She turned away and walked back to the table. With her back to him, she said, "I made that call yesterday to protect Gran. I had no idea you two knew each other. I made a mistake." She turned around and faced him. "Haven't you ever made a mistake…*Johnny?*"

"Dozens. Did you tell her you tried to fire me?"

Her hands went to her hips, and she glared at him. "No. And if you think it will give you a few extra points with her, go ahead and tell her."

"I'm not interested in making points—" Johnny

grinned ''—unless they're with you. How about it, *cherie?* How about a truce?'' He shoved away from the door and moved toward her. ''Doesn't taking that sliver out of your foot count for something?''

Without responding, she sidestepped him and headed for the door. Johnny turned to follow, but she stopped. ''If Gran was faking it, why didn't you confront her with it?''

''Because I agree with you and think she's a decent person. I'm willing to bet if you ask her, she'll admit the whole thing was concocted.''

''You could have told me this during supper.''

''I tried. You cut me off. After that—'' he shrugged ''—I saw my chance to have supper with a pretty woman and decided to sit back and enjoy it. It's been a long time.''

''I don't believe you. Gran wouldn't make me worry needlessly.'' That said, she turned and walked out.

Nicole took a deep breath and summoned her L.A.-cool facade back in place. It had taken an hour to regain her composure after leaving the dining room, but now that she could breathe normally again, she was going to confront Gran with Johnny's absurd accusation.

She rapped lightly on her grandmother's bedroom door. ''Gran, are you still up?''

''Come in, Nicki.''

Nicole opened the door and stepped inside. Gran's room, like her own, was a mix of old lace and polished oak furnishings. A single lamp glowed on a nearby nightstand, and it spilled just enough light into the room to guide Nicole to the bed. Mae was braced against the headboard with a fluffy pillow at her back. She was in a white nightgown, her hair brushed out, the strands thin and flyaway in the dim light.

Nicole didn't want to believe Gran had feigned the dizzy

spell, but she looked for signs that would convince her otherwise and found none: Gran looked perfectly fine.

"I waited up for you," she said, patting the bed to encourage Nicole to sit.

"I want to ask you something," Nicole said, taking a seat and getting right to the heart of the matter. "Did you—"

"Yes."

"Yes?" Nicole frowned. "How can you answer a question you haven't heard yet?"

"Because I know what you're going to ask. Johnny saw through my hoax tonight and he told you, didn't he? I expected he would."

Confused, Nicole asked, "Why did you do it? Why did you pretend you were sick?"

"I've sensed for two days that you haven't been happy with my decision to bring Johnny here. I thought once you got to know him, you'd feel differently. He really is a good boy, Nicki. But it takes time to warm up to him. I was giving you that time."

"It's not going to happen, Gran. I believe he's a chameleon."

"Aren't we all. It depends on the time and place and who's standing next to us, but I believe we all are changing constantly. That boy has seen a lot, Nicki. I'm surprised he's still in one piece."

"He's not a boy," Nicole reminded. "He's a man. A man you haven't seen for fifteen years."

"It doesn't matter. I'm not wrong about him, Nicki. You'll see I'm right, once you've decided to give him a chance."

Nicole threw up her hands. "You sound just like him. 'Give me a chance,'" she drawled in a bad imitation of Johnny's dark voice. "Well, I don't trust him. Or any other man, for that matter."

"And why is that, dear?" Mae reached out and brushed Nicole's bangs out of her eyes. "What has happened to make you so bitter?"

Nicole didn't want to discuss her reasons, but now that she'd said too much, how could she avoid it? She stood and moved to the window overlooking the backyard and a row of giant oak trees. "You were right, there was a man in L.A. His name was Chad Taylor. I fell in love, and he… He walked out on me." She turned around. "I know I'm bitter, but it hurt."

Mae said nothing, as if she sensed there was something else. Nicole groaned, then relented. "You need to know something else. When I called the Pass-By Motel yesterday, it wasn't to find out when Johnny was arriving—it was to fire him." Before her grandmother could say anything, Nicole rushed on. "I didn't know he was a friend of yours. I thought he was some ex-con on parole, is all. A stranger the people in town referred to as 'bad-boy' Bernard. You can understand how that would color my opinion, can't you? Anyway, I apologized for that, and though I'm still not convinced he should be here, I'm prepared to go along with whatever you want. Only, I won't be swayed into liking him. And no more surprise suppers or fake dizzy spells. Agreed?"

A slow grin creased Mae's soft cheeks. "You tried to fire him? And how did he take that?"

"Actually, he told me he was nonrefundable."

Mae clutched her frail chest and laughed heartily. "That's what I would have expected."

"It's getting late." Nicole moved back to the bed and kissed her grandmother on the forehead. "I'll see you in the morning. And remember, no more tricks."

Johnny steered clear of the house on Sunday. He woke early and escaped into the bayou with his cane pole and

the quart of White Horse he'd won the night before playing
poker with Bick. Letting the boat take him wherever it
wanted to go, he dozed until noon, then went hunting for
the best fishing spot for the afternoon.

He hadn't eaten anything all day, so, when he started
on the whiskey around supper time, it was no surprise that
it hit him harder than it normally would have. But he didn't
care. If the whiskey took his mind off Nicole, it would be
worth it. Then maybe tonight he could get some sleep.

When the sun had set, and the day was almost gone,
instead of heading back to the boathouse—not tired
enough, or drunk enough—he thrust the pole into the black
water and sent the boat deeper into the bayou. A slice of
moon was all that guided him as he turned the boat into
another narrow channel and slipped through a maze of live
oak and tall cypress trees shrouded in thick moss. The bugs
were bad, but Johnny paid them no mind as he pulled a
cigarette from his T-shirt pocket.

A clap of thunder sounded, promising a rainstorm before
morning. Undaunted, Johnny shoved the pole into the water and headed north. He saw the light a moment later. At
first he thought he'd gotten turned around, only he knew
he hadn't; the house on the hill was definitely the old farmhouse, and the light was coming from inside.

"What the hell?" Johnny flipped the butt of his cigarette
into the water, dropped the pole into the muck and turned
the boat into the marshy shoreline. He climbed out of the
boat, still keeping his eyes on the house through a veil of
leafy oak limbs. There was no electricity at the house. Was
someone inside with a flashlight? If so, why?

He didn't know how long he stood there, watching and
waiting. A full minute, maybe two. He crept up the bank,
but as he reached the rise, the light went out. He dropped
to his knees and flattened out in the grass. It was so damn

dark out, he couldn't see three feet in front of his face. Still as the night, he waited, listening.

Minutes ticked by slowly. Out of frustration, Johnny swore, wondering if he should rush the house and see who was inside. Another minute passed before he heard a car roar to life. He jerked to his feet, and in an instant he was running flat out. He saw headlights come alive at the end of the driveway, and he steered himself in that direction. The car was backing up onto Bayou Road, turning around. He was too far away to stop it, but too determined to give up. Cutting across the uneven yard and into an overgrown field, pumping his arms and legs, he sprinted through the field as fast as he could in hopes of cutting off the car before it reached the sharp bend on the county road.

At the edge of the field, he jumped the ditch. He could hear the car as it downshifted to make the bend. Relieved that he had made it in time, Johnny stepped onto the dirt road, just as the car came around the corner. The head-lights zeroed in on him. Any second, Johnny expected to hear the driver downshift and swerve to the side of the road. Only the car didn't slow down. To his surprise, the driver gunned the engine, floored it, and sent the car into fourth gear.

''Damn!'' Johnny scrambled to get out of the way, but he wasn't fast enough. The car clipped him high on his right leg and pitched him into the air, tossing him into the water-logged ditch.

Then everything went black.

Chapter 5

The thunderstorm Sunday evening had been reduced to a misting rain by Monday morning. Nicole dashed off the porch and raced to the pickup the moment she saw it pull into the front yard. The passenger door swung open just as she reached it, and she jumped in quickly, slamming the door behind her. "Thanks, I— Oh, my God!"

Nicole didn't need to ask what had happened. It was all too obvious what had happened to Gran's *good boy*—he'd been in a fight. "'Just give me a chance,'" she mimicked. "'I don't plan on causing any trouble,'" she singsonged. "I can't believe Gran can be so naive where you're concerned."

He let her rant and rave for a minute, then put Henry's old pickup in gear and headed down the road. While Nicole fumed, she chanced another look at the bruises that marred Johnny's face. There was a cut on his chin, and a purple welt on his right cheekbone. The long gash on his arm looked nasty. The doctor who had sutured the cut had done a good job: the stitches were small and even. Once it healed, the scar left behind would be no more than a thin white line.

As bad as his wounds looked, Nicole noticed his hair had been freshly washed and tied back. He wore a clean black T-shirt with the sleeves ripped out and another pair of beat-up jeans. He looked impossibly tough and unbelievably composed. Handsome, too, though she wasn't willing to explore that any further than for observation's sake.

She wanted to ask him who the fight had been with, but she kept her curiosity to herself. Remembering what Gran had said about Farrel Craig, she wondered if Johnny had paid the man a visit. If so, she hoped Farrel Craig looked worse than Johnny. She shouldn't care one single bit about who had come out on top, but for some unexplained reason she did. Which was just plain crazy.

"You ask the old lady about the dizzy spell she faked?"

Nicole knew sooner or later he would get to that. She said with as little emotion as possible, "You were right. She invented it."

"She say why she did it?"

Nicole glanced at him. "She thought if we shared some time, I would change my mind about what a 'good boy' you are."

The mockery in her voice made him glance her way. "But that's not going to happen, is it?"

Nicole pointedly eyed his bruises. "I don't think so."

The lazy grin he offered her said he had expected as much.

"If Gran wants to offer you her blind loyalty, that's her business. But don't expect that from me. Gran and I are not made the same way."

He gave her curves the same pointed assessment she had

just given him, then directed his gaze back to the road. "No," he agreed, "you certainly aren't made the same."

The sexual implication behind his words had Nicole feeling self-conscious again. She looked out the window, glad she had picked jeans and a lightweight denim shirt to wear to town instead of cutoffs.

"I need to stop by Tuck's office for a few minutes. You mind if I do that first?" he asked.

"Tuck? Who's Tuck?"

"Sheriff Tucker," he explained.

Nicole shot him a surprised look. "You're going to see the sheriff? Don't tell me you were stupid enough to get caught. I mean, it's bad enough that you were fighting, but if there's a witness who can point a finger, you can kiss your parole goodbye."

"Yeah, that would pretty much screw me."

He appeared perfectly calm. Nicole wanted to scream at him. "Does the sheriff know what happened? Did he order you to come by this morning?"

"No."

"Then why, for God's sake, are you going to see him? If he doesn't know about the fight, he will the minute he sees you. How are you going to explain the bruises? Have you thought about that?"

He rolled his shoulders in a lazy shrug. "I'll have to tell him the truth, I guess."

"The truth!" Nicole's blue eyes went wide. "That's the stupidest thing I've ever heard. The sheriff feels the same as the rest of the town does about you."

Just as they reached the city limits, a flash of lightning cut through the dismal, gray sky, followed by the distant rumble of thunder. Without warning, Johnny pulled the pickup off the road and parked across from Gilmore's Gas and Go.

"What are you doing?" Nicole asked.

He turned slowly and slid his arm along the back of the seat to give her his undivided attention. "Just what do you think I should tell Tuck, *cherie?*"

Nicole scooted closer to the door to avoid his thigh coming in contact with hers. He was staring at her boldly, taking in every detail of her face. She didn't like it when he did that. She wet her lips, thinking. "I don't exactly have a story in mind. Maybe you should just avoid him for a few days. Or maybe tell him you had an accident. You know, walked into a door or something."

"An accident?"

Nicole narrowed her eyes, completely frustrated. "Well, say whatever you want. Say you were in the bayou biting the heads off poisonous snakes and wrestling alligators for no other reason than to count their teeth. Do you think I care what you tell him?" Unable to hold his hard gaze a moment longer, she looked away. Softer, more in control, she added, "I just don't think the truth in this case is going to do either one of us any good. Gran's already making another repair list for you. What about her? If you're sent back to prison, she'll be devastated."

When the silence grew, Nicole looked back and found him staring at her so intently that it made her shiver. "I thought that's what you wanted," he drawled. "For me to pack my bags and disappear."

He was backing her into a corner and trying to get her to say something she had no intention of admitting. "Stop fishing for me to say it," she demanded. "The only reason I care one way or the other is because of Gran and because Oakhaven needs a carpenter."

"There are other carpenters."

"Well, tell that to Gran. She wants you, and I promised her I wouldn't interfere." Nicole didn't want to belabor the point. Besides, they were getting away from the real issue. "It hardly seems worth it," she said.

"What's that?"

"Was one night of raising hell worth another six months in prison? Does your freedom mean so little, then? Does Gran mean so little?"

His eyes narrowed. "Are you so sure that I'm guilty?"

"Are you going to blame *this* fight on someone else, too?"

"No."

"Look, it doesn't really matter what I think. Sheriff Tucker is the man you're going to have to convince, or avoid." Nicole shrugged and tried to sound nonchalant. "The rumor in town is that you're a long shot, anyway."

"You really don't want to know the truth, do you?" He shook his head and sighed. "Siding with the popular vote is understandable, but it's dangerous and gutless, *cherie*."

"I'm not gutless," Nicole exploded. "I just don't take chances on bad investments. Like it or not, that's what you are."

Without warning, he shifted into the middle of the bench seat and slid his arm along the back. He was giving her that look again, only this time it made her feel as though he were burning the clothes off her body, a thread at a time. Nicole tried to look past his battered handsome face, to ignore the heat being generated between their bodies. So much heat that the windows had completely fogged up, and the air inside the cab had turned warm and moist. Finally, he said, "What would you say if I told you I did have an accident? That there was this car and—"

"I'd remind you that it's not me you have to convince," she cut in. "Save the story for the sheriff."

He stared at her for a long moment, then returned to the wheel. He put the pickup in gear, but before he pulled back on the road, he said, "Okay. Have it your way, *cherie*. I'm guilty as hell."

* * *

Johnny stepped inside the police station and tried not to think about the iron cell down the hall. He'd taken Nicole to the drugstore, then dropped her off at the bakery. She told him she was going to be at least a half hour due to the fact that Clair's daughter-in-law, Dory, worked there, and she liked to talk. That had suited him fine—the police station was just around the corner, and he didn't need more than thirty minutes of Tuck's time.

Johnny heard the noisy air-conditioning unit knocking in the window, and realized it had weathered the last fifteen years, as had the creaking wood floors and the dingy gray walls. It seemed nothing had changed in Common.

Well, almost nothing. For years Millie Tisdale had been Tuck's secretary. Now the woman behind the scarred oak desk was Daisi Lavel. She had been a few years younger than him in school, but he still remembered her as the redhead who liked to flirt with him when no one was looking.

She didn't acknowledge him, even though Johnny was sure she had heard the door open. Preoccupied with applying nail polish to nails that were too long to be much good for typing with any speed or accuracy, she had her lips pursed and her eyes glued on her task.

Johnny moved closer to the desk. "Steady as she goes, Daisi."

A glop of polish landed on her cuticle, and her head flew up, ready to chastise the person responsible. Her intention died the instant she recognized who was standing in front of her desk. "Johnny Bernard. My God, you look... You look like your daddy."

"That's what I hear." Johnny grinned. "How are you, Daisi?"

"I'm fine, but I see black and blue are still your two favorite colors. After all this time I would have thought you'd have smartened up."

"Slow learner, I guess."

"No, I don't think that's it. School came easy, as I recall. And physically—" Her eyes drifted over his body with female appreciation. "You look like you could really do a number on somebody if you wanted to, so what's the problem?"

Johnny chuckled. "I don't have any problem, Miss Lavel."

"It's Daisi Buillard now." She leaned back and rubbed her swollen belly. "I married Melvin. You remember him, don't you? The cute one in the family. We're havin' our second in three months. Got a little girl, named Sally. She'll be two this fall. You got any kids?"

"No."

"You sure? A handsome devil like you?"

"No, I don't have any kids." He gestured to the growing puddle on her nail. "Sorry about that."

Daisi reached for a tissue and wiped the glob off her nail. "No biggie."

"I came to see Tuck." Johnny glanced down the hall. "Is he in?"

"Oh, he's in, all right. But he ain't smilin'. Hasn't been since he found out you were comin' back here for the summer. He still hates your guts, you know. But then, I'd hate you, too, if you busted all the windows in my house and stole my dog."

"I suppose I did get a little carried away the night before I left town."

"A little?" Daisi rolled her big brown eyes. "I'd say sprayin' red paint on half the businesses on Main Street and settin' fire to that dead oak in the center of town was more than just a little carried away."

Humbled by the magnitude of what he'd done, Johnny had the decency to flush. "You wanna tell him I'm here?"

One of Daisi's fingers pointed to a metal box tented with

old mail. "The intercom broke a couple months ago." Her eyes danced with mischief. "Why don't you just go on back and surprise him. It'll serve him right for chewin' off one of my ears already this mornin' for not makin' his coffee strong enough."

The phone rang. "Dang." Daisi waved Johnny down the hall. "Good luck. And if I hear any gunshots, I'll remember to duck."

Johnny ambled down the hall. When he came to Sheriff Tucker's office he stopped, his hand poised on the doorknob. He'd gone over what had happened on Bayou Road a dozen times since last night. He figured it had been Farrel behind the wheel. He hadn't seen him, and he couldn't make out the car, but his gut told him it had to be his old enemy, Farrel.

Johnny wasn't expecting Tuck, however, to do anything about it. But a record of the incident on file couldn't hurt. That way if there was more trouble—which there no doubt would be—he'd have a paper trail to fall back on. It might be the only thing that would save him and keep him out of jail if things took a turn for the worst.

If he'd learned anything during his stint in the military, and then in prison, it was that keeping quiet wasn't always the smartest thing to do. Sometimes the more people who knew your business, the safer you were.

He decided to dispense with knocking and took Daisi's suggestion of surprise. Slinging the door wide, he stepped inside unannounced.

The minute Tuck looked up from his desk and saw the condition Johnny was in, he laughed outright. "Well, now. Looks like we got ourselves a problem. Guess your stay is going to be cut short—shorter than even I figured."

Johnny closed the door behind himself, and took a seat in the chair in front of Tuck's desk. Just like the rest of the police station, this room looked in need of more than just paint. A long line of file cabinets ran the length of one dingy white wall. Overhead, an ancient ceiling fan whirled at top speed, vibrating as if it might come apart any minute. A couple of dozen messages and newspaper clippings, some yellowed with age, fluttered on a bulletin board behind the desk.

"So, should I make the call to your parole officer, or do you want to?"

"I already called him," Johnny drawled. "That's why I'm here."

Clifton Tucker leaned back in his chair and crossed his arms over his bulky chest. The fifty-four-year-old man had put on at least twenty pounds since Johnny had seen him six months ago. He resembled a well-fed bulldog, with dull gray eyes and aging curly hair to match.

"So, Bernard, what's your excuse this time? Not that I'll believe it, but we'll go through the motions to keep it all legal-like."

Johnny came to the point quickly. "Someone tried to run me down on Bayou Road last night."

"You got witnesses?"

"No."

The sheriff made a rude noise. "Figures."

Johnny reined in his temper. It would do him no good to antagonize Tuck; the man could make his stay in town miserable if he had a mind to. "I told my parole agent what happened, and he made a record of it. Now I'm telling you and expect you to do the same. That's the only reason I'm here."

Again, the sheriff made a disgusted noise. But he pulled open his top drawer and took out a paper to file the report. "You say this happened when?"

"Around ten last night," Johnny offered.

"Guess it could have happened. Somebody wanting to get even, I mean."

"Like Farrel."

"He's not the only person in town who'd like to see you six feet under, boy. He's just a little more verbal about it than the others." The sheriff narrowed his eyes. "Recognize the car?"

"No." *But it had a sweet engine,* Johnny wanted to say. One that had been worked over and juiced up. The kind of car a grease monkey like Clete Gilmore could put together with his eyes closed. And why not? If Johnny's memory served him correctly, Clete had been tearing cars apart and putting them back together in his daddy's gas station since he was twelve.

Clifton scratched his head, then looked over the few lines he'd written down. "That it?"

Johnny didn't intend to mention the light he'd seen in the window of the farmhouse. He'd gone back to the house to investigate once he'd regained consciousness, but there had been no signs that anyone had been there. He said, "That'll about do it."

Clifton swiped at the sweat hanging from his bushy dark brows, then gave the fan overhead a dirty look. His wilted, tan shirt and the deep circles of sweat ringing each armpit held proof that the fan was failing him miserably. "I'll check around, talk to Farrel and see where he was last night. If I find out that he's got no alibi, and you wind up dead in the meantime, I guess you were telling the truth. How's that?"

No, nothing had changed, Johnny thought, shoving to his feet. But he really hadn't expected a party picnic to welcome him home. And it was doubtful Tuck would get anywhere with Farrel. But that didn't matter. He'd come to make his report and that was all.

He was two steps away from the door when it opened, and a skinny, old man hurried inside. "I need to see you, Cliff."

Johnny thought he recognized the voice. He looked again, studied the man's gaunt face and sharp green eyes. The man was Jasper Craig, he decided. The voice was a little shaky, yet it had a faintly educated ring to it—a drunken educated ring. When he thought about Jasper, he thought about fancy clothes and polished shoes. About an educated man who had made his money too easily, and had spent it in the same breezy manner.

Johnny stared, unable to believe the ragged man standing in front of him could be Farrel's father. What the hell had happened to him? He remembered Nicole saying Farrel had taken over the family lumber business. But he'd just assumed it was because Jasper had retired early. Now it seemed more likely that it was because the man had turned into a pathetic drunk. Johnny eyed his soiled clothes. They reeked of stale whiskey, and there was dirt clinging to him as if he'd just crawled out of a hole in the ground.

Suddenly the old man locked eyes with Johnny. He didn't say anything for a minute, then finally he gave up a lopsided smile. "Hello, boy. You grew up."

"It happens," Johnny answered.

"Plan on staying out at your place, do you?"

"No. The boathouse at Oakhaven."

Jasper nodded, his smile spreading. "The boathouse. Well, that's real nice of Mae. That old farmhouse is in bad shape. Not really fit for staying in." He glanced at the sheriff. "Didn't mean to interrupt, Cliff." He started to back out the door.

"J.P., I thought you needed to talk to me."

"Ah, no. No, that's all right. I can wait."

"Johnny was just leaving."

"No, I'll come back. I just remembered something I got to do."

* * *

She came through the bakery door the minute he pulled the pickup to the curb. Nicole was carrying a small white bag between her teeth, a loaf of French bread tucked under her arm, and a paper cup of coffee in each hand. Despite his best intentions, Johnny couldn't keep his eyes from straying to the rain-spattered shirt clinging to her breasts, or her hip-hugging jeans. She was a sight, and there was no sense denying he was attracted to every inch of her.

He reached over and opened the door. She handed him the cups, then removed the white bag from between her teeth and set it in the middle of the seat. The long loaf of bread went on the dash just before she climbed in. "Dory insisted I take the coffee and doughnuts. She's just like Clair, trying to fatten me up."

Johnny glanced at Nicole's slender curves. She was thin, all right, like a sleek, fine-boned greyhound. He swore silently, then handed her back one of the cups.

"Waiting long?"

"About ten minutes. Did you go see the sheriff?"

"Yeah."

"And?"

"And I'm still here."

She arched a pretty brow, set her cup on the dash, then opened up the white bag and angled it in his direction. He hadn't bothered to eat breakfast. After last night's excitement, just getting up and moving had been all he'd wanted to tackle. He was sore in a dozen places. His right leg and hip were black and blue clean to his butt.

He reached inside the bag and pulled out a cake doughnut. Johnny savored every bite. She offered him another, then another. When the bag was empty and the coffee gone, he draped his wrist over the steering wheel and asked, "Where to now?"

"I have two stops left," she told him. "The post office and Craig Lumber."

Johnny pulled into the lumberyard parking lot moments later, and killed the engine. It was still raining out, the sky still dark, the rumble of thunder in the distance.

"I'll run this letter to the post office," she said. "Then I'll go order the shingles and anything else they don't have on the list." She handed him back the list he'd given her two days earlier. "Why don't you check it over and see if there's anything else you want to add. I'll be right back."

Johnny took the list. He allowed himself a few minutes to appreciate the view of her hurrying into the post office—her long legs and sexy backside giving his heart rate another jolt—then got out of the pickup. He slid the list into his back pocket, and in his normal lazy gait, sauntered through the front door of Craig Lumber.

A quick glance at the desk told him Willis Lavel was half asleep behind the counter. But not for long—the doorbell gave a hellish *clang,* and Willis let out a holler and jumped a good two feet off the high stool he was perched on. He grabbed the counter to steady himself, his gaze searching out the customer who had disturbed his sleep. When he realized who it was, all the color drained from Willis's pudgy face. "Oh, hell."

"Nice seeing you too, Will."

Johnny dug into his T-shirt pocket for his smokes. After lighting up, he took a leisurely drag.

"I got a knife," Willis finally warned. "Try somethin' and you'll be sorry."

If Willis owned a knife, it had to be the size of a fingernail file. Johnny glanced around, noticing for the first time that the office door behind the counter stood ajar. The light was on. Loud enough so whoever was inside could hear him, he said, "Came to pick up supplies for Oakhaven. Think you can put an order together without screwing it up, Will?"

Willis had started to sweat. He swiped at his bald pate,

then reached for his half-used black cigar in the tarnished ashtray on the counter. With shaky fingers, he lit a match and struggled to relight it. "You're gonna have to talk to Farrel about that," he said, puffing long and hard to get the cigar fired up. "But that ain't likely, on account I don't think—"

"That's good, Will. Don't think," Johnny cut in. "Just call your boss out here. I'll do the asking."

The older man gave up trying to light his cigar and disgustedly tossed it aside. "Farrel ain't gonna agree to nothin' that involves you, Johnny," Willis whined. "I ain't never seen one man who can hate another as much as he hates you."

"I've come on business, Will. Oakhaven business."

Just as Johnny expected, his voice carried into the office, drawing Farrel Craig out as if he'd thrown in a baited line and bagged himself a sucker. Farrel was almost as tall as Johnny, but fair where Johnny was dark. His tanned face followed the slender lines of his trim body. His eyes, distinctly green, were deep-set. Insolent.

He wore jeans, snakeskin boots with silver toe caps, and a red shirt too flashy for any kind of real work. Except for an inch-long scar on his jaw and a jog in his nose—both Johnny's doing—Farrel didn't own a blemish, a mole or a freckle.

"You got a lot of nerve coming in here, Bernard," Farrel snarled. When Johnny said nothing, he taunted, "What's the matter, *beggar boy*, they cut your tongue out in prison?"

Like a puppet who had just had his string jerked, Willis started laughing. Once his chuckle petered out and the silence stretched, he nervously picked up his dead cigar and stuck it in his mouth.

"I still got my tongue," Johnny finally said, "and I see you still got a crooked nose."

Instead of getting angry, Farrel grinned. "You look in the mirror this morning? You got more than that. Welcome home, Johnny."

The doorbell clanged once more, and both Johnny and Farrel turned simultaneously to see Nicole hurry through the door. She looked rain-spattered and out of breath, as if she'd made a mad dash from the pickup—which no doubt she had, the minute she learned Johnny wasn't inside waiting for her like some obedient puppy. Before she got her pretty mouth open, Johnny said, "You finished at the post office already, *cherie?*"

He gave her a lazy smile, and in return she gave him a look that could have turned stone into smoldering ashes. "Didn't we agreed you would stay in the pickup, Mr. Bernard?"

She took the necessary steps to close the distance between them. Johnny waited a few seconds before he answered, but when he did he leaned close, whispering, "The lesson here is, if you want to treat a man like a dog, you should remember to bring along a collar and leash so you can chain him up like one. That way you'll always know where you can find him."

"Such a useful tip," she hissed softly into his cheek. "Next time I'll be prepared."

"Could be fun...you trying to put one on me," he drawled.

She didn't appreciate him baiting her, or his smug smile. "We'll discuss it later," she insisted, her eyes shifting to Farrel, then back to Johnny. "Where's my supply list?"

"In a safe place," he assured. "I'll take care of this. All you have to do is choose a color for those shingles we talked about."

"I'll take care of all of it," she insisted. "Now give me the list."

"Is there trouble, Miss Chapman? Something I can help out with?"

Farrel's voice was friendly. Too friendly, Johnny thought, not liking the way his enemy raked Nicole's body with hungry appreciation.

"You can call me Nicole," she told him, "and no, I don't need any help. I do apologize, however, if my worker has been bothering you." She gave Johnny a nasty sidelong glance. "He was told to stay in the pickup."

"It's hard to find good help these days, that's a fact," Farrel agreed, giving his own man a disappointed look. He ran a hand through his cropped blond hair and leaned his arm on the counter. "So, what is it I can help you with, Nicole?"

"I need some building supplies and to order new shingles for my grandmother's house."

Suddenly Johnny was aware that Nicole was leaning into him, her hand on his backside. His body tensed just before her fingers climbed into his right back pocket and stole the supply list. She gave him a pleased look, then floated to the counter with that hip action she'd perfected for the sole purpose—Johnny was sure—of scorching a man's blood and frying his insides.

"Morning, Mr. Lavel," she purred sweetly, charming old Willis into a heated frenzy. "Remember me? We met last week at the bank."

"Sure do. You look mighty fine this mornin', Miss Nicki. It's sure nice, you movin' in with your grandma. My son, Woodrow, thinks so, too."

Johnny was sure Woodrow Lavel wasn't the only man in town thinking he'd just hit the jackpot. Nicole was definitely the apple that would get picked first in this town; she was shiny and new and ripe in all the right places.

She offered a friendly smile to the older man, then unfolded the list and laid it on the counter. Her attention refocused on Farrel, she asked, "I assume Gran's account is up to date?"

"Sure is." Farrel glanced down, half interested, at the material list. "Doing some major repairs, I see. That's quite a list." He slid the list toward Willis. "See to this, Will. And get the boys to tarp the load so the lumber stays dry. I can pick up the tarp next time I'm out that way."

"But you never lend out—"

"Tarp the load, Will!" Farrel's eyes left Nicole's for just a split second and shot Willis a *Get moving!* look that nearly levitated the older man up and pitched him out the door headfirst.

Farrel said, "I've got shingle samples in my office. How about you and me picking that color out over a cup of coffee?"

"That would be fine," Nicole answered.

Farrel escorted Nicole around the counter and into his office. Then, just before he closed the door behind them, he turned back, grinned at Johnny, held up his middle finger and mouthed the words.

Chapter 6

The moon's guiding light vanished the moment Nicole entered the woods. She glanced around warily, then started down the blackened path, ducking from time to time to avoid whatever might be hanging in the tangled foliage overhead. She didn't want to think about the many eyes that were, no doubt, watching her. If she did, she would be struck once again by how crazy it was for her to be going to the boathouse after dark.

Just as she reminded herself of the fact, she stumbled, barely catching her balance in time to save herself a hard tumble. Swearing softly, she stopped to brush her hair out of her eyes.

"Should have brought a flashlight along. That way you could see what kind of snake you're kickin' in the head."

Nicole gasped, then whirled around so fast she nearly fell on her face again. Squinting in the darkness, she saw a match spark. A moment later the glow from a cigarette illuminated Johnny Bernard's handsome face.

He was leaning against a tree, looking relaxed and every bit the bad boy he was. Still, she owed him an apology, and she hadn't wanted to put it off until tomorrow.

"What are you doing out here?" she asked stupidly. "You nearly scared me half to death."

"That must be the question of the night, 'cause I'm wondering the same about you. What brings you out, *cherie?* It's late. Too late for a stroll."

"But not for you?"

"I know these woods. I used to live around here, remember?" He took a drag off his cigarette and sent the smoke into the black night.

"I would have called, but the boathouse doesn't have a phone," Nicole explained, "and I wanted to…" She took a deep breath and let it out slowly. She hadn't been looking forward to this part, but it had to be done. "To apologize."

"Ah, an apology."

She couldn't see his face very well, but she heard the amusement in his voice. "Why didn't you tell me the truth about last night? Why did you let me assume the worst?"

"Did I do that? Funny, I thought I tried to explain. As I recall, you didn't want to listen. Sound familiar?"

"I suppose I deserve that."

"Yes, you do. You've been thinking the worst of me since I got here." He dropped his spent cigarette and ground it out with the heel of his boot. "The bottom line is, you don't know me, and you don't want to."

"That's not true." Nicole swatted at the dozen mosquitoes swarming around her head, glad she had worn a sweatshirt even though it was much too warm. "It's just that—"

"The gossip that arrived later today wasn't what you'd expected. Does that mean you're ready to listen? To trust me?"

Listen, yes; trust him, no. Frankly, she didn't think she

would ever be able to trust a man again. "You knew your visit to the sheriff's office would circulate. That the entire town would be privy to the information before long?"

"That's the way it works around here."

"You think you know everything, is that it?" Nicole was furious. "Did you also expect an apology? Am I playing right into your hands?"

When he didn't answer, Nicole spun around to leave, only to be pulled up short by his hand on her arm. "Easy. Don't go running off all mad."

Nicole pulled her arm free and glared at him. "You set me up."

"No, you did that all by yourself."

She swatted at another swarm of mosquitoes. He reached out and pulled up the hood on her sweatshirt. "Come on. The bugs are making a meal out of you."

Boldly, he took hold of her hand and started deeper into the woods. Momentarily surprised, Nicole followed, as he easily maneuvered the twisted trail as if he shared some secret with the nocturnal animals that thrived on darkness. When they reached the clearing, Nicole saw the bayou in the faint moonlight, and knew where they were.

Inside the boathouse, he ignored the light and guided her through the maze of clutter. Once they reached the stairwell, he let go of her and said, "Wait here."

In the dark, Nicole listened as his booted feet took the stair treads two at a time. Suddenly a muted stream of light brought him into focus at the top of the stairs, and she saw him clearly for the first time since he had frightened her in the woods. He wore trashed jeans, the worst pair she'd seen so far, and a brown T-shirt stretched over his chest. His black hair was damp and loose, as if he'd showered or, maybe, gone for a swim at the pond.

Nicole sucked in a ragged breath, wondering why she

had allowed him to bring her here, why she wasn't in flight back to the house.

"*Cherie,* you coming?"

Nicole pushed the sweatshirt hood off her head, hesitated.

"I don't bite. That is, not unless that's what you like."

His teasing was followed by a suggestive smile. If she had any sense, she thought, she would turn and run.

At the top of the stairs, Nicole slipped past him into the apartment. The day had turned blisteringly hot after the rain, and without any fan the small room felt stifling even with the windows open.

She unzipped her sweatshirt and slipped it off, leaving her in a white T-shirt and jeans. She glanced around, noticing that he had made several changes in the past couple of days. A worn rug lay on the wood floor in front of the rocker, an old-fashioned, metal reading lamp stood behind it. She hadn't thought of him as the type to read, but a paperback novel on the floor beside the rocker claimed otherwise. He had scrounged an old flat-topped trunk from somewhere and turned it into a makeshift coffee table, which sat between the sofa and the rocker. It was all very homey and neat, and she couldn't help but be impressed by the fact that he had invested some time in a few creature comforts.

"You want something to drink?"

Nicole turned in time to appreciate his lazy gait as he sauntered into the small kitchen.

"Soda? Water?" he called out.

"No. Nothing."

While he went to the sink, ran himself a glass of water and drained it, Nicole moved to the sofa and perched on one corner. Another glance around brought her face to face with one of her paintings. It hung over his bed—a picture of Belle Bayou. She'd painted it a few years ago. She remembered sketching for hours near the secluded inlet where the night herons made their nests. Bick had taken her there, and while she had become enthralled with her subject, he had caught a string of catfish. She'd gotten the worst sunburn of her life that day, but it had been worth it; she'd captured the bayou's mystery and its beauty perfectly. She'd sold a number of prints, and afterwards she'd given the original to Gran for her birthday. She was curious as to why it was here.

"Sure you don't want something?" He came out of the kitchen.

Nicole shook her head. "No. I'm fine."

He strolled across her line of vision and seated himself in the rocker. "I'm going to start tearing the roof off the house tomorrow, if it doesn't rain. The yard will be a mess for about a week or two."

Nicole laid her sweatshirt on the sofa beside her. "We'll put up with whatever we have to," she assured him. She paused. "Tell me about last night."

"Like I told Tuck, a car tried to run me down on the county road."

"Are you sure? Maybe the person just didn't see you."

"No, they saw me. I was at the old farm. I still own it, thanks to the old lady and—"

"Wait! Back up. What do you mean, thanks to the old lady?"

"Your grandmother is the reason I came back," he told her. "She's been paying the taxes on the farm ever since I left. Don't ask me why. The place is worthless." He ran his hands through his hair, frustration evident.

"How did you find out you still own it. Did she write you?"

"No, Griffin Black did. He wanted to buy it. I got the letter six months ago. At first I thought there had to be a mistake, so I came here from Lafayette to check it out. I left the courthouse and was headed here when I decided to stop for a cold beer at Pepper's. After that, as they say, all hell broke loose.''

Nicole was beginning to understand—that's *if* she could believe him. ''Do you think it was Farrel who tried to run you down last night?''

''Maybe. Early this morning I called my parole officer, and he suggested that I report the incident to Tuck. He thought having a record of it would protect my position. That is, if something like that ever happens again.''

''Do you think it will?''

He shrugged. ''I'm not going to pretend my being back doesn't matter to some folks. I have a lot of enemies in this town.''

''Why?''

''That's the sixty-four-thousand-dollar question. Some of it I understand, even deserve, but there's a lot that has never made any sense.''

''So now what? What if this person—Farrel or who-ever—tries again?''

''I'll be ready next time.''

Nicole sighed. ''What does that mean?''

''Relax. It doesn't mean I'm going to go looking for trouble. I'm not.''

''Maybe that's what this guy is hoping for. Maybe he's just waiting for you to lose your temper like before. From what I've heard, you have quite a temper when you're—'' Nicole clamped her mouth shut. She was doing it again, listening to the gossip and expecting the worst of him. ''I'm sorry.''

''You get that from Farrel this morning?''

Nicole flushed. ''He did warn me about you. Something about breaking windows and killing a dog.''

''I did break a few windows when I was younger. The

dead dog is bull. Should I take my turn and warn you about Farrel?''

Nicole leaned back into the couch cushions and relaxed a little. "You don't need to. One thing you should know about me, Johnny, I'm no chump. I'm not inexperienced when it comes to men with easy smiles, or who know just the right thing to say nine times out of ten. But that's getting away from the point. If you screw up your parole, you'll be sent back to prison. Don't do it. If you don't have a good enough reason to for yourself, think of Gran. She's the happiest I've seen her in years. I don't pretend to understand why exactly, but I do know your being here is very important to her. And loving her like I do, I'm willing to do whatever it takes to keep her happy. You can't let anyone ruin it for her, you just can't!''

"Take it easy. It won't come to that.''

He started rocking the chair slow and lazylike, his hands resting on the arms, his blunt-tipped fingers dangling limp over the edge. Nicole stood and planted her hands on her hips. "You bet it won't, because you're going to avoid Farrel Craig and anyone else who might try to draw you into a fight. Do you hear? Better yet, there is no reason for you to go anywhere near town.''

"I'm a free man, *cherie*. I'll go where I damn well please, when the hell I feel like it.''

"That would be fine if you only had yourself to think about, but you don't. You owe Gran. You'd still be rotting in prison if she hadn't offered you a job and a place to stay.''

"There's another way of looking at that," he countered angrily. "If she hadn't kept my name on that worthless land deed all these years, none of this would have happened at all. I had no intention of ever coming back here until I got that letter from Griffin Black.''

His bluntness made Nicole clamp her mouth shut. She

turned away, unable to hold his potent gaze a moment longer. Finally, she walked to the window overlooking Belle. The moon had slipped through the clouds, and the picture it made was breathtaking. "Are you holding a grudge? Because if you are—"

"I'm not holding a grudge. The old lady didn't make me break Farrel's nose or pull my knife that day at Pepper's."

The sound of the rocker scraping along the floor warned Nicole that Johnny had gotten to his feet. She waited for him to say something, but instead he came to stand behind her at the window. She could smell his earthy scent, feel his breath next to her ear.

"I'm glad you read Farrel this morning," he drawled. "He's not to be trusted."

"But you are?" Nicole's gaze remained focused on the moon hovering over the bayou, casting gnarly shadows across the still water. She felt him shift his body, his thigh brushing her hip. "Are you trustworthy? Or are you working this situation to your advantage?"

He leaned in, closing the last inch. He was so close, Nicole could feel his warm body against the length of her own. "What would that gain me?"

Nicole turned, and wished she hadn't; it put her practically in his arms. "Not a thing. I told you, I'm no chump." He was too close. She suddenly felt in need of air. "I've got to go." Seeing her sweatshirt on the sofa, she moved around him quickly and picked it up. When she turned back around, he was standing in the doorway.

"Put it on," he said. "Your skin is too delicate for the woods this time of night. Then I'll walk you back."

"I know my way to the house."

"I'm sure you do, but as you pointed out earlier, I don't only have myself to think about these days."

"I was talking about Gran, not me."

"Just the same, I'll walk you back."

Two days later Nicole stepped inside Pepper's wearing a baby-blue, straight jersey shift. The bar was wall-to-wall people. Tonight there was a live band, and everyone for forty miles around had turned out to hear it.

She scanned the crowd looking for Dory. Normally, Nicole avoided bars, but Dory had convinced her that tonight was special. She found an empty table and took a seat— amazing, since every booth was bulging with serious party-goers.

"Hi."

Nicole turned to see a redheaded woman standing in front of her. A pregnant woman. Her gaze fastened on the woman's swollen stomach. She didn't want to stare, but she couldn't help it. She forced herself to smile and cleared her throat. "Hi. I'm Nicole Chapman, and you are...?"

"Daisi Buillard. Mind if I join you?"

"No. Not at all."

Daisi pulled out the only other chair at the table and took a seat. She was dressed in slacks and a cute T-shirt with Baby on Board written on it. "I noticed you right away. I've been meanin' to give you a call and introduce myself, since we're close to the same age—but you know how it is. What with workin' and tryin' to keep the house clean and hubby happy, the days just fly."

Nicole smiled, her eyes straying again to Daisi's pregnant stomach. She tried not to think about her own baby and what might have been, but that was impossible.

Daisi continued to talk, unaware that Nicole was becoming melancholy. "Are you waitin' for someone. A guy?"

"No." Nicole leaned back in her chair and crossed her legs. "I was supposed to meet Dory at seven. She's late. You must know Dory from the bakery? She's—"

"I know Dory. We went to school together. It's not like her to be late. Maybe somethin' came up."

That's all she needed, Nicole thought. If Dory didn't show up, she'd feel foolish sitting alone. She flagged the waitress and ordered a white wine. "Do you want something to drink?"

"A diet cola," Daisi told the waitress.

Another fifteen minutes passed without Dory showing up. While Nicole flagged the waitress for another drink, Daisi motioned for her husband to come over. He was tall and lean. He wasn't the most handsome man in town, but he had kind gray eyes, and it was clear he loved his wife.

"Daisi and I are glad to see someone our age move into town," he said. "There's not many young people making Common their home these days. The norm here is to leave the minute you get out of school."

"Mel and me like it quiet," Daisi interjected. "We bought the corner house on Mill Street." She sipped her drink. "I heard from my mother that you're an artist. That must be excitin'."

Nicole nodded, wishing Gran had kept quiet about her career. "It is," she agreed.

"How's Johnny working out?" Mel asked. "He staying out of trouble?"

Daisi elbowed her husband. "I told you, Mel, those bruises were from an accident. Why do you always have to make somethin' out of nothin'?"

"Maybe because anything having to do with Johnny Bernard usually ends up to be something," Mel challenged.

Daisi and Mel headed for the dance floor a short time later. Nicole watched as Mel pulled Daisi close, and together they cradled their unborn baby between them. It was painful to watch, but she couldn't look away, the past returning with such force that her entire body ached.

She ordered another glass of wine in the hope that it would numb her pain. To her surprise, it wasn't a waitress who brought it, but Farrel Craig. "Hiya, pretty lady." He set the drink down in front of her. "Mind if I join you?"

Nicole had given up on Dory, but as she looked up and saw Farrel staring down at her, she wished her friend would suddenly appear out of a crack in the wall. Trying to be friendly, she faked a pleasant smile. "I don't think I'll be staying too much longer, but you're welcome to the table."

"You don't need to rush off. The fun's just getting started." He pulled out the empty chair and sat. "I've been watching you all evening, and I finally figured it out."

Nicole raised an eyebrow. "Figured out what?"

"The reason you're here. You're dressed for dancing." He held up his hand when Nicole was about to refute his declaration. "Just so you know, it's not you, Nicole. The guys are interested—they're just scared. Not too many women in this town have been educated past high school. You being from California and all, they don't know how to approach you. So they're sitting confused, waiting for someone else to make the first move, to see how he does."

"So you're the designated ice-breaker?" Nicole asked, aware that Farrel was on the verge of asking her to dance. He was smooth, but not the smoothest she'd encountered—no one could be as smooth as Chad Taylor had been, she thought.

"I guess. I've been enjoying the sight from over there." He motioned to a prime booth that had a view of everyone who came in and out. "And just so you know, I came to dance, too."

Nicole glanced toward the band just as they cut loose with another fast-paced, raucous song. Around the stage blinked two rows of pink neon lights. The accordion was loud, the guitar fast-paced, and the fiddler knew just when to challenge the beat with a reckless tempo that turned the crowd wild.

Maybe it was seeing Daisi Buillard pregnant and so happy that made Nicole feel blue, or maybe it was just Farrel Craig's coaxing smile and one too many glasses of wine, but, moments later, Nicole found herself in the middle of the dance floor wrapped in the arms of a man she didn't even like. As he locked his hands around her waist and twirled her into the crowd, he said, "We're going to clear the dance floor, sweet thing. Hang on."

He wasn't kidding about chasing the other couples back to their tables. Nicole thought about the spectacle they were making, then quickly traded one concern for another—maintaining her balance and staying on her feet.

Two songs later, they were the only ones on the dance floor, and the center of attention. Steadily the music grew more frenzied. Ribald hoots came from a nearby table as Nicole's dress inched higher and higher. Worse, the wine decided to kick in all at once, and her heart began to race.

Nicole, face flushed, wanted to stop. She wanted—no, needed—air. But the crowd kept clapping, stomping their feet and shouting encouragement from all sides of the room. On the next song, a slow, steamy Delta Blues, a dozen brave couples took their chances battling Farrel for room on the dance floor. The neon lights were doused, and it was then Nicole realized Farrel was, in fact, the consummate con man Johnny had warned her about. Within seconds, he'd wrapped his arms around her with great care and brought her in to him. Tenderly he began whispering compliments as he stroked the damp hair at her temple.

It was well past midnight by the time Farrel ushered Nicole into the parking lot in front of Pepper's. They had danced for hours and indulged in several drinks, and once outside, Farrel pulled Nicole close and stole a kiss.

His mouth felt hot and invading. Hard. "What do you

say we keep the night going,'' he whispered. "I know a place where we can be alone.''

Nicole struggled out of his arms. "I don't think so.'' She checked her watch. "I didn't realize how late it is. Gran will be worried sick.''

Farrel angled his head. "That's a brush-off if I've ever heard one, Nicole.''

"Sorry.'' Nicole suddenly felt light-headed. "The truth is, I'm not looking for an involvement at the moment. Not even a brief one-nighter. I didn't really come to dance tonight—I came to listen to the music with a friend. But she didn't show and—'' Nicole's stomach rolled, warning her she didn't have long before she'd be too weak to make it to the car without help. "I've got to go,'' she said in a rush. "Thanks for the fun.''

"You're welcome. Anytime you feel like another night of dancing, let me know.''

"I'll remember that.'' A car door slammed from some-where in the middle of the dark parking lot. Nicole squinted and tried to focus, but she wasn't sure if she was seeing the flicker of a match…or nothing at all. She pushed her bangs out of her eyes and started to walk slowly to her car. Not too slowly, but slowly enough that Farrel wouldn't suspect she was teetering on the verge of col-lapse.

She reached her car, dug her keys out of her purse and unlocked the door. Inside, she started the engine and turned on the air conditioner. She glanced toward the bar's front door, relieved when she saw Farrel sauntering inside. She leaned her head back against the seat and closed her eyes. Her head was spinning, and she knew the last glass of wine had been the culprit.

A sudden rap at the window gave Nicole a start. Her eyes flew open, and she let out a cry of surprise that surely was heard through the closed window. To her distress, seeing Johnny Bernard staring through the window at her made her feel worse. She didn't need those soul-searching eyes analyzing her just now. She didn't need him making some wisecrack about her condition, either. Right now, all she wanted was to be sick in private, and without an audience.

He motioned for her to buzz the window down, and after gazing at the panel of buttons for a confused couple of seconds, Nicole turned off the air conditioner, then pressed the upper-left button and watched the window disappear inside the door.

"You all right?"

The warm night air drifted into the car to attack Nicole's flushed face once more, and she instantly felt as weak as a kitten. "I'm fine," she lied. "What are you doing here?" Her words sounded strange, she thought, and the idea had her clearing her dry throat.

He took an impatient drag off his cigarette, then flicked the butt in the opposite direction of the car. Angling his head, he sent a cloud of smoke over the hood of the car. When he locked eyes with her once more, his expression was hard to read. "It's late," he drawled. "The old lady's worried. Especially since Dory called hours ago and said she couldn't meet you. So, what have you been doing for five hours, *cherie?* Or shouldn't I ask?"

"Dory called?" Nicole frowned. "Did she say why she couldn't meet me?"

"There was a small fire at the bakery."

"A fire?"

"Nothing serious. How much?"

Nicole gripped the steering wheel. "How much what?"

"Booze. How much did you have to drink?"

"Excuse me?" Nicole tried to sit up a little straighter. Her stomach did a sudden flip, but she would be damned if she'd let him see just how rotten she felt. She simply wanted to go home, pop a couple of headache pills and fall into bed.

"Drinking and driving is a bad combination."

Did he think he was telling her something she didn't already know? Incensed, she reached for the panel of buttons to buzz the window back up, but he read her intention and had the car door open in an instant.

"Slide over."

Nicole peered at him through narrowed eyes. Suddenly seeing two of him, she groaned softly and blinked in an effort to chase one of him away.

He gave her a nudge. "Come on. Move that cute butt of yours over a few inches, *cherie*. You're in no shape to drive."

"I'm fine," she insisted.

"Like hell."

Before she could argue, the upper part of his body was suddenly inside the car, and he was working his hands beneath her backside.

"Stop that!" Nicole protested.

With little effort, he half lifted, half slid her to the middle of the seat, then climbed in. "You ought to be tanned good for worrying the old lady needlessly," he scolded, slamming the door shut. "And of all things to drink, wine is the worst."

The last comment gave her pause. "And how would you know what I was drinking unless you were spying on me." When he didn't deny it, Nicole clutched at his black T-shirt sleeve so he would have to look at her. "Were you?"

He glanced down at her fine-boned little fist, then locked eyes with her. "You have a nice time dancing with Farrel Craig? Rubbing yourself all over him?"

"I wasn't doing that," she protested.

"Then maybe that grin he was wearing all evening was

just in anticipation of what might happen later if he got you drunk enough. You suppose?''

Nicole wasn't going to dignify that vulgar crack with so much as a peep. Changing the subject, she asked, ''Did you drive the pickup into town?''

He pointed to the middle of the parking lot. It was in the same general area where she thought she'd seen the match spark earlier.

''I'll come back in the morning and get it.'' He put the car in reverse, backed up and left the parking lot.

Once they were headed out of town, Nicole leaned her head against the seat and closed her eyes. She was willing to concede that it was for the best that Johnny drive her home. She was even ready to admit that drowning her misery in a bottle of wine had been idiotic and the most reckless thing she'd done in a while. But seeing Daisi Buillard's swollen stomach had brought the entire nightmare flooding back, all the pain and empty feelings. The helplessness. Her stomach knotted, and she laid her hands there and tried to chase the nausea away. But it wasn't going anywhere.

Johnny glanced at Nicole and saw her holding her stomach. Her head was resting at an odd angle against the seat, and he maneuvered his arm around her and pulled her close so she could use his shoulder for a pillow.

Damn her. What the hell was she doing wearing a dress that showed off every curve she owned, and dancing crazy with Farrel Craig as if they were old friends? He felt his insides tighten, and again the sight of Farrel stealing a kiss outside the bar flashed before his eyes.

He'd never been a jealous man, but at that moment he had been ready to put Farrel's face into a car window— and to hell with his parole. He didn't want to want Nicole Chapman the way he did, and yet there it was. She was a fragile woman, not at all his type, but still he wanted her. He wanted her in his bed, willing and saying his name. No, not just willing, but hot and aroused as hell.

When he had laid eyes on her at the boathouse that first day, all he had wanted was the physical contact, to satisfy himself with a warm, soft female body. Now he realized it was more complicated than just sex. Seeing her tonight with Farrel had been damn painful. He didn't understand it, and he wished to hell he could make it stop. But how?

He heard her moan softly and he pulled her closer to him. "Easy, *cherie*. We'll be home in just a few minutes."

They left the highway and turned off on Bayou Road. When Oakhaven came into sight, Johnny cruised up the driveway as quietly as possible, pulled the Skylark alongside Mae's Buick in the carport and turned off the ignition.

He shifted slightly and looked down at Nicole. She was so beautiful. He couldn't really blame Farrel for making a move on her. A man would have to be crazy not to try. He noticed her hands were still holding her stomach and wondered just how much she had drunk before he'd arrived at Pepper's looking for her. She didn't appear to be the type to get carried away with liquor. Then again, he didn't know her well enough to make that kind of call.

"Hey, *cherie,* wake up," he whispered. "We're home." She moaned and opened her pretty blue eyes, and that's when he saw the tear. Concerned, he wiped it away, then asked, "What is it? Upset stomach? Headache?"

She straightened to sit up, looked away from him as if she were embarrassed. "I'm fine."

He opened the door and climbed out. When he turned around, she was already sliding out his side. He reached out to help her, catching her around the waist. When her feet hit the ground, she swayed slightly. "Come on, *cherie,* get your feet underneath you."

She managed to stand, one arm looped around his waist,

one soft breast pressed into his rib cage. They crossed the yard and scaled the porch steps to the private entrance of her bedroom. Once there, Johnny propped her against the wall to open one of the French doors. Before he got it open, she was leaning against him again, all warm and vulnerable.

He got the door open, then glanced at her. She had angled her head to one side and was looking at him curiously. "Are you really a nice guy, like Gran says?" She pressed her hand to his chest where his heart beat strong and fast. "I hope not. I don't want to like you, Johnny Bernard. Not even a little bit. I want you to be just like Chad, selfish and dishonest."

Her face contorted with raw emotion. She looked like she was one step away from crying again. Johnny didn't know what to say, but it was obvious this guy, Chad, was someone from her past and that he had hurt her. Johnny also figured that if she were thinking clearly, she wouldn't be talking like this, telling him things she deemed her private business. He was curious to know more, but just not this way. Not when she was feeling so low. He said, "Come on, *cherie,* it's time for you to go to bed." He untangled her from his body and set her away from him. "You'll feel better in the morning. Now go on."

He gave her a little nudge toward the door, then started off the porch. He didn't get far before she said, "He didn't ask me if it was all right."

Johnny turned. "What?"

"Farrel. He didn't ask if he could kiss me."

Johnny didn't want to be reminded of that kiss, sure it would haunt him throughout the night as it was. He shook his head. "Go to bed, *cherie.*"

"I will. Only, I can't stop thinking about it. I—"

"Dammit, I don't want to hear it!" Johnny turned away from her, determined to leave.

"You're mad. I'm sorry. It's just that there's this sour taste in my mouth—"

Johnny spun back around. "And just what the hell am I supposed to do about that, *cherie?* I'm fresh out of mints."

At that moment he would have done anything to get her inside so he could get the hell out of there. He was on the verge of doing something stupid, and the longer he hung around—

"I don't want a mint," she said simply, softly. She took an unsteady step toward him, then another and another until they were toe to toe. Slowly, she leaned into him, her sweet scent filling his nostrils, branding him and guaranteeing he was going to spend another sleepless night in hell. "Offer something else, Johnny. Use your imagination."

The thought of kissing away Farrel's taste and leaving her marked with his own had Johnny turning stone hard. God, he wanted to kiss her. Wanted to do that, and so much more.

Her hands stroked up his chest, and she swayed into him. The sultry night suddenly turned stifling hot. Johnny knew he shouldn't do it, even as he lowered his head to meet her halfway. One quick kiss, he promised. Just one…

Her lips were summer warm and satin smooth, and in an instant his plan of offering her *one quick kiss* was shot completely to hell. He slipped his hands around her and brought her slender body in full contact with his. After ravishing her mouth for a full minute, he backed her against the new railing he'd built and kissed her again…then again.

He meant to stop.

Soon he would.

She made a little mewling noise, wiggled against his arousal.

Desire burned hotter than Johnny had ever experienced in his life. He coaxed her mouth open and thrust his tongue deep inside. She wrapped her arms around his neck and clung to him. Her ready response sent another jolt of desire ripping through his aching loins; at the same time blood surged hot through his veins. His heart knocked against his chest like a jackhammer.

His hands moved to her hips, his fingers working her dress up her slender legs to caress her velvet thighs. Boldly, his fingers found the elastic edge of her panties. He was losing control, and she was letting him.

He was breathing fast—too fast, he thought. He stopped for a moment to catch his breath, and that's when it hit him: she was drunk, and he was climbing all over her, making him no better than Farrel Craig or that man from her past. Grounded, Johnny pulled his hand out from under her dress and took a giant step back.

"Dammit, *cherie,* what the hell are you trying to do to me?" Swearing again, he thrust his hand through his loose hair. Then, before she could answer, before her fuzzy head had a chance to clear and grasp just how damn close she had come to ending up on her back, Johnny melted into the shadows.

Chapter 7

Nicole left for New Orleans before breakfast. She didn't want to take a chance on running into anyone: not Gran, not Clair nor Bick. Least of all, Johnny.

Johnny.

Nicole ran a finger over her lips as another sharp mental image assailed her. Had she really begged him to kiss her?

She wanted to believe it was just another naughty dream. But she knew that was just wishful thinking. The entire kiss, every heat-filled moment, could still be felt. She was burning inside and out, floating on some strange, erotic wave of pure bliss. A never-before experience, which made it all the more distressing.

How could she have sunk so low?

She really had had no business staying at Pepper's after Dory hadn't showed. And the wine had been mistake number two. The doozy had been allowing Farrel Craig to control the evening, then steal that miserable kiss.

Looking back, she realized the entire evening had disaster written all over it. And Johnny showing up to witness the whole thing, then playing white knight and chauffeur all in one, had been the *coup de grâce*. It was more than just humbling to know she had allowed him to see her in such a pathetic state. She felt not only ashamed, but humiliated.

And considering what had happened between them on the porch, she feared her disgrace wasn't over yet. Surely he would make an issue out of that wicked kiss he'd planted on her lips. And more to the point, of how readily she'd accepted.

Furious with herself, Nicole snapped off the radio, pressed her sandaled foot to the floorboards and sent the speedometer well past what the county road could handle. Anxious to forget last night, she turned her thoughts to New Orleans and the new gallery Gran had told her about. Maybe if she started working again things would get back to normal sooner.

Since she had been a little girl she had wanted to paint pretty pictures and to be taken seriously for her artistic talent. She'd wanted the reality of snaring her dream and building on it. She'd worked hard for it, battled the odds and prevailed. And the heady pleasure she had gotten from her first sale had been euphoric. She would never forget that phone call or the overwhelming feelings that had nearly choked her and rendered her speechless. Yes, if only she could paint again, she knew she would be able to get back to her old self.

She saw *him* just as she careened around a curve in the road. She was two miles from town, planning to hook up with highway 18 and take the river road straight into New Orleans. Too late, she realized she should have gone cross-country.

He wasn't hitchhiking, simply walking with purpose toward town. *I'll get the pickup in the morning* is what he'd told her last night. Why hadn't she remembered that until now?

Evidently hearing the car approach, he slowed his pace and glanced over his shoulder. Nicole cursed her luck, sped past him, then slammed on the brakes. Her flashy car did a little dance as it came to a screeching halt. She tried to remain calm as she glanced into the rearview mirror and watched him stroll to the passenger side, using that famous loose-limbed gait he appeared to have owned since birth.

Nicole took a deep breath and braced herself as he opened the door and climbed in. When he slammed the door shut, she winced and wished the four headache pills she'd taken before leaving the house would hurry up and corral the pounding behind her eyes. She managed to put the car into gear, and sailed off down the road. Out of the corner of her eye, she saw him roll his broad shoulders against the leather seat and stretch his long legs out in front of him.

His beat-up jeans and T-shirt hugged him shamefully, only serving to make her more nervous as she remembered how wonderful it had felt being pressed against all that hard muscle. His boots were dusty, his jaw unshaven. He looked great, his hair loose and shiny in the morning light.

He slanted her a look, and she jerked her eyes back to the road. She could feel his gaze drift slowly over her. The gallery she was going to was on Julie Street in the warehouse district. Nicole had dressed for the occasion in a straight skirt in orange sherbet and a silk tank in white. She hadn't felt up to fussing with her hair, but she'd managed to twist it into a stylish knot. And though her hands had been a bit shaky, she'd bravely attempted the five-step make-over regime she'd picked up from an old friend that promised a miracle in just ten minutes.

"Thought you'd be sleeping in today."

Nicole braced herself for the attack. "No. I'm going into

New Orleans today. And where are you off to this morning?'' she asked before she realized the question was a loaded one.

''To fetch the Dodge.''

He gave her another long look. Nicole gripped the steering wheel and tried to breathe more quietly. Keeping her eyes on the road, she said, ''I want to apologize for what happened last night. I wasn't myself. I was…''

''Drunk,'' he said bluntly, when words failed her.

''No. That's not exactly true. I was…I never meant to let things get out of hand. I was just trying—''

''To get Farrel Craig's taste out of your mouth. Yeah, I remember.''

His tone was sharp, harsh, the words ending the subject with finality. Nicole gave him a sidelong glance. Was his anger directed at her? She frowned, annoyed with the idea. Actually, he should share some of the blame. He was the one who had insisted on driving her home.

No. She couldn't blame him for what had happened last night. She had been the one to let her emotions lead her astray. She was the one who'd had too many glasses of wine. And in the end, she was the one who had asked him to kiss her.

No, she hadn't asked. She'd begged.

''Sleep all right?''

They were on the outskirts of town, passing Gilmore's Gas and Go. ''I did, yes,'' she lied. Actually she'd gotten sick not five minutes after he had stormed off the porch. She'd sat by the toilet for two hours before dragging herself to bed.

The town was still half asleep when she swung into the deserted parking lot at Pepper's Bar and Grill and pulled up next to the pickup. She left the car idling in the hope that he would get the hint she was in a hurry, but he didn't budge. Instead, he reached across the seat and slipped her dark sunglasses off her face. In slow motion, his arm slid along the back of her seat, bringing his body close, his face mere inches from hers. He drawled, "Let's have a look-see."

Nicole blinked her bloodshot eyes and prayed her makeup covered the dark circles outlining them.

"Wine's no good when you've got serious drinking to do, *cherie.* You feel all right?"

"Just a little headache," Nicole admitted. "I'll be fine."

He looked at her, his eyes searching hers. Finally he said, "That's what counts."

He gave her back her dark glasses, and Nicole gladly slipped them on. "Johnny, about last night—"

"If anyone was to blame, it was me," he said quickly. "I had the clear head, remember? I should be the one apologizing, only—" he offered her a lazy smile "—I've never been any good at saying I'm sorry if I'm not. Holding you felt real nice. It's been a long time, and I'd be lying if I said I wished it hadn't happened."

"But—"

"Thinking about it too much and trying to analyze it to hell isn't going to change anything. If you want to forget it happened, *cherie,* that's your right. Me, I don't intend to forget any part of it. In fact, I don't think I could even if I wanted to. You drive safe now, you hear?"

The gas gauge shouldn't have been sitting on empty. Johnny's first thought was that someone had siphoned the tank dry overnight, but as he drove into Gilmore's he knew better—they were waiting for him, just like old times.

Knowing he'd been set up, Johnny stepped from the pickup without the slightest hesitation. As in the old days, the three of them were wearing smug grins—Farrel standing in the middle with Clete on his left and Jack Oden on his right.

Johnny wasn't really surprised. He'd always known Farrel would bring a fight to him sooner or later, only he'd hoped for better odds. But he shouldn't have. Farrel had never been much of a fighter; he was always too worried about getting dirty and feeling pain.

No, it didn't look as if Farrel had changed his tactics. He still didn't know how to fight any other way than behind a couple of front-runners. The truth was, no one had taught him how to take pride in his own ability. He needed to win, and that was all that counted. But sooner or later a man had to lose.

Only, Farrel wouldn't lose today. The question wasn't *if* Johnny was going down, it was how soon. There was no denying he'd be kissing the dirt before this was over. No doubt in his mind at all.

Well, hell, nothing like a little discussion between enemies early in the morning to get a man's blood pumping and put his life into perspective, Johnny decided. Only, this time he wasn't a vulnerable kid anymore. He'd learned a few moves of his own.

He sent the cigarette he'd had pinched between his lips to the asphalt and crushed it out with his boot, then stepped away from the pickup. Henry's Dodge was in good condition, and he didn't like the idea of scraping the paint or putting a dent in it once the party got rocking.

With a five-star smile, Farrel pushed away from the wall of the gas station. He was wearing black jeans and a black T-shirt. "Kinda feels like old.times, don't it, Johnny? I've got you cornered, and there's nowhere to run." He gestured to his sidekicks, and they pulled wide, fanning out as if it were high noon at the O.K. Corral. "You remember the fun we used to have—you, me, Clete and Jack? It's like a reunion, don'tcha think?"

Johnny didn't answer, but he had to agree—it was exactly like old times. Except that Clete's body had gone to fat—about three hundred pounds' worth. And Jack looked like life had played a cruel joke on him—his red hair had gone completely gray and had thinned to a mere ten hairs on top of his head. His teenage pockmarked face had worsened, too, giving him several hellish scars on both cheeks and across his forehead. He looked meaner than ever and angry at the world, with plans on getting even that very minute.

"I think he's gonna run," Jack warned, cracking his knuckles. He turned his head and spat a stream of tobacco a good ten feet.

"He ain't gonna run," Clete assured. "Not *Swampy*. He's treed and he knows it. And you know what we do when we tree a coon, don'tcha, *Swampy?*"

"You girls plan on standing around sweet-talking me all day, or are we gonna get to it?"

Johnny's wisecrack had Clete jerking his crooked hat down farther over his ears and Jack snarling like a wild dog. But Farrel only chuckled. "All right, then, let's do it, Johnny."

The joke put the boys back in a better mood, and when they saw Farrel start to advance they followed his lead. Hands loose at his sides, Johnny watched as Clete started to circle left while Jack moved right.

Farrel hung back. But that was no surprise; he always moved in after the dust had settled.

It was after dark when Nicole wheeled into the driveway. Her arms loaded down with packages, she sprinted across the yard in the rain to reach the house. The day had gone better than she had ever imagined it could, considering the way it had started out. She had met Frank Medoro, the new gallery owner in New Orleans. He was maybe thirty-five, good-looking, and spoke with a refined French accent. Best of all, he had recognized her name and had even seen some of her work. Excited, she had accepted his lunch proposal, and before she had left the Palace Café on Canal Street, he had invited her to his summer exhibition in a few weeks.

"I'm so glad you're home," Clair said as she greeted Nicole at the door.

Nicole let Clair take her packages. "The French Market bag is for you." She pointed to the wrapped package. "That one's for Bick. It's some of those special cigars he likes from Dumar's. Is something wrong? You found my note this morning, didn't you? You knew I went to New Orleans, right?"

"Yes, we knew. I'm sorry about last night, honey. Dory felt bad about not being able to meet you. One of the ovens caught on fire at the bakery. You know how it is when you're in business for yourself. She appreciated the call you left on her answering machine this morning."

"I'll give her a call again tomorrow." When Clair's worried expression remained, Nicole realized there was something more. "Clair, what is it? Is it Gran?"

"No, Mae's fine. But something is wrong, honey. It's Johnny."

"Johnny? What's wrong with Johnny?"

"Mae's in the study. I'll let her tell you."

A wave of panic flooded Nicole's senses as she hurried past Clair. When she reached the study, she flung open the door. "Gran? What's happened to Johnny?"

Mae turned away from the French doors where she had been sitting in her wheelchair half the day. Her cheeks were tear-stained. "Nicki, dear, I'm so glad you're home. Johnny's gone. No one has seen him since last night, and I'm terribly worried."

Nicole immediately felt a rush of relief. "Don't be," she soothed. "I saw him this morning."

"You did? Was he all right?"

"He was fine." Nicole was determined to ease her grandmother's mind. Gran looked awful. She didn't want to detail her morning conversation with Johnny, but if she had to, she was willing.

"Did you talk to him? Did he say anything about what his plans were for today?"

"No. I just assumed he would be working." Nicole crossed the room, crouched in front of Mae and took her hand. "Don't worry, Gran. Johnny is more than capable of taking care of himself."

"I know. But I keep remembering what took place a few days ago on the road. If anything happens to that boy, I'll never forgive myself. It's my fault he's here, my fault for everything."

"Gran, you're not responsible. Yes, I know about the land deed and your paying the taxes. Johnny mentioned that, but you didn't make him draw his knife at Pepper's. Really, you're getting all worked up over nothing."

"Then where is he, Nicki?"

That was a good question, one Nicole couldn't answer. "Maybe he took the day off and went fishing," she offered.

"No, he wouldn't do that," Mae argued.

Nicole stood and walked to the French doors. Through the screen she could hear the active nightlife in the distant bayou. She scanned the woods beyond the road. It had stopped raining, and the air was ripe with the smell of magnolia blossoms. "Where are you, Johnny," she whispered. "Stop worrying Gran and show yourself."

She turned, wanting to ease Gran's mind, but she didn't know how. The only thing that would make her grandmother breathe easier would be Johnny walking through the door.

It was odd how he had wormed his way into their lives, she thought. He hadn't been there a week and already most everything that happened centered around him. Gran's mood hinged on whether he came to breakfast and showed up for supper. Clair's menus had been altered to satisfy Johnny's palate. Even Bick searched him out and tagged behind him like an awestruck admirer.

What was it about this man that had attracted the people in this household so easily? What was it about him that had attracted her?

Yes, she admitted she was attracted to him, only not in the way everyone else was. Her attraction was based on something more, something far more dangerous. She couldn't deny she'd had a wonderful time in New Orleans today, but Johnny hadn't been far from her thoughts. His dark, intense gaze—the one he had offered her before he'd climbed out of the car—had been with her all day. And then there was that burning kiss that hadn't stopped smoldering since he'd planted it on her lips last night.

Ironically, even his slow-moving style and lazy drawl made him more exciting than any other man she knew. She hadn't thought she would look at a man with a sense of desire ever again, but she'd been wrong. Until a few days ago, she had promised herself she would never allow another man into her life, but somehow she had.

"How was New Orleans?" Mae managed to ask.

"Hot and crowded. I met the owner of that new gallery. I'll tell you about it tomorrow." Nicole faced her grandmother. "Did you call Sheriff Tucker and report Johnny missing?"

"No. I was afraid to. I didn't want him thinking Johnny skipped town."

"Could he have?"

"No. Johnny's a good boy."

Nicole could hear the pride and love in her grandmother's raspy voice. It was clouded with emotion and worry, and her heart went out to her. "He'll turn up, Gran. He will."

"Bick's out searching for him. I've been hoping and praying. That boy walked out of my life once before, and now that I've got him back I don't want to lose him a second time. I failed him once, but not this time, Nicki. I won't let it happen this time."

"Failed him? What are you talking about?"

"I should have tried harder. Made him feel welcome here. I should have insisted."

"He knows you care about him. I'm sure he knew back then, too."

Mae let out a long, tired sigh. "I'm not so sure, Nicki. And it's something I've lived with for fifteen years."

Without warning, Clair swung the study door open and rushed into the room. "Bick found him," she nearly shouted. She looked at Nicole, then Mae. "He found him at the farmhouse. He's been beaten badly."

"Oh, dear Lord," Mae gasped.

"Beaten!" Nicole cried. "Why? How?"

"Bick didn't give me any details. He just said I should tell Mae that Johnny's at the boathouse. He said not to worry, but you know Bick. He never stutters unless he's riled good. And he was making a mess of his words."

"Nicki! Where are you going? Nicki!"

From the porch, Nicole shouted, "To the boathouse! I'll let you know how serious he is as soon as I can." Then she was off the porch and running toward the woods as fast as her sandals would allow.

By the time she made it to Belle, Nicole was panting and clutching her side. She didn't remember when her hair had slipped from its knot, but when she reached the boathouse it was hanging in her eyes and the gold clip was gone.

Inside, she met Bick coming down the stairs. "How is he?" she asked anxiously.

"They kn-knocked him around p-pretty good, Miss Nicki."

"Who are they?"

Bick shrugged as he moved past her. "He w-won't say. But to do damage like th-that, th-there had to be more than one walking on him at the s-same time. Whoever done it s-sure got more than one piece of him." Bick jerked his baseball cap lower on his head. "Don't l-look so worried. I-I'll fix him up best I c-can."

"You? Shouldn't we take him to the hospital?"

"He said no fuss."

"I don't care what he said," Nicole snapped. "This is no time to be stubborn."

"Well, you b-best talk to him. He said no doc."

"I'll handle it. You go back to the house and fill Gran in. Assure her that he'll be all right." Nicole paused. "He will be, won't he?"

"Oh, h-he'll make it," Bick guaranteed. "It's just gonna slow him d-down for a spell."

"He did tell you what happened, didn't he?"

"I know what happened," Bick declared. "H-he got beat."

Nicole sighed in exasperation. "Just explain it as best you can to ease Gran's mind. Tell her I plan on taking Johnny to a doctor as soon as possible."

"Good luck with that, Miss Nicki. You want me to head back here in a little while, after I talk to Mae?"

Nicole was losing patience. "No. If he doesn't agree to a doctor, he'll have to settle for me."

"You got any training in busted ribs?"

The color drained from Nicole's face. "Busted ribs?"

"My guess is two, maybe three."

As Bick headed back to the house to do as she asked, Nicole climbed the stairs and let herself into the room. She hadn't expected it to be so dark. Brought up short, she waited a minute while her eyes adjusted to the darkness.

"Bick, that you?"

The pain in his voice sent a spasm of fear through Nicole's entire body. She took a deep breath to calm her nerves and made her way farther into the room. "No, Johnny. It's me, Nicki."

Silence.

"Johnny?"

"Dammit, *cherie,* get the hell out of here."

"I'm not leaving." He was on the bed; she could see his shadowy figure. She stopped by the rocker and turned on the small lamp. "Oh, God!"

He was lying on his back, shirtless in a pair of faded jeans. His face was badly bruised; one eye, his good one, was blackened and completely swollen shut. His lower lip was split, and blood had dried in the corner of his mouth. He had a cut on his forehead, and his bare chest and stomach were a mass of dark ugly bruises. A three-inch cut started to the left of his navel and disappeared into the waistband of his jeans.

There were two empty whiskey bottles on the bed beside him.

Yes, he'd definitely been beaten. But amazingly enough, he still looked tough and resilient lying there sprawled the length of the bed.

Nicole marveled at his durability; at the same time she felt angry and sick over what had been done to him. She glanced at the empty bottles, sure the liquor had been used to ease his obvious discomfort.

She moved to the bed and eased down beside him.

"You need a doctor, Johnny. Bick thinks you have broken ribs.

"It looks worse than it is. I don't need anything but a day off." He offered her a half smile. "You think the boss lady will give it to me?"

Nicole studied his face. He was a little drunk, but not inebriated. "Let me call Dr. Jefferies. Please?"

"How was New Orleans?"

"I didn't come here to talk about what I did today. I've come to drive you to the hospital." She held out her hand to offer him help in getting up. He made no move to take it.

"Did you come by yourself?"

"Yes." Her nursing skills were limited, but if he wasn't going to go to the hospital, Nicole would be forced to use them. "Come on, let's go. You can't—"

"Shh. My head's pounding. Don't be a nagging wife."

Nicole clamped her mouth shut and glared at his battered face. "I wouldn't have to be if you would listen to reason."

"You look good," he drawled. "What I can see of you. So when are you going to start patching me up so I can feel your hands on me and think about something else besides how much I hurt?"

Instead of getting angry, Nicole went into the bathroom and quickly put together some supplies to clean his wounds. She found a small enamel pan beneath the sink and filled it with hot water, then collected several towels, antiseptic and a bottle of pain relievers from the medicine cabinet.

"You could have internal injuries," she scolded, returning to the bed. "I still think—"

"I'd know it, if I did. And I don't."

She'd have to take his word on that, Nicole decided,

because she couldn't very well carry him through the woods and put him in the car by herself. She got busy cleaning the cut on his forehead and washing the dried blood from his face. She tried not to think about his comment earlier, even though she knew he was conscious of her touching him.

She eyed the cut on his belly, hesitated as to whether she should unzip his jeans. When she glanced at him, she found he'd opened his eye and was watching her. "You can leave it if you want," he said.

"So you can get an infection?" She forced her hands to move. After she'd unsnapped his jeans, she slowly slid his zipper down halfway. Luckily, the cut wasn't deep and only moved past his waistband an inch. She dipped the cloth in water once more and began to remove the dirt carefully from the wound. "How did you get this?" she asked.

"Don't remember."

"Sure you do. Why won't you tell me?"

"Because it's not important."

She rinsed the cloth and went back to work. He sucked in his breath when the cloth brushed over the cut. "Sorry. I've never been any good at this kind of thing."

"You're doing fine."

"Well, it's the least I can do. After all, you took that sliver out of my foot, remember? And last night you rescued me from driving home intoxicated."

"But I was already rewarded for that."

Nicole was fully aware of the heat that had surfaced between them. He reached up and brushed her bangs out of her eyes so he could see her better. "Does remembering our kiss make you uncomfortable, *cherie?*"

"Yes. You make me uncomfortable," she admitted. "Especially when you look at me like you're looking at me now.'' She knocked her bangs back into place, then went back to work. After she'd put a bandage on his belly, she reached for one of two elastic wrap bandages she had brought from the bathroom. ''I'll help you sit up, then I'll wrap your ribs. I think that's all they would do at the hospital. That and X-ray them. Are you sure you don't want to go to the hospital?''

''No.'' He groaned as he struggled to sit up. Nicole quickly reached out and gripped his shoulders as he dropped his bare feet to the floor. Disgusted with his inability to handle the task on his own, he cursed crudely.

When he finally looked as if he was going to stay upright without falling over, Nicole kneeled between his legs. ''You'll need to tell me if this gets too tight.''

She could feel his heavy breathing on the side of her neck as she leaned forward and started wrapping his ribs as carefully as possible. Being this close to him only served to remind her of last night, and a little shudder went through her.

''You smell good,'' he drawled lazily, lowering his head so that his face brushed her hair. His cheek slowly moved against hers.

Nicole's hands stilled. ''Johnny, please don't.''

Ignoring her plea, he slipped his arms around her and locked her between his hard thighs. ''What did you do in New Orleans today? Bick said you were gone all day. Meet someone?''

''Actually, I did. A very nice man,'' she admitted.

His mouth brushed her ear, and Nicole sucked in her breath and closed her eyes. ''Want me to wipe the taste of him away?''

''It wasn't like that.''

She was treading in dangerous water again. Frightened, she jerked hard on the bandage.

"Ouch! What the hell was that for?"

"To remind you that I'm trying to be nice, and you're trying to take advantage of the situation." She finished the job quickly, then stood and went into the kitchen. When she returned, she offered him a glass of water along with four pain relievers. "Here. Your body is going to hate you in the morning, but at least this will get you through tonight. Tomorrow we'll move you to the house. It'll be easier to care for you there."

"The house? No way. I'll be fine right here."

"We'll talk about it tomorrow. For now, you need to get back in bed. Only—"

"Only what?"

She lowered her gaze, a solid lump forming in her throat.

He followed her interest. "If you're worried about getting me out of my pants, don't be. You can close your eyes and feel your way through it."

It amazed her how he could make jokes when he looked so awful. Still, Nicole didn't want any part of what they were discussing. "If you have enough strength to be a wise guy, then I imagine you can't be as bad off as I first thought. The pants are your problem."

That said, she busied herself rinsing the pan out at the sink. Luckily, by the time she returned, he had somehow gotten his jeans off and was back in bed. She picked up his discarded jeans from the floor and draped them over the foot of the bed. His eyes were closed, and she didn't say anything to him for fear he'd fallen asleep.

Bick came by and asked her if she wanted him to stay, or if there was anything she needed. She told him no, and that he should go and get some rest himself. In the morning they would move Johnny into the house. She suggested her room, since she didn't think climbing up and down stairs would do Johnny's ribs any good.

"Have Clair pack a few of my things and put them in my old room upstairs," she told him. "And tell Gran not to worry. Tell her Johnny hasn't lost his sense of humor. It's safe to say he's going to live."

Chapter 8

Johnny slowly climbed out of bed and pulled on his jeans. It had been three days since his run-in with Farrel and the boys. He could see out his blackened eye now, and it no longer hurt to take a breath, though he sucked air with more care than usual. He'd been staying in Nicole's bedroom at the house. He felt funny about it; making her move out hadn't been necessary.

All the fuss had actually embarrassed him. He had told the old lady and Nicole more than once that the boathouse was where he wanted to be. Yes, he looked like hell—that he hadn't debated. But he would mend whether he stayed at the boathouse or the big house. All he needed was time.

The process would be slow when it came to his ribs. He was sure a couple were busted, but he had denied it to the women, saying they were only bruised.

When the knock at the door came, Johnny wasn't surprised. A morning routine had been established, and about this time Nicole brought him breakfast in bed. Only, this morning she wasn't going to find him there.

Angry all over again that she continued to wait on him like a slave for hire after he'd told her time and again not to, he put on his best ugly face and nailed her with a look that said *I eat little blondes for breakfast* the minute she swung the door open and stepped inside. She ignored his exaggerated scowl from where she stood by the window, and carried the breakfast tray to the nightstand and set it down.

"Clair made pecan waffles," she announced. "She tells me they're one of your favorites."

"I'm getting out of here, today," Johnny told her.

She turned and looked at him where he stood soaking up the morning sunshine. "I think that's an excellent idea. Maybe it'll improve your mood. I'll have Bick come by and take you for a walk."

He turned back to the window. "I'm not some damn dog. I don't need to be 'taken' anywhere. My legs work just fine. I don't need a nurse any longer, either, so consider yourself fired."

"Has the maid service been that awful? What, the sheets not crisp enough, sir? Or is it the food? Clair will be crushed to hear you don't like her waffles."

She was mocking him, and he had a mind to...what? He turned away from the window, his eyes fully on her molded curves straining the confines of her slippery white shift. What she'd said was anything but the truth. Actually, the service had been the best he'd ever had. He couldn't remember anybody ever bringing him hot food and worrying about crisp sheets. But it was something he could get used to real fast if he let himself. Only he wasn't going to. As soon as his parole was over, he was on his way out of Common for good.

"What I'm saying is all of you have better things to do. I'm just the hired help, remember?"

She shrugged, then headed for the door, stopping before she opened it. "Can I get you anything from town?"

"Like what, a color book?"

She laughed. "I was thinking more on the lines of a magazine or a book, but if you have your heart set on coloring…"

So that's why she was dressed up: she was going into town. He gave her another slow head-to-toe, stopping when he spied her pink toenails. Her white sandals showed off her slender feet and narrow ankles. Her knees were a favorite with him. But best of all, he liked her naughty long bangs, and the way they half hid her beautiful blue eyes. "What are you going to do in town?"

"Gran's garden club meets today. I told her I would drive her."

"Come here."

"What?"

"You heard me."

"No." She shook her head. "I'll bring you food, a color book from town if that's what you want. But you've been scowling at me since I came through the door. In fact, you've been downright mean for days. I'll keep my distance, thank you."

Johnny dragged a hand through his hair, then started toward her. "So why have you been putting up with me if I've been such a bastard?"

"Because it makes Gran happy."

He'd hoped for a different answer. "You won't have to too much longer."

"Shall I start celebrating now or after I buy the party balloons?"

Johnny stopped a foot away from her. "Since I've taken your bed, how do you like sleeping upstairs?"

"I was only using this room until Gran's ankle got better. Actually, I like the room upstairs." She checked her watch. "I've got to go. Clair should have Gran ready by now, and your breakfast is getting cold."

She turned to leave, but Johnny reached out and caught her hand. "When I talked to Mae yesterday, she said she didn't think you had been sleeping very well." He brushed his thumb beneath her right eye. "Dark shadows, *cherie*. Still pacing late at night?"

"Mae? Since when did you start calling Gran anything but 'old lady'?"

"Since yesterday," Johnny admitted. "She asked me to do her a favor. Made me promise before she told me what it was. I was conned before I knew it."

She smiled, and Johnny was reminded of how much he liked her mouth, of how soft and sweet it was. Of how many times in the past three days he'd wanted to drag her down on the bed and kiss her.

"So, tell me why you don't sleep."

"I'm sleeping fine. It just takes me a little time to unwind." She slipped her hand out of his.

"And why is that?"

"There are millions of insomniacs out there."

"Good answer, but I don't think you're one of them."

"Let's change the subject. Is this going to get to be a habit? Are you going to get beat up weekly or monthly?"

"That depends."

"On Farrel?"

Johnny had never given any names. But the situation being what it was, he supposed Farrel was everyone's logical choice. "Has he confessed to something I should know about?"

"I don't think so. Should he?"

Johnny shrugged guardedly, knowing she was trying to get him to falter.

"You've had plenty of opportunity to tell me what happened. I've asked often enough," she prompted. "I'm beginning to wonder if what Bick said isn't closer to the truth.''

"Oh?" Johnny shifted his stance, his hands finding his back pockets. "And that would be…?"

"Bick says there was more than one. He said the only way anyone would get the jump on you was if you were outnumbered or caught by surprise."

"Sounds like Bick talks too much and shouldn't be scaring little girls with such tall tales."

"Oh, he wasn't telling me," she announced. "He was talking to Gran. I was eavesdropping. Was he right?"

Again Johnny didn't answer. The truth was, he didn't want Nicole, or anyone else at Oakhaven, involved in his problems. Choosing sides would be dangerous for her, especially if she chose his.

He had asked her to give him a chance days ago, but now he wasn't so sure that had been a good idea. He didn't want to put Nicole in an awkward position—not when she was intending to make Common her home.

"Not giving up their names doesn't make this go away," she continued. "If anything, it's just letting those men off the hook so they can do it again. And next time—"

A sudden rap at the door cut Nicole off. "Nicki?" It was Clair. "Pearl Lavel called for a ride to the church. Mae says you better hurry along. Pearl will huff like a steam engine the entire way if she's late."

"You better go," Johnny said.

She glanced at his breakfast tray. "I hope the food isn't too cold."

"It'll be fine," he assured.

"If you're feeling cooped up and restless, maybe you could spend some time in the study figuring out renovation costs. Gran's been after me to get some totals for her, but I'm not very good with figures. I hear you are, though."

When Johnny made no comment, she continued, "I don't expect you to do it for nothing. The hours would be added to your paycheck."

"I wasn't thinking about that," he told her. "I'll sit down this afternoon and see what I come up with."

"Nicki?" Clair was again in the hall. "I'm putting Mae in the car."

"Bring me back some cigarettes, would you?" Johnny asked. "I ran out last night and—"

"I think a color book would be healthier. Maybe this would be a good time to quit blowing smoke."

Johnny rested his shoulder against the wall and studied her bloodshot eyes. "I'll quit the day you go to bed before midnight and sleep straight through the night. Deal?"

"You're offering that deal because you think I can't do it."

"No." Johnny gave up a lazy smile. "Call it incentive. Wouldn't you like the satisfaction of seeing me suffer from withdrawal?"

"It does have a certain appeal. Especially since you've been such a nightmare of a patient." She opened the door and stepped into the hall.

"Cherie?"

"Yes?"

"Keep your opinions about this mess to yourself while you're in town, would you. These folks are funny. They might not always like everything their own do, but if an outsider starts riling them up they usually band together like wolves. You and Mae don't need to be caught in the middle of the war against me."

"It's called Red Flame." Daisi struck a pose, her long fingernails wiggling against her cheek.

"They look stunning," Nicole complimented, noting the

color was a perfect match to Daisi's red-striped maternity dress.

"I love red." Daisi giggled, then glanced appreciatively at Nicole's slender figure. "I wish I was that thin, but even before I got pregnant I didn't look like that. God, you must eat practically nothin'."

"I'm just naturally thin, I guess," Nicole admitted.

Daisi wrinkled up her button nose. "I hate that line, but I won't hold it against you. I'll be the first to admit bein' pregnant doesn't do a woman's figure any favors, but it sure makes my nails grow."

Nicole's gaze shifted to Daisi's swollen stomach. She tried not to dwell on the fact that there was a baby nestled inside, growing and gaining weight. A healthy baby. It was so hard getting past the emptiness, the deep ache that never seemed to go away for very long. The guilt.

"It was real nice of you to give Mama a ride to the church."

Nicole kept her smile fixed. Pearl Lavel was not one of her favorite people. Daisi's mother had huffed and sniffed and evil-eyed the back of her head the entire way from her house on Willow Street through the short five blocks to the Saint and Savior Baptist Church. That the woman had a daughter as nice as Daisi was a God-given miracle.

"How did you know I drove her?" Nicole asked.

"One thing you'll get used to around here is that everybody knows everybody else's business. Just like what happened to Johnny. We all knew about that by breakfast the next mornin'."

"And just what version did you hear?" Nicole knew she shouldn't have said anything. Johnny had warned her to keep her opinions to herself, but maybe Daisi knew something that could be helpful.

"What are you askin', Nicki?"

"Johnny hasn't given out any names. Do you have any?"

"Sure. I've got three. Woody said Clete Gilmore is walkin' around town with a limp and two teeth missin'. And I know Jack Oden has a broken jaw 'cause I saw him in the clinic the other day when I went for my checkup. I haven't seen Farrel's broken nose, but I've heard it's worse than the last one Johnny gave him six months ago."

Nicole listened while Daisi spilled every piece of gossip she'd heard on the subject. She didn't say anything, just listened, thinking all the time that Bick had been right—they'd stacked the odds against Johnny from the moment he climbed out of the pickup at the gas station. And the way Daisi talked, it was nothing new.

"I heard Johnny's been flat on his back," Daisi continued. "Is he gettin' better?"

"He's up," Nicole informed her. "Do you know why it happened?"

Daisi leaned forward, lowering her voice. "There doesn't have to be a reason for Farrel to go after Johnny. They've always hated each other."

"Are you sure? I don't think Johnny lies awake nights trying to figure out ways to rearrange Farrel's face."

"Maybe not, but they've always fought."

"Did you know Johnny very well in the old days?"

"We went to school together." Daisi grinned. "I had a bad crush on him when I was in the sixth grade. But then, I think most of the girls in town did. Only, none of them would have wanted to admit it. It wasn't cool to like the poor boy in town, if you know what I mean. And the Bernard family—they were the poorest around." Daisi glanced down the hall. "You can go back and see Sheriff Tucker. He don't have nobody back there with him."

"Thanks." Nicole walked down the hall and stopped at

the first door she came to. After taking a deep breath, she knocked.

"Come in."

"Sheriff Tucker?"

He looked up from his desk as Nicole walked in and closed the door. "Miss Chapman, what a surprise."

"Is it?" She took a seat in front of his desk.

He pointed to his coffee cup. "Can I offer you some?"

"Thank you, no." Nicole gazed around the dingy room, her gaze falling on the news clippings that covered the wall behind his desk. Some of them were yellow with age, making them look twenty years old or more.

Sheriff Tucker sat back in his chair and folded his arms over his thick chest. "So what can I do for you, Miss Chapman?"

"I'm sure you're aware that three days ago Johnny Bernard was badly beaten. I was wondering what you're planning on doing about it."

"The way it works here, little lady, is if there's been a crime committed, I get involved. If there's no proof of one, I don't. And no one has come forward and pressed any charges. My take on the matter is that Johnny and Farrel went a few rounds at Gilmore's. It isn't the first time, and I'm afraid it won't be the last. I don't mind telling you that's why I didn't think too much of this here deal the parole board set up. Johnny back in Common just doesn't make good sense. Actually, I'm giving him the benefit of the doubt in this instance by ignoring what happened."

"Meaning?"

"Fighting is a parole violation, Miss Chapman." The sheriff mopped his brow. "I could have him sent back to Angola if I wanted to."

"But he was a victim," Nicole blurted out.

"Johnny Bernard, a victim? Now that would be a first. I've seen the boy in action."

"He was defending himself," Nicole pointed out.

"You obviously haven't seen Clete and Jack. Farrel won't be winning no prize with his looks for some time, either."

"You're saying Johnny defended himself too well!" Nicole couldn't believe what she was hearing.

"No judge in his right mind would look at Johnny's rap sheet and call that fight one-sided, the deck stacked or not. Johnny got a piece of all three of them boys—a big piece."

"Johnny did not start that fight. He was only acting in self-defense. A man would have to be stupid to pick a fight with three men all at the same time. And from what I've seen, Johnny Bernard is far from stupid."

"You don't have to convince me of that, little lady. No one said Johnny isn't smart. Still, if I pursue this thing, it won't go well for him. Now, you may not like hearing that, but it's the truth. I think leaving it alone would be for the best."

"So there's no recourse?"

"Not at this time."

"And if it happens again?"

"Like I said, Johnny's on parole. He's supposed to be keeping his nose clean. The truth is, Miss Chapman, he's been in trouble most of his life. I think the first time he slept over in my jail was age nine. It's true, some of the things that happened weren't always his fault, but most of the time they were."

He gave her a long look, as if seeing her anew. "The folks in town, frankly, got their bellies full of him years ago. They aren't feeling too charitable where he's concerned, and that's their right. We're all trying to do the best we can around here. Honestly, I'll be happy when the summer's over and Johnny clears out."

"I called Johnny's parole agent and explained the situation,'' Nicole announced matter-of-factly. ''He said he was going to call you.''

The sheriff's blue eyes narrowed dramatically. It was the first time he'd shown any emotion since Nicole had entered the room. ''You seem awfully interested in sticking your pretty nose in Johnny Bernard's business, missy. Does he know?''

''Actually, no, he doesn't. But I imagine with the way the gossip in this town flies, he will soon enough.''

''You can bet on it. In the meantime, I suggest you back off. We're not ignorant around here. We don't need to be told what to think, or how to do our jobs.''

''I have no desire to take over your job, Sheriff Tucker. But Oakhaven has a lot riding on Johnny Bernard's health and his ability to work.'' Nicole stood. ''I apologize if I've offended you. I just wanted you to know that I'm not any more ignorant than you are, and if Johnny Bernard is flat on his back in bed more than he is on his feet, I'm going to be damn mad. My father was a lawyer, and if I need legal advice, I know one of his associates would be happy to give it to me. Have a nice day, Sheriff Tucker.''

''Is that what you wanted, *cherie?*'' Johnny asked that night as he slowly entered the study to find her sitting at the desk going over the figures he'd worked on that afternoon.

Nicole glanced up, surprised that she hadn't heard him enter the room, and even more surprised at how well he was moving. ''You did all this in one afternoon?''

''A few hours.''

''That's amazing.''

He smiled, then stepped through the door and closed it behind him. Holding onto his smile, he moved slowly across the room and rounded the desk. Leaning over her shoulder, he began to point out the additions he'd made on repairs and the cost of each. "The kitchen floor is soft," he said. "It'll need a new underlayment. And you'll need to decide if you want another wood floor laid down or linoleum."

"Wood."

"It'll cost more."

"But it would look better, don't you think?"

"Yes."

"Then if Gran says yes, it's all settled."

"I found several ceiling cracks in the upstairs rooms," he told her. "I added those repairs to the list, and the material to fix them, too."

He was so close, Nicole could feel his warm breath on her neck. One of his big hands rested on the desk, and the size of his arm was twice that of hers. She closed her eyes for a moment and tried not to think about what it felt like being in those powerful arms.

She gazed up at him. "You really are a carpenter, then? It's what you want to do with your life?"

He arched his dark brows as he looked down at her. "Right now Oakhaven needs a carpenter, so I guess that's what I'll be."

"And if we need a plumber?"

"Then I'd go find a wrench," he drawled.

And if I needed a lover? Nicole would never let him know what she was thinking, but since the kiss on the porch she had been thinking about it more and more. It was crazy—insane, in fact—yet she couldn't stop thinking about what it would be like with him.

They stared at each other for a moment. Nicole felt her heart skip a beat. She wet her lips, her gaze drifting over his face, inspecting him slowly. The cut on his forehead was no longer an angry red gash, and his black eye had faded. He certainly had a tolerance for pain, she thought.

Nicole envied that about him. She wished she could

store her pain in a neat little box in the back of her head and open it only when she needed a reality check. Instead she was haunted by it daily, forced into reliving it nightly.

"What are you looking at, *cherie?* What are you thinking?"

Nicole realized she'd been caught staring and musing. "I— You didn't overdo today, did you? Clair told me you went for a walk and that you went alone."

"You worry too much."

He really did look fine in more ways than one, she decided. None of what had happened to him had diminished his sex appeal. He was still affecting her breathing, still making her nervous. Still making her yearn for things she would be better off without.

Nicole shoved the chair to one side and stepped around him. She walked to the French doors and gazed outside. It was another sweltering night, the air heavy, filled with the scent of magnolia blossoms. She'd changed back into a pair of cutoffs and a yellow T-shirt the minute she'd gotten back from town. Her feet were bare. "I've been concerned with the amount of money Gran will need for the restorations. I wish there was some way to recoup the expense."

"Want one?"

His quick reply surprised her, and Nicole turned to look at him. "You have an idea?"

"Why not put cane back in the fields? That way, Mae's savings would stay intact. And Oakhaven stands on its own feet again. It's a profitable business."

The idea had never occurred to Nicole. "A sugar plantation, like when Grandpa Henry was alive?"

"Why not? Griffin Black is making money at it. Why not us?"

Us. He'd said *us.* Nicole's heart started to pound. "But

I don't know anything about running a sugarcane plantation. I don't even know that I want to.''

"It's just a thought. I could look into it, at least, if you'd
like. It'll be a pile of work, and this first year all we'd do
is get the fields in shape. But by next spring everything
would be ready to go. Before I leave I could check out
who might be interested in working for you. That way,
they'd be lined up for next spring.''

When I leave. To hide her disappointment, Nicole
quickly turned to gaze outside. Funny how unexpectedly
things change, she thought. A week ago all she wanted
was Johnny Bernard out of their lives. But now… Now
she couldn't imagine him gone. Suddenly she was angry.
Angry that he had disrupted her life in the first place. Angry that she had let him.

She faced him. "It wouldn't work. Not without a foreman to keep it all running smoothly. No, forget it. I'll get
the money another way.''

"At least let me check—''

"I said no!''

He slanted her a puzzled look. "What's wrong, *cherie?*
A minute ago you acted like the idea was worth checking
out.''

"I was being polite.''

He started toward her. He looked a little angry, or
maybe disappointed. When he finally stopped, he was so
close that Nicole could see his pulse throbbing at the base
of his throat. So close, she could smell his musky male
scent. She took a step back and felt the window against
her spine. "Let's just drop it.''

She turned her head to avoid his eyes, but he reached
out, cupped her chin and turned her face back to his. "Let
me help you.''

"Me? How can you help me when you can't even help
yourself? Half the town hates you, and Sheriff Tucker isn't

going to do a damn thing about those men who—'' Nicole knew in that brief second she'd said too much.

''You talked to Tuck today?'' He was frowning.

''Yes.''

''Where?''

''At his office.''

''You went to see Tuck after I told you to keep out of this?'' He released her chin. ''Why?''

''Gran and I have a stake in your well-being. If you can't work—'' She didn't go on. He was glaring at her, so angry he was clenching his teeth.

''Don't worry, I'll make sure I get the work done,'' he told her.

''That's not what I meant. I only—''

She clamped her mouth shut as he turned and headed for the door. After swinging the door open, he turned back to look at her. ''I warned you to keep your opinions to yourself. If you make enemies in this town, *cherie,* you'll have them for the rest of your life. Take it from someone who knows.''

''I'm not afraid of the people in this town,'' Nicole snapped, feeling defensive.

''Well, you should be. These people are a crazy bunch, some more than others. But if they decide not to like you, you won't have a chance in hell of changing their minds later.''

''And what would make them not like me? Speaking out on your behalf? Facing Sheriff Tucker and telling him I think Farrel Craig and his 'boys' were out of line and should be arrested for assault?''

''Dammit, *cherie,* do you have any idea what you've done?''

''Don't tell me, I've just been condemned.'' Nicole

clutched her throat as if someone had ahold of it and was choking the life out of her. "Will they beat me up, too?"

Johnny's answer to her theatrics was dead serious and final. "If anyone lays a hand on you, I'll kill them."

Chapter 9

Two days later Johnny moved back to the boathouse and found a rat snake nailed to the front door. He removed it, tossed it in the bayou for fish bait, then went up to his room. He was getting tired of the harassment. Still, there was more than one reason to keep his cool. There were too many people depending on him right now.

Feeling surly, he scanned the small apartment, found it unchanged, then headed back outside. On the dock, he untied the boat and climbed in, ready to spend Sunday afternoon by himself. He'd had enough of Mae's fussing and Clair's oversize meals. And he'd played so many hands of cards with Bick, the man had nearly lost his entire stash of White Horse.

Mostly, he'd had enough of Nicole and her newfound silence. She hadn't spoken to him since the night they'd fought. Of course, he hadn't tried to speak to her, either. He was still mad as hell at her for deliberately going against his wishes.

The afternoon heat had steadily climbed into the nineties. Johnny stripped off his T-shirt and tossed it in the bottom of the boat, then picked up his pole and thrust it deep into the water. Giving a solid push, the boat surged forward, cutting through a thick patch of spider lilies and pickerel weeds.

He closed his eyes briefly as the familiar bond he shared with Belle wrapped its magical fingers around him, and for a moment he was a kid again, exploring the narrow channels leading everywhere and nowhere. He'd gotten lost a hundred times as a small boy, but eventually he'd learned every secret channel and switchback Belle owned. He'd even braved the black bog long before he'd known it was the nesting ground for monster alligators like old One Eye.

The sky was clear, and there was just enough breeze to keep the heat moving. The bayou branched off in a maze of tiny channels. Johnny maneuvered around the cypress knees, chose the hidden gate most often missed, and in an instant disappeared through a veil of Spanish moss.

Around the next bend stood the old farmhouse. He pulled the boat into the shoreline and tied it to an old post left over from what had once been a dock. Holding his ribs, he hiked the overgrown path, stopping when he'd made it to the top of the hill.

Funny how, standing there, so many memories rushed back to him. The strongest were the Sunday afternoons he'd spent with his mother and father on the hillside. He closed his eyes, remembering how they used to lie side by side and look at the sky. How they would take turns telling each other made-up stories. Once they'd gotten talked out, they would doze off, holding hands.

His family had been beggar-poor, Johnny admitted, but what they had shared so briefly had been worth gold. They had loved one another honestly and completely. God, how they had loved one another.

He took a deep breath, then eased down on the hillside to sprawl in the tall grass. The sun felt good on his face, and he let go of the tension that had been keeping him restless the past few days. After a time he turned his hands palm-side up and pretended *they* were once again beside him holding his hands. He took a deep breath and let it out slowly, allowed the sun's rays to seep into his bones, and damn if he didn't fall asleep just the way he'd done back when he was a kid.

Only, it wasn't his mother's voice jarring him awake an hour later. It was Nicole's.

"Johnny?"

"Mmm..."

"Are you all right?"

Her sweet voice sent pure desire snaking through Johnny's blood. Through half-open eyes, he watched her sink to her knees in the fragrant grass a foot away. After noticing she had on those too-short jean cutoffs again and a skimpy red T-shirt, he reminded himself he was still angry with her, and she with him.

"Johnny, wake up."

"I'm awake. I heard your car a mile away," he lied, rolling slowly to his side and raising up on one elbow to rest his head in his hand. His booted feet, he crossed at the ankles. "So we're talking again, is that it?"

"You walked out on me, remember?"

"With good reason."

She rolled sideways onto one hip and tucked her feet close. "I'm not going to say I'm sorry, because I'm not. You told me if you're not sorry, you shouldn't say it. So it goes for me, too."

Hearing his words thrown back at him made him frown. "Sometimes I should keep my mouth shut," he grumbled.

She smiled, then gazed at the farmhouse. "Are you going to fix it up?"

"The house? Hell, no. There's no point. It needs to be leveled."

She shoved a loose strand of hair behind her ear, and directed her interest to the bayou. "It's beautiful here. Belle is picture perfect."

The bayou was beautiful, Johnny agreed silently. But not as beautiful, nor as perfect as the woman sitting next to him. He couldn't deny how much he enjoyed looking at her. How much he liked being close enough to smell her womanly scent. She was driving him crazy, making him want her more and more with each passing day. It was ironic how one small woman could do so much damage to his insides in such a short amount of time.

Frustrated, feeling suddenly reckless, he reached out and grabbed Nicole's ankle, jerking her off balance and onto her back.

"Johnny! What are you doing?"

She tried to shake off his hand, but he hung on while he got to his knees. Flattening out his hands on either side of her tiny waist, he effectively pinned her to the ground. "So you like me, is that it?"

"What! Are you crazy?"

Grinning, he said, "Why else would you pay a visit to Tuck? Don't be shy, *cherie*. You can admit it to me. It'll be our secret."

A defiant gleam sharpened her blue eyes. "Me, like you? An arrogant ex-marine, ex-con, ex-who knows what else. I don't think so, Johnny Bernard. Now get off me and let me up."

"I've caught you staring," he goaded.

"Neanderthals are rare in California," she reasoned. Johnny hooted.

She scowled at him. "It's really nothing to be proud of. Or don't you know what a Neanderthal is?"

"So are you interested in kissing this Neanderthal again?"

She went still. A warm flush darkened her cheeks, while at the same time she defiantly answered, "No."

Johnny leaned closer, drinking in the scent of her. "I think you're lying. I think that's why you came looking for me."

"The afternoon sun has cooked your brain," she insisted, squirming beneath him and pushing gently on his chest. "Let me up."

Johnny shook his head, liking her hands on him. "How about we strike a bargain?"

"No." She shoved a little harder.

"Ouch!" Johnny rolled off her onto his side and clutched his ribs, while Nicole scrambled to her feet. "It serves you right. I— Oh, God!" She dropped to her knees beside him. "I didn't mean to— I'm sorry, all right?"

"So she says after she drives my busted ribs into my lungs."

"Busted? They're busted?"

He heard her suck in her breath, and opened his eyes to see her looking worried and afraid. "Hey, I was just kidding."

"No, you weren't. You've known all along, haven't you?"

Johnny sat up slowly. "They're mending fine. You like to fish?"

She wrinkled up her nose. "Not really."

"Boat rides?"

"Sometimes," she said cautiously.

Johnny glanced up at the blue sky overhead. "Great day for a boat ride."

"Are you asking me to take a boat ride with you, Johnny Bernard?"

She cocked her head to one side. Johnny relaxed, enjoying her smile and her shapely curves accented in her well-fitting cutoffs. "Yes, mama, I guess I am," he drawled. "I'll show you a side of Belle that's rarely seen. Cypress trunks eight feet across."

"There isn't such a thing," she challenged.

Johnny stood and headed down the hillside to the bayou. "If I'm lying," he called over his shoulder, "I'll work the next week for no pay."

By the time he reached the boat, Nicole was trailing him. Grinning to himself, Johnny helped her into the boat, warning her to watch her step, then climbed in after her. Knees bent, his balance cemented in the boat, he deftly maneuvered them away from the grassy bank with the long push-pole, then traded the pole for a paddle and sat down.

In the blink of an eye, the shoreline vanished, as Johnny sent them deeper into the swamp where the sun wasn't able to follow. Giant cypress—their massive, twisted trunks submerged in the brackish water—closed in around them, crowding the narrow channel, some stretching eight feet across at the base, just like he'd said.

An hour passed. The scenery turned wilder, more remote. He pointed to an alligator gliding along the muddy bank. "Be a good girl, *cherie,* and keep your hands in the boat."

She did as she was told, inching her tiny backside into the middle of the boat.

They skimmed over a carpet of water lilies so thick it could easily have been mistaken for solid land. "What did you do in L.A.?" Johnny asked, maneuvering them around a cypress knee.

"Does it matter?"

He slanted her a curious glance, detecting a note of challenge in her tone. "Virgil couldn't remember what kind of work you were doing there."

"Virgil?"

"Yeah, I asked him what he knew about you that first day after our phone conversation. I wanted to find out about the woman who was bent on firing me without even laying eyes on me."

"I didn't need to see you to know you were trouble," she told him.

"Still think so?"

"Yes." She paused, then softly said, "No."

"So who's Nik Kelly?"

She'd been enjoying the scenery. Suddenly, she stopped and looked his way. "Are we playing twenty questions?"

"Something like that." Johnny grinned. "So, who's Old Nik? The guy sure has made an impression on somebody around here. There're paintings everywhere by him. One in every room. Mae even insisted I hang one at the boathouse."

"She did, did she? Do you like the painting?"

Johnny liked the painting very much, but if the artist turned out to be a close friend of Nicole's, he wasn't so sure he'd like it for much longer. He said, "It's all right."

"Just all right? Then you're not interested in art?"

"I don't know much about it," Johnny admitted.

"Most people don't. But it's not the knowing that's important. It's whether you like what you see or not. Or maybe it's not even about that. If it makes you give it a second look, makes you stop and think for just a second, then it worked." She ran a hand quickly through her hair, sending it away from her face, only to have her long bangs fall back into her eyes. "Actually, *Old* Nik lives right here in Common. Would you like me to introduce you sometime?"

That the guy lived in Common surprised Johnny. Still,

he shook his head. "No, thanks. I don't think we'd have much to talk about."

"That's too bad. I think *she'd* enjoy showing off her collection of paintings to you."

Johnny's brows knit quizzically. "She?"

Suddenly Nicole extended her hand the small distance that separated them in the boat. "Johnny Bernard, meet Old Nik. The paintings are mine."

She had completely taken him by surprise. "You're the artist?"

Enjoying the trick she'd played on him, an impish smile parted her irresistible lips. Then, like a naughty child, she giggled with delight. It was the prettiest sound Johnny had ever heard. "I really had you going," she boasted proudly. "You should see your face."

Johnny shook his head, finally giving up a grin. "Why Kelly?"

"That was my mother's name. Alice Kelly. Everyone called my father Nik instead of Nicholas. I just put the two together," she explained.

Johnny glanced at the wilderness surrounding them, the gnarled trees, all the shades of color that made up the landscape. "It takes a special talent to make all this come alive with a brush and a bunch of wet, slippery paint."

She considered what he'd said. "I never thought of it quite that way, but I suppose it does."

He looked back at her. "I'm impressed."

"I'm flattered that you are," she admitted. "I've been selling in a gallery in L.A. for about four years. And it looks like I might be doing the same in a gallery in New Orleans if things work out. I've considered turning the attic into a studio. Actually, it was Gran's idea."

She stopped herself from going on. Johnny noted that the animation had drained from her face and that she now looked a little ill at ease. "Fixing the space so it works for you would be no problem. All you have to do is tell me what you want.''

She allowed a small smile. ''That's nice of you to offer. Maybe I'll take you up on it a little later. After the more important things at Oakhaven get done. I told Gran I was taking the summer off, so there's no rush.'' She batted away an irksome fly. ''My parents never liked the idea of my being an artist,'' she confessed. ''They said no one would pay me to paint pretty pictures, and I should go to law school so I could become a partner in my father's law firm.''

''Did they eventually understand?''

''Not really. I always wanted their approval, for them to see me as a success. I guess all kids do. Now, hopefully a little wiser, I think what matters most is how you see yourself. If I had children I would…I'd try to teach them that. Try to let them be whoever they need to be, not what I need them to be.''

''Sounds like your kids are going to be lucky having you for a mom.'' His comment made her look off into the bayou, her face as solemn as Johnny had ever seen it. ''Sorry, did I say something wrong?''

''No, you didn't. I haven't been around kids much. And I never had a lot of friends.'' She looked back at him. ''You were an only child, too, right?''

''Yeah. And you already know my status with friends.''

Aware that her mood had darkened, Johnny was curious why, but he didn't think asking would be wise. This was the most Nicole had talked to him since they'd met, and he wasn't ready to squelch it by getting nosey. She had a right to her past, just like he did. Though he couldn't deny that he was eager to know how *Chad* fit in—and why, when nighttime came, she got as restless as a cat.

''I'm boring you,'' she said suddenly. ''This all must sound ridiculous to you. First I tell you I'm an artist, then

I start getting philosophical. I must sound like a complete idiot.'' She looked away, embarrassed.

"No, don't do that," Johnny drawled, reaching out to turn her face back to look at him. "Don't be embarrassed, *cherie*. Not with me. Never with me."

The words hung between them. They stared at each other while a chorus of crickets trilled. Then an alligator's low growl echoed through the channel, sending several birds into flight.

"I don't usually talk so much," she said, still looking embarrassed. "How about if you talk for a while."

Johnny dropped his hand from her cheek. "I've never been much of a talker, either," he admitted.

"Well, since I told you something about me, I think it's only fair you share something with me. One of your secrets.''

"Secrets? I don't have any secrets," he told her. "I'm an open book.''

She laughed richly. "Liar. A secret," she insisted. Then with more care and in a sultry, quiet voice. "One no one else knows.''

The intimate request fell into the silence. It was followed by the two of them sharing another long look.

Finally, Johnny said, "Something no one else knows, hmm…'' He scratched his chin. "How about I show you, instead?''

"I knew it!'' Her eyes lit up like those of an anxious child. "You have buried treasure in the swamp?'' she speculated. "You buried it long ago and now you've come back to dig it up.''

Moments ago they had shared a special heat-filled look; now they were sharing laughter. Johnny couldn't remember when he had really laughed with a woman, when he had felt this damn good.

It would take twenty minutes to travel to the *secret*

Johnny had decided to share with Nicole. Once their laughter died out, he reminded her again to keep her hands in the boat, then steered them into another hidden channel and headed north. North into the black bog.

Deeper…deeper still, they slipped through a watery maze so remote and overgrown, it was like stepping back in time to a place no human had ever traveled. Only, there were a few who had braved the bog. Once, Johnny had tried to outrun the sheriff by way of the bog, only to be caught and arrested for vandalizing the Saint and Savior Baptist Church. He hadn't been responsible for the broken windows, but he had paid for them nonetheless.

The boat cut soundlessly through the water while egrets and cranes watched from their nests—as did the white ibises, and the shy night herons. An abundance of bofin, spotted gar, crayfish and bullfrogs went about their business in the unseen depths beneath.

Nicole's artist's eye absorbed everything as Johnny pointed, naming various animals one by one—a sleeping barred owl overhead, a red-eyed slider that had come alongside the boat, a tree lizard as red as a brilliant sunset. She seemed genuinely fascinated, and soon began asking questions—questions Johnny liked knowing the answers to. He liked the way she seemed openly impressed with what he knew, and it served to prompt more conversation between them.

He saw the king snake hanging in a tree long before Nicole did. It wasn't poisonous, but he pointed it out, anyway. "Harmless," he assured, maneuvering the boat away from it to ease Nicole's mind.

She nodded, then offered him that impish smile he was fast growing fond of. "Harmless? Like you?"

"Yeah, just like me." He grinned, steering the boat toward a narrow strip of land. He stood, then leaped onto a spongy green carpet, watching Nicole's eyes grow wide as the ground beneath him moved. It sank away slowly, bobbed, then stabilized somewhat.

"Johnny! That's not land!" she warned. "Hurry, get back in the boat!"

Her concern was touching. He said, "Easy, *cherie*. It's fen. Moving land." He held out his hand. "Come on."

"Are you crazy? I've heard stories about people thinking they were safe out here, then they disappear and never come back. Get back in the boat!"

"Out here you don't listen to the stories, *cherie*. You listen to me," he told her, holding out his hand. "Always."

She raised her stubborn chin. "Forget it. I'm not leaving this boat."

"Come on, Nik Kelly. Trust me."

"Johnny, please. I can't."

"Yes, you can." He stretched his hand out to her. "Come on, you won't be sorry. Trust me…just this once. Then the next time will be easier."

She chewed on her lip, glanced around. "If I come, will you—"

"I promise."

"You don't know what you just promised."

Johnny shrugged. "It doesn't matter. Whatever you want, I still promise."

She stood slowly, grabbed his hand and hung on tight. "Oh, God! I must be crazy."

Then she did as he'd asked. She trusted him.

The minute her tennis shoes sank into the spongy green fen she let out a startled shriek that flushed a couple of dozen nesting birds from the trees overhead. The sound they made taking off startled her further, and she nearly jumped out of her skin and into Johnny's arms.

She clutched him tightly. So tightly, in fact, that he gritted his teeth against the pain that shot through his vulnerable ribs. But it didn't matter. The warm feeling of her curvy body against him far surpassed his discomfort, and he enjoyed the moment like a greedy beggar.

After she had regained her composure, he tied up the boat and led her into the dense woods, the ground still moving beneath them. "How far?" she asked tentatively, her voice almost a whisper.

"Just a little farther." He squeezed her hand reassuringly, and she squeezed back.

There was no path to follow, and as soon as they reached the woods, they were surrounded by thick, green foliage. After several twists and turns, Johnny drew them to a stop, pointing toward a massive cypress.

For a long time she simply stared. Finally she breathed, "This is...unbelievable."

The amazement in her voice said it all, both her surprise and delight duly noted. Nonetheless, the idea of her seeing such a private piece of his past made Johnny feel as exposed and vulnerable as he knew it would. But maybe it was worth it, seeing her so in awe of something that was his and his alone.

"I said I'd show you my secret," he reminded. "I built the tree house at age eleven."

"At age eleven?" She angled her head to one side, amazement gleaming in her bright eyes. Then she smiled, and Johnny felt as if he'd been born anew. "I take it no one knows this is here?"

"I don't think so."

"So it's a secret only we share?"

He gazed down at her. "That's what you asked for," he drawled softly. He took her hand and tugged her along behind him until they were standing beneath the massive limbs, heavy with tattered moss trailing from its sweeping branches. He hadn't intended to show her this place when he'd bragged about the giant cypress, but here it was for her to see—a tree that would make a monumental statement if he'd ever let anyone know it was here.

He released her hand to let down an old rope ladder he'd put together years earlier. Finding it still sturdy enough to hold his weight, he climbed on. "I'll go first." He looked over his shoulder. "To evict the unwanted guests."

Even with bruised ribs, he scaled the ladder with agility, then disappeared into the moss-covered shack built around and into several high, sturdy limbs. A moment later he emerged with a snake in each hand. The brown snakes could easily have been mistaken for cottonmouths, except for the fact that they were missing the black bands and yellow underbelly of their deadly cousin.

"Oh, God!"

"Easy, *cherie*. They're friendly. When you meet up with a snake remember, don't move fast, but don't freeze up either." Johnny gave the snakes a mighty heave, and the reptiles suddenly became airborne. "Okay," he encouraged, pointing to the ladder. "It's your turn. I'll hold it steady."

She hesitated only a moment, then grabbed the ladder and started slowly up. Seeing how delicate she looked climbing twenty feet into the air suddenly made Johnny nervous as hell. The minute she was close enough for him to lay hands on her, he reached out and snared her around the waist. Then, in one quick motion, he swept her inside the dark shack.

As she clung to him, her head fell back, her slim body molding to his. Breathless, she said, "Your secret is wonderful. Thank you for sharing it with me."

Her eyes were glittering with pleasure, her body warm and arousing pressed against him. Johnny's blood raced through his veins. "Thank me another way, *cherie*," he whispered. "Kiss me."

The request smoldered between them, as sultry and poignant as the moody, black bog surrounding them.

A minute lapsed.

Slowly, Nicole went up on her tiptoes and brushed his lips with a seductive feather-light kiss.

Johnny didn't move, didn't breathe. Not until he felt her shudder and move against him. Then he drew her tightly to him and deepened the kiss. In answer, her lips parted, her clever pink tongue turning into a fish lure, dancing and teasing him senseless.

They spent the rest of the afternoon exploring the swamp together. Johnny didn't kiss her again, not after the heated passion they'd shared in the tree house. Not after the way she had sugarcoated the moment by whispering his name and rubbing her soft body against him.

The sun was low on the horizon when they arrived back at the farmhouse. Johnny walked Nicole to her car, where it sat in the driveway, and she left not saying much. He watched her drive away, then returned to the boat, troubled by a vague feeling that someone was watching him.

Nicole closed the book she was reading and glanced once more at the clock on the nightstand. Nine-thirty. Sighing, she swept the sheet aside and climbed out of bed. It was ridiculous to think she could attempt to go to bed at a reasonable hour. The ritual had been set months ago; she needed at least two hours of pacing to unwind. Tonight, maybe three.

She could hear the patter of raindrops on the windows. It was one of those lazy rainy nights, the kind that make a person restless. Anxious. Something she didn't need more of tonight.

She padded to the second-story window and looked out. Her bedroom window overlooked the front yard and offered an unobstructed view of the oak-lined driveway.

Johnny had gone into town. Gran had said he was spending the evening with Virgil.

He'd been gone for hours, and after what had happened a week ago, Nicole didn't see why he didn't just stay away from town altogether. At least until he felt a hundred percent again. What if Farrel tried something a little more creative this time? What if this time he didn't stop at a few broken ribs?

Nicole's stomach knotted as she thought about the possibility of Johnny taking another brutal beating, or worse. She wrapped her arms around herself, not wanting to think about it but unable to think of anything else.

Today had been one of the nicest days she'd had in months. The entire afternoon had been an artist's dream come true. Johnny had taken her places she would never have seen on her own. He had explained so much, made her feel important enough to share his secret, and had completely swept her away on an amazing adventure right in her own backyard. She'd seen cypress that resembled giants, just the way he had promised, and Spanish moss so thick that it had veiled them like a live blanket.

Even before today she had loved Belle, but now she felt oddly connected to it. And she had Johnny to thank for that.

Gran had insisted he was special. Today he had shown Nicole not only Belle, but a side of himself she suspected only a rare few had cared enough to see.

Trust me, cherie, he'd said. And she had; for the first time in months, she had trusted a man. Looking back, she had actually put her life in his hands at least a dozen times today, and he had not once failed her.

She stared out the window, anxious to see lights coming up the driveway, lights that would confirm he was safe. A minute turned into two, then three.

Desperate for a diversion, angry with herself for not

being able to drive Johnny from her thoughts, Nicole stripped off her chemise and grabbed a loose cotton shift from the closet. Abandoning the idea of wearing a bra, and after retrieving a pair of blue satin panties from her drawer, she dressed quickly, then headed downstairs. After finding a flashlight in a drawer in the kitchen, she escaped outside.

Warm raindrops greeted her as she stepped off the porch. At first she thought she would try out the swing in the backyard, but instead she found herself in Gran's flower garden. Another half an hour passed, and soon Nicole left the garden behind and crossed the road. Once she entered the woods she turned on the flashlight and let the shining beam guide her to the swimming hole. If anyone knew what she was planning, they would surely think she had lost her mind.

Over the past few weeks she'd gotten adept at maneuvering the wooded trails. Flashlight in hand, she easily arrived at the swimming hole unscathed. Turning out the light, she laid it down in the grass and waited a moment until her eyes adjusted to the darkness. It only took a few seconds before she could see the shadowy outline of the water lapping the grassy bank. She kicked off her wet canvas shoes, then swept her rain-soaked shift over her head and let it fall at the water's edge. Naked except for her panties, she slipped into the water.

An hour later, feeling less anxious and relaxed enough to maybe fall asleep once she returned to the house, Nicole waded to the bank in search of her discarded shift and shoes. Wringing out her wet hair, she glanced around the dense buttonbush.

"Looking for this?"

Nicole spun around, her wet panties clinging to her curvy bottom, her arms quickly covering her bare breasts. "Johnny? How long have you been standing there?" she gasped, speaking to the ghost who still hadn't materialized, but knowing it was him by his unmistakable black-bayou drawl.

"Long enough." The formidable shadow shoved away from the shelter of a tall oak and stepped into the misting rain. "Kinda late for a swim. Weather's not the best, either."

Nicole's heart began to pound wildly. Her body started to tremble when she saw her dress in one of his big hands. "Toss it," she implored.

At the mention of her dress, he glanced down at the sodden garment as if he'd forgotten it was there. Only a few seconds lapsed, but it seemed like forever before he did as she asked and tossed her dress—to the other side of the buttonbush.

Nicole sucked in her breath as he started to advance on her. Stunned, she took a step back and felt the water lap at her feet. "Johnny, what are you doing?"

"What we both want me to do. What your eyes have been begging me to do to you all day." His powerful hands locked solidly around her elbows, and he pulled her up against him. Nicole's eyes went wide. She made a strangled little cry that could easily have been mistaken for that of a creature of the night, but he ignored it and thrust his hand into her wet hair, tipped her head back and quickly covered her trembling mouth.

The kiss was hot. Desperate. Possessive. His tongue probed, searched, forced her mouth open to delve deeply. Not breaking the kiss, his hands slid around her and cupped her behind the knees, lifting her into his arms. Then they were moving, heading in the direction of the boathouse.

Nicole wrapped her arms around his neck and burrowed

her face against his rock-hard shoulder. "Your ribs," she whispered.

"Shh," he silenced.

He smelled earthy and warm. Rain-soaked. Nicole brushed her lips against the pulse throbbing at the base of his throat, whispered more concern for his ribs. He told her again that she worried too much and wrapped his arms more securely around her nakedness, fusing her to him as if she were his most prized possession.

Halfway to the boathouse he stopped. "We're not going to make it, *cherie*. I'm not going to make it," he amended, sliding her from him. He pulled her beneath a live oak with high branches that created a natural umbrella from the misting rain. Backing her against the tree, he sought her lips, giving her no time to think or to question the right or wrong of it. She kissed him back, her fingers sinking into his loose, wet hair. He leaned into her, rotated his pelvis urgently. The feel of his arousal through his damp jeans had Nicole moaning softly, liquid heat bubbling up inside her.

His rapid breathing caused his chest to heave in and out like a bellows, and when his hands closed over her breasts, palming them, kneading her warm flesh, Nicole bit her lip and arched into his big hands. He dragged callous thumbs over both aroused nipples, playing with them, at the same time keeping his eyes on her face, gauging her response, her need.

"You're so beautiful," he drawled, then bent his head and drew one ripe nipple into his hot mouth. Nicole again arched into him as every internal muscle responded all at once.

His kisses trailed lower to her abdomen, licking, stroking. Then he was kneeling in front of her, his hands settling on her waist, his tongue delving into her navel. Nicole gasped and felt her knees go weak. His hands moved lower, brushing the satin wedge between her thighs. "Say yes, *cherie*," he murmured. "Say you want this. That you want me as badly as I want you."

He was giving her a way out, she realized. Letting her escape at the last possible minute, if she needed to. He had stopped touching her, and she looked down to see he was staring up at her, waiting for her answer.

"I want you," he drawled softly, "but if I misread you this afternoon—"

Nicole silenced him by brushing her fingertips over his full mouth. "You didn't misread anything."

He stared at her a moment longer, then his fingers began caressing her satin mound through her panties, keeping his eyes still watchful on her face. Nicole trembled in answer to his silent request, and again felt as if she were being robbed of air.

"Time's up," he drawled. He kissed her flat stomach, his fingers moving past her panties to find her sex swollen and wet with desire. He moaned against the soft flesh of her stomach and gently parted her.

Nicole made a little starved noise in the back of her throat as his fingers entered her, testing, seeking, becoming familiar with her body. He was setting her on fire with one frenzied wave of heat after another. Panting, she twisted her body in a desperate plea. "Oh, Johnny! Ohh—"

The urgency in her voice had him withdrawing his fingers. Standing, he kissed her again, then hooked a finger in either side of her panties and snapped the elastic as if it were a single thread. Pulling the damp satin forward, he let it drop.

"Unzip me," he instructed, tearing his rain-soaked white T-shirt off and tossing it aside.

Nicole ran her hands down his hard belly. With trembling fingers, she worked his zipper down. Another shudder ripped through her as she reached for his rigid shaft, her fingers closing firmly around him.

"No, *cherie*," he groaned, grabbing her wrist. "I won't last two seconds with your hands on me."

He released her wrist and shoved his jeans past his buttocks, then quickly lifted her, urging her to wrap her legs around his waist. Without ceremony, he gripped her naked bottom and guided her down on his erection. Nicole's head fell back and her body shuddered violently. His hips strained upward, eased into her farther. She closed around him, her body willingly accepting him.

He let out a slow torturous moan of approval, and with one powerful thrust he was deeply seated inside her. But he wasn't there long before he lifted her as if he would leave her completely, then swiftly brought her back down over him. The air in his lungs rushed out while his hips strained again, bucking upward. He penetrated her again, then again in several solid mind-numbing thrusts.

He swore she was killing him. But it was Nicole who thought she would be the one to die as passion enveloped her and a flood of liquid heat shot past the burn of being stretched so completely. She gasped in sweet agony and clutched at him as his violent release sent her spiraling over the edge. She caught her lower lip between her teeth, closed her eyes and hung on as he carried them through the tempest, his endurance endless, his hard body controlling the tide, giving and taking at just the right moments. And when it was over, Nicole, shaken to the core, knew she would never forget this moment or the man named Johnny Bernard.

Johnny watched her as he slowly lifted her off him and set her bare feet gently to the ground. Righting his jeans, he kept silent, letting her have time to catch her breath. Feeling shaky himself, he bent and scooped up his T-shirt, looking for a cigarette. Realizing he must have lost them in the foray, he swore and tossed the shirt back to the ground.

He couldn't explain why he had ended up at the swimming hole. He supposed the water had simply beckoned, and he had answered the call. The lazy rain was to blame, he decided. It had lured him, tempted him. But the moment he had laid eyes on Nicole gliding on her back in the water, he knew a higher power had brought him here.

He glanced at her now as she reached for his T-shirt and pulled it over her head to conceal her naked body. He'd ruined her panties, but she picked them up anyway and tucked them neatly into her little fist. She didn't look at him as she stepped from beneath the tree and tilted her face up to the night sky. It was still raining, a fine, almost invisible mist. She stood perfectly still like a fragile statue.

Johnny waited for her to say something, anything, so he could gauge her emotional state. But after a minute passed she simply started walking toward the path.

Surprised, he asked, "Where are you going, *cherie?*"

"To find my shoes and dress."

"You okay?"

She turned to face him. "I'm fine."

Was she really fine? He had tried to be gentle, to go slow, but he'd found out the first time he'd kissed her that slow would never come easily where Nicole was concerned. The minute he had her in his arms, all he could think about was having her as quickly and as completely as possible.

"Look, I thought this was a mutual—"

"It was."

"Then what the hell's wrong?" Johnny hadn't meant to

sound so angry, but she was confusing him. One minute she was moaning and saying his name; the next she was acting as if they were strangers.

"Nothing's wrong, Johnny," she assured. "I just don't want to analyze what just happened. It's obvious we both needed a feel-good session. Let's just leave it at that."

Her comment was like a pail of cold water thrown in his face, and Johnny took a step back. He'd heard it called a lot of things before, but never that. Yeah, it had felt good all right, damn good. And he'd be the first one to admit that he'd had a sexual craving the size of the Gulf since he'd gotten out of prison. That, however, had had nothing to do with tonight. This hadn't been planned—but it hadn't just happened, either.

Angry that she had him trying to justify it in his mind, he taunted, "Well, then, the next time you feel needy, you let me know. A 'feel-good' session with you beats the hell out of playing poker with Bick any day of the week. In fact, we could set up a schedule if you like. Twice a week sound good? Or do you get needy on a daily basis?"

"Go to hell," she spat, and spun around to head down the trail.

With lightning speed, Johnny caught up to her, grabbed her elbow and pulled her around to face him. Quickly, he slid his free hand over her bare bottom, and when she tried to wiggle free, he squeezed, restraining her easily. "Don't," he grated. "Once barely took the edge off. Unless you want me inside you again right now, don't fight me."

"It would be by force this time," she snapped.

Johnny felt her tremble. Boldly, he moved his hand over her naked buttock and watched her shudder once more. "I don't think I'll have to force anything, *cherie*. We fit better than my custom-made boots, and like it or not, when something feels that good, that right, you usually get spoiled and don't want to settle for less.''

"You arrogant bast—"

He lowered his head and kissed her hard and fast. Then, releasing her, he left her standing in the sultry mist while he headed down the path to fetch her clothes. Over his shoulder, he said, "I'll be back with your things. Don't move. If I have to run you down, we both know who'll win."

Chapter 10

She'd known him less than three weeks, and yet she'd let him touch her and make love to her with the familiarity of a long-time lover. Nicole could feel her cheeks burn with the memory of what he had done to her and how she'd responded.

She wanted to shift the blame, wanted Johnny's broad shoulders to carry the weight of what had passed between them. She wanted to accuse him of using her, but she knew that wouldn't be fair. Not when she wasn't so sure she hadn't used him a little herself. Exorcising the past from her mind—Chad, specifically—hadn't been painful at all when the man she had given herself to last night had the power to consume her body, mind and soul.

Oh, she would never forget the baby. Nothing and no one would be able to erase the memory or the loss of her innocent baby girl. But since Johnny had entered her life, the pain of Chad's rejection had steadily diminished. And after last night, Nicole was almost feeling as if she owed Chad a debt of gratitude for walking away.

She knew now she had never loved him.

She wasn't proud of the fact that she might have used Johnny, that subconsciously it might have been her intention all along. No, it wasn't something to be proud of. But the alternative was much worse: she couldn't possibly be falling in love with him.

Love… No, she wasn't about to let Johnny Bernard worm his way into her heart. Though he'd done a good job so far.

She plopped down on her bed, determined to pull herself together. She rubbed her tired burning eyes, sleep having eluded her until only a few hours ago. After Johnny had walked her to the house last night, she had paced in earnest, until her feet hurt and the lip she kept chewing was raw.

The thought of seeing him at the breakfast table in a few hours was suddenly giving her a stomachache. What she really wanted to do was run off to New Orleans again. But what would that solve? When she got back she would still have to face him.

Their fevered lovemaking flashed in her mind, and Nicole squeezed her eyes shut. Normally she didn't like overpowering, take-charge men, but last night Johnny had controlled her every move, and she couldn't have been happier. He'd taken her to a place she'd never been before, an erotic haven she had only fantasized about in her most private dreams. Desire—yes, she desired him in a dozen carnal ways.

But she wouldn't love him. She couldn't.

Nicole swore and headed for the closet. She was half dressed when she heard a loud rumbling noise outside. She turned to the window with her T-shirt in hand. When she drew back the curtain, she wasn't prepared for what she saw: four huge, green tractors were being unloaded from long trailers.

"What on earth!" She watched as one by one the tractors were backed off the trailers and outfitted with plows. Moments later they headed into the overgrown fields.

Realization dawned as to what was happening and, just as quickly, as to who was responsible. Furious that Johnny had dared to take charge of another part of her life, Nicole finished dressing in a flurry of motion, jammed her feet into a pair of tennis shoes and raced downstairs.

She crossed the road in a blaze of anger, her arms swinging at her sides, talking to herself as she went— giving Johnny a verbal beating with each step. If and when Oakhaven became a sugar plantation, it would be Gran's decision, not that of some handsome ex-con. And the sooner Johnny Bernard learned his place around here, the better.

Johnny heard footsteps on the stairs just seconds before the door flew wide and banged hard against the wall. There wasn't time enough to pull his pants on. Hell, there wasn't time enough to climb out of bed.

One eye open, he saw Nicole march into the room and head straight for him. He sat up, dropped his feet to the floor. She hadn't been too talkative last night when he'd walked her back to the house. In fact—

He saw her pull her tiny fist back. It registered what she aimed to do with it seconds before she swung at his head. "You've got a lot of nerve...Bernard!"

Johnny ducked just in time, coming fully awake in an instant. "What did I do? I couldn't have done it today because it's—" He squinted at the clock on the wall. "Hell, it's not even six o'clock."

"I know what time it is," she snapped.

He guessed she did. She looked bright-eyed and awake, as if she'd been up awhile. She sure looked pretty in her tight little cutoff jeans and yellow T-shirt with pink lips tattooed all over the front of it. "So, what's got you so riled, *cherie?*"

"Four green tractors. That's what!"

Johnny rolled off the bed, dragging the sheet with him. His sore ribs protested the quick movement, and he groaned as he straightened. "So what's up with the tractors? I told them to stay out of the front yard. They didn't tear something up, did they?"

"That's the problem. You had no business telling them anything."

"Sure I did," Johnny argued. "I got the okay from Mae a couple of days ago. That's why I went into town last night to see Virgil. I knew he would be able to help us out with a name or two. This time of year most of the crews are busy with their own crops. I thought he might be able to call in a favor for us with his brother, Martin."

"You cleared it with Gran?"

"Sure. What did you think, that I'd go ahead on my own?"

"Why didn't you tell me about it last night?"

Clutching the sheet around his waist, Johnny ran his gaze down her curvy body. "We weren't exactly talking business last night—not doing much talking at all, if you know what I mean."

The look she gave him could have boiled water. "I should have expected you to gloat at some point. Well, you had your fun, last night and now this morning rubbing my nose in it. I hope you've enjoyed yourself because it'll be the last time you will at my expense."

Johnny studied her face. Now that he was awake, he noticed she didn't look as well rested as he'd first thought. It made sense; he'd lain awake for half the night himself. He turned contrite. "Sorry, *cherie*. I wasn't gloating."

"Save it. It's not worth talking about." She turned and was out the door more quickly than she'd come.

Johnny swore, dropped the sheet and reached for his jeans. In the heat of pulling them on and shooting the zipper north, he nearly castrated himself. "Son of a—!" Barefoot, rubbing his crotch, he took the stairs three at a time.

Just as she was about to open the outside door, he caught up with her, shot his hand past her and flattened it against the door. In her ear, he whispered, "Don't leave mad."

She whirled. "Okay, I won't leave mad. I'll just leave."

"You forgot something."

"I didn't forget anything."

"Well, I did."

"What? Is there something else you've forgotten to mention about those green monsters in the fields?"

"No." He paused for just a moment, then drawled, "What I forgot was this." He lowered his head and kissed her. He didn't give her time to protest, and he didn't allow himself to get carried away. Once he ended the kiss, he took a step back and ran the back of his hand along her cheek. "Good morning, *cherie*." Then he turned and strolled back upstairs, leaving her speechless, the taste of him on her pretty parted lips.

"I just don't understand why you didn't tell me," Nicole demanded of her grandmother. They were on the front porch, Mae tending to her prize azalea in the corner. The sun was baking the grass in the front yard and baking Nicole, too. She would have preferred to be inside in front of the fan, but she was determined to get used to the blessed heat even if it killed her. Which it no doubt would.

"I told you, Nicki, it just slipped my mind."

"Nothing slips your mind, Gran, unless you want it to," Nicole insisted. "I thought something as important as becoming a sugar plantation again would be something you'd want to share with me."

"Yes, I suppose you're right, Nicki. I should have discussed it with you first. I should have explained our financial situation, too. I'm not broke, by any means, but selling the fields, or making them turn a profit, would certainly help us down the road."

Nicole slipped into the wicker chair next to her grandmother. "I told you I'd help. You know I've got money from Dad's half of the law practice. And when I sold Mom and Dad's house—"

"Nonsense, Nicki. You'll do no such thing. That money is for you and your own family. For your children's future."

"I don't plan on having any children," Nicole blurted out, then wished she hadn't spoke so quickly. Gran was completely taken aback.

"No children! But children are wonderful little creatures, Nicki. They're the future. This doesn't sound anything like you. What's happened to change your mind about a family? About babies?"

"Nothing, Gran. You're right, children are the future. And someday maybe I'll want to settle down. I just don't think I would be a good mother right now. Not with such a demanding career."

Gran looked slightly mollified. Nicole felt guilty. In truth, she would never allow herself to go through another pregnancy. She was too afraid.

"You and Johnny didn't say two words to each other over breakfast. Has he done something to upset you? You two aren't fighting again, are you?"

"He should have told me about the fields," Nicole countered, "as you should have."

"I'm sorry, Nicki. I made the decision by myself, and that was wrong of me."

"No, that's not what I'm saying. It was your decision

to make. Only..." Nicole sighed. "I guess I just didn't want to be the last to know."

"You're right, of course. When Johnny brought it up, well, I was just so excited, I told him to see Virgil about it right away. Virgil's brother has a plantation east of here, a very successful plantation. I knew if anyone could help us out and quickly, it would be Martin Diehl." Mae looked satisfied. "I'm so glad Johnny's come home. This is working perfectly. Better than I'd planned."

"Planned?" Nicole stiffened. "What do you mean 'planned'?"

"I know that look. I said I wouldn't do anything sneaky again, and I won't." Mae went back to grooming the azalea. "When I said 'planned,' I was talking about the fields. I think this is going to be the answer to everything. I'm just surprised I didn't think of it myself."

Nicole pulled into Pepper's parking lot and climbed quickly out of her car. Already late to meet Daisi, she hurried inside wearing jeans and a funky scoop-neck ribbed tank in slate blue with two dozen tiny buttons down the front. The bar was darker than she remembered. Except for that one night weeks ago, she'd only been inside Pepper's over the noon hour, when the sun's rays shot through the transom over the double front doors. Gran loved the Wednesday lunch special—sausage gumbo and a slice of Bosco pie made with extra pecans and Pepper's best whiskey. Clair had tried to duplicate the legendary pie, but she still hadn't discovered the secret. Pepper swore he'd disclose it the minute she promised to leave Bick and marry him.

She stood in the doorway until her eyes finally adjusted to the dim lighting. When she spied Daisi at the half-circle bar, talking to her brother, Woody, Nicole started toward them.

The talk in town was that Woody had a terrible crush on her. He looked up, and when their eyes met, Nicole smiled. She seated herself on a red leather barstool next to Daisi. "Hi," she said, when Daisi spun around.

"You made it. Great!" Daisi glanced at her brother. "See, I told you she'd come." She looked at Nicole. "Didn't I tell you he was cute?"

"Oh, hell, Daisi," Woody grumbled, blushing red. "Shut up."

Nicole let her gaze travel the length of Daisi's brother. Yes, he was cute; he had a nice set of dimples, and kind eyes the color of caramel pie. His attractive long blond curls had been bleached from working outdoors in the hot sun, and it accented his tanned cheeks. His body was a working man's body, lean and muscular. The package was fine, more than fine. Still…

She blinked away the vision of Johnny Bernard's face. All day she'd felt depressed, as if she'd lost her best friend. Which was ridiculous—friends didn't purposely keep things from one another. And that's what Johnny had done by not including her in Gran's decision to go back into business.

"Nicki?"

Nicole blinked, then said, "Sorry I'm late."

"That's okay. Woody thought you weren't goin' to show. But I told him you were the type to keep your word."

"I lost track of time," Nicole explained. "I started cleaning out the attic. I've decided to turn it into my painting studio."

"I'll have to come see." Daisi gestured toward her brother. "Woody will bring me sometime, okay?"

"Sure," Nicole said.

Just then Toby Potter, the local loudmouth, walked by and gave Nicole a long, interested look, then a playful wink. "You better watch yourself tonight, gal. Farrel had all the fun last time, but tonight me and the boys won't be sittin' back watchin'." He glanced at his competition. "I see old Woodrow here's got the same thing in mind. There's likely gonna be some scrappin' goin' on to see who wins the first dance."

Woody gave the truck driver with the shaggy red beard a nasty look. "Go cool off, Toby. Miss Nicki's dance card is full up tonight." He glanced back at Nicole to see if he'd overstepped his bounds.

Nicole nodded, then smiled. At the moment she would have agreed to just about anything Woody suggested. Toby Potter looked as if he hadn't bathed in weeks, and the toothpick he was chewing on was as black as the grease under his fingernails.

"Well, Woodrow," Toby was saying, "I'll fight ya for that dance card. Your call—fists or something more meaningful?"

Nicole's eyes widened. Oh, God, she thought, Toby outweighed Woody by at least fifty pounds. And what did he mean by 'something more meaningful'?

"You boys can discuss this without us girls," Daisi said, dismissing Toby as if he weren't even there. "My back's achin', and I need a comfortable chair to sit in." She reached out, grabbed Nicole's arm and hauled her off the stool. "Come on, girlfriend. Let's find a table. Pepper, bring me somethin' pretty. Somethin' sweet—no liquor for me. Nicki, what do you want, wine?"

"No! I mean, not tonight. I'll have the same as you."

"Make that two pink lemonades, Pepper," Daisi hollered.

Pepper had a towel moving on the bar in time to the music playing on the jukebox and a fat black cigar poking from between his fleshy lips. He never looked up from polishing the bar, but he called back, "It's comin' up, darlin'."

"Hey, Pepper, I'm empty," a man yelled from the other end of the bar. "Stop trying to spit shine that old thing and tend to your customers."

"Hold your horses, and say 'whoa,'" Pepper called back. "Ladies come first around here. I'll bother with you soon as I get them settled." He served Nicole and Daisi their drinks moments later. "Here ya go," he said, setting down the drinks. "My specialty. I call it Sunrise on the Bayou."

It looked too pretty to drink, Nicole thought, the glass tall and narrow, a slice of lemon and a slice of orange stacked on a plastic stick topped off with a cherry.

"You need anythin' else, you just give Pepper a holler. I'll be listenin' for them sweet voices."

After Pepper stuffed himself back behind the bar, Daisi said, "Lucas Pelot's band is playin' later. You ever hear them?"

"No," Nicole admitted, pushing the fruit stick aside and taking a sip of her drink.

"They're really somethin'. Lucas can finger that accordion of his better than anyone I know," Daisi boasted.

They were seated at a table just on the outside edge of the dance floor—the floor Nicole recalled being whirled around just two weeks earlier in Farrel's arms. She had been hoping Farrel wasn't here tonight, but she glanced around and, to her disappointment, noticed him standing at the end of the bar with a drink in his hand. When their eyes met, he lifted his glass and smiled. Nicole didn't reciprocate. She had no intention of furthering a friendship with a man who could be party to a gang beating such as the one he and his friends had given Johnny.

He had called her twice, so Clair had said, leaving messages both times for her to call him back. But Nicole had ignored the requests.

"So, how are things?" Daisi asked. "I haven't seen you in days."

Daisi's question forced Nicole to focus her attention back on her new friend. "Like I said, I've been working in the attic, and I've been sketching, too. There's a gallery owner in New Orleans who is interested in my work."

"I bet the sketches are wonderful."

Nicole hadn't told Daisi anything about the past year in L.A. She hadn't told anyone, actually. She'd wanted to, and she really felt that Daisi would be the one to understand. Only, with Daisi being pregnant, Nicole thought it would be too awkward, the part about the baby. And Daisi just might start worrying about her own pregnancy. Nicole didn't want that. The truth was, having babies was as natural as breathing. Just because it hadn't been for her didn't mean Daisi wouldn't enjoy the wonders of motherhood.

"How are you feeling?" she forced herself to ask. "Is the baby moving? She's fine, isn't she?"

"She? I didn't say it was a she." Daisi laughed. "I told the doctor I didn't want to know." She sobered, glanced at her blooming stomach. "Is it the way I'm carryin' it? Have you heard somethin' I should know?"

"No." Nicole felt a little foolish. "I'm sorry, it was just a slip. I think of all babies as girls."

Daisi relaxed. "Don't let Mel hear you say that, 'cause he wants a boy."

Woody suddenly appeared. "Lucas just finished warmin' up." He set his bottle of beer on the table. "You still willin' to dance with me, Nicole?"

The band started things off with a traditional Cajun song called "Jolie Blonde." At Daisi's encouragement, Nicole took Woody's hand and let him lead her onto the dance floor.

A night of dancing was just what she needed, Nicole decided as she settled herself in Woody's capable arms. Only, this time she was going to stay away from the wine—and Farrel Craig.

From his booth on the far side of the bar, Johnny watched Woody Lavel tripping over his grin as he swept Nicole onto the dance floor for the sixth time. He wished to hell he hadn't seen her come in. And he wished to hell that after he had, he'd left Virgil to his own demise and gotten out of here. But he hadn't. And now it was too late; he wasn't going anywhere. Not with the way Woody was feeling more confident with every song. And with Farrel, leaning on the end of the bar and eyeing Nicole the way he was.

"She sure is perdy." Virgil glanced at the dance floor. "Why don'tcha ask her to dance? Yo' want ta. I can see de way ya look at her, boy."

"I don't dance," Johnny drawled. But he did want to hold her close, only not here. Not in a crowded room full of people. He wanted to go somewhere private with her, somewhere he could have her all to himself.

"Well, maybe it's time ta learn," Virgil was saying. "Woodrow's gettin' de cream tonight. Yo' okay with dat?"

Johnny glanced at his friend. "Shut up, old man."

"Doan take my head off 'cause yo' doan know how ta dance. No point. 'Tain't my fault."

Woody's hand captured her small waist and drew her closer. Johnny's chest constricted, as he remembered how it felt being that close to her, touching her, loving her.

"Doan tink she'd mind, do yo'? Thought Mae said yo' two were—"

"Shut up, Virg."

Lucas Pelot's band hit the last chord on a hip-swinging

tune and immediately went into an up-close, touchy-feely ballad. Out of the corner of his eye, Johnny saw Farrel slide off his stool. Virgil saw it, too.

"Now doan go feedin' trouble with stupidity," Virgil warned. "Tuck'll toss yo' in de slammer if'n yo' get crazy."

Johnny watched warily as Farrel shouldered his way through the crowd and tapped Woody on the back. The younger man turned to see who was intruding on his party, and when he realized who it was, his face fell. He wanted to argue with Farrel, but in the end he backed off, and Farrel slipped in to take his place.

Johnny could see Nicole's body tense from across the room. And he would have come to her rescue if he hadn't known her as well as he did. She looked fragile, vulnerable as hell, but she was made tougher than anyone knew. If she didn't want to dance with Farrel, she'd say so.

He got to his feet. "I'm going home, Virg. Thanks again for getting Martin to turn the fields over."

"Does dat mean yo'll be stayin' ta run things for Mae? Folks tink dat's jus what it means. Down at Red's dere takin' bets yo' be movin' back ta de farm soon."

"Don't waste your money on that bet, Virg." Johnny started for the door. He was almost there when he heard *her* above the music and the laughing crowd. "I said I don't want to dance with you. Now let go."

He glanced over his shoulder and saw her struggling against Farrel's hold. He wasn't aware of it at the time, but suddenly he'd changed directions. A number of dancing couples saw him and scrambled back to their seats. The music stopped, a violin chord dying slowly.

Johnny recognized Nicole's fighting stance from that morning. Quickly he grabbed her around the waist and pulled her back against him, just as she was about to drive her fist into Farrel's surprised face. "Easy, *cherie*," he drawled in her ear. "He's been known to hit back. Even women."

Much to Johnny's disappointment, Nicole didn't appear to be any happier to see him than Farrel. "Let go!" she demanded. "He deserves a black eye, and if he tries to hit me back, I'll blacken the other one."

Johnny hung on to her. "Let's go outside and cool off."

She shook him off. "I'm not going anywhere. He's the one who should go out and cool off. I'm no dumb blonde." She spun around, glaring at all the men enjoying the show. "Did you hear that, guys? Find another game."

"But we like this game, honey," Farrel mocked.

The men at the bar roared with laughter.

Johnny's already crappy mood deteriorated further. He said, "The fun's over. Come on, *cherie.*"

"That's where you're wrong, *beggar boy.* It's just beginning," Farrel taunted. He started to reach out and haul Nicole back into his arms, but Johnny grabbed his wrist and squeezed. "The lady's not interested. She's made that clear." He released Farrel's wrist. "Lay a hand on her again, and it'll be the last time you use that hand."

The crowd grew quiet.

"Did you hear that, everybody? He threatened me," Farrel shouted. "Not too smart in front of witnesses, Bernard."

Johnny shrugged, then spun Nicole around to face him. "Come on. Or do you want me to finish what you started?" Grinning for the first time since he'd seen her enter the bar, he added, "One helluva choice, ain't it? Watching a barroom brawl that'll likely end with me in the slammer, or leaving through the front door with the most unpopular man in town. One way or another, come tomorrow, the gossip will be ripe."

She made a face at him, then struck out for the door with her nose in the air.

Farrel called out several vulgar taunts, trying to bait Johnny into a fight, but Johnny wasn't interested. Farrel wasn't worth another jail sentence.

When he caught up with Nicole outside, she was breathing fire. "If you're expecting a 'thank you,' you can forget it. I didn't need your help in there."

Johnny glanced around at the people gawking. "Can we go? Or do you want to make a scene out here, too?"

"I'm not going home with you," she snapped.

"Oh, and why is that? You suddenly afraid of me? Or afraid of what might happen if we're alone?"

"Nothing is going to happen. And, no, I'm not afraid of you."

Johnny started toward the car. "Good. Let's go."

She hurried after him. "I'm driving. Do you hear? It's my car and—"

Johnny called out over his shoulder. "That's a deal. It'll leave my hands free."

She called him a nasty name, made a quick direction change and raced past him to climb in the passenger's side.

Laughing, Johnny got behind the wheel.

Chapter 11

From his perch on top of the roof, Johnny heard a truck shift into low as it headed up the driveway. When it stopped in the front yard, he glanced down and saw it was one of Farrel Craig's delivery trucks loaded down with supplies. It was a surprise, to say the least. He had expected Farrel to cancel the order and refuse their business after what had happened at Pepper's a week earlier.

"I got those shingles Miss Chapman ordered," the man hollered, climbing out of the truck and slamming the door.

The afternoon sun was hot enough to fry spit. Johnny hooked his hammer in the leather pouch strapped to his waist, then backhanded the sweat from his brow. He came off the roof using the extension ladder leaning against the side of the house. Once on the ground, he unhooked a leather tool belt and laid it on the workbench. A jug of water sat nearby, and he lifted it and dumped it over his head. Shaking like a dog, he picked up the T-shirt he'd discarded hours ago, dried his face off, then pulled the shirt back on.

"I could have come in and picked up the shingles,"
Johnny told the truck driver. "We don't need the added
expense of a delivery charge when I got a pickup right
here."

"Miss Chapman requested the delivery weeks ago," the
driver informed him. "The boss didn't tack on no extra
charge. In fact—" he handed Johnny the invoice "—it
looks like he gave her a helluva discount."

Johnny took the invoice and scanned it. His nostrils
flared when he saw just how generous Farrel's discount
was. He jammed the paper in his back pocket, wondering
just what the bastard was up to.

The two men worked side by side until the load was off
the truck, and when the truck pulled out, Johnny eased
into a chair on the front porch. Sweat dripping from his
brow, he ran a hand over his face, then through his hair.
Eventually his eyes drifted toward the open French doors
that led to the study.

He wondered if Nicole was still inside. He'd walked by
earlier and spied her seated at the desk. Conversation between them had been reduced to one-liners since he'd
driven her home from town a week ago.

He stood, stretched, then sauntered to the open doorway.
Leaning against the jamb, he saw she was still there, still
punching keys on a small calculator. She made a mistake,
swore softly, then repeated the number sequence. Satisfied
this time, she wrote the total in the appropriate column in
a black ledger.

"Since when do you do bookkeeping?" he asked.

"Since I refused to ask you for a favor." She hit another
set of numbers on the calculator.

Her all-business attitude had Johnny's reined-in temper
slipping a notch. He sauntered into the room, stopped at
the desk and turned off the calculator. "I don't mind doing
it."

Her fingers stilled on the keys, and she slowly looked up. "Well, maybe *I* mind."

Damp strands of hair had come loose from the casual twist she'd secured at the back of her head. The warm day had flushed her face, adding more color to her already comely complexion. The pale blue sundress she wore made her already stunning blue eyes more radiant. The low neckline and narrow straps lured his eyes to the exposed swell of her soft breasts and a touch of sun-kissed cleavage.

Johnny kicked himself for noticing, felt his jeans turning uncomfortable, but then noted she was giving his wet T-shirt a long, hard look, too.

When she saw that he'd noticed her interest, she said, "Did you fall in the swamp, or has it started to rain?"

He shrugged off the sarcasm and went looking for a chair to sit down in. He was sweat-stained and dirty, so he chose the wood rocker. "Craig Lumber just dropped off the shingles."

She arched a brow. "My call must have worked."

"Call?" Johnny dug the bill out of his pocket and tossed it on the desk. "It must have been some call to get that kind of discount."

She picked up the bill and scanned it. Smiling, she said, "Yes, it must have made quite an impression."

Johnny stiffened. "Beg forgiveness?"

"Something like that." She sat back in her chair and folded her hands in her lap. "Driving to New Orleans for supplies would have cost us double. It was much easier just to make amends."

Johnny tried to keep from getting angry. "I'm curious. What does it cost these days to make amends?"

"I don't know what you mean."

"Sure you do. What did you promise him, *cherie?* Dinner and a movie? Or was there something more substantial involved?''

"You have a filthy mind," she snapped.

"No. I just know Farrel, and how low he can stoop.''

"Think what you want. I really don't care.''

Johnny bit down hard on the inside of his cheek. He didn't like feeling jealous, but there it was. That damn green monster was biting him again. The truth was, if anyone was going to scratch her itch, he wanted it to be him. She was in his blood now, and there was nothing he could do about it but suffer. "I'm just looking out for you. Mae would want me to," he reasoned.

"I'm a big girl. Gran knows I can look out for myself.''

"That's not what she tells me. Just this morning she asked me if I'd consider driving you to New Orleans next weekend. She's afraid you're going to get mugged, or worse.''

Nicole looked stunned. "You told her no, of course.''

"No, I said I'd discuss it with you. But I'm game.'' Johnny allowed himself the pleasure of studying her pretty mouth, then he looked back at her eyes. "Maybe a few days away would do us both some good.''

At his words, her face contorted and her lips thinned. "Thank you, but no thank you. My plans are already set. Now if there isn't something pertaining to your job we need to discuss, I'd like to get back to work. You should, too.''

"I'm taking my morning break," Johnny informed her, sliding more comfortably into the chair.

She shoved back her chair and stood. "Fine. Take it outside.''

He knew full well that he should do as she said, but as he got to his feet, instead of heading for the open door, he started toward her. When she backed up, he smiled and helped her along with a little shove that neatly put her against the wall. "Feel needy today?"

"Stop it."

"It's been a few weeks. You must be—"

"Go away!"

"Can't. I'm yours for the summer, remember?"

His words brought a flush to her cheeks, and she squeezed her eyes shut. "Please, don't."

The idea of touching her again had been driving him crazy. He'd tried to stay busy, to ignore it, but she was on his mind twenty-four hours a day. Disregarding how dirty he was, Johnny leaned into her and pinned her more firmly against the wall. "Look at me," he drawled softly in her ear.

"Johnny, please," she panted, struggling against him to free herself.

He shifted his body more solidly against her, allowing her to feel his full-blown arousal against her belly. Angling his head, his lips brushed her temple. "You feel good, *cherie*. Smell good, too."

"You don't," she countered.

"I've been on the roof since six." He ran his hand up her bare arm and the shiver he felt go through her body tormented his condition further. He wanted her, right here, right now.

He moved quickly, kissing her not gently, not experimentally, but like a man who had been lying awake nights dreaming about what they'd already shared.

The kiss deepened...deepened.

She didn't fight him, and when he realized she wasn't going to, he slid his hands around her waist and pulled her away from the wall so his hands could glide freely over her curves. She sucked in a little gasp when his hand cupped her backside and pressed her more firmly into him.

A moment later he felt her small hands drift up to his shoulders.

Rocked by a sudden, swift possessiveness, Johnny kissed her again, then again. He could feel her heart racing. Feel her fingers grip his shoulders.

"Johnny…"

He claimed her mouth again, stroking his hands up her spine, then tangling his fingers in her hair. The fragile clip holding her hair went to the floor. Minutes ticked by. Johnny and Daisy were unaware that they were being observed from the front porch. Mae Chapman sat silent in her wheelchair with a satisfied smile parting her lips and happy tears glistening in her aging blue eyes.

Nicole stood at the railing on the front porch and watched Johnny amble across the lawn toward her with that loose-jointed gait that made her heart race. She'd been avoiding him for days, thinking that if she did, she would be able to forget what was happening. But it hadn't helped; she knew she was falling in love with him. Hopelessly in love with a man who intended to leave in less than three months' time.

"You get packed?"

"Yes." Nicole watched him scale the porch steps. He was in another white T-shirt, his jeans ragged but clean. His hair was damp, suggesting that he'd just showered, but he'd neglected to scrape off the shadow clinging to his jaw.

She stepped back from the railing. Her white cotton dress—a loose shift with an irregular hem—fluttered in the breeze as she turned and slid into one of the wicker chairs. Barefoot, she tucked her feet beneath her, then indicated he was welcome to take the other chair. He declined, opting instead to lean against the railing.

"You still taking off in the morning?" His hand found his hip, hooked a thumb in an empty belt loop.

Nicole remembered how taut his muscles were in that area, and the memory made her mouth go dry. "Yes. Early morning. Take care of Gran?"

"Sure."

His response was simple but sincere. He shoved away from the column and jammed his hands in his back pockets. "I called my parole officer. He gave me permission to leave town for the weekend." His eyes searched her face.

"No." Nicole shook her head. "I'm going alone."

He nodded as if he'd expected her to hold firm to her decision. "You watch yourself. A lot of crazies living in Sin City."

Nicole closed her eyes briefly. She loved his husky, bayou drawl. Loved the way he showed his concern, even though it was half hidden behind his tough exterior. She was beginning to read him. Not always, but half the time at least. And what she'd learned was that there was a soft, sensitive side to Johnny Bernard. A side she had wanted to deny existed from the very beginning. But Gran had known it was there all along, and that's why she had felt he was worth the trouble all those years ago. He was a good person, honest and noble.

"Things have been going well, don't you think?"

"Seem to be," he agreed.

"I appreciate your working so hard for Gran. This is the happiest I've seen her in years."

"It's because you're here that she's happy."

"Maybe it's both of us," Nicole conceded.

"About this party you're going to—"

"It's an art exhibit, not a party." Her teasing tone was meant to lighten the moment, but when his expression didn't change, Nicole wondered what he was thinking. He looked a little on edge tonight.

"So you're not meeting anyone there?"

Nicole shook her head. "No. I'm going because the gallery owner is interested in handling some of my paintings. It's called networking."

"Where are you staying?"

"The Place d'Armes in the French Quarter. It's small and quaint. I stayed there once before with my parents." She climbed out of the chair. "I want you to do the bookkeeping again. Will you? I know what I said before. But I was being—"

"Stubborn," he finished for her.

"Yes, I suppose I was."

He stepped forward, and she took a step back.

It just wasn't fair, Nicole thought. God help her, she didn't want to love this man. He was going to break her heart, and this time she feared it would never mend.

"I've got to go inside," she offered quietly. "Thank you for helping Gran out this morning." She gestured to the treelike azalea in the corner. "I dreaded repotting that thing. It meant a lot to her that you cared enough to help."

He took another step toward her, invading her space. They stared at each other for a long, tense moment. Nicole's heart skipped a beat, and she noticed Johnny's breathing had turned erratic. Finally he said, "Thank me another way, *cherie*. Kiss me."

The familiar words made her shake her head. "No," she whispered. "No, I won't."

He didn't move, didn't ask again, but he didn't back away, either.

Tomorrow, Nicole reasoned. Tomorrow she would start weaning herself away from him. Tomorrow she would be stronger. Tomorrow she would have the distance between them and she would be able to think more clearly. She wouldn't have to look into those see-to-the-soul eyes across the breakfast table, or be teased into a frenzy by his black, hypnotic drawl. Yes, tomorrow would be soon enough to face the truth.

Slowly she slid her hands up his chest and lifted her mouth to his. The kiss was warm and sultry. She meant to keep it simple, uncomplicated. But he had other plans, and she lingered on the porch much longer than she'd intended. Much longer.

Chapter 12

He fit in as if he were one of them, and no one suspected otherwise. No one, except Nicole.

She stood in the pristine gallery's arched doorway, her knees weak and her heart in her throat. Johnny was at the other end of the spacious room, his back to her, gazing at a portrait of a naked woman draped over a piano as if dead. He wore snug, faded jeans, free of holes, his custom-made boots, and a navy blue shirt that Nicole had never seen before. The shirt looked new, and it clung to him with an expensive sheen that made her breath catch. His hair was loose, riding his shoulders, and the jet-black color in the gallery light made him stand out like a black knight in the crowd.

She glanced around, taking in the room full of artists, and spied Mr. Medoro at the same time he spied her.

"Ah, Nicole, I'm so glad you decided to come," he said as he hurried toward her.

She smiled and forced her legs to move through the doorway. "Yes, I'm here."

"Tomorrow we will talk about your wonderful talent. But tonight—" he gestured to the walls "—we will enjoy the work, no?"

Nicole nodded, accepted the gallery owner's arm, and soon was whisked into a crowd of artists. She was introduced to each one of them, and the circle tightened around her. She answered their questions, smiled and nodded, but all the time she was gazing off in various directions, trying to locate Johnny. At one point she saw him standing with three women. One, a curvy brunette, was clinging, trying to get him to share her glass of wine, which he declined. Another time, he was standing with Mr. Medoro. Together, they were studying an abstract wooden sculpture with two heads. Distracted by questions and meaningless conversation, it was almost an hour before she broke free of the crowd to search for Johnny.

"Your paintings are better than all of them."

Nicole closed her eyes as she felt his presence behind her, his warm breath upon her neck. A tingle ran down her spine. She didn't turn around, and instead said, "And you're an expert, right?"

"I know what I like," he drawled, moving closer. His hands came up to stroke lightly down her arms.

Nicole finally gave in and turned. They were toe to toe, so close that his soft shirt brushed her bare arm. "What are you doing here?" she finally asked. "You were supposed to stay at Oakhaven and take care of Gran."

"Actually, she's why I'm here. She was stewing about you all day, sure you were going to be kidnapped or robbed. She insisted I come and be your bodyguard."

Nicole couldn't stop staring at him. He was there, dressed for the occasion, looking remarkably sexy and amazingly relaxed, though she doubted he had ever set foot in an art gallery in his life.

Grinning, he leaned forward and whispered, "Have you networked enough? I'm starved."

"You don't like your catfish?"

"Huh? No," Johnny said, "the food's always good here."

"You've been here before?"

Mulates was one of New Orleans's famous Cajun restaurants. Johnny liked the cozy atmosphere and the dim lighting. That's why he'd suggested it and asked the hostess if they could have a small corner table in the back.

"I lived here for a few years," he confessed. He didn't mention being a dishwasher for this very restaurant at age seventeen.

Her surprise was subtle, a mere lifting of one delicate eyebrow. "After you ran away?"

"It was a good place for a kid to get lost. An easy place to find work."

He tried not to stare too long at her pretty mouth. He wasn't going to make her uncomfortable by ogling her bare shoulders or licking his chops like a hungry dog, either. But the slippery, little black dress outlining her curves continued to raise hell with his heart rate and the comfort of his jeans.

She had twisted her shiny blond hair up in a messy knot that showed off her mole and accented her slender neck. He had always thought she was naturally beautiful. Tonight she was stunning, turning every head at the gallery as well as in the restaurant.

She smiled, sipped her wine. "So what do you think about Mr. Medoro and his gallery? Will I fit in?"

"I think you'd fit in anywhere. In fact, I suggested to him that he give you your own exhibit."

Her eyes widened. "You what?"

"You're too modest about your talent," Johnny scolded

gently. "You've got to speak up. Let them know how good you are."

"I speak up," she argued.

"Yeah, when you're chewing me out." He grinned, letting her know he was teasing.

She rested her elbow on the table and propped her small fist beneath her chin. "If I've ever chewed you out, it was because you had it coming."

Johnny sat back and watched her. "You like getting all dressed up and going to galleries?"

"Sometimes. But I'm not crazy about surprises."

"I suppose now we're talking about me?"

"We're talking about you, yes." Her smile turned impish. Suddenly she giggled. "You looked relaxed, but I think it was all an act."

"Why do you think that? Was my suffering that obvious?"

"Not to that woman cooing in your face."

Her comment about the overbearing woman with huge red lips made Johnny's grin widen. "She wanted to know how long I was staying in town."

"And you said…?"

"I didn't know."

"So have you arranged a late date with her?"

He wasn't sure if she was teasing or if she was jealous. Jealous, he hoped.

She reached across the table and touched the cuff on his new shirt. Johnny gazed down at her hand where her small fingers played with the fabric. When she realized her error, she quickly withdrew her hand. "I've never seen you in anything but a T-shirt. This is nice."

"I'm not much for clothes. Still, I wouldn't deliberately embarrass you, *cherie*." He paused, saw that both their plates were empty, and said, "You ready to head back to the hotel?"

"Yes. I agreed to meet with Mr. Medoro in the morning to discuss some sketches I've done. I'd like to turn in early."

"But you won't. Instead you'll pace the floor, right?"

"Not funny."

A horse-drawn carriage was just passing by as they reached the street. Johnny flagged the driver and lifted Nicole into the white carriage. It felt good to touch her. So good, in fact, that he slipped the driver an extra fifty to take a longer route back to the hotel.

Forty-five minutes later, after enjoying the glowing streetlamps, the music coming from Bourbon Street, and the sweet aromas that were so much a part of New Orleans, they reached St. Ann Street. Johnny lifted Nicole from the carriage, and they entered the Place d'Armes Hotel, a two-story structure in the heart of the French Quarter. It had a historic courtyard brimming with flowers, and was well known for its quaint charm.

Inside the elevator, Nicole unzipped the gold purse she had slung on her shoulder and went fishing for her room key. "Where are you staying?" she asked. "You never said."

"Actually I got a room here," Johnny told her.

She looked up, unable to hide her surprise. "Here? You're kidding."

He took her key from her hand, and, when they stepped off the elevator, he followed her to her room. Once he'd unlocked her door, he stuck his head inside, flicked on the light and glanced around. "Did you remember to lock the balcony door before you left for the gallery?"

"Yes. Well, I think so."

Her hesitation made Johnny scowl. He shoved the door wide and stepped inside. He found the French doors unlocked. Swearing, he made a quick check of the room, then stepped out onto the balcony. It was narrow, surrounded by a wrought-iron railing. A large potted plant in the corner camouflaged the adjoining balcony. Against the aging brick wall sat a small table and two chairs.

He glanced across the lantern-lit courtyard and found all the other balconies empty. Below, two couples relaxed in the secluded octagonal pool, which was half hidden by palmettos and flowering vines.

He stepped back inside, laid her key on the dresser, then headed for the door. "If you need something I'll be—"

"I won't. But thanks, anyway."

She seemed anxious to get rid of him. Disappointed, Johnny stepped into the hall, and, before he could turn around, she closed the door. For a few minutes he just stood there. He didn't know what he had expected, but he knew what he'd been hoping for.

He pulled the key to the room next door out of his pocket and headed inside. It had taken some time to convince the desk clerk to give him the room next to Nicole's, but a few unexpected cancellations had helped out. Fate, again.

The room was dark and cool. He ignored the lights, pulled his shirt from his jeans and unbuttoned it. The balcony beckoned, and he unlocked the narrow doors and shoved them open. Patting his shirt pocket, he took a cigarette and cornered it in his mouth, then slipped into the sturdy wrought-iron chair.

Two cigarettes later, he closed his eyes and breathed in the warm night air. The heavy scent of azalea blossoms, ripe and sweet, drifted to him, and he tried not to think about Nicki for a moment, especially her undressing and getting ready for bed.

He had just lit his third cigarette when *her* balcony doors opened. He sat silently, glad the mammoth azalea plant on her balcony hid him from sight. He watched as she stepped to the railing, the lit lanterns below giving her silhouette a golden glow. He noticed she'd let her hair down, but she still had on the skinny black dress.

Mesmerized, he watched her arch her back like a cat and angle her head to smell the fragrant night air. Her profile was beautiful, delicate. Curvy. Exotic. When she ran her fingers through her hair, he wished it were his fingers having the pleasure.

All evening he had kept his hands off her, but it hadn't been easy. Swearing inwardly, deciding it was too much—watching and not touching—Johnny stood to go back inside.

"I'm not chasing you away, am I?"

He stopped dead in his tracks, glanced down at his cigarette, then dropped it and crushed it beneath his boot. "How did you know? The smoke?"

"Yes. It's your brand."

Johnny turned and moved to the railing. "Raunchy habit. I took it up in the joint."

She faced him. Offered him a sultry, needy look. Later Johnny would say it was that *needy* look that had started the next chain of events. But who could say whose need was stronger?

"You're killing me," he admitted.

"Am I?"

"You know you are. Come here."

She shook her head. "I don't think so. If you're suffering…good. At least that way I don't feel quite so alone."

Her admission was as unexpected as it was arousing. "You don't have to suffer, *cherie*. Neither one of us does."

She drifted toward the railing, staying just out of reach. "No gloating later?"

"None."

"And I'll stay the entire night?"

"If that's what you want, yes."

"Will we share breakfast in bed?"

"If we wake up before noon."

Johnny sucked in a deep breath as she took two steps closer, making it possible for him to reach out and touch her. But he didn't lay a hand on her. Slowly he leaned into the railing and kissed her. Only after he felt her shudder did he reach for her, and then carefully, so he didn't bruise her body on the wrought-iron that separated them.

After a long kiss, he slid his hands around her waist and lifted her over the railing. She slid against him and wrapped her arms tightly around his neck. They kissed once more, this time hungrily.

His hands tightened, forcing her breasts to flatten against his chest. "I like feeling you against me," he murmured.

Her hands moved from around his neck and slipped inside his open shirt. Gently, her fingertips stroked his flat coppery nipples. "I like the feel of you, too," she whispered.

Johnny closed his eyes and dragged in a ragged breath. "Yes, you're killing me."

Her smile told him she enjoyed his agony. She lowered her head, her lips following her hands in a series of featherlight kisses over his bare chest. "Don't die yet. You promised me breakfast in bed tomorrow, remember?"

He recaptured her velvety lips. Devouring her softness, he plundered her mouth. He felt her arms move back to his neck, her clever little tongue teasing him, inviting him inside.

"Why?" he panted next to her ear. "Why are you letting me have you, *cherie?*"

She ran her fingers through his hair, rubbed her body against him. Nose to nose, lip to lip, she whispered, "Because you take my breath away, Johnny Bernard. You snatched it away from me weeks ago, and you're doing it again right now. No one has ever made me feel the way you make me feel. So have me Johnny, if that's what you want. It's what I want.''

Her admission nearly took him off at the knees. Johnny pulled her close, kissed her again, then lifted her into his arms and carried her back inside. He laid her on the bed and stretched out beside her. She turned into his arms, arched against him and said his name. His fingers caught the hem of her dress. Drawing it upward, he stroked her silky thigh.

At the feel of her, eager and needy, Johnny rolled to his back and pulled her on top of him. ''Straddle me,'' he murmured.

She shoved her dress clean to her waist, then did as he asked. When she lowered herself over him, the feel of her slender thighs brushing his hips made him groan, and he gritted his teeth against the sweet agony of it all.

She spread his shirt wide and trailed light, teasing kisses across his hard chest. Johnny moaned again. ''More,'' he demanded. ''More.''

In answer to his plea, her hands continued to caress the hardness of his chest; at the same time her knees squeezed his waist, and she moved against him. ''Yes, more,'' she whispered. ''More than once. Promise you'll love me all night long, Johnny.''

''All night,'' he promised. ''Take your dress off.''

''Help me,'' she sighed breathlessly.

At her entreaty, he pulled her dress farther up her slender body. Then, giving the slippery thing a fast jerk, he let it fly. ''Drop the lace,'' he said, staring at her full breasts.

She reached around, unhooked the black bra and let it fall to his chest. Brushing it aside, she leaned close and teased his chest with her aroused, hot nipples. Another ragged moan ripped from his chest as Johnny felt her seduction take him past the brink of sanity. She tortured him further by sliding her hand along the inside of his thigh. Her fingers flattened out to cup him through his jeans.

He heard her breath catch with the realization of how badly he desired her. *Needed* her.

Before he lost his head and took her too fast, Johnny quickly pulled her off him and heaved himself from the bed. Gazing down at her, he said, "We're going slower this time. There's no reason to hurry. We've got all night."

She smiled a slow, sexy smile. "I had no complaints about the first time."

"Is that right?" He grinned. "You liked me acting like a wild animal?"

"Actually, I did."

He pulled off his boots, then unzipped his jeans and sent them to the floor along with his underwear. Standing in front of her in all his naked glory, he watched as she slipped off the bed, slowly hooked her fingers into her panties and shoved them past her thighs. Before they reached her knees, he had her on her back once more and was peeling the satin past her ankles.

"You've changed your mind, then?" she asked when he covered her quickly.

"What?"

"I thought we were going slow," she teased.

"Next time," Johnny promised. "Or the next."

Nicole blinked awake. She lay still for a minute, aware sunlight poured through the open balcony doors. Slowly she rolled to her side. Johnny lay on his stomach, one arm draped over his head, the other dangling off the side of the bed. His lips were parted, his eyes closed. His broad, naked back beckoned her to reach out and touch him, but she held back, intrigued with the idea of watching him sleep without his knowing.

He stirred, and the movement drew Nicole's attention

to his long, powerful legs. Even relaxed in sleep, he looked tough as nails.

She inched closer, his heat drawing her body like a magnet. The way he had made love to her last night had been incredible. She closed her eyes for a brief moment, unable to fight her feelings any longer. It was true, she loved him. Loved the way he made love to her. The feel of him. The way he smelled, talked, tasted.

She simply loved every inch of Johnny Bernard.

His eyelids fluttered, and he rolled over. "You like watching naked men sleep, *cherie?*"

Nicole smiled. "It has a certain appeal, yes. How long have you been awake?"

"Long enough." He stretched, rolled sideways. Eyes smiling, he stole a kiss. "Good morning."

Nicole arched into him and felt his arousal against her belly. "Johnny…"

"Shh. Don't say anything. Not yet."

"Breakfast in bed. You were serious?"

The door between the two hotel rooms stood open. Nicole, freshly showered, struck a pose wearing a short lavender satin robe. "Of course, I was serious."

"How long?"

"How long?"

"How long before they come knocking with the food?"

"Thirty minutes."

"Come here."

"No."

"Why not?"

"I have an appointment with Mr. Medoro in two hours. I have to get dressed soon."

She wasn't going to make the appointment. Johnny had plans of his own. He loved loving her, loved making her sigh and say his name. He loved her eyes, her sweet lips.

Touching her soft skin drove him crazy. No, she wasn't going to make her appointment with that long-haired Frenchman.

"Come here."

"Johnny…"

"Okay, I'll come to you."

In an instant he was out of bed, stalking her. Nicole whirled around to dash back into her room. The minute Johnny realized she was heading for the bathroom, he cut her off, forcing her back toward the bed. She stumbled just as he reached for her, and together they landed on the unused double bed.

They were laughing as their eyes locked. Slowly, simultaneously, they sobered.

"I want you again. In *your* bed this time."

"Johnny…"

An hour later Johnny watched Nicole rescue their breakfast tray, which had been left outside his door a long half hour ago. When she returned, she placed the tray in the middle of the bed and sat cross-legged, tucking her robe around her.

"The food's cold," she grumbled, lifting the cover off the seafood omelette.

"Still looks good," Johnny said, popping a slice of banana from the fruit cup into his mouth and chewing with a satisfied grin. He had pulled on a pair of white underwear and now stretched out on his side across the bed.

Nicole cut a small piece of the omelette and sampled it. She speared another forkful and offered it to him. "Want some?"

For an answer, Johnny opened his mouth, took hold of her wrist and steered the fork between his teeth.

She fed him two more bites, then set the fork down, her

attention averted by the puckered scar on his thigh. Slowly, she traced it with her finger. "Where did you get this?"

"In prison."

"A knife fight?"

"No." Johnny picked up the fork and gripped the handle. Raising it, he acted out the scene. "A lot of guys in the joint use whatever they can steal and make them into weapons—forks, spoons, a scrap of metal."

"That's awful. It must have hurt terribly. Did you provoke someone?"

Johnny grinned. "No, I didn't."

"But you did fight back, right?" She gestured to the fork. "With one of those?"

Johnny laid the silver fork down. "No weapon. I'm an ex-marine, remember? If you know how to use your hands, they can be just as deadly as any knife."

"And are your hands deadly?"

Johnny gave her body a long heated look. "I don't know, are they?"

She blushed red. "You are really bad."

"You didn't think so a little while ago," he teased.

She motioned to his scar again. "Stop trying to distract me. What happened after the guy stabbed you?"

"We went a few rounds, then afterwards he spent a couple of days nursing a half-dozen busted ribs and a bruised windpipe, and I got a week in solitary for defending myself a little too good."

"Solitary? That wasn't fair."

Johnny laughed. "Fair? Not much is fair, *cherie.* When I was a kid there was always somebody wanting to see me facedown in the dirt. It wasn't fair, but it didn't change things."

"Farrel?"

"He was a regular. That's how I first met Mae," Johnny admitted. "I used to sneak through the cane fields to keep from being beat up by Farrel and the boys. It usually worked, hiding out in the fields. When it didn't, I hid in Henry's pickup. She found me there once. I guess I'd fallen asleep. After that, she used to leave apples and oranges in the pickup for me. Sometimes comic books. I'd lay on the floor, have an apple, and read until Farrel got tired of looking for me and went home. Then I'd stuff the comic books under the seat and head home.''

When Nicole lowered her eyes, Johnny reached out and gripped her chin. ''I didn't tell you that for pity, *cherie*.''

''I don't pity you, but I do feel bad. Didn't your father or mother ever try to stop them from persecuting you?''

''My father was being harassed most of the time, too. He would come home from work some nights with his face so black and blue, I wondered how he could see to walk home.'' Johnny glanced around, feeling the need for a cigarette. ''Don't go anywhere, I need to find my smokes.''

She put a hand on his arm. ''Last night you said it was a bad habit. So today, do something about it.''

''I suppose a deal's a deal.''

''Meaning?''

''You didn't pace last night 'til midnight did you?''

She smiled. ''No, I didn't, did I?''

''Slept straight through, as I recall,'' Johnny confirmed. Sobering, he said, ''I'd still like to know the story behind it.''

''The story?''

He knew she knew what he was talking about. He drew her close, kissed her. ''Who's Chad?''

She gave him a look of surprise. ''How did you know his name?''

''The night you got drunk you mentioned him. Not enough to explain anything, but enough for me to know he hurt you somehow. Who is he, *cherie?*''

She glanced away, then faced him again. "Chad was one of my college professors. When my parents died, he was there for me. At the time, I needed someone older and wiser. He fit the bill perfectly."

She tried to leave the bed, but Johnny hung on to her. "What happened?"

"He changed his mind. Maybe he got bored. I don't know. The reason isn't important."

"Hard to believe that it was boredom. There had to be more to it."

She narrowed her eyes, bit at her lip. Finally she lowered her eyes and stared at her hands folded in her lap. "He wasn't honest with me. He talked about the future, even mentioned marriage. I got careless."

"Careless?"

"All right. Pregnant."

Johnny tensed. "And?"

"You should see your face. Why is that such a scary word for men to hear?" She laughed bitterly.

"I'm not scared. Surprised, is all. You don't look the careless type."

"Well, don't worry, having sex with me won't make you a daddy. You can breathe easy."

Johnny frowned. "I don't deserve your anger. I'm not Chad. Now finish the story."

"It's the old story, really. Student falls for her art teacher, gets pregnant, and he walks. That's it." She turned away.

Johnny sat up, gripped her arms and forced her to look at him. "That's not the end of the story. What happened to the baby?"

She tried to pull away, but he wouldn't let her. "Easy, *cherie*. Take it easy."

"I—I lost her, okay! I lost her in the fifth month." She swatted at his arm to make him let go, but instead Johnny

pulled her close and cradled her in his arms as she started
to cry. He didn't know what to say. *I'm sorry* seemed
inadequate, so he opted to say nothing. He just held her.

They fell asleep in each other's arms. Some time later,
Nicole woke up and realized she'd missed her appointment
with Mr. Medoro. "My appointment," she sighed. "I forgot my appointment."

Johnny continued to hold her close. "Shh. He'll understand. We'll call him later."

She sat up. "You knew I had an appointment. Why
didn't you wake me?"

He tugged her back into the circle of his arms. "I was
hoping to convince you to spend the day in bed with me."

"All day?"

"All day." He swept her robe off her shoulders to expose a perfect breast.

"Johnny…"

"The first time I saw you," he said huskily, "I wanted
to throw you to the floor in the boathouse and rip your
clothes off. Did you know that?"

"You did?"

"Those long legs of yours, your pretty knees. I had just
gotten out of prison, *cherie*. What the hell were you thinking of, showing up dressed like that?"

"You weren't supposed to be there, remember? You
said three-thirty or four. I had given myself plenty of time
to drop Gran's note off, open the windows, and leave well
before you ever saw me."

"Then I guess it was fate."

"No, just bad timing."

"*Bad* timing?" Determined to put the sparkle back in
her blue eyes, Johnny pretended to be offended. Then, just
as quickly, his grin turned mischievous, and he lunged at
her. Nicole screamed as he began tickling her and wrestling with her on the bed. It wasn't long before he had

pinned her beneath him. Seconds later the laughter ceased. Slowly, he kneed her legs apart and eased himself between them. "Spend the day in bed with me, *cherie?* All day?"

"All day?"

"Starting now."

"Now?"

Johnny glanced down at her naked breasts, and before his eyes her nipples pebbled. Smugly, his gaze locked with hers once more. "I'll take that as a 'yes.'"

Chapter 13

After taking a dozen pictures of Belle and the old farm-house on the hillside, Nicole found herself inside Johnny's childhood home. She'd decided days ago on the way back from New Orleans that she wanted to paint it. Johnny had been talking about tearing it down, and she wanted to cap-ture it on canvas before it was gone, or at least have photos to work from later.

It was just the sort of picture that would sell at the gal-lery in New Orleans, she thought, though she wasn't so sure she would be able to part with it once it was finished.

And she would finish it. She was back working again, spending at least five hours a day secluded high in the attic. Since she and Johnny had returned from New Orleans, it was as if a great burden had been lifted from her shoulders. She was working daily, and sleeping through the nights, and it was absolutely wonderful.

How and why it had happened, she wasn't sure. But she knew Johnny was partly responsible. Or maybe he was entirely responsible. He'd filled up the empty hole in her life, and in her heart, as well.

The interior of the house was dark because the windows had been boarded up. Nicole carefully walked through each room; the crude, less-than-efficient kitchen, the adjoining living room with just a few dilapidated furnishings. Two small bedrooms, one with a ragged mattress rotting in the corner.

She realized something that she hadn't been aware of until now—Johnny's childhood had been more than simply hard; it had bordered on child neglect. He'd lived without running water or electricity, and most likely without a real bed, if the tiny room with the old mattress in the corner was, in fact, his.

In that moment, her heart went out to that small boy who must have ached for a normal life. Was that why Gran had worked so hard to befriend him and then to protect him? Was that why Johnny had finally given in and accepted her in his life all those years ago?

Since they had returned from New Orleans, he seemed different. Up by six, working shirtless until supper time. He hardly stopped to rest. And after supper, instead of relaxing on the front porch or playing cards with Bick, he spent hours in the study tending to the bills and renovating costs.

He hadn't brought up leaving Oakhaven in a very long time. Still, Nicole was sure he intended to go back to Lafayette as soon as his parole was over. Just thinking about it made her want to cry, but the truth was, Johnny had never made any promises to her. She had known all along that he would be leaving at the end of the summer. She wouldn't pressure him into staying. Yes, if he told her he had changed his mind, she would be thrilled. She might even be brave enough to confess her feelings. But it was just wishful thinking, his staying. Wishful, dangerous thinking, when the odds were that he would leave as suddenly as he'd come.

When the door groaned open, Nicole was just returning to the living room. Face to face with Johnny, she stopped dead in her tracks.

"What are you doing here, *cherie?*"

"I—I was photographing the outside of the house, and..." Nicole flushed. "I was curious."

"Curious?"

"Maybe that's the wrong word." She noticed he was sweat-stained and dirty. His bare chest gleamed with a sheen of perspiration. She didn't care. In a second, with the slightest encouragement, she would slip into his arms and forget everything but the feel of his powerful arms around her.

"No, I think *curious* is the right word," he said, closing the door. He glanced around, his eyes taking in the stark surroundings. "It looks bad, but it really never looked good." He gave her a half smile.

"I'm sorry."

"I told you before, I don't want your pity."

"I don't pity you, but I do wish things had been different for you." She broke eye contact with him and moved to stand near a small stone fireplace. She wasn't there long before she felt him come up behind her. "I saw you from the rooftop," he said softly. "I wondered where you were off to, so I followed." He nosed in close. "I'd like to touch you, but I'm ripe."

Nicole turned around. "It never stopped you before. I like you any way you are, even 'ripe.' We haven't had much time together since we came back from New Orleans. You've been working day and night."

"So, the pretty lady is feeling needy today, is that it?"

"Don't tease me, Johnny."

He bent forward and kissed her without laying a hand

on her. "We could go to the swimming hole. I could wash up, and you could strip for me." He wiggled his dark eyebrows. "I'd like that."

"I'd like that, too."

He moved in to steal another kiss, then hesitated. "Do you smell smoke?"

"Smoke?" She watched him turn away and stride quickly back to the door. He tried to open it. No success. "Johnny?"

"Dammit!"

"Johnny?"

He slammed his shoulder into the door. Then again.

"Johnny! Is the house on fire?" Nicole could smell the smoke now. She hurried to one of the boarded-up windows and tried to peek out through the slats, but had no luck. "When did you board up the windows?" she asked.

He spun around, his gaze taking in the windows one by one. "Hell, when was that done?"

"You didn't do it?"

"No."

"Oh, my God, Johnny. We're trapped!"

Johnny rammed the door once more before he gave up and hurried to one of the newly boarded-up windows. He couldn't believe he hadn't noticed them before now, but he'd followed Nicole, and all he'd been thinking about was catching up with her and getting some time alone with her. Checking the windows, he found they had been nailed shut from the outside, making them impossible to open.

A rumbling noise alerted him that the fire had taken root and was growing fast; the smell of gasoline confirmed things were going to heat up in a matter of seconds. The moment he thought it, he saw live flames eating through the wall. As they licked across the tinder-dry ceiling, black smoke began to fill the room. He dragged Nicole to the floor. "Stay down," he instructed.

He remembered the old root cellar, just as an explosion rocked the building and a spray of live flames sailed through the air. Quickly, he pulled Nicole beneath him to shield her. He grunted as something solid struck him low on his back, but he didn't take time to acknowledge the searing pain. A thick fog of gray smoke was filling the room, blinding them. He knew they were running out of time.

Dragging Nicole with him, he belly-crawled toward his childhood bedroom, hoping against hope that he hadn't gotten turned around in the smoke-filled room. Overhead, the trusses were creaking, only seconds away from crashing down on them.

"Come on," he shouted, demanding that Nicole follow him as he felt his way toward his small bedroom. His throat was on fire; his eyes felt like two hot coals. He knew Nicole must be feeling the same way, and he was afraid for her. Moving faster, he dragged himself deeper into the pea-soup smoke, knowing that if they were going to survive—and by damn, they were—he had to get them into the root cellar.

When his shoulder banged into something solid, he swung his right arm to the side and confirmed, with great relief, that it was the doorjamb.

"Johnny…"

Nicole's voice sounded weak. He hardly heard it for the roar of the wild flames eating up the wood. With urgent purpose, he pulled her close, just as another explosion sent more debris crashing down around them. Quickly, he flattened himself out on top of Nicole, until he was sure no more flying debris would harm her. Then he swiftly hauled himself upright again.

Swinging his arm out like a blind man who'd lost his

cane, Johnny made contact with his old mattress. The minute he had his bearings, he located the trapdoor beneath it and thrust the heavy door open. "Come on, *cherie,* we've got to hurry. Down here."

When she didn't respond immediately, Johnny scooped her up, drew her close to his body, then dropped into the hole, cradling Nicole against him.

The force of the ten-foot drop ended with a bone-jarring jolt. It knocked the wind out of Johnny, and he groaned in agony as he lay there trying to get past the pain. Just as he was sitting up, another explosion ripped through the house, verifying that the ceiling had caved in.

"Johnny, where are we?" Nicole began to cough.

He pulled her close and hugged her tightly. "We're in the cellar. Catch your breath. We can't stay here long."

When he could move, he got to his feet and ushered Nicole to a safe corner of the cellar, then he climbed up the skeleton ladder, half eaten away by age, and pulled the trapdoor closed. Feeling the heat in the floorboards, he dropped back into the hole, knowing they didn't have long before the floor overhead caved in on them.

Anxiously, he began to search for the tunnel he'd dug as a kid. It had been useful when Farrel and the boys were hot on his trail, had saved his hide a number of times when he was too far from the house to escape them. He sighed with relief as he found the narrow tunnel, then checked to see if he could still fit through it. To his surprise it seemed wider than he remembered, but he didn't consider why that was, only that it was the only escape route they had, and that he was thankful for it.

He heard her coughing again and hurried back to her. "This way, *cherie.* There's a tunnel."

She squinted up at him. "A tunnel? Down here?"

"I dug it when I was a kid. I hope you're not claustrophobic,'' he teased halfheartedly, trying to pull a smile from her frightened face.

''Would it matter?''

''No. Where I go, you go.'' When she said nothing, Johnny reached down and hauled her up. She was trembling, completely exhausted, but she was *alive,* doing better than he had expected. He gave her a quick kiss, then urged her toward the tunnel. ''I'll go first, just in case there's an animal living in there.''

Johnny saw what looked like artificial light soon after they entered the tunnel and made the first turn. The distant glow became brighter as they crawled toward it. Five minutes later, on hands and knees, Johnny and Nicole entered a tiny underground room lit by a single lantern burning in one corner.

In the other corner, clutching a bottle of whiskey, sat Jasper Craig.

Chapter 14

Johnny took in the small hand-dug room with keen interest. When his gaze moved back to Jasper Craig, the town drunk was sitting straighter, his back against the dirt wall. "What the hell are you doing in here, old man?"

"I'm doing nothing," Jasper mumbled, glancing at Nicole, then back to Johnny. "I—I heard loud noises. Something happened, didn't it?"

"Yeah, something sure as hell did," Johnny agreed. "Somebody just set fire to my house with a gas can. That is, after locking us inside. You know who would want to do that, or am I looking at the man responsible?"

"Me?" Wide-eyed, Jasper shook his head emphatically. "Not me. I'd never burn down Madie's house. Never." He licked his pale lips. "I wouldn't hurt her son, neither."

The mention of his mother made Johnny frown. "Why would you care one way or the other?"

Jasper suddenly surprised Johnny by offering him a smile. He relinquished his hold on his bottle, setting it beside him, and reached for a covered wooden box.

"Easy, old man," Johnny warned.

Again he said, "I'd never hurt Madie's son." He flipped open the top of the box and began fumbling through an array of possessions. Finally he found what he was searching for and pulled a gold locket from his stash.

Johnny recognized the locket immediately. It had been his mother's, but it should have been in his drawer back at the boathouse along with his father's cheap watch. He reached out, snatched the older man's wrist and took the locket. "This is mine. What the hell are you doing with it? You steal it, old man?"

"I didn't steal it," Jasper argued. "I took it back, is all. It ain't yours. I bought it, paid top dollar years ago. Had it engraved. Madie would want me to have it back."

Johnny examined the locket, but saw no signs of engraving.

Jasper said, "Look behind the picture."

Johnny opened the locket and carefully peeled out the small picture of himself. Sure enough, as Jasper had promised, Johnny found a small engraved inscription: *To my Madie, Love J.P.*

Jasper wiped his nose on his sleeve. Then, in a conspiratorial whisper, he said, "We were in love." Pointing to the locket, he said, "That proves it." He dug once more into his box and handed Johnny a picture. "This is my favorite, but I got lots more if you want to see."

Rocked off balance by Jasper's claim, Johnny stared at the two people in the framed photograph. It was easy to recognize his mother. Jasper was a little harder to identify—the years hadn't been kind. *We were in love.* The possibility of that seemed remote, but then, his mother was awfully young in the picture.

Nicole leaned over and eyed the picture. "Is it your mother?"

"Yeah, it's her," Johnny confirmed. He tossed the locket back to Jasper, but hung on to the picture.

Jasper caught the locket, stared at Johnny for a minute, then tucked it back in his box.

They were three feet away from where Jasper sat. He smelled bad—a mix of stale liquor and urine. His pale blue shirt was soiled with dirt, his gray pants torn at the knees. The first time Johnny had seen Jasper in Tuck's office he'd noticed the dirt on his pants, and now he knew why—the old man had been spending his days in the tunnel with his whiskey and that box of memories.

His gaze shifted deeper inside the tunnel. A draft of air floated into the small space, causing the light to flicker and the foul smell to rise and drift. An old cooking pot sat on a dead fire, a gunnysack not far from it. Johnny asked, "What's in the sack?"

"Supper," Jasper answered. "Frogs, mostly."

Johnny heard Nicole suck in her breath, and he squeezed her hand to reassure her that it was all right. "Farrel know about the tunnel, old man?"

"No. He comes looking for me sometimes, though. I hear him calling to me, but I don't answer. He don't like me being here."

"Anyone else come around?"

The old man hesitated, looked away. "No. No one else."

"You sure?" Johnny watched the old man's eyes blink several times. "Don't lie to me," he warned.

"No one else knows I come here. Just Farrel."

The sack moved, and Nicole gasped.

Jasper turned and whacked it hard. "No reason to be afraid," he said. "They're just frogs."

"So tell me your story, old man," Johnny encouraged, finally handing the portrait back. "Tell me about my mother and you."

Jasper nodded, the topic obviously one he enjoyed. "We grew up together. I lived on the hill just out of town. Still do. I don't know if you knew your mama was adopted. Old Glady Keen took her in, mostly to have someone to do her work for her, I always thought."

"I knew about Mrs. Keen."

Jasper scratched his chest. "I wanted to marry her, but my folks didn't think she was right for me. I had to sneak out of the house to see her." Jasper sniffed, then wiped his nose again on his dirty shirtsleeve. "It was all my fault," he muttered. "We were gonna run away and get married. But first I had to take a trip to Baton Rouge with my folks. I met Farrel's mother there." He shrugged dejectedly. "I ended up getting Nora pregnant. I could say she tricked me, but I was a young buck back then. I thought I could have whatever I wanted. An affair out of town didn't seem all that terrible. A lot of men kicked up their heels before they tied the knot. Only, I got caught. In those days you did the right thing and owned up to your mistakes."

Johnny vaguely remembered Farrel's mother. A fancy dresser. Skinny. A blonde with a plastic smile and cold green eyes. She'd left Jasper before Farrel turned ten.

"Madie was my only love," Jasper admitted, "but I ruined it. She refused to talk to me after I came home and word got out that I was engaged to Nora. A few months later there was talk she was seeing Delmar Bernard. It didn't make any sense. Sure he was a good-looker, but he was Carl Bernard's son. She had no business getting mixed up with a Bernard, and I told her so. Only, she told me I didn't have any right to tell her nothing. She said Delmar was a good man, honest, and that all the rumors were just that—rumors." Jasper flushed. "You won't like to hear this, boy, but those stories weren't rumors. They were all true. I know 'cause I seen it with my own eyes."

Johnny held up his hand. "What rumors?"

"Your grandpa Carl was a womanizer. A no-good wife stealer! That's what." Jasper's nostrils flared. "He busted up half a dozen families in this town, sweet-talking the women into forgetting who they had promised themselves to. Nobody in town talks about it anymore, but that don't mean it didn't happen. We that knew the truth just let it die along with your grandpa."

"Only, you didn't let it die, did you?" Johnny accused. "My father and I paid daily for that old sin."

Jasper lowered his eyes. "That's true. In some ways you're right. But the pain ran deep, boy." He faced Johnny once more. "Your daddy could have passed for Carl any day of the week. That black hair and those eyes kept the memory alive for many of us."

"My father was a decent man," Johnny argued. "He loved my mother and was faithful to her."

"I believe he was. Only, to me, that just made things worse. I was angry that he had won my Madie, and every chance I got, I beat the hell out of him for it. The truth is, I hired him at the lumberyard just so I could take him apart whenever I wanted to. And I did, plenty of times. I'm not proud of it, but he had my Madie. Don'tcha see, boy? He owned my life."

"So you beat him up because *you* made a mistake." Johnny shook his head, so angry that he could hardly sit there a minute longer. If Jasper weren't so pathetic, Johnny would have reached out and strangled the bastard.

Jasper's face twisted in pain. "I don't deserve to live. I know it. You'd have every right to hate me. I hate myself." He squeezed his eyes shut, the pain of living continuing to tear him in two. "She was mine, she'll always be mine," he mumbled.

Johnny never once glanced Nicole's way, but he knew she was silently absorbing everything Jasper Craig said.

Unconsciously, she had slid close to him, her small hand tightly clasped in his, her shoulder pressed against his arm. "So who set fire to my house, old man? Farrel?"

"No. My son hates you, but if he was going to kill you, I think he would have done it long ago."

That made sense—Johnny felt much the same way. In fact, that's what he'd told the judge at his trial. "Then who?"

Jasper's eyes widened. "I don't know. I—I can't say."

"Can't...or won't?"

"Carl had a lot of enemies. Some of those men could never forgive their wives. I don't know, boy. I don't know who it is," he said again. "I'd never hurt Madie, and hurting you would hurt her. I come here to talk to her and be with her. Farrel won't let me keep this stuff in our house. I have to leave it here. I hide in the tunnel so Farrel can't find me when he comes looking for me, but I don't hurt nobody."

"Farrel knew about my mother, didn't he?"

Jasper nodded. "He overheard me and Nora arguing about her when he was real young. I was sorry about that."

After Jasper stubbornly refused to leave the tunnel with them, Johnny and Nicole belly-crawled a quarter mile, and emerged from the underground hole just west of the house, a few yards from the shoreline of Belle. Gazing toward the hillside, Johnny saw there was nothing left of the house, just a pile of rubble.

The past was starting to make sense now. Johnny had always wondered why the town had hated the sight of a Bernard, and now he knew. He turned back and stared at Nicole. "How are you?" He gently touched a nasty bruise on her shoulder. "That's going to hurt like hell in the morning."

She looked him over in much the same manner, concern in her eyes. "You look worse than I do. You've reopened the old cut on your arm." She spun him around and examined his back. "And there's a bloody gash on your back that needs tending."

He turned and took her hands in his. Slowly, he brought them to his lips and kissed each palm. "I'm not worried about me," he drawled. "You sure you're not hurt anywhere else?"

"No, I don't think so."

"Maybe I should have a look-see to make sure," he teased, trying to lighten the moment. "Come on. Mae must have seen the smoke. She'll be worried."

They started toward the driveway. Nicole said, "Will you report this to Sheriff Tucker?"

"I suppose so, but it won't do much good. We don't have a suspect."

"Should you call your parole officer?"

"It wouldn't hurt." He glanced at her once more. "You sure you're okay?"

"Yes."

She had dirt smeared on her face, her clothes were torn, and she had a number of tiny cuts and bruises on her arms and legs. "Starting now, I want you to stay close to Oakhaven. Until I get some answers, we're going to have to be extra careful."

"All right—as long as you promise to be careful, too."

"I promise."

"If Sheriff Tucker turns a blind eye like last time, who will help us?"

That was a good question. Johnny didn't know how to answer, but he didn't intend to worry Nicole about that right now. Again he was struck with how close he'd come to losing her. He had never minded putting himself on the line before, facing bad odds or worse. But gambling with Nicole's safety was one thing he wouldn't do. He was in love with her, had been for weeks, maybe even from the moment he'd laid eyes on her. But today, those feelings had been magnified, and the fear of losing her had shaken him like nothing else ever had. It had also opened his eyes to a new truth—one that would change his life forever if he was brave enough to face it head-on.

"This is Detective Archard from New Orleans, Gran," Nicole said by way of introduction. "He's a friend of Johnny's parole officer. He's here to investigate the fire."

The tall sandy-haired man shook Mae's hand. "Sure is a beautiful place you got here, Mrs. Chapman." From where he stood on the front porch, Ryland Archard gazed out over the freshly plowed fields. "Looks like good soil out there."

"If you don't mind me saying so, how would a New Orleans detective know anything about it?"

The detective smiled and turned to give Mae his full attention. "I'm from Texas, Mrs. Chapman. We didn't plant much for crops, but we sure grew a lot of beef."

"So can you help us, Detective?" Nicole asked. Johnny had joined them on the porch, and she found herself drawn to him for moral support.

"Like I told Johnny, Miss Chapman, I'll try my best," Detective Archard said.

Fifteen minutes later Johnny and the detective were on their way to see Sheriff Tucker, leaving Mae and Nicole alone on the front porch.

"I just can't believe someone set fire to the farmhouse," Mae sighed. "Thank God, Johnny followed you, and thank God, he dug that tunnel years ago."

"Did you know about Carl Bernard?" she asked. "Was Jasper Craig telling the truth? Were there women in town who were intimate with Johnny's grandfather?"

She was standing at the porch railing, and when Gran

made no comment, she turned around. "Did you hear what I— Gran, what's wrong? You look as pale as a sheet."

Mae turned her head away and gazed across the front yard. The sun was setting and the sky was streaked pink. "Carl was a handsome man, Nicki. Just like Johnny. He could charm a woman out of her dress before she realized what she'd done. His only crime was liking women and enjoying their company too much. All women—short, tall, thin, heavy. He didn't discriminate, and I truly believe he loved them all in his own way. He had such a smooth way about him—a gentleman in rags, I used to call him."

Mae's voice had turned wistful, as if she felt the need to speak reverently about a man the entire town thought was the devil himself. Nicole's heart started to pound. "Gran…?"

"Yes, Nicki. I was one of those women. I cheated on my Henry with Carl Bernard."

The shocking admission momentarily stole Nicole's voice. Finally, she said, "Gran, you don't have to say any more. It was a long time ago, and he probably tricked you. He—"

"No, Nicki, he didn't trick me. He may have seduced me a little with his smooth manner, but I knew what I was doing. He was the kind of man a woman just had a hard time saying 'no' to." She turned to look at Nicole. "I'm sorry if I've shocked you. You must think I'm a terrible old woman."

Nicole didn't think that at all. Gran had just admitted to being human. Everyone made mistakes. Nicole herself had made several in the past year. "I don't think you're terrible." She spoke quietly. "I love you and think you're wonderful—that will never change. You could have ignored the truth, but you didn't. You didn't put all the blame on Carl."

"It was time I told you."

"And I need to tell *you* something," Nicole said suddenly.

"What is it, Nicki?"

"Remember when I told you about Chad? Well, I left out the most important part." She stopped suddenly, took a deep breath, then charged on. "I got pregnant, Gran. That's the real reason he walked out on me. He didn't want to be a father, and I—I wasn't so sure I wanted to be a mother, either. But there I was, pregnant, and in a blink of an eye, alone."

"Oh, Nicki, you should have told me. You must never think you're alone. This is your home, I'm family."

"I know, but I was ashamed." Nicole wiped the tears from her eyes. "After weeks of crying my eyes out, I got angry. Angry at Chad and then at myself. Even angry at the baby. But then the most wonderful thing happened. A few months later I felt her move inside me. My baby moved. From that day on, my life meant something. Then—" Nicole turned away, stared out into the front yard. "Then one night I woke up with violent stomach pains. By the time I got to the hospital, I was already in labor."

She forced herself to face her grandmother once more. "I lost my little girl, Gran."

"Oh, Nicki, I'm so sorry. Come here, dear."

Nicole wiped the tears from her cheeks, then knelt by Gran's chair. "I should have told you sooner. I just didn't know how. But when you told me about Carl, I—"

"You didn't feel like you were the only imperfect one in this family."

"Oh, no, Gran. I would never judge you."

"Hush, dear. It's all right. Life is hard to live, but we do the best we can. And whether we want it to or not, life goes on."

"Did Grandpa Henry forgive you?" Nicole asked.

"Yes, he did. Many of the men in town didn't, though. Griffin Black disowned his wife. Pearl Lavel's oldest sister left town in shame, not telling a soul where she was going. Frank Gilmore's wife left four small children behind. And there were many others who sold their homes and moved away. Some with their husbands, some without. It was a horrible time for this town, but Henry and I got through it together."

"You didn't end up hating Carl Bernard, though? Blaming him just a little?"

"No. Like I said, he never forced me into anything I didn't want to do. I could have said no."

"And he was married, too?"

"Yes. His wife left him finally, when Delmar was in high school. Like some of the others, she ran off in the middle of the night and never let Carl know where she'd gone. Delmar turned out as handsome as his father, and I think that was salt in everyone's wounds. Delmar in Carl's image only kept the scandal alive. Carl died of a stroke at fifty-five. Delmar stayed on the farm, and not long after high school he married Madie. The rest you know."

Nicole moved to the wicker chair next to Mae and sat. "So do you think maybe Griffin Black or one of the others is responsible for the fire?"

"It's very possible. But Griffin remarried soon after, and now all he thinks about is buying up more land and making money so that fancy young wife of his can spend it. I don't believe he's living in the past any longer."

"So who else, then? Think, Gran. Who have you forgotten about?"

Mae sat quietly for a moment, thinking. Disgusted, she said, "I just don't know. Most of those people moved away or are as old as I am."

"Then maybe the person we're looking for isn't old,"

Nicole decided. "Maybe Jasper Craig is lying to protect Farrel."

Suddenly, Nicole wanted to speak to Johnny, to touch him and make sure he was all right. He had told her to stay close to Oakhaven, but she felt he should be taking his own advice. Glancing toward the road, she prayed he would come home soon.

Nicole paced the floor in the study. It had been hours since Johnny and the detective had gone to town. What was taking so long? Three full hours had passed.

She stopped in front of the window and looked out. The sky was dark, and it had started to rain. She was growing anxious. *Terrified* was a better word. Had something horrible happened to Johnny? No, she wouldn't accept that. He was with Detective Archard. What could happen?

Again she searched the long, dark driveway, hoping to see lights. "Where are you, Johnny? What's going on?"

Twenty minutes later, Nicole snatched up her keys and headed out the front door. It took her less than ten minutes to get to town. Once there, she checked the police station, only to find it dark; the green Blazer the detective owned was nowhere in sight. She decided to drive the streets in search of them, noting it wouldn't take very long since the town was so small.

She ran the streets north and south first, then started on the east-west route. She was ready to give up when she noticed the Blazer parked in the back lot of the Pass-By Motel. Relieved, she pulled in alongside the Blazer, then got out of her car. The lot was dark, and the hotel was lit by a single light coming from Virgil's office.

Nicole was headed for the office when she heard a noise. Spooked by what had happened at the farmhouse two days earlier, she flattened herself against the building and clung there a minute. Frustrated, she hissed softly, "Damn you, Johnny. The things I do for you."

"Are you keeping a record so you can get paid later, *cherie?*"

Johnny's silky drawl was right next to her ear. Nicole gasped and nearly jumped out of her cutoff jeans and tennis shoes. She whirled around to find him standing with his hands on his hips and his dark eyes narrowed.

"I thought I told you to stay put." His voice was tight and not at all friendly.

"I've been waiting at home for hours. I thought you were probably lying in some ditch somewhere. Honestly, couldn't you have called?"

"And tell you what?"

His inconsiderate answer struck a nerve, and Nicole turned defensive. "Sorry for cramping your style." She glanced behind him to see if they were alone or if Detective Archard was close by. As far as she could tell, they were alone.

He saw her glance over his shoulder and turned slightly. "You expecting someone?"

"No. Are you?"

"What kind of question is that? I've been with Ryland Archard since I left Oakhaven. He's one helluva cop. Best of all, he's in my corner."

"But would he be if he knew the whole story?"

"Meaning…?"

Nicole knew she shouldn't have brought up his grandpa. Still, it made her angry that the man had dared to disrupt so many lives and hurt so many people, her own family included.

"I asked you a question, *cherie.*"

"I just meant your grandfather was a…"

"A womanizing bastard," he finished for her. He stood

tall and straight, towering over her, his hands on his lean hips. "Are you suddenly thinking I'm the same?"

"That's not fair." Nicole felt the challenge and didn't back down. She jammed her hands on her own waist and glared back at him. "I didn't say that. I'm not comparing you with him."

He moved closer, so close Nicole was forced back against the wall. "Am I scum in your eyes now, *cherie?* Have I soiled you?"

"Stop it. I'm just upset and worried. And—"

"And that's why I want you back at Oakhaven. Ryland's been picking Virgil's brain about the old days, trying to get a lead on who this crazy might be. So until we know who it is, I want you home where you'll be safe. Now, be a good girl and do what you're told."

Nicole resented his condescending words, as well as being sent home like a naughty little girl. "Okay, fine." She moved past him.

He grabbed her arm. "Don't do that. Don't walk away mad."

"Let go, Johnny. I'm not some helpless child who needs to be told when to go home. I sure as hell don't need you telling me to be good and do what I'm told, either. Now get your hands off me!"

When he released her, she started back to the car. She'd only taken three steps before he caught up with her. He didn't touch her, but he kept pace.

They reached her car in short order, and to Nicole's surprise, as she attempted to open the door, Johnny captured her around the waist and whirled her into his arms. Holding her next to his hard body, he nuzzled her neck, then kissed her ear before whispering, "I don't want anything to happen to you, dammit. Right now that's the most important thing to me. If I'm acting a little crazy, *cherie,* it's only because I care. But that doesn't give me the right to talk to you like I did. I'm sorry.'' He pulled back to gaze down at her, then he lowered his head and kissed her.

Nicole didn't want to be a clinging vine, but she gave in to her emotions and slipped her arms around Johnny's waist. Soon the kiss turned long and deep, and when they finally parted, Johnny said, ''We might be out half the night. If I find out anything, I'll call you. I promise.''

''Just don't be a hero, Johnny,'' Nicole pleaded. ''Don't take any chances. I don't want to add more pressure to the situation, but you have to know I love you.'' When he would have said something, she quickly pressed her fingers to his warm lips. ''No, don't say anything. I didn't come here to spill my guts, and I don't expect you to say anything back. Just be careful.''

Nicole met Daisi Buillard in front of her house on Mill Street at ten-thirty. Unlike the other times they'd met, tonight Daisi wore sloppy jeans and a T-shirt, her feet shoved into a pair of black tennis shoes. Her pretty hair, she'd stuffed under a baseball cap.

''I can't believe I'm doin' this,'' she said, climbing into the car and handing Nicole the key. ''If you get caught, both our backsides are gonna be lunch meat,'' she said bluntly.

Nicole took the key. ''I appreciate your lending me the key. I couldn't have broken into the police station without it.''

''Are you sure you should be doin' this? Why not just wait until tomorrow?''

''Sheriff Tucker hates me. He wouldn't help me any more than he'd help Johnny. I have to do this tonight.'' Nicole glanced at Daisi, suddenly not so sure she should have involved her friend in something illegal. Especially breaking into the very place where she worked.

"Woody doesn't have a chance, does he? You really got it bad for Johnny Bernard, don't you?"

Nicole's smile was a little sad. "I love him, Daisi. But I'm not so naive as to think that love will get me what I want. I've resigned myself to the fact that Johnny's leaving soon. It hurts—only, it would have hurt so much more if I hadn't gotten to know him. He's a good man, Daisi. He truly is a wonderful man."

"Woody's goin' to be heartsick. Oh, well, I'll still be your friend," Daisi teased, "even though I was hopin' we'd be sisters someday."

"You're the best, Daisi." Nicole leaned across the seat and hugged her friend. "I'll get the key back to you. I promise."

She left Daisi at the curb and turned the corner on Cooper. Avoiding Main Street altogether, she turned off the headlights and headed into the alley. After parking under a massive weeping willow, she slipped from the car and crept along the side of the building, keeping a watchful eye out for any passerby. If she saw someone, she intended to walk past the station house and round the block as if she were just out for a stroll.

Luckily, the streets were empty as she neared the door, and she slipped inside with relative ease. She locked the door from the inside, then stuffed the key in her pocket.

She had been ready to head home just as Johnny had instructed when she decided there might be something in the files in Sheriff Tucker's office that would shed some light on who might be out for revenge.

The small flashlight she'd taken from the glove compartment would come in handy, and she snapped it on and directed the narrow beam down the hall. With hurried steps, she passed Daisi's desk and headed for Sheriff Tucker's office. Outside his door, she stopped to catch her breath, then turned the doorknob. She sighed with relief when the door opened, and she eased into the office. As she scanned the room with the flashlight to get reacquainted, the beam of light passed over the file cabinets along one wall, then the sheriff's desk, strewn with papers. She was moving toward the row of files when she heard a noise—

Oh, God! She froze, then turned off her flashlight.

Holding her breath, she listened as footsteps started down the hall. She knew whoever it was had to have a key, and it didn't take too much imagination to figure out who that was. Nicole scrambled toward the file cabinets to hide. She nearly fell on her face in the dark as she tried to reach the narrow space along the wall. Sucking into the tight gap, she crouched low and held her breath.

The door creaked open moments later. A flashlight—the beam the size of a searchlight—illuminated the room. Panic seized Nicole when the flashlight zeroed in on her hiding place. "You really are starting to annoy me, Miss Chapman," Sheriff Tucker said. "Crawl out of there."

Nicole felt herself shudder as Clifton Tucker strolled forward, roughly gripped her arm and hauled her out of her hiding place. "I'm sorry," she said, trying to think of a way to explain. "I know this looks bad, but—"

"Nothing happens in this town without me knowing about it, Miss Chapman. Nothing."

Nicole snapped her mouth shut, surprised by the deadly tone in his voice. His eyes had taken on a glassy quality, she noted, and had narrowed in the bright light. At that moment she realized the truth. "It's you, isn't it? You're the one—"

The words barely out of her mouth, Nicole swung her flashlight at Clifton Tucker's head as hard as she could. The weapon made a sickening *thud,* and the sheriff groaned in pain and staggered back. Free, Nicole scrambled for the door. Just as she thought she would escape, he lunged at her and grabbed her around the waist. Her flashlight clattered to the floor as his strong arms lifted her and threw her into one of the metal file cabinets along the wall. The impact made Nicole see stars.

Then nausea rose up in her throat—and everything went black.

Chapter 15

Farrel had an airtight alibi for the afternoon of the fire, as did Clete Gilmore and Jack Oden. The last name on Johnny's list had been an old-timer who lived in Assumption Parish, some thirty miles away. But Tweed Bowdeen hadn't even remembered who Carl Bernard was—Tweed had had a stroke and had been housebound for several years. Johnny and Ryland were forced to admit they had hit a dead end.

"It's late," Johnny said, once they were back on the road heading home to Common. "Let's call it quits for tonight."

"Sounds good," Ryland agreed. "We'll sleep on it, and get an early start in the morning."

Ryland Archard was one of the NOPD's toughest, and he was used to getting stonewalled. But he was also used to working a number of angles, and looking at trouble from both sides of the law. He said, "I've got two days before I have to be back. There's still time, and a few rocks we haven't overturned. Keep the faith, Johnny."

Johnny had never had much faith in cops, but then, he'd never met a cop like Ryland Archard. The man was honest and straightforward. A regular guy with a normal-size ego.

Johnny checked his watch and found it was past eleven. The weather had turned sour, with thunder rumbling like a bowling alley on a Saturday night, and sheet lightning dancing across the black sky.

Ryland reached over and snatched a cigarette from Johnny's T-shirt pocket. "I need to quit, but it's not going good."

Johnny nodded. "I've quit."

"The hell. What are you doing with smokes in your pocket, then?"

"As long as I know they're there, I don't need them. Sounds crazy, I know. But it's been working so far." Johnny grinned. "It was Nicole's idea."

The detective grinned back, flashing his straight teeth. "You meet a woman, and she helps you quit smoking. I meet a woman, and start up. Lucky bastard." Ryland's smile widened, then he took a long drag off his cigarette.

Johnny's thoughts turned to the dilemma he'd been wrestling with all day. Finally, he asked, "If we can't solve this thing, what are the odds of getting my parole moved somewhere else, real quick-like?"

"It can be done," Ryland assured. "I'll work on it, if and when you decide that's what you want."

"I think I do. Nicole and Mae have been put in an awful position since I came to town. I don't want to see either one of them hurt any more." Johnny cracked the window to let the smoke from Ry's cigarette filter out, then sank into the seat and closed his eyes. "Wake me when we get back to town, will you?"

They were on highway 20, Johnny dozing, when Ryland hauled on the brakes and pulled to the side of the road. "Hey, partner, your lady's car just sailed by."

Johnny suddenly came awake. "Can't be—I sent Nicole home hours ago."

"No mistake. She just sped past us like a lightning bolt."

"Then run it down," Johnny demanded. "Move!"

Ryland did an on-the-spot U-turn while dropping the clutch from first into third. Within seconds the Blazer was in fourth gear, the accelerator on the floor. When the Skylark slowed down to turn off the highway onto the county road, Johnny said, "It's her car, all right."

When the car hit a straight stretch, Ryland saw his chance to floor the Blazer and speed past it. Once out in front, he cut right and skidded to a stop, forcing the Skylark to the side of the road. The Blazer was still bouncing when Johnny leaped out into the rain and angrily stalked toward the car.

Before he reached the door, however, it was thrust open, and he came face to face with a wide-eyed Jasper Craig. "It's good to see you, boy. Thought I'd have to take him on by myself."

"What's going on, old man?" Johnny hollered over the thunder.

"He's got her. Cliff took your lady."

"What?"

"I was scared. I should have told you he was the one. He's the one who burned down Madie's house. He's done other bad things, too. Real bad things."

Johnny froze, feeling his world tilt. A moment later, he rallied. "When? How?"

"I saw you two in the parking lot at the Pass-By. I heard what you told her about going home, but she went to Daisi Buillard's house instead, then to the police station. She had a key, and I watched her go inside. Then Cliff showed up. When he left a little while later, he had your lady with him. I'm scared he might already have hurt her, boy. She wasn't moving when he put her in the trunk of his car.'' Winded, Jasper gasped for more air; his breath was laced with whiskey. "I didn't know what to do. I waited a bit, then got in her car and decided to follow Cliff. It's just a good thing she left the key in the ignition."

Fear gripped Johnny, and he squeezed his eyes shut for a minute to absorb Jasper's words. If anything happened to Nicole he'd never forgive himself. If anything happened to her, he didn't want to live.

Johnny and Ryland rushed back to the Blazer and Johnny directed him to the farm. Jasper followed at high speed in the car. They found Sheriff Tucker's car parked there.

"See," Jasper pointed, "I was right."

With a flashlight Ryland had produced, Johnny tracked Clifton to Belle Bayou. Needing a boat to follow him, they backtracked quickly to the boathouse, and untied two boats.

"Follow me," Johnny instructed as he sent the pole deep into the water and pushed one of the boats away from shore into the black bayou. He knew full well how dangerous the swamp could be, especially at night. But he wouldn't let it end like this, he promised. He had been a fool tonight not to tell Nicki he loved her, but he *would* tell her. He'd tell her everything he'd been holding back since he'd made love to her at the swimming hole weeks ago.

It wouldn't be too late, he promised. He wouldn't let it be too late.

Nicole woke with a pounding headache and rain showering her face. Her head spun, and she moaned softly. For a minute she couldn't think, then she remembered what had happened, and with the memory came the realization that she was no longer in Clifton Tucker's office, but in a boat. Slowly, she sat up.

"It's about time you woke up. Just so you know, I didn't want any of this to happen. The score was already settled years ago. I just wanted Johnny to go away and never come back."

"Why is it so important that Johnny leave town?" Nicole winced as pain shot through her temple. The slightest noise, even her own voice, made her head want to split in two. "He's a good man."

The sheriff swore. "Them Bernards—they were always good at getting the women to fall for them."

"You don't want to hurt me, Sheriff Tucker. Take me back."

"I can't. They're on to me by now. That damn fool Jasper has probably told them how Delmar really died."

"What do you mean how Delmar really died? Johnny's father died in a hit-and-run accident on Bayou Road, that's what Gran told me. Are you saying it didn't happen that way?"

"No, it was a hit-and-run." The sheriff grinned. "Just not an accident."

A lump formed in Nicole's throat. Was he saying he'd killed Delmar Bernard—that he'd run Johnny's father down on the road? Or had he covered for the man responsible?

Another bolt of lightning ripped across the black sky as Clifton Tucker, caped in a black slicker, poled the boat deeper into the bayou. Nicole shivered as the rain soaked her to the bone, making her clothes feel like a cold, wet blanket.

She didn't want to surrender to this madness, but if she jumped from the boat she would surely die. The swamp was full of alligators and poisonous snakes. The least bit of splashing would bring them to investigate. She shuddered at the thought, remembering Johnny's words. *Be a good girl and keep your hands in the boat,* cherie. *No sudden moves.*

The image of an alligator clamping its jaws around her, or a snake touching her with its kiss of death had Nicole feeling dizzy with fear. She squinted into the darkness, trying to grasp where they were, but it all looked the same—a bleak promise of black water and certain death. She felt tears sting her eyes. She didn't want to cry. Didn't want to die.

There had to be a way to escape. There had to be something…

Shaking violently, Nicole squinted into the darkness, noting that the boat was gliding very close to a stand of cypress. Was there a shoreline close by? The swamp was so deceiving, she couldn't be sure.

She studied the water, then felt the boat bump into something. It wasn't exactly solid, but— Fen? Could it be fen? With no time to debate her decision, Nicole said a silent prayer, then exploded off the wooden seat and grabbed a passing tangle of vines. The boat tilted as she caught a fistful of the thick, ropelike vines and hung on.

"No! Come back. No!"

Clifton's angry voice only spurred Nicole on, making her more determined than ever to get away from him. Head still spinning, she didn't look back as she swung her body into the air, then let go of the vine. Keeping her shaky knees bent, she set her feet. The ground beneath her bobbed once, twice. The third time she went down and came back up, the ground stabilized.

A flood of emotion engulfed her as she realized she was, indeed, standing on fen. Sweet, wonderful, *fen.* She could have cried out with joy, but there wasn't time. She turned and ran, fighting her way through the thick vines, determined to get as far away as possible before Sheriff Tucker came after her.

She found the tree house by accident, practically stumbling into the giant cypress facefirst. When she gazed up and saw massive limbs supporting Johnny's tree house, she started to cry. Leaning against the giant tree, she worked at catching her breath.

"Miss Chapman. Do you hear me? I would have done it quick, killed you fast and painlessly. Now the swamp will make you suffer."

His voice urged Nicole into action, and she jerked the rope ladder down and began to climb. Refusing to consider what she might find inside the tree house, she stepped into the shelter just as a flash of lightning lit up the sky. For no more than a brief second, she saw the snake coiled up in a dry corner, and it stopped her in her tracks.

This one's a harmless milk snake, cherie.

Well, it was too dark to see underbellies, Nicole noted. *Think,* she told herself. What else had Johnny said?

Don't move fast, cherie. *But don't freeze up, either.*

Nicole forced herself inside, taking slow, even steps. "You can stay right there," she told the snake, "and I'll stay over here."

Unable to see whether the snake had moved, she had to blindly trust the reptile—and fate. "Fate and Johnny," she whispered softly. "He'll come for me. I know he'll come."

She forced herself to breathe evenly, and began to pray that Johnny would find her sooner rather than later. She refused to think negative thoughts. Instead, she wedged herself into the corner and clung to the wall. At least she didn't have to worry about freezing up; she couldn't have stopped shaking if she tried.

Clifton's voice above the thunder was the lucky break Johnny needed. He turned the boat toward the black bog and sent the pole into the murky water with swift, strong, purposeful strokes. Five minutes later, he heard Clifton's voice again. This time he was calling to Nicole, taunting her about dying in the swamp.

The reality of the situation made Johnny's blood run cold. With renewed energy and his keen sense of direction, he pushed on. He told himself the swamp was his home; he'd traveled every inch of it in daylight and darkness. He would find Tuck, but most importantly he would find Nicole. He had to.

He spotted Clifton's boat pulled into shore some ten minutes later. They ran their boats onto land, and Johnny led Detective Archard and Jasper through the thick woods. It was Johnny who first saw the sheriff stumbling around as if he himself were lost.

"Tuck!"

The sheriff spun around, drawing his gun at the same time, his flashlight zeroing in on Johnny's face. "That you, Johnny boy?"

Johnny squinted through the misting rain. "Why, Tuck? What's going on? Where's Nicole?"

"It ain't my fault she's gonna die, it's yours," Clifton said. "None of this is my fault. If you had stayed away, this wouldn't be happening. It was all over. The debt paid."

"Tell him all of it." Jasper suddenly appeared alongside Johnny. "Tell the truth, Cliff. Tell him how his daddy died."

Clifton angled his head and stared at Jasper. "You wanted Madie for yourself as much as I wanted justice for my daddy. It wasn't my fault she got sick and died before you could marry her. If she had lived you would have called me a hero instead of a murderer. Don'tcha see, J.P., we had to do it."

Jasper shook his head. "I didn't do nothin'. I didn't know what you'd done until after. I would have never agreed to murder. Never!"

"But you kept my secret for twenty-two years."

"What secret?" This time it was Ryland's voice.

"Carl Bernard seduced my mama, and my daddy shot himself when he found them together. I had no choice after that. The Bible says 'an eye for an eye.' That's why I ran Delmar down on the road that night."

Johnny was sure he hadn't heard right. It was too crazy. Sheriff Tucker was responsible for the hit-and-run accident. "You killed my father?"

"Delmar always walked home from town. No one questioned it." Sheriff Tucker raised his gun and pointed it at Johnny.

Detective Archard said, "You've just confessed to murder, Sheriff Tucker. It's all over. Put the gun down."

It was then that Johnny came out of the gray fog that had enveloped him. Crying out, he charged Clifton, knocking the bigger man off his feet. He threw a hard punch to the man's jaw and reached for the gun.

"No, boy. No!" Jasper hurried forward. "Don't hurt him, Cliff. He's Madie's son. Don't hurt the boy."

The gun went off, a deafening *crack*. It all happened so fast that in a matter of seconds it was all over. Johnny threw a hard right to Clifton's jaw and then muscled the gun out of his hand. When he looked up, he saw Jasper crumpled on the ground, a bullet hole in his chest.

"Old man!" Johnny crawled over to where Jasper Craig lay unmoving on his back, vaguely aware of Ryland rushing to apprehend Sheriff Tucker.

"Boy?" Jasper fought for air. "Listen now. There ain't much time. You tell Farrel I'm real sorry. Tell him you two are even now, that it's time to make peace. Go to the tunnel and get my things. I want them with me." He reached for Johnny's hand and gripped it urgently. "Promise me, boy. I need my things."

Johnny nodded. "You have my word, old man. You'll have them."

Jasper smiled, then nodded. "Good boy. Your mama was a fine woman. You remember that. Your daddy, too. We just wanted the same thing, and I was a sore loser."

"You should have stayed back, old man. Kept clear."

"It was time I did something right. Selfish, really. I've been needing to see Madie real bad for a long while now. This time, when we meet, she'll be happy to see me. She'll know I did something good for a change. She'll smile, maybe even forgive me. You remember my box, boy. I need my box with me."

Those were the last words Jasper Craig ever spoke.

Johnny looked over at Clifton Tucker. Ryland was putting handcuffs on him. "You bastard! Why?" Johnny scrambled to his feet, his fists raised.

"Johnny, no!" Ryland grabbed him by the shoulder. "Listen to me. He's crazy. What you do to him now won't make any difference. Let the law handle it. Remember what we came here for. Nicole's out there somewhere, and she needs you to find her. Go!"

Ryland's words shocked Johnny back to reality. He turned and scanned the darkness once more, then yelled, *"Cherie!"* He wiped tears out of his eyes as he struggled into the woods. He couldn't remember the last time he'd cried. His mama's funeral, he supposed.

"Johnny!"

"Cherie!"

"Here, Johnny. I'm in the tree house!"

Moments later he was standing beneath the giant cypress. When he saw her appear in the doorway of his tree house, he nearly collapsed with relief. A moment later he was lifting her off the rope ladder and hauling her into his arms. Cradling her against him, he buried his face in her hair.

"Johnny? I heard shots. Are you all right?"

"I'm fine," he drawled, still holding her close. "Give me a minute, *cherie,*" he said, unable to let go of her just yet. When he finally loosened his hold minutes later, he told her what had happened.

"I'm so sorry, Johnny. It's all so terrible."

"He's crazy." Johnny hung his head. "Jasper's gone. The old fool was trying to help me and Tuck shot him."

Raw emotion took him over the edge. Johnny pulled Nicole close and buried his head in her hair once more. After a few minutes passed, he set her away from him and smiled down at her. "The good news is you're safe. You aren't hurt, are you?"

"A bump on the head is all. I'll be fine now that you're here. I knew you'd come. Thank you."

"Thank me another way, *cherie.* Kiss me."

The townsfolk were in a state of shock. And yet the gossip lines were humming; the phone at Oakhaven hadn't stopped ringing all morning.

What had amazed Nicole most about the people of Common was their sincere effort to make amends to Johnny.

The truth was, for years Sheriff Tucker had manipulated the people of Common, and they had come to realize that fact quickly, with alarming clarity—something that more than convinced Nicole they were genuinely good people. Yes, the truth had shaken the town of Common to the core, but it had also given the people back their dignity. And for that, Nicole believed they truly thanked Johnny.

Last night, when they had gotten back to the house, they'd spent an hour explaining to Gran what had happened and why. Next, Farrel had to be called, and Johnny and Ryland had spent several hours closed in the study with him. Nicole hadn't asked Johnny what had happened between them, but she knew whatever had been said, their feud had ended.

Ryland had been wonderful handling all the details last night, and again this morning. The incarceration of Sheriff Tucker had gone smoothly, and before he'd left to go back to New Orleans he'd promised to look into Johnny's parole deal. It was amazing how quickly things could be expedited when you knew the right people, Nicole thought. And Ryland Archard certainly knew the right people. Good, honest people—people like himself.

All in all, last night had ended the hostility toward the Bernards. It had also explained Jasper Craig's self-destructive obsession with liquor, and Farrel's constant need to wreak vengeance on Johnny. Sheriff Tucker had been a victim in many ways himself. Though Nicole was glad he would be locked up, she found it hard to hate him.

She parked the car at the end of the driveway and walked up the road leading to the hill where the farmhouse had stood. As she neared the hillside, she saw Johnny sitting in the grass overlooking Belle. The morning sun was hot, but there was a gentle breeze, and his loose, gorgeous hair moved freely around his shoulders.

He had been so protective of her last night, and she of him. She supposed they had looked ridiculous clinging to each other the way they had, but no one had said a word. Later, in the early hours of the morning, he had come to her bedroom and made love to her. Such fierce, passionate love that she had cried the entire time.

She reached the hillside and silently sat down beside him. Just being near him made her happy, made her thankful to be alive. God, how she loved this man.

He turned to look at her. "So, *cherie,* what's so important that it couldn't wait until noon? I told Mae I'd be back by lunchtime."

"Yes, I know. Ryland called from New Orleans. He said the parole board will be reviewing your case. He says you'll be a free man in a matter of weeks, if he has anything to say about it. I thought you'd want to know."

He dismissed the news with a slight nod. "You feel like talking?"

"If you want."

He turned and looked straight into her eyes. "I wanted to talk last night, but you couldn't stop crying." He grinned. "That was new. At first I thought I was hurting you."

"You stole my breath again," Nicole confessed. "My reaction was just a little different this time. So, what is it you want to talk about?"

"Last night, before all hell broke loose, you told me you loved me. Remember?"

"Yes." Nicole wanted to reach out and touch him, but she held back. He looked suddenly very serious, and it made her nervous. Was this it, then? Was this where he told her he appreciated the time they'd spent together, but that he was leaving nonetheless?

"Do you still?"

Of course, she still loved him. "More than ever," she admitted. "But I told you—"

"Shh." He reached out and touched her lips with two fingers. "It's my turn. I've been sitting here trying to figure it out. How best to say what I need to say."

Nicole couldn't keep quiet. "I know you plan on leaving. I've always known. I've been preparing myself." She offered him a soft smile in the hope that he hadn't heard the lie in her voice. "It's okay, really. I—"

"Is it? You want me to go?"

"No!" Nicole said in a rush. "But I don't want you to feel—"

"To feel what?"

He brushed her hair out of her eyes, and Nicole welcomed his warm touch. Savored his gentle side. "I—I want you to do what you want," she said. "That's all."

"Whatever I want?"

"Yes."

"It's all up to me?"

"Yes."

"So I can love you?"

Nicole couldn't breathe. Did she dare hope?

"I love you, *cherie*. 'You've got to know that I do' is what you said to me last night. Well, you've got to know that I love you, too."

He *loved* her. Nicole could hardly sit still a moment longer without touching him, without knocking him over and kissing him senseless. "And?"

"And if I stay, I'm not living in the boathouse. And I'm not sleeping alone, either."

He was moving in. That was doable. More than doable. Nicole tried to contain her smile, but it was spreading fast. "So?"

"So, *cherie,* what do you think? Are you going to marry me so Mae can stop matchmaking?"

Nicole couldn't believe what she was hearing. "This isn't some guilt thing, is it?" she asked suddenly. "I mean—"

With one quick movement, he had her on her back, and he was towering over her, his dark eyes narrowing slightly. "No guilt." His eyes softened. "And about kids…we'll go slow. If and when it happens, it'll be because you're ready. No pressure."

"No pressure," Nicole agreed, so in love with Johnny that she could hardly contain her tears. "You can't take it back," she whispered, feeling the first tear wet the corner of her eye. "Now that you've asked, it's a done deal. Right?"

"Are you going to cry?"

"Probably."

He grinned. "Because I'm stealing your breath again?"

"Yes." Nicole squirmed beneath him, running her hands down the length of his strong back, needing so badly to feel his strength. "Should we seal the deal with a kiss?"

"Just a kiss?" Johnny's eyes turned heavy-lidded, and as needy as Nicole's. She wrapped her arms around his neck as he eased his weight onto her prone body. It was going to be gentle and tender this time. He whispered the promise in her ear. Unhurried, he swore. But as usual the kiss turned hot and demanding the minute their lips touched, and what followed sizzled, then burned.

They ended up late for lunch to tell Mae the good news.

* * * * *

0606/108/MB038 V2

Escape to...

19th May 2006

16th June 2006

21st July 2006

18th August 2006

0706/51 V2

THE CRENSHAW BROTHERS
by Annette Broadrick

Double Identity

Jude Crenshaw's blond, craggy good looks made it easy for him to woo innocent, sweet Carina Patterson. The skilled secret agent intended to secure the information he needed before anyone got hurt. But suddenly the one thing he couldn't do was walk away…

Danger Becomes You

Delta Force agent Jase Crenshaw knew no one would be looking for him in the remote cabin. No one to point a finger of blame. But then innocent Leslie O'Brien arrived, running for her life, and their unexpected encounter could save them both.

❧

SECRETS OF PATERNITY by Susan Crosby

James Paladin had agreed to be a sperm donor to his best friend's wife. With conditions: 1) Caryn was not to know. 2) When the boy turned eighteen, all secrets would be revealed. That time had come…

BEDROOM SECRETS by Michelle Celmer

Playboy Tyler Douglas loved everything about women, but after a recent embarrassing encounter, he was avoiding them. Until Tina Deluca, with her sweet innocent face, offered to help him with a sensual course in lovemaking.

❧

SLEEPING ARRANGEMENTS by Amy Jo Cousins

Addy Tyler had to be married to gain her inheritance, and her groom of convenience was the handsome Spencer Reed. Their marriage was supposed to be a paper one, but their sleeping arrangements changed everything!

ROCK ME ALL NIGHT by Katherine Garbera

She was late-night's favourite DJ, Lauren Belchoir. Her soft, sexy voice on the radio had haunted him, and hotshot producer Jack Montrose intended getting to know the woman behind it—*intimately*!

On sale from 21st July 2006

Visit our website at www.silhouette.co.uk

0706/14 V2

MILLS & BOON®

Live the emotion

Blaze™

GOOD, BAD...BETTER *by Cindi Myers*

She's a good girl determined to be bad. He's a bad boy with
a hidden good side. He's perfect for a steamy summer fling
before she leaves town. But the hotter the nights get, the more
intense their affair becomes!

UNZIPPED? *by Karen Kendall*

The Man-Handlers, Bk 2

What happens when a beautiful image consultant meets
a stereotypical computer guy? Explosive sex, of course!
Shannon Shane is stunned how quickly she falls for her client,
Hal Underwood, and she just can't keep her hands to herself.

TEXAS FEVER *by Kimberly Raye*

Holly Faraday, owner of Sweet & Sinful desserts, is thrilled
to learn she's inherited her grandmother's old place. That is,
until she learns that her grandmother was the local madam
– and the townspeople are hoping she'll continue the family
business!

BORN TO BE BAD *by Crystal Green*

Deep undercover. That's how far tabloid reporter Gemma
Duncan will go to get her story! Then New Orleans' naughtiest
playboy, Damien Theroux, lures her into his world of steamy
games and forbidden temptations…

On sale 4th August 2006

*Available at WHSmith, Tesco, ASDA, Borders, Eason,
Sainsbury's and most bookshops*

www.millsandboon.co.uk

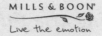

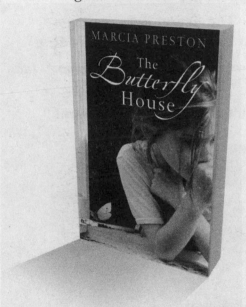

"People look at me and they see this happy face, but inside I'm screaming. It's just that no-one hears me."

While breaking the news of Princess Diana's death to millions, reporter Isabel Murphy unravels on live television. *But Inside I'm Screaming* is the heart-rending tale of her struggle to regain the life that everyone thought she had.

21st July 2006

MIRA